# Jack
# Of
# All
# Trades

## Ian Stewart

# CONTENTS

# 1 Billy the Kid

"Billy! *Billlllllllyyyyyyyyyy!*" The voice bounced across the flats, startling a group of basking mudlarks who scrambled for the safety of a nearby sump, hooting in fear. Flotation chambers insufflated rhythmically. Skeeters whined. Nothing else stirred. *Tarnish it, where is the child?* "Wyllam!"

Terpsichore Jarneyvore leaned heavily on the verandah and sighed. She went to the corner, where her house faced on to Swidger Street. It wasn't a street in the conventional sense, just a long muddy strip between neighbouring rafts. No sign of Billy there, either. She shrugged, and went inside the house. The ornament shelf was dirty again, speckled with tiny spots of dried mud from the weekend's storms. It always got into the house no matter how tightly the doors were sealed. To take her mind off her errant offspring she picked up a damp cloth and set to work, moving the ornaments as she wiped. She stopped when she reached Jole's memogram, picked it up, smiled back in reflex at the happy face. The smile faded. Jole Jarneyvore had been seconded to the Space Department to take part in the first exploration of Sharraby Breach. He had disappeared while on active duty, and was presumed dead.

Five years later she still found it hard to believe he was gone.

Five long, empty years, filled only by young Wyllam. Terpsichore Jarneyvore was a stolid, unimaginative woman, who could neither control her son nor understand him. She stared into the memogram, seeing Billy in his father's face. Billy had taken Jole's death badly, becoming not so much a tearaway as an enigma. Such a strange child...

She went out to the verandah and shouted again, but nothing stirred around the fringes of the swamp. She opened up the tiny box that sat between Jole's memogram and a pair of PAXIAL prisms and took out a ring with a translucent green stone. Where Jole had got it from, she had no idea. He had been in an unfathomable mood, sitting alone in his study or tinkering aimlessly in the workroom. Then, just before leaving for Sharraby Breach, he had handed her the box, asking her to give it to Billy when he came of age. And there was a message to impart, a verbal one, along with the ring: *beware Etonians*. She had wept, although she understood neither ring nor message, because Jole Jarneyvore's trade was predicting the future, and she knew that her husband had predicted that he wasn't coming back.

She heard the wet slap of footsteps on the planking, and snapped the box shut.

"Moom?"

Large, dark eyes in thin, tanned faced. Slim, bony, but athletic, and now decorated with a cheeky grin. Billy could be an engaging child at times.

Those were the times to watch out for.

"*There* you are. And *covered* in mud as usual. It's time for school, Billy! Hose down that slicksuit and get yourself over to the landing-stage for the school tove *at once*."

"Yes, Moom."

"Don't you 'yes, Moom' me, you cheeky little troon, or I'll call the Sump-boglin to nibble your toes while you sleep!"

"Aw, Moom, you know I don't believe that kids' stu—"

"Would you rather believe the back of my hand?"

"No, Moom." Billy hosed himself vaguely clean, and sauntered down to the tovestop, his school bag slung over one shoulder as if it was an independent entity that was merely along for the ride. He joined the twenty or so kids from Raft 4177 just as the battered old tove sloshed to a halt at the mooring post. The chattering rabble clambered aboard, to sour looks from the browning Grynth pilot. The tove cast off and lumbered across the mudflats in a cloud of steam.

Grover's World was one huge mudball. Its glutinuous swamps covered the planet's surface, varying in depth from fifteen metres to over a thousand, a mud ocean with no land. It swarmed with living creatures — lazy, fat wollagongs, skittish mudlarks, irritating swamp-skeeters, assorted mudslingers, slobbers, boggies, shronk, and quagmoles. There were gelatinous growths of squelp and oozing sponge, and sticky colonies of quolyp infested any floating object. A gigantic sun glowed cool red, dominating the sky.

Billy had asked himself a thousand times. Why would anyone in his right mind choose to live in a dismal midden like Grover's World? But he knew the answer.

Mud.

Lucre was never more filthy than on Grover's World, where mud and money were synonymous. Grover's World wallowed in ooze with the joyous abandon of a pronking shronk. Within its beslimed biosphere there flourished an unprecedentedly rich variety of organic macromolecules — a vast, self-renewing source of chemical feedstock. Only ten years ago Grover's World had been an uninhabited mudball, too far from the main starlanes to permit official settlement, too near for more exotic tastes. Now it was an industrial boomworld. Thousands of corporations, large and small, had descended on it to suck profit from the mire.

With them had come the family Jarneyvore.

The people of Grover's World lived on complexes of rafts, tethered in tension-webs, sprawled in loosely-knit groups along the planet's equator. The rafts were supported by massive flotation chambers shaped like blunt sausages. To keep the quolyp at bay the chambers were alternately deflated and inflated. The slow pulsation dislodged the incrustation before it could gain a hold. Mobile extractors prowled the planet's surface, filter-feeding for organics just as the legendary whale had strained terrestrial seas for krill. According to the more literary inhabitants the machines' colloquial name, *mobies*, derived from this analogy rather than the obvious acronym.

Billy would never admit it in front of his classmates, but there were times when he actually *liked* school. Electronics was his favourite, and he was well into building a Bell-Galactic system-scrambler. True, the teacher thought it was a mail scheduler, but Billy had replaced the sealed RNA biochip by one that he had custom-cultured in his mother's vitrovarium. When he finished it, the phone company was going to get a surprise. He also liked languages (he was fluent in Merkan and Grynth standard, with some pidgin Barasshanti and a smattering of Femmish), radiation technology, polymathics, quag chemistry, and cybergenetics. His perfect memory helped, though he deliberately made mistakes to avoid attracting attention — the other kids would have made life a Sump for him if they'd thought he was cleverer than they were. His teachers recognised that his outward brashness hid a quick intelligence, and when they weren't cursing him — which was seldom — the more perceptive ones were impressed by his breadth.

The trouble began as soon as he got off the tove. The swimnastics coach was waiting. "Well, it's young Jarneyvore! Go to the Principal's Office! At once!"

"What for?" The teachers had long ago ceased to expect politeness from Billy Jarneyvore.

"You'll find out. Just go." Billy went. Along the way he discarded several sensitive items from his schoolbag, concealing them in a hole behind the main drainage channel. He transferred others to a secret pocket in his codpiece. It was best to be prepared.

The Principal was named Maloysius Long. The Long family was prominent in Grover's World commerce — Maloysius's sister Wylgeta owned LPC, a polymer-producing corporation with outlets on a dozen worlds. Wylgeta had inherited the lot when their father died; Maloysius had been shut out, and hated her for it. The fact that the sister had a flair for business, whereas Maloysius was unimaginative — and the suspicion that their father had understood this only too well — just made matters worse.

Maloysius Long was also unshakably straitlaced and could not abide independent minds. Certainly not if they undermined his authority. Billy Jarneyvore managed to combine all the orthodox forms of unorthodoxy with a few unorthodox forms of his own, and his instinctive reaction to authority was to flout it. The two saw eyeball to eyball rather than eye to eye. In fact there was only one person on Grover's World that Billy disliked more, and that was Mayor Graspmudgeon. Every time you turned on the HV all you ever saw was the preparations for Graspmudgeon to open the new spaceport. Huh! Better than Tinky and Turkey, admittedly, but all it really proved was that Grover Holovision was in Graspmudgeon's pocket. Billy knew that the mayor was taking bribes from construction companies. But he couldn't tell anybody because he'd found out by illegally tapping Graspmudgeon's private phone line. Anyway, who'd believe a kid?

Why did Long want to see him? Billy could guess. The previous night he had been skulking around the substructure of the Principal's dwellingplace, which was on the same raft as the high school, looking for a suitable place to infect the floorboards with a virulent strain of dendrophage. He had just located the perfect spot when the floor opened above his head, knocking him from his perch into the mud. Catching a quick glimpse of a half-open trapdoor and a head in silhouette, Billy had lain flat and pretended to be a dead wollagong pup. When the head disappeared, accompanied by confused shouting from within the building, he had crawled off between the understruts. At that moment someone had shone a torch through the trapdoor. At the time Billy thought he hadn't been spotted; but now he was sure that Old Longjohns had recognized him. Or maybe he had just guessed it was Billy — a natural enough deduction given the history of their relationship.

Wyllam reached the Principal's office, hesitated, swallowed, and knocked on the door. A disagreeable voice told him to enter.

"Jarneyvore." Long had a face like a desiccated bloodhound. He made the name 'Jarneyvore' sound like some disgusting thing that lived in the swamp and stuck to people. To be fair, it often was. "So! What have you got to say for yourself?"

"You haven't asked me anything yet."

Long shot him a sour glance. "Don't try to pull the mud over my gills, Jarneyvore. I've made allowances because you don't have a father to keep you in line, but this time you've gone too far!"

*I do have a father. Jole isn't dead. He's just missing. One day I'll find him...*

"I'm suspending you pending an investigation by the Constabulary."

"I ain't done nothing!" said Billy indignantly. The linguist in his head protested at the atrocious grammar, the logician observed that the statement was both grammatical and true because a double negative counted as a positive, and the actor overruled them both. Billy wondered why Old Longjohns was getting so snorty around the orifices about a harmless prank. *He's never threatened me with the phoz before.*

"*Someone* did something," said Long flatly. "Someone who knew how to break computer security codes. Someone who knew how to tap into the datastream of the Luticultural Bank. There is only one person in this school with that kind of warped talent, and that person, Jarneyvore, is *you*. Admit it!"

A number of thoughts jostled for attention in Billy's mind. The first was that he had not the faintest idea what the Principal was talking about. The second was that Long's behaviour didn't ring true — his speech-patterns were awkward, as if he were acting out a prepared script. The third was that there was a large phozbug poorly concealed behind a pot of cydrangulas on Long's desk, and the prepared speech was for its benefit. All of which meant that he was being set up... But *why?*

"Admit what?"

"That you embezzled the school charity fund for handicapped Barasshanti younglings. You're a thief, Jarneyvore."

\* \* \*

Barasshanti.
Femm.
Grynth.
Humans.

The Quaternity. At its best, a loose-knit federation, four species each looking after its own ends. At its worst, a complex, shifting power-struggle. The Grynth... Humans and Grynth seemed to have more in common than the others, even though the Grynth resembled a cross between a gorilla, a polar bear and an Old Anglish sheepdog. Maybe because they did. Maybe because the Grynth had a very human sense of humour, when they cared to show it. Maybe because it was Humans and Grynth who had founded the Quaternity — only in those days they called it the Duality.

The Femm... Except for their jointy legs, they looked almost human, until you took a close look at their version of teeth, a single bony ridge along each jaw. But their viewpoint was so alien that neither Humans, Grynth, nor Barasshanti had any idea which way they would jump next. The Femm were suspicious of Human-Grynth cooperation.

The Barasshanti... Encased in hard shells, upright turtles whose lobster limbs terminated at improbable hooves. They were by nature suspicious of everything — especially other Barasshanti — and they were convinced that the Femm's appearance of distrust was actually camouflage for covert collaboration. This was actually highly implausible. The Femm had joined the Quaternity only because the combined weight of the other three species made it too risky to stay out. It was generally believed that their long-term political aim was to break up the Quaternity, permanently. So presumably the Barasshanti maintained their illogical position in order to mislead —

Such is the stuff of Quaternity politics.

Lobachevskii Sector, in which Grover's World resides, is noted throughout the galaxy for Sharraby breach, a dust-filled slash of spatiotemporal disruption roughly a light-century in length. According to one theory it is the relic of a wandering repulsar, which ricochetted through the area at translight speed during the early unfolding of the universe from the primal singularity, accompanied by a gravitic shockwave that created a permanent dislocation of the continuum. This theory is disputed by others on the grounds that no repulsar has ever been observed. Its protagonists hold this fact unsurprising, all repulsars having disappeared from the universe some twelve billion years ago.

An early resolution of the dispute is not anticipated.

On SpaDe spacecharts, Sharraby Breach is annotated with the black zigzag that signifies unpredictable danger. The Space Department is the main operational arm of the Quaternity. Billy hated SpaDe, because it was SpaDe that had dispatched his father on the ill-fated expedition to Sharraby Breach. By logical extension, Billy hated all forms of authority. He hated its rituals, its trappings, and its arrogant assumptions. He hated how it pushed people around, how it exploited them, and how it discarded them. If he were in charge he would rule by anarchy. Intellectually he was aware of the contradiction, but emotionally he was too immature to resolve it.

Terpsichore Jarneyvore was his mother, not authority, and Wyllam loved her fiercely; but he could never bring himself to say so, perhaps because he didn't realise it. SpaDe stood for the unreal, unseen, infinitely distant Quaternity, loathed all the more because he knew absolutely nothing about it.

But, as a matter of everyday experience, authority on Grover's World came in two forms: schoolteachers and constables. Schoolteachers loomed large in Billy's life, and he tolerated them because they possessed, albeit in feeble and dim form, a priceless commodity: knowledge. Billy knew instinctively that knowledge was the key to the universe. If anything would get his father back, it was knowledge. But when they weren't teaching, teachers were a tedious nuisance. "Hose down, Jarneyvore!" "Sit down, Jarneyvore!" "Eyes down, Jarneyvore!" They were all down on Jarneyvore.

The second incarnation of authority on Grover's World, the phoz, offered him nothing to compensate for its nuisance value. But between Billy Jarneyvore and the local constabulary there existed a reluctant respect, mainly because each knew exactly what the other was up to. The constables respected Billy because it was so damnably difficult to pin anything on him, even when his guilt was as plain as the whiskers on a wollagong. Billy respected the phoz for the gruff sense of fairness with which they carried out their duties — only once had he been punished for something he hadn't done.

* * *

Long waved a sheaf of holofax printouts. "You're a thief, and I've got the evidence to prove it!"

*Thief.* A shameful word. The unfairness of the accusation made Billy feel sick. He liked his fun, certainly, but he was — in his own way — honest. He realised that Long must have some kind of evidence, and that it had to be faked. Why was the Principal going to such lengths over a practical joke, when he could get Billy into plenty of trouble just by telling the truth? It didn't make sense. The fund for handicapped Barasshanti younglings was something that he would *never* tamper with. Hadn't he organized the sponsored wallow-in on its behalf? Billy was about to to protest his innocence when it dawned on him that his charitable action might easily be viewed as a ploy to bolster the size of the fund before plundering it.

When the door opened to reveal two uniformed constables, it also dawned on him that the phozbug was live. "This is the culprit, officers," said Long, trying unconvincingly to sound disappointed. "Little Billy Jarneyvore. I've given him his chance, but the silly child refuses to admit his guilt. Maybe *you* can get him to tell the truth."

The constables advanced into the room. Long was astonished when Billy began to cry. Hard-as-iron Jarneyvore, who usually showed all the emotion of a hibernating quagmole? The Principal watched in amazement as the child fumbled in the waistband of his slicksuit and drew out a moderately clean handkerchief. The boy wiped his eyes, blew his nose loudly, then burst into tears again and dropped the handkerchief on the floor. He dredged another from his waistpouch.

Long felt an acute attack of guilt. He'd never seen Billy Jarneyvore shed a tear in his life.

Come to think of it...

There was a bright purple flash and a noise like a thunderclap as the moisture-sensitive chemicals impregnating the first handkerchief exploded. The room vanished behind a pall of grey smoke. Billy pulled the second handkerchief — actually a thin-film filter — over his nose and crawled along the wall to the door. He opened it as noiselessly as he could and crept out into the hallway. Then he set off down the corridor at a fast trot. If Long was trying to frame him he wasn't going to hang around and argue the merits of the case: he was going to keep his freedom and use it to find out what on Grover's World was at the bottom of it all.

From behind came coughs, and cries of "Stop him! Stop that boy!"

The astropology mistress barred his way. Billy plugged his ears with chewing-gum and activated a shrieker capsule disguised as a fastener on his kneepouch. As the earsplitting howl filled the building the teacher fell to her knees, moaning and holding her head. Billy jumped over her, shot down the stairs, and hit the main concourse at a run, heading for the refectory balcony. Two more shriekers cleared the way. His back foot launched him on to a dining bench, his front foot hit the balcony rail, and he dropped ten metres to the swamp. He hit with a resounding splat and disappeared beneath the slime.

His pursuers looked down from the balcony rail, stunned. A single semicircular shockwave rippled across the mire, upsetting basking mudlarks as it passed. Their puzzled hoots could be heard faintly, disappearing into the distance.

The crowd on the balcony stared in growing horror at the mud. Nothing disturbed its surface.

\* \* \*

Grover's World is unusual in one respect other than its mud. The influence of Sharraby Breach had disrupted the usual processes of planetary formation. Stars near the Breach have few planets, and those that do exist are either too close to their parent star for human habitation, or too far away. Grover's World is the only habitable planet anywhere near the Breach, and then only by accident. It is the innermost planet of the red giant Willington 708 kappa, known locally as Basketball, with a diameter of ninety-six million kilometres. The planet orbits only eight million kilometres above the star's surface. But so cool is the star that the planet maintains a pleasant temperature, and the great red globe is a spectacular sight, almost filling the daytime sky.

However, Grover's World pays a price for its habitability. Though the radiation is low, the gravity is not. The planet is too far inside the star's gravitational well for freewave broadcasting to be possible. All interstellar communication to and from Grover's World must be relayed — by outmoded radio, at intolerably slow lightspeed — to the freewave transmitter stationed on Willington 708 kappa II. This planet, the second and last in the system, is a further twenty-three billion kilometres out, and colloquially known as Icebox.

Usually Icebox orbited in splendid isolation, but not on this occasion. Trailing it by some twenty degrees of arc was a solitary Femm cruiser. It was there for the same reason that the installation on Icebox was there: critical freewave radius. Its single passenger had to maintain contact with his superiors. But the delay in communication with his agent on Grover's World was a constant irritant. For the hundredth time Hymllyr Tubbytt debated whether to send a shuttle, but the danger of alerting SpaDe was, as always, too great.

       \* \* \*

Billy had had plenty of time to think things through while lying immobile in the mud. *After you have eliminated the impossible*, as his holovix heroine Shirley Combs was wont to say, *whatever remains, however improbable, must be the truth*. Blatant nonsense, because you could never be absolutely certain that what you thought was impossible really was. But a reasonable punt position... so punt. *Something* had triggered a series of inexplicable acts on the part of the school Principal. Now, apart from the incident beneath the floorboards, Billy had done nothing for several weeks. In fact he'd laid off harassing Long in the hope that he wouldn't be suspected when that personage's floor fell in.

Ergo: Long *had* recognized him under the floor. So why had he invented a quag-and-mudball story about the charity fund? *And* gone to the trouble of faking holofax printouts as evidence? Come to think of it, Old Longjohns could hack about as well as a wollagong could hang-glide. *Hypothesis 1*: Long had hired someone to produce the fakes. That would be expensive. And dangerous — Long would lose his job if the truth ever came to light. Ridiculous. *Hypothesis 2*: somebody had done it for him, voluntarily. Same problem. And why would anybody want to do such a thing? Hmmmm.

Billy blew a small bubble and looked through it at his watch: three minutes. Not time to move yet. Back to the brainwork. Long couldn't have acted alone. Billy cast his mind back to the previous night. The trapdoor opened, a head appeared in silhouette... *had it actually been Long?* He replayed the scene in his mind. No, the head was broader, the neck more stumpy... Then there had been some confused shouting... how did it go? Something like *wallop my grandma with featherless hippos*... That was idiotic. All hippos are featherless...

*Woullomig! Ranmurr taf edrellyss xsiphphou!* Femmish for "Look out! There's somebody down there!" That's what is was: Femmish! When it comes to getting results, the subconscious is a wondrous creation. It doesn't so much jump to conclusions as launch itself at them from a ramp.

But why would Long have a Femm in his house? Because he was involved in an illicit deal with the Femm. Now it was starting to make sense. When they'd seen Billy under the floor they'd panicked, so they had to fix things so that nobody would believe a word Billy said, before the kid blew the whistle on the deal. Whatever it was.

So... what the Sump was it that they thought Billy had *seen*? He reviewed the mental record. Mud below, boards above... A standard inspection trap for underpinnings... the usual network of struts and flotation chambers... a rectangle of light picking out puddles of water amid the sluggish quagmire.

Nothing unusual there.

The *presence* of a Femm in Long's house? Curious, but not enough to excite comment... it could have been a visiting Quaternity educationalist, for instance...

But there must have been something...

' "*Is there any other point to which you would wish to draw my attention?*" asked the constable.

' "*To the curious incident of the shronk in the night-time.*"

' "*The shronk did nothing in the night-time.*"

' "*That was the curious incident*," remarked Shirley Combs.'

Of course! A 'live' flotation chamber exhibits slow, rhythmic breathing, to discourage infestation by quolyp. But the flotation chamber underneath Long's house was *covered* in quolyp. It must have been dead.

No one allows their home's flotation chamber to die. But Long had. *Why*?

He had to take another look.

\* \* \*

Billy waited until dusk. Then he made his way to the nearby dock and borrowed a pair of skoats — ski-like flotation boots that could be used to walk on the glutinous mud with the aid of two poles, each ending in a hollow sphere the size of a large wallowmelon. He skoated under the raft until he neared Long's dwelling. Then he removed the skoats, lodging them temporarily at the junction of several cross-struts, and made his way towards the flotation chamber, crawling along the main beams just below the flooring.

He took a close look at the flotation chamber. Definitely dead. Curious...

Billy arranged himself in the most comfortable position he could find and settled down to wait. The mournful honks of mudlarks lamenting the setting sun died away. From afar came the sepulchral drone of a cow wollagong calling to her offspring. Night fell on Grover's World. From his boot Billy took a soft plastic mask with nitesite lenses, and pulled it over his eyes. Several hours passed.

It was the creaking of boards above his head that first alerted him. He watched as the trapdoor opened and someone shone a torch in a wide sweep. But he had chosen his position carefully and he couldn't be seen. Then a shadowy shape clambered through the opening, followed shortly by another: Long and his Femmish companion. They clambered awkwardly along the inspection catwalk to the flotation chamber. There was a pause while Long produced a small object — probably a magstripe card — and inserted it somewhere. Then they disappeared.

Billy wasn't totally surprised. As he had expected, they had gone *inside* the chamber. Normally that wasn't possible: faulty chambers were deflated and detached for repair. They must have cut an opening, which explained why the chamber was dead. They must have done something to make the chamber look as if it were still inflated... maybe a chemical rigidifier. That argued careful planning. But for what?

Billy crept closer. He pressed an ear to the quolyp-infested skin of the chamber, and confirmed his belief that it would make an effective sounding-board. He could hear every word from within.

"... improvement," said Long.

"Yes. The new strain is crowing well." That was the Femm. The accent was unmistakeable: typically they mixed up c's and g's. Not always, but often enough that you noticed. "Its degenerative properties have ingreased by one hundred and sixty percent."

"Is it ready yet?"

"Soon, soon... we must be certain that it will keep crowing in the natural egology."

"Right. But it must affect only the strains of bacteria used by LPC. I don't want a planet-wide disaster!"

"Of gorse," said the Femm. "That was all decided long ago. Yes... a high destrugtive factor is indicated. By tomorrow we will know whether it can be sustained."

"Tomorrow! Ah, then I'll have them right where I want them! Wylgeta will regret the day she inherited the Long Polymer Chain! "

"Be calm, and wait. Tomorrow, if all goes as expegted, you may release the organisms. But be careful."

"Don't worry," said Long. "I've waited a long time for this. I'll be as cautious as a boggie in a shronk-midden."

It sounded as if the conversation was coming to and end. Billy wiped stray quolyp from his ear and retreated among the girders, just in time. Long and the mysterious Femm emerged from the flotation chamber and climbed back through the trap. It slammed shut.

You didn't have to be a genius to grasp the plan. The Femm had supplied Long with some destructive organism — the odds were on a tailored virus — intended to disrupt the activities of the Long Polymer Chain. Presumably by damaging the microorganisms that produced its feedstock.

But why would the Femm involve themselves in Long's personal vendetta?

The short answer was that they wouldn't. So there had to be something in it for them. Something big. Everyone knew that the Femm had only joined the Quaternity because the combined powers of Humans, Grynth and Barrasshanti were just that bit too much for them. They weren't willing partners, and they spent most of their time hatching plots to break up the alliance. Every little bit of sabotage helped. Divide and conquer.

The Femm had told Long that the virus would damage only the activities of the Long Polymer Chain. Clearly this was a lie — so the damage would be much more widespread. The entire economy of Grover's World was at risk! Hmmm... why use Long at all? Because the Quaternity authorities would have little trouble reconstructing what had happened, and they needed a non-Femm scapegoat. Long was too consumed by hatred to realise that he was being manipulated.

Billy had to get into that chamber. But Long had used a magstripe card, which meant that there was a heat-sensitive alarm. Naturally, Billy knew how to disconnect something as simple as an alarm — if he could get inside the chamber. He could get inside — if he could disconnect the alarm.

A pretty puzzle.

How does a boggie evade a pack of odour-sensitive shronk? It camouflages its odour in a pongonia patch. How does a burglar evade a heat-sensitive alarm? He camouflages his body heat. Time for a trip to the school laboratory.

An hour later Billy had bypassed the school's locks and liberated an assortment of equipment. Tools, electronic components, a reel of wire, a flask of liquid nitrogen, a pump, a jar of chemicals, and assorted hoses and pipes. And, in a cage, the school's pet mudlark, affectionately known as Oozak.

* * *

He cleared away a patch of quolyp. Then he cut a circular groove in the flotation chamber's plastoid skin, not quite penetrating it, and glued a handle to it. He rigged the pump and liquid nitrogen to produce a small snowstorm, and sat under it until he was worried that the chattering of his teeth would alert Maloysius Long. Then he wiggled the handle until the cuts gave way, climbed through, and disabled the alarm before he could warm up enough to set it off. He replaced the plastoid disk, taped it in position, and switched on the light.

The chamber had been rigged up as a makeshift workshop. There was a lot of expensive equipment, not all of which Billy recognised. In the middle was a sealed canister marked 'Viral Containment Unit. DANGER!! DO NOT OPEN!!' The canister was connected by tubes to a sealed glass dish, inside which was a layer of culture medium. A few greenish blotches with red centres dotted the surface — dead or dying bacteria. In this way the Femm had proved to Long that the virus would help him ruin LPC. The unit was also connected to a flask, to collect a liquid that the organisms were producing.

Billy ran off some of the liquid into a syringe. He looked at the caged mudlark. *Dammit. Sorry, Oozak old friend. Grover's World needs a volunteer for a suicide mission, and you're elected unanimously by circumstances beyond my control.* He injected the liquid into the creature's neck-vein, hating himself for doing it. If he was right, it wouldn't take long.

The ecology of Grover's World — as Mz. Fligg was wont to emphasise in her Grovography class — is a single complex network of cause and effect. Feedback-or-be-fedback. The unicellular microorganisms that infested the mud provided food for swamp-skeeters and crustacea, which in turn fed the mudlarks and wollagongs, boggies and shronk. The waste products of the higher animals in turn nourished the microorganisms.

Break the chain at any point and the whole cycle dies. And the weakest link is the mudlarks.

Twenty minutes. Oozak continued to snuffle around its cage, rooting out swamp-skeeter larvae. But it didn't sound quite right. The snuffles were becoming laboured... It was clearly in trouble. It rolled on to its side, convulsed twice, then was still.

A single tear rolled down Billy's cheek. *Sorry, Oozak. So sorry. No time, no choice. They will pay dearly for this.*

The Femm had tailored a virus. It was a masterly achievement. It did two things simultaneously. First, it killed the species of bacteria used by LPC. But that was just a blind. Its main job was to kill mudlarks, which it did by persuading another species of bacteria to produce a chemical that poisoned the creatures. The Femm would have chosen a species of bacteria that was common all over Grover's World. Now they had their virus, and were exploiting Long's family feud to distribute it. Come daybreak, and Long would know that 'his' virus was working. By midday he would have released it. He would have no idea what he had really done...

Billy could go to the constables... no. They'd sling him in the pokey for stealing the charity fund. They wouldn't believe him. A plague of dying mudlarks would convince them, but by then it would be too late.

He could steal the virus. But Long would just breed more.

Billy sat, and thought like he had never thought before. Shirley Combs never gave up, no matter how hopeless things seemed. Not even when arch-villain Morry Hardy had marooned her on an asteroid with less than an hour's oxygen. So Billy the Joat would not give up, either, however impossible —

An idea came. Something he'd read about in *Holovix Weekly*. It would take some basic hacking, but he already had most of the codes, and he knew where to get the rest.

He set to work. An hour passed. The task completed, he made sure everything looked undisturbed, and removed all of his gear through the hole in the plastoid. A quick coat of polysolv and a smear of quolyp, and nobody would ever know he had been there.

\* \* \*

Nyjel Grawlvyre, Chief Constable of Grover's World, had a big job on his hands. Today was the opening of the new spaceport, and he was in charge of security for several dozen visiting dignitaries, the most prominent being the Seventh Assistant Sub-Undersecretary for Transportation from the Sector Directorate on Aphélix. He had been working like a squabber all morning making final checks. Now the ceremonies were about to start. He sat in front of a bank of holovix monitors, trying simultaneously to watch raftboard approaches, airspace, and the ceremony itself.

Mayor Graspmudgeon was clasping hooves with a Barasshanti delegate from Tacktongle IV when Grawlvyre realised that the event wasn't going as scripted. On the giant replay board that GWHV (the local holovix franchisee) had set up to give spectators a close-up view of the laying of the foundation-plank, there appeared a series of flash messages.

EMERGENCY INTERRUPTION
THIS MAN IS A CRIMINAL
I'LL PROVE IT

Grawlvyre gaped in astonishment as, on his monitor in slightly fuzzy close-up, there appeared the bloodhound features of the school principal. The Chief Constable had met Maloysius Long a few months earlier at a reception, and taken an instant disliking to him.

Next, the square shoulders and heavy head of a Femm.

The Chief Constable blinked in surprise. He knew there were a few Femm on planet, but none had any reason to be with Long. He turned up the sound.

"...ready?"

"Yes. Gontinue!"

"I'm releasing the virus," said Long, lifting a large canister and tipping it on end. "Kill their bacteria... ruin them..." Fluid gushed out. "I've done it! I've broken the Long Polymer Chain! I've finished that bitch Wylgeta for good!" He broke into a curious little dance. Grawlvyre had no idea how the transmission had occurred, but the word 'virus' tripped his relays and he knew that his job might depend on taking it seriously. He grabbed a communicator and began bellowing into it.

\* \* \*

The school hall was packed. At the podium stood the Mayor. He had been speaking for over an hour. Behind him sat threescore local bigwigs, all Graspmudgeon appointees, all as corrupt as he. On a seat to one side was an increasingly bored Wyllam Jarneyvore.

The Mayor listed a number of civic activities that were in the offing, and reminded his audience that only two weeks remained until Waghort night, when the Quaternity would celebrate the Battle of Gladstone's Gap. Thanks to the controversial actions of Milverton Waghort, the Humans had lost this famous battle to the Grynth, and were eventually obliged to join forces with them in what later expanded to become the Quaternity. Each person commemorates the event in one of two ways — either by burning an effigy of Waghort so that his unspeakable treachery will never be forgotten, or by constructing a likeness of Waghort and setting it alight so that his astonishingly far-thinking sacrifice of the short-term aims of his own species will be a shining beacon to future generations. These conflicting interpretations of that ancient event still cause heated disagreements and often lead to rioting. Waghort Night would have been banned long ago except that it is enormously popular among the juveniles of the Quaternity, who get to set off firecrackers and roast munchmallows in Waghort's embers.

It is also an excellent way to get rid of old socks.

The Mayor concluded his speech by reminding all of his listeners to give generously to the Graspmudgeon Fund, a charity whose activities were curiously vague. He then rambled off into a lengthy paean of praise for Grover's World's educational system. "...and it is a tribute," Graspmudgeon droned on, "to the educational expertise of this administration, and to all of its officials, that this *brilliant* young man" — he acknowledged Billy's existence for the first time in the speech — "was afforded the opportunity to develop his unusual talents. Our enlightened approach to educational breadth has paid handsome dividends..."

*Indeed it has*, thought Billy. *Mostly in diverted Q funds going to your private account with the Nomes*. He smiled shyly. *But what really irks me is the way you're taking the credit for what I did*.

"In recognition of which I now call upon young Wyllam Jarneyvore to step up to the podium and receive this citation to honour his sterling work on behalf of the community."

Billy rose, still smiling. *Big fat hairy deal. I save the planet's economy and you give me a piece of paper and a pat on the back. And you give the impression that what I did only counts if it has your approval*. He bowed stiffly as he took the beribboned scroll from Graspmudgeon's plump hand.

*Saved the planet's economy...*

"Thank you, your wormship," Billy mumbled politely and ambiguously, and stepped back. His mind had taken on a life of its own.

*Saved the planet's economy...*

Why *were* the Femm involved in a plot to destroy Grover's World? A random act of sabotage? Nuts. This was the boondocks. Divide and conquer was all very well, but there must be more effective ways of hurting the Quaternity than screwing up a one-shronk planet. There must be more to it, much more. Grover's World, the Quaternity, SpaDe, the Femm. They were all part of something, something *big*...

A faint creaking sound interrupted his deliberations and reminded him where he was, and what was about to happen. Billy stepped back, trying to move at a natural pace. Graspmudgeon was coming to the climax of his peroration, lavish self-praise for fiscal rectitude.

The creaking became louder. The assembled toadies exchanged puzzled looks. The Mayor launched into his final paragraph. "...and my administration has made an especial point of wasting —" he looked closely at his script — "I mean, *avoiding* wasting — public money on unnecessary repairs. Take this school, for example —" The floor beneath them sagged, then with an earsplitting crack it gave way. They slid together in a tangled, screeching heap as it collapsed, dumping them all into the mud beneath.

"Oh my," said Wyllam Jarneyvore to a hall full of horrified parents. But he was thinking: *I* knew *that dendrophage would come in handy*.

# 2   Jack Of All Trades...

The years slid past like skeeters down a slobber-hole. Billy Jarneyvore reached the age of majority and received his father's ring and the accompanying message about Etonians. Neither made the slightest sense. He hung the ring round his neck on a chain, tucked the message away in an attic corner of his mind, dropped out of Grover High without graduating, and found himself a job.

Several jobs.

For instance, he worked as a trainee holovix technician. He was promoted when he found a way to increase the bandwidth of the channels used as local links for HV cameras, so that a single controller could handle 20% more information at a negligible extra cost. He was fired when they found he was using the extra information capacity to run a network-wide sweepstake on the company chairman's extramarital infidelities.

He worked as a mechanic, putting toves and pleasure-craft through their annual swampworthiness test. He was doing well until he dug out from the archives of City Raft an obsolete by-law that had never been repealed, and failed the entire fleet of Graspmudgeon taxitoves for failing to carry a spare wheel.

Space-struck, he wangled a job with an archaeological dig on Thorneycroft, the nearest of the worlds on which PAXIAL relics had been found. The name masked ignorance: **P**resumptive **A**dvanced **X**tragalactic **I**ntelligent **A**lien **L**ifeform. (Well, you couldn't pronounce PAEIAL, could you?) They were xenoarchaeology's greatest mystery. Millions of the prisms, all apparently identical, had been scattered across a known twelve worlds by some long-extinct spacefaring race. The prisms were white, about the size of a stick of chalk, hexagonal in cross-section, with a spiral pattern inscribed on the flat end. They promised secrets of unknown technology. They were allegedly used for purposes that, depending on the school of thought, ranged from nuclear grenades to the equivalent of disposable razorblades. Their promise was all the more tantalizing in that nobody had ever been able to make any PAXIAL artefacts do anything whatsoever, except sit enigmatically and ornamentally on the mantelshelf, which they did in huge numbers throughout the inhabited galaxy. There had been a brief craze for PAXIAL prisms, and you could find them in any junk shop. Jole Jarneyvore had brought a few home, and Terpsichore still owned several.

Junk, nothing more. But...

The prisms must have had some purpose, otherwise why make so many, distribute them so widely? The PAXIAL homeworld would surely be a find beyond price. And there was the intellectual challenge too, of course, as his employer impressed upon him during the first ten minutes.

It was a spectacular dig. About two weeks in, Professor Wigbogger dug up an entirely new kind of PAXIAL artefact, a remarkable pale blue hemisphere that occasionally flickered as if its power-source was still feebly active. Functioning PAXIAL technology! The Professor issued press-releases, appeared on HV chat-shows, and explained at interminable and enthusiastic length that the new artefact was the most important archaeological find since the Olympus egg. It was significant, it was provocative, it was stupendous, it was —

*A fake,* said the older and wiser heads of the Xenoarchaeologic Institute, when they finally got a close look at it. Wigboggler wasn't as big a fool as the incident had made him appear. It wasn't all that hard for him to work out who had designed it, who had built it, and who had planted it. Wyllam Jarneyvore, responsible for all three, was given a one-way ticket back to Grover's World.

Next, under an assumed name, he took a job as a temporary assistant financial advisor with the law firm Witherspoon, Huggins, and Ruggle. In a bizarre incident, the entire contents of Mayor Graspmudgeon's secret accounts, together with those of a number of assorted Groverian bigwigs, were accidentally dumped into the main computer of the Interstellar Revenue Service. His Worship, plus bigwigs, shortly departed Grover's World on a lengthy vacation to a Quaternity SPD (Special Planet for Deviates). Jarneyvore, who was on duty at the time, denied responsibility for the accident, which he maintained had been caused by an unusual conjunction of a solar flare in Humphrydavy Sector and the appallingly pathetic design of the IRS nodal buffer-flushing algorithms. He might have kept his job, but a number of prominent and respected citizens promptly withdrew their accounts from Witherspoon, Huggins, and Ruddle. The Sector Manager was unimpressed by Billy's argument that this proved something about those clients. "What do you think a financial advisor is *for*, Jarneyvore? Of course they've got something to hide! Our job is to help them *hide* it, not to broadcast it all over the Quaternity!" However, after this incident, Billy's enemies — and he was making many — began to treat him with the same sort of respect that one would show to a forty-foot bogodile at the height of the mating season.

Among those enemies — though at this time the young Jarneyvore had only just begun to suspect it — was the organization that his father had warned him about. Billy dug out a tenuous link between Graspmudgeon and a bunch of entrepreneurs who called themselves 'Etonians'. *Beware Etonians.* He resolved to find out more about them. But this particular trail was dead on arrival. Billy was impressed: someone had mounted a really high-powered cover-up.

He took a job with the Space Department, hoping to track down material pertaining to his father. He expected to have his application refused on the grounds that he was a security risk, but they hired him at once. He couldn't decide whether that was significant. He found nothing, but he did learn how to reset the sprinkler system at SpaDe Headquarters on Aphélix, just in time for the Midsummer Ball. SpaDe's investigative team couldn't prove anything, but soaked wives of space-admirals have a habit of getting their way, and Billy shortly fell foul of an obscure regulation about matching shoes and the Department was regretfully forced to dispense with his services.

He took a job dehoozing mobies. It was manual work, ill-suited to the application of his talents, and as a result he managed to keep the job for long enough to earn some money. Bearer-check in hand, he surprised everyone by presenting himself to the registrar of Grover University demanding to be enrolled for a degree.

"What degree?" the registrar asked. She didn't normally deal directly with student applicants — or "customers", as the Board preferred them to be called — but she made it a rule never turn down a potential client, so she rummaged in a drawer and found a prospectus for him to read.

Three hours later Wyllam Jarneyvore was still mulling over the advantages of becoming a Bachelor of Cosmodynamics, compared to certain drawbacks of the otherwise more attractive Diploma of Shronkology, and wondering whether he could keep open options in zero-energy proton resynthesis, semantic poetry, somactid ecology, and the sociotopology of globular feudalism. Oh, and could he join the trapeze-golf team?

Hermione Ginghyllys had been a registrar for twenty years, and she diagnosed the problem immediately. "Jarneyvore, you don't want to take *a* degree."

"Miz?"

"You want to take them *all.*"

Billy admitted that this appeared to be the case.

"And I bet you haven't thought which Guild to join, or what kind of job you want to get at the end of it all, either."

"But I have," Billy protested. "That's the problem! You see, I'd quite like to be a plunchnologist, which is why I think I should go for the certificate in socioorganic architecture... or maybe an armiger-cybernaut, in which case the seminars on equivocal disbezzlement would be better. Then again, what I'd really like to do is become a company director. Which is why I'm interested in the course in carpentry."

"What has carpentry got to do with it?"

"I want to chair the board."

Hermione Ginghyllys sighed. "Your problem, Jarneyvore, is that you're a born dilettante."

Billy thought that sounded like a really interesting job. What did you have to do to become one of those?

"A dilettante, Jarneyvore, is someone who dabbles. In art, science, or literature. You seem to be aiming at all three, with politics, philosophy, and whippet-breeding thrown in."

Jarneyvore was offended. "I do *not* dabble! I take everything seriously!"

"Jarneyvore, you can't take *everything* seriously. You've *got* to specialize. Join a Guild. Otherwise you'll just end up as a Jack of all trades."

Billy sat bolt upright in his seat.

"That's it! Miz Ginghyllys, that's *it*!"

He shot out of the room, leaving a pile of course leaflets and a puzzled registrar, who never did understand what it was that she had said.

# 3   ...and Master of One

Boomworlds, in the haste of exploitation, tend to sidestep the bureaucratic niceties of more established domains. It is, for example, possible to obtain work without possessing various paper qualifications normally demanded of its citizens by the Quaternity, or without being a member of one of the specialist Guilds. In consequence, boomworlds attract a less than conformist breed; and such people, especially in concentration, engender a less than orthodox variety of problems. Fortunately, though, a stringent workload keeps these individualists in check most of the time.

But not always.

As a case in point, consider the plight of Wyllam Jarneyvore, now in his early twenties, and a joat by trade. He had not anticipated returning to his homeworld, but in the event it was inevitable. He was outwardly cheerful by nature, and inwardly apprehensive by virtue of having been — well, apprehended. The penalty for tampering with the freewave communication network was twelve months on Jeremiah's Revenge.

In most respects he was an average sort of person. He had grown neither short nor tall, slim nor stout, though he had remained bony. His complexion was neither pale nor sallow. His dark wavy hair was close-cropped at the back and cut long at the sides in the height of last year's Aphéligian fashion. Thick eyebrows clung to his forehead like terrified caterpillars on a mountain ledge. Below were the same large almond-shaped eyes, their irises dark brown with specks of blue. With his unremarkable physique he might have made an excellent spy, blending unseen into the crowd — but in point of fact his ill-matching clothing made him stand out like a wollagong in a beauty parade. He wore a ruffled yellow shirt embroidered in black cross-stitch, scarlet pantaloons cut tight at mid-calf on the left leg and mid-thigh on the right by lace bows, green fishnet hose, calfskin boots studded at the toes with artificial emeralds, a lospided blue tunic that had seen better days, and a conical woollen hat with a long gold tassel attached to its brim. He considered himself a snappy dresser and never could understand why nobody else shared this assessment. His hands were long-fingered and dextrous, their nails blunted, broken, and grimy. His right hand was backed with dark hair, but the back of his left hand was newly hairless from a chemical experiment that had gone wrong. His palms were calloused but the skin was plump and pink. They bore contradictory signs: the hands of a workman, the hands of an intellectual.

He was both.

He sat in the rear compartment of a four-man tove as it skimmed between the rafts and among the cables that tethered them. Like much of Grover's world, the tove was mostly orange-brown in colour, and liberally streaked with green. However, here and there it was possible to detect patches of metallic blue.

The uniform of the constable sitting beside him was the identical shade.

Two days previously, Jarneyvore had been eating his breakfast on a balcony above the boardwalks of Raft 5077, observing the shifting domain structure of pockmarks etched by the rain on the murk below. Still not fully awake, he had opened the morning mail, wondering for the ten thousandth time how he could break into the SpaDe computer network and find out what had really happened to his father.

The first envelope had brought forth a credit-note, of satisfactory but not generous dimensions, in recompense for assistance in troubleshooting a hormone imbalance in the cyborg controller of an underwater city on Nueva Zimbabwe. He had tucked it on a shelf, behind the PAXIAL prism that he had kept as a memento of events on Thorneycroft. Then he had opened the second envelope, which disclosed a tax waiver on that item from the Interstellar Revenue Service in recognition of his absence from Sector of Domicile for a period of not less than twenty-two days... but what was this? A tax *demand*, for the very same transaction?

An explanation, all too plausible, was soon forthcoming. Grover's World, not the most developed in the galaxy, would have routed the information to the sectorate on Aphélix. Even though freewave was essentially instantaneous, the relay to Icebox was not. The tax demand was routine but the waiver was not, and therefore had not yet been processed. A retraction would certainly follow, after some confusion, the IRS being notoriously inept at unravelling leapfrogged communications.

The whole thing would probably outrun *The Moletrap*, now in its seventy-third excruciating year. (The constable did it.) Jarneyvore saw it as one more example of the pernicious effects of authority, even though he was slowly coming to accept with grudging grace the tangled red tape of the Quaternity. It was better than a four-sided war. Though less exciting. What made it worse was that the IRS was a human institution, and most of its staff were still drawn from human ranks. One was entitled to a little empathy from one's own race — or so it seemed to Jarneyvore's muzzy brain at that early hour, history being overwhelmingly against that particular philosophic standpoint.

Why couldn't *they* be made to feel frustrated for once? Why couldn't —

Perhaps they could.

He hastily put the thought out of his head, mindful of the unattractive prospect of Jeremiah's Revenge. It surfaced later that day when he was engaged in tedious reconstruction work at the Frozen Freight Terminal. This time he thought long and hard about the technical problems, which were attractively difficult, but by no means insoluble...

An evening with Mary Carey, a buxom rosy-cheeked outdoor girl who looked like a vegetable grower but actually worked for the telephone company (she claimed she only went out with him because he was the first person in two decades not to remark, when first introduced, that her name rhymed) submerged these thoughts again. Until the perfect method bubbled up, unheralded, from his subconscious. At approximately one o'clock in the morning he spent twenty minutes in a public booth punching digits.

The result, thirty-four hours later, disrupted IRS communications from Hickory Gulch to the Greater Magellanic Cloud.

\* \* \*

The pryship *Pontryagin*, a SpaDe research vessel, floated at the edge of Sharraby Breach like a snowflake beside a crevasse. Like all spacegoing vessels, it was equipped with PhaDER gear, equipment for travelling faster than light. The full name is Phase Dislocation Existential Relocator. The device is based on the fundamental physical principle that the material universe is merely an insubstantial frill on a far deeper and more important structure known as phase space — that each point of ordinary space-time is merely the material tip of a vast, intricate fractal iceberg, nearly all of which points out of the world in which we fondly imagine we live. As, of course, does most of *us*. Particles of matter do not, in fact, exist in ordinary space-time at all. They are merely the shadows in space-time of probabilities that are distributed over these extra orthofractal dimensions. One popular way to rescue the classical picture of space-time is to pretend that each of its points has associated with it a hidden orthofractal phase, which determines this distribution. Because of singularities left over from the Big Bang, these orthofractal phases do not vary continuously from point to point; instead there are dislocations in phase space across which the phase *jumps*. Particles of matter can be transported across huge distances of space in small amounts of time by concentrating their probabilities near phase dislocations, then shoving them across the jumps, and spreading them back into what is erroneously known as the 'real' world — a process known as phading. A typical phade takes only a few nanoseconds, though it can take *hours* to set one up when there's heavy traffic.

Quaternity philosophers have long debated the reasons why the universe should be constructed in such a ridiculously complicated and deceptive manner. One school of thought points out that without faster-than-light transport, a galaxy-wide civilization like the Quaternity cannot exist, and it is obviously foolish for creatures that live in a galaxy-wide civilization to ask why the universe is constructed in a manner that permits the existence of a galaxy-wide civilization. Because, if it wasn't, they wouldn't be asking that question. This argument is known as the Anthropic Principle, and its adherents are as numerous as they are naive.

However, some great thinkers believe that such reasoning applies only to intelligence — the time-honoured argument that intelligent beings should not be surprised that the universe is constructed so as to permit the existence of intelligent beings, because if it were not then there would be nobody around to ask awkward questions about their own existence. In point of fact, this reasoning is fallacious. On the jungle world of Owoooh there lives an incredibly stupid animal known as the Florid Bungus. It suffers from a terrible dread of heights, but has evolved to run up a tree at the first sign of danger. Because Owoooh is an incredibly dangerous place, the Florid Bungus spends much of its life clinging in terror to the tops of tall trees thinking "Why am I here?" This demonstrates that the universe could perfectly well be constructed so as to give rise to creatures asking awkward questions about the meaning of existence without suffering any compulsion whatsoever to produce intelligent life. Unfortunately the Florid Bungus is far too unintelligent to communicate its thoughts to anybody else, so this particular fallacy has never been exposed.

Whatever its philosophical status, the PhaDER is the glue that binds the Quaternity together. However, phading is not without its perils. Phasemesh failure can strand a ship in a region of space that bears no relation to its destination. But most of all, spacegoers fear *escalade*, a term that designates a rare phenomenon in which phase resonance grows without limit. The *Astronaut's Almanac* describes the result in its characteristic style: 'Expansive forces increase exponentially until they exceed by several orders of magnitude the design tolerances of the structural material.'

*Pontryagin* was exhibiting the classic symptoms of escalade. Its phasic halo, normally a frigid blue, was yellow streaked with orange and red. In the few seconds before it shattered into a formless cloud of ionized particles, *Pontryagin* transmitted a freewave message to Quaternity Central: a carefully profiled waveform which resolved itself en route into a sequence of coded soliton pulses.

\* \* \*

Jarneyvore traced the tove's progress on a map of the city that he kept in his head. It disturbed him more than he cared to admit when he realized their destination was the Space Department. For, according to the Doctrine of Disconnected Powers, SpaDe had no right to be involved in IRS affairs.

He recognized the SpaDe official at once: Joze Palgandra, local Defence Secretary and a Grynth to boot. Like all Grynth he was large and hairy; his fur a dull beige except for the tips of his ears, which were black. He had the musculature of a giant ape, the dentition of a feline predator, and the subtlety of an oriental potentate. His deep growling voice spoke with the ingrained confidence of someone who knows that his authority will be backed to the hilt by an organization of boundless capacity and power. He was intelligent enough to cultivate the appearance of clumsiness, making it easy to underestimate him, which was how he liked it. He was a political animal, an operator, but one with a streak of — humanity is the word, species notwithstanding — which he tried to hide but exercised when necessary. To those who saw through his act, Palgandra was impressive: to all, he was authoritative.

The Joat hated authority and was determinedly unimpressed, not least because he *did* see through the faked clumsiness, but his mind was already looking for the points of maximum leverage, because he knew the Defence Secretary would be a tough opponent... *Defence?* He began to relax. It wasn't the IRS business after all.

Palgandra looked up sharply from his desk and snorted. The sound appeared to come from his large hairy ears, but in fact it came from twin orifices just behind them. "You are Wyllam Jarneyvore. Otherwise known as Billy the Joat." It was not a question and it elicited no reply. "We live in interesting times, Mr. Jarneyvore. My Specialists seem to agree on only one thing: they desperately need the services of a joat." Billy relaxed imperceptibly. Palgandra leaned forward, and snorted again. "I take it that a *joat* is some kind of polymath?"

"Jack-Of-All-Trades. A dilettante with depth. Not a Specialist, and utterly different from a Generalist. I'm the glue that binds the intellectual world together. Without the specialists, I'd know nothing. Without me, they find it hard to talk to each other, so they don't. With my able assistance, they do, and things happen that never would have."

Palgandra shuffled papers. "You keep strange company."

"To be a good joat you need to cultivate all possible sources of information."

"The records say you have made important contributions to Quaternity research. Also that you possess an incurable urge to tinker with mechanisms in ways embarrassing to those in authority. My psychologists tell me that this is a characteristic of successful joats, a price we must pay if we desire their services." Palgandra's skepticism was palpable.

"Look, Palgandra, there's a lot of cultural pressure towards specialization," said Billy. *Dammit, that walking doormat's getting me on the defensive.* "To resist that, you have to be a bit weird. A distrust for established authority is part of the mind-set."

"Such as reprogramming a police tove to perform ever-decreasing circles around the Eros Raft?" Billy did not react. Palgandra looked directly at him. "Or worse. Someone with your particular mind-set saw fit to tamper with the IRS freewave network."

Billy decided that his relaxation had been premature.

"He gained access to the Bell subdirectory here, and from there he got into the main Directory on Aphélix. That trick uses three classified commercial codes — one to tap the maintenance channel, one to link to directory update, and one to unlock the software protection system. Using Bell's private language he then entered a self-erasing parasite that transposed the numbers of IRS branches whenever a call was made between them. The subdirectory feeds in batches to the main one, with a delay of about twenty hours, and nothing happened until this morning. When the effect became noticeable, but before it was clear what it was, the Comptroller followed standard procedure and put out an all-branch alert." *Just as I'd expected*, thought Billy with satisfaction, until he remembered where he was. "Because the alert is automatically routed by freewave through the telephone system, the effect was to randomize all twenty-four million branch numbers." Palgandra paused for breath, and Billy seized his opportunity.

"Mr. Secretary, I don't see why you want *me*. The IRS must have records of the original numbers; if not then I'm sure Bell does. It would only take a day or so to upload them. Tell me, what's SpaDe doing in a purely IRS affair?"

"It isn't a purely IRS affair. The Directory is their problem, but ours is more serious. We lost a pryship out near the Breach."

"Doing what?"

"I can't tell you. It's top secret."

"It's highly dangerous, too. Erratic, uncontrollable time warps; lots of energy flux. Very unstable area." He didn't mention that the

Breach had taken his father from him, though it was almost certain that Palgandra knew. "I can't imagine what SpaDe would find in the Breach to interest them." He was fishing now.

"No, you can't," said Palgandra, refusing the bait. "What concerns you is a different, though intimately related, matter." The Grynth pressed a button on his desk, and after a few seconds a quiet, slightly shifty looking human entered. "Allow me to introduce Chief Cryptologist Mauris Harllan. Harllan, this is Mr. Jarneyvore, a joat. Please explain to him our unfortunate difficulty."

Harllan cleared his throat. "Er — Mr. Jarneyvore... You are, no doubt, acquainted with trapcodes?"

The Joat looked thoughtful. All commercial concerns used trapcodes, but they kept them under wraps, so it wouldn't do to appear *too* knowledgeable. "I'm a joat," he said, as though this was answer enough. When the silence had stretched to breaking-point, he decided he should perhaps be more forthcoming. "Um, well, yeah... I know a *bit* about trapcodes. Main thing is, they're unbreakable, with thousands of pages of theory to prove it. The encoding algorithm can be made public without compromising the decoding algorithm. It's a standard method for transmitting classified industrial and military information."

Harllan nodded. "Yes. The technique uses two large primes and..."

The Joat knew a lot more about trapcodes, and although he had no wish to reveal this, he also had no wish to sit through a description of them again. "Mr. Harllan, I really don't think that now is the time to go into such fine detail." Momentarily Harllan looked offended, but he was intelligent enough to take the point. Billy turned to Palgandra. "So something happened with a trapcode. What?"

"We use one for SpaDe reports. Yesterday evening the computer stopped decoding. The primes were erased. It forgot the decoding algorithm."

"Change the code. Get a new computer."

Palgandra shook his head. "The code is changed automatically every twenty-four hours. The computer is in full working order. We have lost exactly one day's reports. Unluckily, they happen to include the one from the missing pryship."

Billy frowned. "How did the computer get wiped?"

"The algorithms," said Harllan, "included a randomizing element. Based upon the current contents of the BG directory on Aphélix."

"BG is the Bell-Galactic telephone company," put in Palgandra, unnecessarily.

"It was in a protected segment of the core," added Harllan. The Joat began to worry, though nothing showed in his expression. He enquired softly, "*How* protected?"

"Totally."

"Sorry, let me rephrase that. Protected *how*?"

"ERS."

"Engulf/Rewrite/Scramble." *That explains a lot — and I'm in trouble. Joat, generalize thyself!* "I've — er — I've heard of better methods."

"It's a standard cryptographic technique," said Harllan, falling back on the defensive. "Until now we hadn't realized it was unsatisfactory."

Billy leaned back in his chair. *Oh, gods.* "Dr. Harllan, in the last three years there have been at least fifty technical papers in the journals of the Guild of Programmers that discuss potential flaws in the ERS method. But of course they aren't in the *cryptography* journals, are they? So you've never read them."

"I have more than enough work to do keeping up with my professional speciality," said Harllan, in a huff.

"That's no excuse. Tell me: while you were pursuing your professional speciality so singlemindedly, did you discover that it is impossible to auto-protect ERS on a concealed program unless you use an irregular tag?"

"No. I don't see how —"

"The point is that if someone feeds in a self-erasing parasite it may be *attracted* to the tag. That preempts the rewrite instruction, and the scrambler gets absorbed. What *should* happen is that the parasite is engulfed, the decode algorithm is rewritten, and the parity echo is scrambled to delete any memory of the protected segment... but without an effective rewrite, you lose whatever was in the space that the parasite subver—"

"I really don't think that now is the time to go into such fine detail," said Palgandra. The Joat had the decency to look sheepish.

"Self-erasing parasite?" asked Harllan. Billy gave him an exaggerated stage smile but said nothing. Palgandra broke the icy silence. "I see what you mean about Guilds not talking to each other. But I must tell you, Jarneyvore, that the IRS parasite looks remarkably like your handwriting."

"How can you tell, if it's erased itself? You can only tell it was there because of what it did."

"That's *exactly* the part that looks like your handwriting."

"It could have been a disgruntled Bell employee. A disgruntled SpaDe operative. With freewave, almost anyone in the galaxy with access to the right information."

"Except that we know the parasite was entered here on Grover's World." *I've often wondered if they could do that. I'd have preferred to remain ignorant.* "But not only are you the sole person on planet with the knowledge to pull such a stunt *and* the personality to do it," continued Palgandra, "you're also the only person on planet with any chance of putting it right."

"Naturally. So impressive is the record of Wyllam Jarneyvore, joat extraordinary, that restoring vanished numbers from a computer, or breaking an unbreakable code, will be scarcely enough of a problem to trouble the great mind." He got to his feet. "Why me? You could phade every joat in the Quaternity over here if you felt like it!"

Palgandra snorted enigmatically. "But I don't feel like it, Jarneyvore. First, there is a proverb about too many cooks. Second, your record is genuinely impressive and you are on the spot. Third, we have in fact put other joats to work on the problem. But *you* have much better motivation."

"Motivation?"

"*We* know you're responsible for this; *you* know you're responsible for this. As a citizen of the Quaternity you are enlisted in the Defence Reserve. We may have to send out another pryship; I can ensure that you are on it. As latrine assistant, unless I can find a less exalted rank." Palgandra leaned both elbows on the desk, and there was a long silence before he continued, "I won't have to do that, of course. You tell me why."

"*Agneth*," the Joat said with false confidence. It was a Grynth form of racial pride, translating loosely as 'honour' or 'face', but neither term really captured it. On matters of agneth, the Grynth were as immovable as a black hole event horizon.

Palgandra emitted a series of snorts, the Grynth sign of amusement. "*Agneth?* You don't warrant *agneth*, Jarneyvore. There's nothing the least bit *gnethaly* about you! Try again, something sensible this time."

"Um. You have my personality profile on record. It tells you that I won't produce good ideas under threat. That I wouldn't cooperate. That I'll fight SpaDe through every court in the Quaternity. You need my cooperation now, not in twenty years' time."

"Close," said Palgandra. "But not close enough."

"So what's your theory?"

"Your personality profile also records that beneath that brash exterior lurks an altruist."

"Crap."

"By accident, your little scheme has blown up into something serious. You may not admit responsibility, but you *feel* it. You would like to help, to undo the damage you did."

*I'd give my right arm to get on a pryship going to Sharraby Breach, too,* thought the Joat. *But not as a latrine assistant. However, this could be a golden opportunity to dig around in SpaDe's files...* He shrugged. "*You* might say that. *I* could not possibly comment."

"You wish to remain silent so as to incriminate yourself?"

"You said that, not me."

The Grynth rubbed its eyes with the back of one paw, a sign of anger kept under control with growing difficulty. "I think I see a way out of this impasse. Joatry requires recognition from no Guild, and involves no specific qualifications. It is a freelance profession. I imagine that you would have no objection to undertaking a SpaDe commission — subject to the negotiation of a mutually acceptable fee?"

"What do you deem mutually acceptable?"

"Double your usual rate."

"Now that, Mr. Palgandra, is a generous offer. I could hardly *refuse* you without running the risk of being interpreted as incriminating myself."

"No, you couldn't."

"Naturally I accept your generous commission. The Quaternity can afford it. Though an action carried out for personal gain hardly amounts to altruism."

Palgandra shook his head. "On the contrary, it is often the purest kind."

\* \* \*

The problem, as Palgandra explained it, was exacerbated by politics, and went well beyond the mysterious loss of one pryship. Humans and Grynth were worried that *Pontryagin*'s disappearance had been engineered — most probably by the Femm but conceivably by the Barasshanti — while hoping fervently but without conviction that it hadn't. Privately, each species was a bit worried that other might be involved, but as founding fathers of the Quaternity they had long ago come to a mutually beneficial working arrangement. Feelings were running high, and the Barasshanti had accused Humans and Grynth of conspiring to conceal the real reasons for *Pontryagin*'s loss, in order to cast suspicion on *them*. As ever, the Femm remained inscrutable.

This at least was the surface. However inaccurately waves on an ocean reflect the true turmoil beneath, they are an unmistakable sign that turmoil does indeed exist.

The Joat's first step was routine — the only one that was. He set the wheels in motion to convene a cabal — an *ad hoc* gathering of Specialists whose combined areas of expertise would encompass all fields likely to be relevant. Add one joat and stir, and you have a group of people who can talk to each other and whose pooled resources have a fighting chance of finding a solution.

If there is one.

Grover's World was ill-equipped, and its communications were slow. Jarneyvore located the cabal on Aphélix. While his commandeered cruiser was calibrating its PhaDER grids he initiated two long shots — a core search to see whether the decoder still existed somewhere in the BGD memory, and a codebreaking sequence of his own invention whose chance of success was, to be candid, less than that of a boggie surviving a lightning strike. Instructions for both were recorded for immediate transmission on demeshing, prior to planetfall.

\* \* \*

The furniture was comfortable and casual. There was a bank of terminals hooked into the main SpaDe reticule by freewave link. Jarneyvore had also insisted on a blackboard and chalk — obtained after some confusion from the Aphéligian Museum of Obsolete Technology — and a plentiful supply of coffee, acceptable to all participants except the Femm, for whom a species of groundnut performed a similar function. Across three species, a scientist is a machine for turning coffee into ideas.

Chief Cryptologist Harllan was there, though under protest. He had objected to Jarneyvore's (lack of) qualifications — until it was pointed out that while there were some twenty-seven thousand cryptologists in the sector, there were only three joats. Also present was Maralyn Chanopy, computer specialist; compact and spiky with a sharp mind and a mouth to match. A trio of Grynths formed a statistics team that had worked with Maralyn when the code system was installed. They conferred in one corner at the threshold of hearing. Pazh ap-Rozby, a Barasshanti electronics expert, was riffling through a pile of logistack profiles using a robomanipulator attached to one forehoof, with a sceptical look on his alien features. But then, Barasshan always looked skeptical. Except when they looked actively suspicious. Mizzlizllyn Dirijjee, a Master Mathematician and a Femm, balanced a bowl of *kaata* nuts on one leg-joint and gazed blankly at the floor. He was either deep in thought or asleep, you could never tell with Femm.

As background, Harllan explained the intricacies of trapcodes. The process was simple, elegant, and effective. The encoding algorithm required knowing only the product of two particular two-hundred-digit primes. But to decode a message you needed the primes themselves, known only to the computer that had created them. To obtain the prime factors by factorizing the product would take, given good fortune, some forty trillion years. The Joat recalled an apposite quotation from an ancient number theorist: "Suppose the cleaning lady gives $p$ and $q$ by mistake to the garbage collector, but that the product $pq$ is saved. How to recover $p$ and $q$? It must be felt as a defeat for mathematics that the most promising approaches are searching the garbage dump and applying memo-hypnotic techniques." True then, and just as true now. Though he wondered what a cleaning lady was.

Maralyn wanted to know how accurate the estimate of forty trillion years was. Mizzlizllyn opened one eye, muttered "ludigrously optimistic," and closed it again. No one queried this.

"I would like to know more about the encoding program," ap-Rozby put in. He scratched his carapace gently with his unencumbered hoof. "Since the computer has forgotten the two primes, and we are assured that nobody else knows them, I assume that only the computer ever had access to that knowledge. How was this achieved?"

This was Maralyn Chanopy's territory. "I can answer that one, Pazh — though I doubt it will help."

The Joat looked sharply at her. "Why not?"

"Well... that program was designed to be foolproof. It makes use of a rumdog to —"

"A *what*?"

She blushed. "Silly Specialist jargon. A random number generator. We use it for a pre-encoding computation. It produces the two primes, at random."

"Any chance of getting a copy of this — er — rumdog?"

"It's a standard software package."

The Joat's ears pricked up. "Isn't that dangerous?"

She looked at him blankly. He expanded. "I mean, if the rumdog is available on the open market —"

"Oh. I see. No, that wouldn't make any difference. The important thing is to get the best one available. It doesn't help to know how it works. Random is random, you know."

"Are you a statistician, Maralyn?"

The question came not from the trio of Grynths, but from Pazh ap-Rozby. It startled both Maralyn Chanopy and Wyllam Jarneyvore.

"You know perfectly well that I'm a programmer, Pazh."

"Even so, surely you've heard of Rozby ap-Fordd?"

"The Nobel winner in statistics! Yes. Rozby? Relative of yours?"

"He was my herdfather. When I was a young boy I was playing *krapph* — a Barasshanti game of chance — and I said something about how structureless chance was. I still remember his reply."

"What was it?"

Ap-Rozby smiled — a rare feat for a Barasshan. "He told me, 'there is no such thing as "random". Even the disorder in the universe is structured. Randomness is merely evidence of a pattern that temporarily escapes the Barasshanti mind.' "

One of the Grynths spoke. "I studied Rozby. In his six-disk *Marginalia of Metastatistical Methodology* he also said, 'there are no patterns in the universe beyond those our minds impose on it.' "

"Did he? I wonder what the context was... I thought I should mention what he told me. Rozby ap-Fordd seemed to think it was important."

"I think Pazh has a point, Jimi." The speaker was another of the Grynths: Hari Jaxxon. Human names were in vogue amongst the Grynth. "Especially in this context. You don't generate random numbers by writing a random program. All they ever do is hit loops."

Billy nodded. "So how *do* you generate random numbers, Hari?"

Jaxxon told him.

When generating random numbers it is necessary to be certain that they really are random. To do this requires detailed knowledge of the rules that govern their formation — a paradox, since known rules cannot be truly random. Its resolution is to be found in the behaviour of insect populations. Under suitable, carefully controlled conditions, population numbers can fluctuate violently and without pattern. It had been found, not without surprise, that such fluctuations can occur even with deterministic breeding rules, owing to effects that the entoecologists dubbed 'chaos'. The mathematicians, less desperate but still betraying their ignorance through their terminology, called them 'strange attractors' and attacked them using symbolic dynamics and ergodic theory. They are analogous to turbulence in the population drift. A byproduct of the analysis is a simple algorithm for generating random numbers by a deterministic process.

Billy digested this. "Can we duplicate the computation used for the decoder?"

"That's not the point!" said Maralyn excitedly. "We already know the listing for the program. I *told* you, it's standard."

"Chaos?"

"We prefer to call it PLiER — Positive Liapunov Exponent Recursion — but, yes, it does use that kind of technique."

"Well," said Billy, "I think it *is* important, Maralyn. If the standard program had been nondeterministic, we would have been in real difficulty. Run one of those twice, and the second time it does something quite different from the first. At least with a deterministic program you get repeatable results."

Maralyn came close to stamping a foot. "Whoever heard of a nondeterministic program?"

"I believe that the Femm have developed a range of nondeterministic hardware," said ap-Ropzby. "What would a program for that look like?"

"I was thinking of some work of Wallach at MSU," said the Joat. "What she does is —"

Jaxxon stepped in to defend Maralyn. "I think the pair of you are chasing a herring's nest. You can't just duplicate a rumdog computation by running the program again. Can you, Maralyn?"

"Damned right, Hari! You have to know where to start."

"Explain that, please, Maralyn," said the Joat.

"Look. You take any fixed program and run it on a machine. Now run it again. What happens?"

"The same thing."

"Exactly. Will a random number generator be any use if it repeats the same list of numbers every time you start it up? No. So what you do is incorporate into the program a starting-point that changes from one occasion to the next—a seed. Like the date. Or the time. Or the longitude of Sirius."

"So to reconstruct the decoder," said Billy, "all we need to know is the date when it was run?"

Jaxxon grinned, but shook his head. "Not so easy. That's a little too obvious."

"What *do* we need to know?"

Jaxxon sighed. "That decoder was intended to be *unbeatable*. We had to use something that could never be guessed, or even if it was guessed, could never be reconstructed."

The Joat leaned back, spread his arms. "Let me guess. When I talked to Palgandra he mentioned... right. The contents of the BG directory on Grover's World?"

"You got it."

\* \* \*

Jarneyvore reported to SpaDe headquarters on Aphélix. He had been wondering why such an important operation had been left to a minor official, but it soon became clear that Palgandra was a ringer. He obviously held a much higher rank than the position of Defence Secretary on a boondock world indicated. This reinforced his feeling that Humans and Grynth were engaged in cloak-and-dagger activities in Sharraby Breach. He vested his hopes on a glimpse under the cloak, and resolved to watch out for the dagger.

After making him cool his heels for half a day, SpaDe HQ sent him straight back to Grover's World to report to Palgandra in person. Typical. It might have been just bureaucratic channels, or internal politics. Whatever the explanation, the Joat was happy to be back on home territory — until he saw Palgandra's reaction to his news.

"I can reconstruct the decoding algorithm if I can find the missing primes," said Billy. "In fact I could run the random number generator again and make the *computer* find the primes. But first we have to initialize the program, and to do *that* we have to know what was in the BG directory, here, three days ago."

"And that...?"

"...is impossible. They keep no records of past list—" Palgandra tipped his head back and howled like a banshee. Then he demonstrated a vocabulary of profanity that extended across several dozen languages and all four species and made the Joat distinctly envious. He tore the legs off his chair and used them to beat the sofa to death. Then he took a deep breath, sat down amid the wreckage, and said "That's a pity."

"Yeah," agreed the Joat. "I suppose there's a minuscule probability that a galaxy-wide search could turn up a list, but the likelihood of an error, or something being missed out, is enormous. I can't see any way to get accurate information. And just one bit out of place in a trillion will give totally different results. Butterfly effect."

"Ask Bell Central?"

"The local directory does transmit them an update. In fact, that's what's used to initialize the code. But the central directory doesn't record outdated listings, so we're three days too late. The version we want has been overlaid twice since."

"So to put the matter succinctly, Mr. Jarneyvore..."

"It's a bugger."

"Quite."

\* \* \*

Mary's phone bleeped. "Billy! You're back! Is everything all right?"

"So-so. I'd like to talk it over with you. You know, bounce ideas around a bit. Sometimes that helps, and you're a good listener."

"If that's meant to be flattery, Wyllam Jarneyvore, it's a bit backhanded. You ought to say that I make an intelligent contribution to the discussion."

"You do."

"Yes, but *you're* supposed to say that, not me!"

Billy started again. "Are you free for dinner tonight, Mary?"

"Maybe."

"Scrab Vietnese at Chu Minh's, dancing at Pook's, followed by a tove ride and cocktails on Windy Mire?"

"Bribery beats flattery any day. Splash by at eight-thirty."

Midnight found them both seated at the perimeter of the R&R raft, adrift on Windy Mire, served by chauffeured toves from the nearby shore.

"...but Billy, there must be *something* you can do."

"I wish there were, Mary. But wanting a solution to an impossible problem doesn't create one. We got a lot closer than I'd have expected. We can beat the code, but only if we can get hold of a key that was wiped three days ago."

"Do some kind of microscopic analysis of the memory-banks? Look for traces of what was there before?"

"Can't be done with enough accuracy, I'm afraid."

"Nothing showed up in any audit-trails?"

"No. They keep records going back forever of who called whom and when, but they don't keep directories. There's no way short of time-travel."

"It's rotten luck."

The Joat gave a wry smile. "Huh. With *my* personality profile it's not. It's inevitable. Civilization — to use a polite phrase — likes to think it moves on nice, smoothly oiled wheels. My function is throwing a wrench in the works."

"Don't blame yourself. It's not your fault that the IRS sent you a tax demand when they shouldn't have. That's what started it all."

"That's true. If they hadn't been so penny-pinching about freewave equipment —"

"Billy, you know they can't use freewave this close to Basketball."

"Oh, right. Because of the gravity-well."

"Exactly. They have to use a relay, and the messages take about twenty hours to reach Icebox, where the freewave station is. It's not a cost-cutting measure. I know someone in the radio-room where they handle that sort of thing. Janys Burrows, you know her?"

"Is she the slim one with the long blonde hair and nice legs?"

"Ooooh, you *pig*! No, she's short and dumpy, not your type at all."

"Mary Carey, quite con... oops, sorry. I know you're sensitive about that. But you won't give up, will you?"

Mary worried at the problem like a shronk with a sumpslug. "I don't see how you can be so certain that it's totally impossible."

"Mathematics. Lower bound complexity estimates. Mizlizzllyn insists that his lower limits on the codebreaking time are foolproof, so sneaking in the back door is the only chance. Trouble is, there's no back door."

Mary leaned closer and touched his hand. "You'll find a way, Billy. Don't be discouraged."

\* \* \*

A message from the Joat woke her up at three o'clock in the morning. "Mary, you're beautiful." It was a nice compliment, though a strange thing to send, and a stupid time to send it. A bunch of swamp-lilies delivered at breakfast time would have been the normal tactic. But then, Billy *was* strange. And stupid, as often as not, come to think of it.

Only later in the day, when she tried to get in touch and Billy's concierge informed her that he had left for SpaDe headquarters long before dawn, did she begin to wonder whether the message had greater significance.

By that time Billy the Joat and Pazh ap-Rozby were in deep space with a shipload of electronic equipment.

\* \* \*

"Was Palgandra surprised when you told him you'd cracked the uncrackable?"

"*Was* he? He surely was. Dammit, so were Pazh and I. When we told him how we'd done it, though, he was plain annoyed."

"Why?"

"Well," said the Joat, "it disclosed a rather nasty security leak."

"Yes, I suppose it would, breaking the unbreakable."

"I gave him a head start setting it right, though. I rewrote all the protection routines for him."

"Why did you bother?"

*Good question*, thought Billy, *and one I shall evade*. "In return for an explanation of what happened to *Pontryagin*. I can't tell you much, for legal reasons. But they were trying to investigate something involving the Femm. Ironically, it's all inconclusive. The whole political thing is still up in the air. They found out *what* happened to *Pontryagin* — it went into escalade and blew up. What they *don't* know is why it did it. Some say accident, some say sabotage. So now everyone's arguing again. But I'll tell you something..."

"Yes?"

"*Somebody* was up to no good. Whatever it was, they won't find it so easy to keep it under wraps from now on."

"You can't give me the real dirt on the code, either, can you?"

The Joat shook his head in a manner that indicated that on the contrary he could. "Everything's got to be changed anyway, Mary." He leaned back against a cushion, and gazed at a point just in front of his nose to focus his thoughts. He presumably didn't realise that this made him look like a lovesick boggie. "I should've thought of it right at the start. To duplicate the decoder, all I needed was the contents of the directory, three days ago. After it had been sent to Bell Central and wiped. Nothing to it, really." He pretended not to notice her hands bunching into fists. "If they'd sent it by freewave that really would have been the end of the trail. But they didn't, because they couldn't, for the same reason that the IRS couldn't, which is what caused it all to begin with." He paused for breath. "Ironic, isn't it. They sent it by radio, squirted in a tight beam to Icebox. As you reminded me, it takes radio nearly twenty hours to reach Icebox."

"Oh, *I* see."

"Yes. What happens if you go about three and a half times as far out? Apart from it getting even colder?"

She nodded. It was all clear now.

"I should have got the solution sooner, but I hadn't known they'd used radio. No, that's a bad excuse — I should have worked it out from the timing. But I didn't get to thinking about it until you mentioned your friend in the radio-room."

"I told you, Janys is short and dumpy."

"I was thinking about radio, not Jinette Wossername —"

"Nice try but no dice. Joats have eidetic memories."

"Mine's very selective... It took time to make the connection. If you hadn't kept worrying at the problem, I might never have thought of the answer. I'm grateful."

"Don't mention it. Let me just see if I've got it figured out right. By going that far out you get to a place where the message takes oh, perhaps... seventy hours? to arrive."

"Exactly. Out in deep space, strung out as a stream of tiny radio pulses, is yesterday's directory. Further out, the day before's. It's ludicrous really: a whole series of telephone directories, getting fainter and fainter and older and older, wandering off to infinity. I wonder if somewhere in the distant depths of intergalactic space some incredibly ancient and intelligent race is picking them up? Maybe the mysterious PAXIAL are listening in. I wonder what they make of an endless stream of telephone numbers?

"But that's beside the point. All you have to do is phade out to the right place, and switch on your recorder. With good equipment, a week's delay is no problem. And Pazh's equipment is *very* good, especially if you bear in mind that he had to read up an obsolete technique in about an hour, cannibalize a whole heap of Bell's spares, and add a few gadgets of his own. We made several recordings, phading out just a little further each time, to fill in any gaps and resolve errors. Then we shipped it all back home, dumped the current directory — Bell played sweet Sump about that, I can tell you — fed in the recording, and ran the program. To test it, we fed in a coded message and saw whether it decoded correctly. It did, ergo QED."

"Ipso facto, genius."

\* \* \*

The Joat had told a few white lies. He knew a lot more about what was happening in Sharraby Breach than he would admit. In fact, he knew a lot more about what was happening in Sharraby Breach than SpaDe would ever have imagined. They had let him have physical access to their computer. It was a far bigger security blunder than the radio transmission of the directory.

However, he still didn't know *enough*.

He did know that there was some sort of power-play going on, Humans and Grynth against Femm. The Barasshanti, on the sidelines, had their suspicions... but they always did, and their evidence was weak, so on the sidelines they would stay, no doubt until it was too late. The Femm were mounting unusual activity around and probably inside Sharraby Breach. Humans and Grynth were worried enough to have sent a SpaDe pryship into that dangerous area. The Femm were worried enough to have planted a saboteur on board. *Pontryagin*'s captain had said as much before he died.

Jole Jarneyvore had been lost on a SpaDe expedition to Sharraby Breach. Another escalade? If so, Jole really was dead.

But something told his son that it wasn't so. The Femm knew what had really happened, and why. Until he found out more, he would have to play a waiting game.

* * *

Some three months later, Billy the Joat assembled a small electronic device, took a tove to an obscure quarter of the city, checked for a tail and sidled into a booth when he was sure he wasn't under surveillance. He affixed the device to the console like a limpet, then played an arpeggio on the keyboard. Two two-hundred-digit numbers appeared momentarily on the screen, then flashed off, to be replaced by their product. Below this he printed the public encoder.

The numbers matched exactly.

Using the limpet he erased all record of the transaction and exited the booth. A hundred yards further along the boardwalk, the limpet plopped into deep mud.

The main thing Billy needed in the search for his father was information. What better source than SpaDe's own computer?

# 4   The Malodorous Plutocrats

"But I don't *want* a sound-microscope!" said Billy the Joat. "All I want is an ordinary fibroptic wormrunner, size seven, with remote squirm control and laser spotwelding capability. You *must* have some of *those* in stock!"

Yaffa Varian, the grizzled Grynth proprietor of the Thriftex Part Mart, one of the most popular hobby shops in the slummy Brixton area, shrugged expansively. "Yez. But there wuz a cargo strike on Godzilla II, and then there wuz magnetic storms in McGonagall Sector, and the shipment wuz impounded on Ballantrae." His fur was browning in places and he wore a khaki overall to conceal some of the worst patches. Yaffa Varian found it hard to grow old gracefully.

"Ballantrac? The excisemen there are the biggest sticklers for regulations this side of the Magellanic Clouds! You'll *never* get the shipment out!"

The Grynth shrugged again. "Tell me about it," he snorted. "I've put in a replacement order already, but there's a six-month backlog."

The Joat groaned, and swore an ancient but still potent oath. A good oath, like fine wine, matures with age. "Look," he said, "I've got a contract to service a dozen fusion baffles for Deneb Mercantiles, and I need that equipment." He waved a hand at the racks of gadgetry; the festooned tubes, wires, and polycompatible connectors; the dumpy plastic crates of heavy machinery; the shelves of universal componentry in colour-coded boxes. "You must have *something* that will do the job."

Varian pursed his lips. "I've got a size nine without remotes," he said finally. "You could probably cannibalize a B7-c borer for those, and spotweld with an arc instead of a laser."

"That's 'ark' as in Noah? I'd need three hands with equipment that obsolete."

"I could lend you an autolimb."

The Joat became indecisive. "Those things are expensive to rent."

"I can get one cheap." The Joat didn't ask how; that was Varian's business.

"Sure," said Billy. "No sweat. Of course, the job'll take three times as long as it should, and be five times as tricky. Fortunately," he went on modestly, "I'm an autolimb virtuoso and I can handle it. How cheap?"

"The equipment? Same as a size seven 'runner plus attachments, since that wuz what you wanted."

"No," said Billy. "The autolimb."

"Free of charge."

"Rubbish!"

Another shrug. "Of course, as a reciprocal gesture of friendship, I'd appreciate the purchase of one of these fine sound-microscopes..."

Billy the Joat's reply was drowned out — though his gesture, hardly one of friendship, was not — by an amazing noise. It began as a high-pitched whine, growing in seconds from the level of a swamp-skeeter at springtime to that of a six-bore quartz drill encountering a flint obstruction; it sashayed into an irregular grinding sound terminated by a rapid burst of three whiplash cracks; it ended in a bone-jarring rumble that vibrated mud and raft like a blancmange in rut, shaking the building to its baseboards and causing a fine dust to drift down from the ceiling, filling the air with its particles. It faded slowly into the distance.

Joat and junk-merchant gathered their wits. "What wuz *that*?" enquired the Grynth.

"If we were on one of the wargame worlds in Rim country," said Billy, "I'd guess at a Q-class battlecruiser on a bombing run. But," he added, "since this is Grover's World, the only thing I can imagine is a Mitsui Mark VIII sportsyacht making a supersonic approach. And that's stupid," he went on, "because it's illegal, and the only people who own Mitsuis are ambassadors' daughters, football players, sensorium stars, and politicians... and none of them would want to come within thirty light years of *this* dump."

But is *was* a Mitsui. And its owners were *just* the type of people who would have one.

* * *

"...and they've bought half a dozen raft blocks over by Shumly Marsh," added Mary, finishing a lengthy account of the newcomers' activities as gleaned from the offices of Bell-Galactic Telephones Inc. "Right on the edge of the Brixton slums. I can't understand why they chose it."

The Joat explained. "It's right in character for an Etonian family."

"Etonian?"

SpaDe's computer had been very helpful about the Etonians, and Billy was now an expert, although he still had no idea why Jole had warned him against them. "They want contrast. They go in for ostentatious wealth, shown up to greatest effect."

"On *Grover's World*?"

"Yes, I can't understand that either. Though we hardly lack money, thanks to the chemicals in our ubiquitous mud."

"It's about all we *don't* lack," said Mary. "We don't even have freewave."

"They'll be rich enough to bring in anything they want," said Billy, "including miniaturized phaskets to send messages. But it is a bit ironic."

"In what way?"

"The dynasty goes back to Rudolph Eton. He *invented* freewave. Funny old sod, Rudolph was... Complete eccentric, but he had flashes of brilliance, maybe even genius. A very creative mind... when it wasn't smashed on booze. He stayed sober long enough to secure the freewave patent. You can imagine what the revenue was before the intellectual property rights lapsed — and that was a lot longer than usual because that much money doesn't just buy good lawyers, it buys good judges. The money went to his head and he decided to found a dynasty." He ticked the names off on his fingers as he spoke. "Started well: Rudolph, Rudolph II, Rudolph III, just like the ancient Anglish kings.

"Rudolph the red-nosed?"

"Probably would have been, but then there was a family feud, after which the leading Etonian was Wynstun II — "

"What happened to Wynstun the first?"

"Younger brother of Rudolph II, I'm only giving you the main vine in the family jungle. Next, the first female top frog, Deirdry II. Who begat Eshelby III who begat Wynstun IV who begat Rudolph IV who begat Suzella who begat Deirdry III. The current dynast is Rudolph V. There was an elder brother Bly, but he died nineteen years ago. His kids, Sherryl, Eshelby VI, Filip, and Kenith, have always been a bit peeved because when Rudolph V inherited the throne they were automatically relegated to the minor league. The first in line now are Rudolph's kids — Tory, Dwina, and Maggi. I mention this because Sherryl and Eshelby VI are the ones currently gracing Groverian society with their presence. Along with a very nasty piece of work called Kray Harrow, who's an Etonian via the wrong side of the sheets. The family uses him to lean on anybody who makes a nuisance of themselves. A thug, but an intelligent thug. Very dangerous."

"You seem to know a lot about them."

"My job, knowing things. Anyway, when Rudolph — the original Rudolph — hit it big, he became a real show-off. He set up his legacy so that his descendants had to be not only wealthy, but *conspicuously* wealthy. Their income is still enormous, of course: they diversified. They must have a hard time spending it."

"They could do worse than shove some my way," said Mary. "Even so — why come here, of all places?"

"For that matter," said the Joat, "why did we let them in? Etonians always cause trouble."

\* \* \*

Twelve rafts to the south and four east, and twenty minutes earlier, Joze Palgandra had asked the same question. As the top-ranking local SpaDe official he was also in a position to obtain an answer.

Which he did not like.

"So we can't kick them out," he snarled at his Second Undersecretary.

"No, sir."

"Not even that Harrow character? He gives me the creeps."

"Nothing official ever proved, sir."

Palgandra inspected the ceiling, as if seeking a spider. Actually, seeking inspiration. None came. "*Why* can't we kick them out, Worthington?"

"They've acquired a controlling interest in Consolidated Sludge, sir. And ConSludge has a twenty-year franchise to filter organic macromolecules from the mud. We can't deport franchisees, it wouldn't do our business image much good."

"True. But even so," said Palgandra, "I don't see why they had to *come* here. They could have set up a holding company."

"Unfortunately not, sir. There's a new Quaternity edict — a copy is on your desk, sir — dealing with the exploitation of scarce resources. Access is restricted to local companies, where 'local' is defined by a criterion of domicile."

"You mean they have to live here." The other nodded mutely. Palgandra gestured out of the window. Brown and green slime spread endlessly to the horizon, under a brooding orange sky. "You call *that* scarce?"

"No, sir, not by planetary standards. But by sector criteria, some of the organics are very scarce. Especially kata-chelated-dibenzopoly-5\*-phenyloxylazophospholine-22."

"Good gods," said Palgandra. "What's that?"

"Damned if I know, sir."

\* \* \*

The Etonians lost no time in transforming Brixton to suit their tastes. A fleet of tenders followed hard on the Mitsui's heels, crammed to the phase-coils with equipment and possessions (eighty per cent of the latter, as required to satisfy the new domicile criteria). Existing buildings on the newly purchased rafts were demolished, and a Barasshanti company skilled in high-speed construction moved in. Elegant, slender towers sprouted skywards, encircled by spiral walkways and exotic gardens in artificial environment pods; fragile arches spanned the channels of slime that separated the rafts; squat domes housing communication equipment and power supplies proliferated like measles.

An open area at the very centre was the subject of intense activity. Elliptical in shape, a hundred metres by fifty, it was completely levelled. A squad of Femm technicians sunk a deep permacrete-lined shaft, and departed as quietly and suddenly as they had appeared — only to reappear a fortnight later with an immense hovertransport, which positioned itself above the shaft while a large featureless oval capsule was installed. After that everything was obscured by scaffolding and plastic sheeting for a while. When these came down, they revealed an opulent structure whose design resembled a Femm brood-palace from the Reductionist period, but executed entirely in glass. The external rooms were faced with flat, transparent panels. Within these were displayed jewels; valuable paintings; sculptures, hologravings; precious metals and scarce minerals; cabinets of rare perfumery and spices; ancient books and tapes; antique furniture; hand-crafted carpets from Shiraz IV — even a collection of priceless ash-period Grynth mosaics. In compliance with Rudolph's wishes, the Etonians paraded their wealth.

Chief Constable Otis Pigge shook his heavy jowls incredulously. Such a display, on the fringe of such a disreputable area, represented an irresistible challenge to every crook on planet. And, to judge by the seven hundred per cent increase in tourism, every crook off planet as well. Pigge prophecied that within two days there would be nothing left but an empty glass shell.

Yet, a month later, the contents were more opulent than ever, and not a single item had vanished. Pigge was confounded, and the underworld was frustrated: the building seemed impenetrable. The glass — if glass it were — was unbreakable; there were no locks to pick; and submersible toves encountered an invisible barrier in the murky depths beneath the raft. When in desperation one offworld criminal brought up a battery of laser cannon, the beam ricochetted back off the glass and wrecked his projector. The event was sufficiently unusual to attract the news media, and the aspiring thief was interviewed several days later in his hospital bed.

* * *

"They've set up an inflex screen," said Billy the Joat, addressing the blue cow-wollagong on his mug of coffee, having noticed the headline. He distractedly leaned his left elbow on a slice of toast, thickly spread with three-fruit marmalade, as he thought the implications through.

"They've set up an inflex screen," stated Chief Constable Pigge in horror. "I want it shut off immediately. Get me a court order."

"They've set up an inflex screen," said the Second Undersecretary to Joze Palgandra. "Big Pig has tried to get it shut off again, but the Etonians have the approval of Quaternity Central."

"I can't believe that's true," said Palgandra. "Those things generate undesirable pollutants when used in a planetary atmosphere." He pinched his nose. "They *smell*, Worthington. They smell *dreadful*."

"QuatCent says this one has a newly developed suppressor system, sir."

Palgandra was skeptical. "And has this newly developed suppressor been field-tested?"

"I gather we *are* the field-test, sir."

* * *

At first it seemed to work. But slowly a nauseating smell began to build in the immediate vicinity of the screen. After a time, gawping visitors on nearby rafts began to sniff uncertainly. Soon faint emanations could be detected kilometres away.

It is a characteristic of inflex screens that the odours they generate cannot penetrate the screen itself. The Etonians could ignore the problem they were causing. In fact they rather enjoyed it: it suited their personalities and heightened the contrast between their lifestyle and that of the remainder of Grover's World.

Yaffa Varian placed an order for a quarter of a million noseplugs, sale-or-return.

Quaternity Central unaccountably refused to revoke approval for the screen.

Chief Constable Pigge fumed.

And then he received an unexpected phone call from... Eshelby Eton VI. Who had been robbed of several dozen priceless artefacts. Big Pig had dreamed of this moment. He could scarcely believe that fortune had so smiled on him. When he checked with his superiors on Aphélix he discovered it hadn't. He was so upset that he high-tailed it over to SpaDe headquarters.

"You mean," said Palgandra, "that we not only have to put up with these dreadful people, but we have to *assist* them?"

"Actively," said an exasperated but subdued Pigge. "We must — quote — leave no swamp unturned — unquote. And fast, or we're *both* out on our necks. It stinks — metaphorically as well as literally."

Palgandra paced the carpet, thinking fast. Situations such as these had occurred before in his career, but not at his present high level. How to reconcile these circumstances with *agneth*? The loss of face would be hard to bear, he'd be the snorting-stock of the entire sector! He pulled his thoughts together. "That's crazy. I can't imagine how they could have so much pull in Quaternity Central. They must have something we don't know about."

The Chief nodded. "They do," he said. "Katch-22."

"Eh?"

"Kata-wozzit-dibenzo-something-or-other."

"Ah, I remember. Kata-chelated-dibenzopoly-five-star-phenyloxylazophospholine. Twenty-two."

The Chief brightened. "You've heard of it, then?"

"Oh yes," said Palgandra. "It's a chemical. The Etonians have cornered the market in it. Though I have no idea what it's used for." He paced the floor at an accelerated rate. "This is a very singular problem," he said. "And it needs a very singular person to solve it."

Pigge grunted. "I presume you have someone in mind."

"I do indeed," said Palgandra with a sigh. "You recall the affair of the erased trapcode?"

"How could I forget?" said Pigge. "It is indelibly linked in my memory to another incident, involving a police tove and the Eros raft. But," he added, "I suppose that doesn't count in such desperate straits."

"No, it doesn't." Palgandra's mouth twisted in a grimace of pain and resignation. "He's the only choice."

"I confess," said Pigge, "I agree. Those Etonians," said Pigge, "are even worse," he continued, "than Billy the Joat."

\* \* \*

While the Chief Constable of Grover's World and the Space Department Secretary for Defence were reconciling themselves to the idea that the planet's future depended on the unique services of Wyllam (the Joat) Jarneyvore, that worthy individual was busy rifling the files of SpaDe's computer reticule using his own illicit circuits. He knew he had to be very careful not to set alarm-bells ringing, and he extracted the information in brief episodes at irregular intervals.

So far he had found out that his father had been co-opted to join an expedition under Commander Vikta Mookpace, which set off to explore Sharraby Breach in the year 436 QC when Billy was four years old. They had departed in the research vessel *Edwin Hubble*. Mookpace was a Grynth veteran, and his crew were entirely Grynth or Human, as were the technical experts who had been seconded to the project. The vessel left under heavy secrecy, and every attempt was made to conceal its activities, especially — reading between the lines — from Barasshan and Femm.

It had arrived at Sharraby Breach and was never seen again.

What Billy was now trying to find out was why something so risky had been undertaken at all. The files that he needed were kept at one of the highest levels of security clearance, on Aphélix. He anticipated little trouble penetrating the Aphéligian data reticule, but to get round the security he would need some very expensive equipment, much of the expense taking the form of bribes.

The Joat needed money, and he needed it quickly. But, after that embarrassing incident on Winterwelt — hardly his fault, they should have told him that the mountains were hollow, then he wouldn't have used so much explosive — the demand for his services was temporarily at an ebb.

But something would turn up soon.

On cue, the phone rang.

Two minutes later Billy the Joat was on his way to SpaDe HQ as fast as his skoats would sklide him.

\* \* \*

"That's a tough brief. Find out who cracked a tamper-proof inflex screen, and how. Locate the stolen property. Satisfy QuatCent that this has been done to the Etonians' satisfaction. The Etonians will be so eternally grateful that they will switch the screen off before the smell renders Grover's World uninhabitable, incidentally removing all protection from their incredible hoard of valuables. Better still, they will cheerfully move off planet, abandoning their franchise to filter Katch-22, which — whatever it is — appears to be valuable enough to have attracted them to this unprepossessing dump in the first place."

"You can do it," said Palgandra.

The Joat bowed elaborately. "Your wish is my command. I'll need an open-ended contract — nine hundred a day plus all expenses."

"*Nine hundred*? That's a bit steep!"

"Eight-fifty?"

"Five hundred a day."

"Not enough."

"Plus a bonus of twenty-five thousand if you succeed."

"Put it on disk and I'll countervalidate it."

\* \* \*

A joat is a person with a finger in many pies. And, by nature, a pie in many faces. A joat has an eidetic memory, a knack with machinery, a gift for improvisation, and a taste for practical jokes. A joat can build up a broad picture from sketchy information, and manoeuvre with a sure touch without having the foggiest idea what is happening. A joat's skills range from linguistic dexterity to quark-engineering, from xenoentomology to synchronized skliding. In a universe of Specialists, a joat lubricates the scientific, industrial and bureaucratic machinery — often in the manner of a banana-skin as it lubricates the sole of a boot. In a universe where status is granted according to specialities, a joat is an individualist who cooperates only grudgingly with authority, which, so the joat imagines, does not apply to the joat. Authority comes to terms with joats only because joats get results. Joats never come to terms with authority.

Wyllam Jarneyvore, a prince among joats, had a personality to match.

His first step was to put out feelers among the less desirable elements of Grover's World society — the petty criminals and informers. As Chief Pigge, in his cups, had eloquently put it, the skin on the underworld porridge. The Chief, in a show put on for the benefit of QuatCent, had already done the same, but got no results. The Joat expected to do better.

Yurik the rosp (Receiver Of Stolen Property) was having a bad day. No sooner had he risen than he had accidentally snipped off an ear-tuft that he had been trimming to a rakish angle for six months. Then a Constabulary snoop had come within a hairsbreadth of catching him red-handed examining a ten thousand kroon mollucite bracelet which Woli the Snief had separated from the wrist of an offworld tourist, who'd presumably come to gawk at those confounded Etonians. And now his damned fool assistant Bronthx had paid out good money for a dozen ten-unit cartons of hideous table-lamps from gods-knew where. He fingered the demolished ear-tuft in despair and wondered if anything was going to go right.

The door optic bleeped.

A customer. Yurik ran a pawn shop as a front.

The snood — as Yurik referred to his non-professional customers — was a gangling human clad in pale violet shorts, a blue-and-white check body-warmer with green arm-windings, and a flat pork-pie hat with a red velvet band that hung down his back like a queue. A blue veil, depending from the hat, covered his features. He wore battered sneeglers on his bony feet, and the big toes peeked from their open ends.

"Can I help you, my good sir?" said Yurik. It came out more like "Knyelpya mguudzurr?"

"Pozzibly," said the snood. "I yam looking for some gifts for a small zelebration I yam planning. I want zomething out of ze ordinary."

A Stonksman, by the accent. Yurik concealed a snort. This snood wasn't going to improve his day. "How many guests, mguudzurr?"

"About a hundred." Yurik's heart missed a beat. Mayhap Lumenifer, the Goddess of Lambent Effulgence, would bedeck his day with lightness after all. And that gave him an idea that brought a warm flush to his hairy ears.

"Lamps," he said.

"Hunh?"

"You're in luck, mguudzurr. I have just this morning taken delivery of a hundred and twenty antique lamps from the ancient ruins of Zandernoid Spex. They have been discreetly modified to function on modern electrical supply. Kindly permit me to demonstrate."

The snood watched while Yurik opened a carton and extracted a bottle of sickly yellow fluid, adorned with a tarnished plastic trim failing valiantly to resemble silver. A layer of green goo occupied the bottom few inches. As the bulb below warmed it, the goo began to heave convulsively. A large blob detached itself, rose writhing, split into two medium-sized blobs and several small ones, sank slowly back and reunited itself with the seething morass below.

"Fifty kroon," offered the snood.

"I can't let them all go for that," said Yurik the rosp. "Maybe one carton..."

"I meant fifty kroon each."

*Six griffs! A profit of five hundred per cent!* "As I was saying, maybe one carton for a thousand... but to you, half price."

"There's a condition attached," said the snood, drawing back the veil from his face. "I thought you'd have recognized the voice behind the phoney accent, Yurik. You're slipping — I yam sorry to say."

The rosp's face fell with disappointment. "Gods help me, it's Billy the Joat. It ain't my day at all. What the blut do you want?"

"What does a joat ever want, Yurik, old friend?"

"Information."

"For which I will pay generously — and, to make it look above board, take off your hands those hideous old lamps."

Yurik's features brightened.

"For twenty kroon apiece."

They dulled again, then a grin split the furry face. "What sort of information?"

The Joat wrung his hands to warm them. "Some items of value were removed yesterday from the home of a very wealthy citizen, a newly-arrived immigrant who's caused something of a stink around here."

"I catch your drift." The rosp drooped his jowls and looked infinitely sad. "But I ain't got a clue, Billy. Honest. I swear on my mother's grave."

"If you ever had a mother she'd be cast in concrete on a river-bed," said Billy. "Give."

"No, honest, there ain't nothing to give. You know me, Billy — if anyone had sniffed a whisker it'd be Yurik the rosp. But there's nary a twitch on the grapevine. It ain't an underworld job, truth."

The Joat's surprise was manifest. Maybe Pigge wasn't incompetent. Maybe the underworld really wasn't involved.

"All right, Yurik." He turned to leave.

"The absence of information," stated Yurik, "is itself information of a kind."

The Joat gave it careful thought. "True. But information of lesser quality and hence lower value."

"How much lower?"

"Fifteen kroon per. One point eight griffs for the whole batch, one hundred and twenty junk lamps. Just to keep up appearances, you understand?"

*Well, it's still a profit.* "You're getting a real bargain, Billy, never forget it." Yurik packed the cartons on to a trolley, to wheel them across the boardwalk to the Joat's private tove. He whistled to himself in happiness.

He wouldn't have been so pleased if he'd been able to read the Joat's mind. Billy knew full well that there was no such thing as the ruins of Zandernoid Spex. But he also knew — as Yurik the rosp clearly did not — that his purchases were indeed antiques, of Twentieth Century Terrestrial origin, worth at least five hundred kroon apiece.

    \* \* \*

*The underworld*, thought Billy, as he sped across the swamps with twelve valuable cartons on the back seat, *knows nothing about it. By inference, the underworld had nothing to do with it. Which implies offworlders or amateurs.* The most tempting suspects, the construction crews, he ruled out immediately. They had left the planet before the crime was committed. *Though that need not prove anything*, he thought, provisionally ruling them back in again. *A construction worker might have concealed a robot within the screen, programmed to depolarize the generator and decamp with the goodies. Or left a timer to do the depolarizing, with a robot or a living accomplice working from the outside. And what about a self-erasing parasite in the program for the automatics? Or...*

On thinking about it, there were so many possibilities that the security-minded Etonians must have done something to prevent any such tricks.

Surely.

Billy reached for the phone.

Five minutes later he put it down, having augmented his grudging admiration for the Chief Constable. *Almost as good as old Grawlvyre had been, before he retired.* For Pigge had had similar thoughts, and had gone beyond them, to run a few checks.

The Etonians had put all of the construction workers under mindbinding — a kind of hypnosis, which restrains its subjects from specified actions while leaving their faculties otherwise unimpaired. *At fifty thousand apiece*, thought Billy, *security doesn't come cheap. But then, the Etonians don't think about money they way most of us do. They should have mindbound the whole damned planet.* But even the Etonians' wealth would hardly stretch that far... and in any case mindbinding was voluntary. The Joat wondered briefly if someone had found a way to get round it, then discarded the thought. Anyone that clever would never be caught anyway.

He ruled the construction crew out again.

On Katch-22 he had more success. According to persistent rumour, the substance was involved in the production of a cancer-suppressing drug, much valued in the central worlds by aging diplomats and officials. (It would have been much valued elsewhere, but the supply was restricted.) This explained the Etonians' influence. The catch was, he noted, that this influence vanished the moment they left the planet, along with their franchise. Which was a fascinating thought. Katch-22 indeed.

Billy set the library database to work digging up literature related to inflex screens, and went to interview the Etonians.

Kray Harrow wouldn't let him in.

Kray Harrow wouldn't let anyone in. The inflex screen was configured to depolarize only for the members of the household. If the Etonians wished to talk to visitors they received them on one of the adjoining rafts. Harrow was totally paranoid about letting anyone into the main building itself. Look, but don't touch.

Billy pointed out — very politely — that this made his investigations difficult, but the argument squeezed no mud. In the end, Harrow grudgingly offered a telephone interview, and the Joat settled for that, even though he had hoped to get a closer look at the inside rooms of the house, hidden from public view. The Etonians displayed their possessions, but preferred privacy for themselves. The contradictions in their psychology fascinated him.

If anything, the Etonians were even harder to deal with than Harrow; but eventually Sherryl Eton condescended to talk to him. Over the video circuit he saw that she was tall, well-formed, with short cropped hair dyed jet black, tipped with silver. She wore a clinging dress of real silk, a hand-made creation from the fashion circuit, looked like Bogolyubov except that the drape was wrong, more in the style of Lapiste. However, the Joat's attention was mostly on what the material was draped *over*. It was lust at first sight. He noted in passing that a triple row of emeralds formed a belt round her waist, and her feet floated two inches above the floor on magnetic levity-pumps. She looked beautiful and innocent and she sent tingles all over his body. *Beware Etonians, Jole said... But maybe I'll make an exception for this one if I get the chance...*

"Jarneyvore." She looked at him and smiled. *And maybe Jole was absolutely right.* It was like being on the wrong end of a king cobra. "A joat. How delightful. To what do I owe this unaccustomed pleasure?" She was watching him very closely, while trying to appear casual.

He asked a few routine questions. She had already furnished a list of the stolen goods to Constable Pigge: the Joat could obtain a copy by phone if he wished. No, she had no idea who might have access to the building, and neither did the rest of the family. It should not have been possible.

"There is no known way," said Billy, "to penetrate an inflex screen. But somebody did. Could they have interfered with your household robots using a radio beam, a laser, anything like that?"

Instead of answering, she stood up, and walked into an adjoining room. Her movements were lithe and fluid, like a cat. Well, not *exactly* like a cat. Mind you, somewhere in the universe there might be an exceptionally sexy cat with a smile like a king cobra — let's not leap to conclusions. The phone, presumably held by a robot attendant, followed her, while Billy watched on the screen. The room was windowless, with a soft artificial light. One wall was a featureless plane surface, and it was black. "An inflex screen," she said, "from the inside. It lets light out, but it lets *nothing* in. No radiation of any kind. No solid matter. No particle beams. Not even freewave." She touched a switch and the surface cleared. Through it Billy could see parklands, and beyond them the city. Songbirds, imported by the Etonians, sang in the bushes, and distantly he heard the mournful honking cacophony of a draggle of mudlarks. "Partial polarization," she said, "for visible light. Like this, a laser beam could enter." She pressed the switch again and the blackness returned. "We keep it like *this*. That demonstration is the first time I or anyone else have used this switch."

"The phone link? That must get through somehow."

"The phone link was built in when the screen was set up. It's monitored to prevent unauthorised use."

"I see... You know, you're creating an awful smell with that screen," said Billy.

"I do not concern myself with the problems of the lower orders. The smell keeps the tourists away. I have noticed one curious thing," she added. "The birds seem unaffected by it." They listened for a moment to their twittering. "Perhaps they don't have a sense of smell. I advise you to emulate the birds."

\* \* \*

Palgandra was unimpressed. "It's not much, Jarneyvore. Big Pig got most of that information days ago. All you've done is confirm that the crime was impossible."

"I did find out what Katch-22 is used for," the Joat reminded him.

"Public knowledge. All you had to do was ask."

"Ask the right people. *You* didn't know."

"*I* wasn't trying to find out."

Billy rose to his feet. "I'm doing my best, Mr. Secretary, and we're not licked yet. By tomorrow I'll know more about inflex screens than their inventor. *Somebody* cracked that screen, and if they can do it, so can I."

Palgandra gave an ambiguous snort and looked glum.

Billy's researches into inflex screens were extensive, but yielded little that he didn't know already. The mechanism that generated the field was of Femm origin; and while a little strange, as was everything Femmish, it was based on accepted physical principles. The generator was customarily housed in a sealed unit with its own power-plant, and it required heavy lifting gear and portable neutron shielding to make any adjustments to it.

The screen itself was a gravitic singularity: a delocalized black hole that produced a gravitational field only along its own surface, creating a barrier impervious to any form of radiation or matter. It functioned like an infinitely thin pseudo-rigid shell — in fact much of the engineering theory treated it as one. It could be marginally polarized to permit the entry or exit of a band of electromagnetic radiation — light or radio — by a subsidiary mechanism, which altered the surface gravity field. It could be fully depolarized to permit entry and exit of material objects (such as the Etonians and their money), and the associated security systems appeared completely watertight. Billy doubted that the machinery itself offered any interesting possibilities, although access to the controls was a different matter. But that, again, required some sort of penetration of the field.

The smell was an unavoidable side effect. A spherical gravity field must have singularities, for topological reasons. If there existed a gravity field on a sphere without singularities it would be possible to smooth the sphere along the force-lines of the field. But it is impossible to comb a hairy ball smooth, which is why Grynth, like most other furry animals, have partings down their tummies. Therefore spherical fields cannot be smooth everywhere, so they must have singular points. Theoretically the curvature of the tangential field becomes infinite at a singularity; in practice it gets very large and the theory breaks down. Localized pressure under twisted conditions ties up innocuous nitrogen, carbon dioxide, and water into complicated organic knots: ketones, isocyanides, hydrazines — none of which would win any prizes in a perfume competition. Given the odd atom of sulphur it is possible to form mercaptans, which are worse.

It was a fascinating example of how higher mathematics can cause a bad smell. But, bad smell or not, nowhere within its capacious memory could the library find any method to penetrate or shut down an inflex screen from the outside. Which just left the Shirley Combs principle: *after you have eliminated the impossible*, and so forth. If an outside job was impossible, could it have been an *inside* job?

Who *was* inside?

A multitude of Etonians. *Beware Etonians.* There'd be plenty of backbiting and infighting among a bunch like that, but it was hard to come up with a really convincing motive. Sherryl and Eshelby VI were presumably united by their common hatred of Rudolph V and his brood of usurpers. *Sherryl... now that's a woman and a half.* Eidetic memories have their advantages, and he replayed their meeting in his mind, paying close attention to its visual aspects... With a jolt he shook himself out of a fruitless and quite possibly highly dangerous reverie. *Whenever you think of Sherryl Eton, remember her smile.*

*The crime, Billy, the crime.* The value of the missing goods was insignificant compared to their total wealth, which tended to rule out fraud. No, it didn't fit. Joats rely on a highly developed intuition, and Billy's told him that Etonians were not the culprits.

Servants? The Etonians had none, only robots.

Now that was a thought. Robots. Could the crime have been committed by a *robot*? That really was ridiculous, a robot could have no conceivable motive. Of course, an outsider could have subverted a robot's programming... but that put the problem back where it had been before, because an outsider could have no access to any of the Etonians' robots.

And Harrow never allowed any visitors within the screen. *What do I do, Shirley, when* everything *is impossible?*

Billy considered another possibility. Perhaps some item of equipment, some valuable artefact, was not what it appeared to be. For example, an autonomous robot, capable of shutting off the screen temporarily. Though that was a little far-fetched, because they would surely have security snoops to inspect everything they bought or were given. However, that was at least a potential weak link. If there *was* anything of that nature, it would have to be something acquired since they arrived on Grover's World. Nobody could have anticipated their arrival, it was so utterly improbable, which meant that no offworlders could have laid plans ahead of time. No, it was an opportunist crime, committed by someone *here*.

If it wasn't some disguised item of equipment, it had to be outsiders. If you could transmit a radio beam through the screen then it would be relatively easy to subvert the program of one of the lower echelon robots, such as a cleaner. They were conventional models with radio-directed supervisory programs. You'd have to know a few codes, of course, but Billy could have laid hands on those himself. The trouble with that theory was, radio can't penetrate an inflex screen.

Nothing can.

\* \* \*

He called Chief Pigge. To the Chief's credit, he had already thought about automatic machinery infiltrated under some other guise, and had obtained from the Etonians a list of their Groverian purchases. It wasn't very long — clearly Grover's World had little to offer — and it included a few artworks with Quaternity certificates of authenticity that would be hard to fake, together with a few mineral specimens purchased from, of all places, the Thriftex Part Mart. Among these, the only unusual one seemed to be a large cluster of gemstones of Femm origin, known as pphollery. The Joat looked the word up in his Femm-Galaxic dictionary, but found only the words pphol, meaning 'shine', and llery, meaning 'howl', both of which he knew already. *Shinehowl?* It didn't make much sense.

However, the mention of the Thriftex Part Mart reminded the Joat of Yaffa Varian. Varian, in his own area, was a somewhat erratic microjoat. His trade required the same unorthodox combination of talents. In technical matters his knowledge was unparallelled for its breath, though its depths were fraught with reefs and sandbars, which could easily cause a wreck.

Even the great Shirley Combs sometimes had to consult her sister Mycroft.

\* \* \*

"Pphollery," said Varian, "is very rare stuff. I picked up a lump from a prospector who wuz down on his luck and had some... *awkward* problems that had to be settled. Quickish."

"Why didn't he sell it to the Mining Department?"

"That wuz related to the awkward bit. Look, I'd really prefer not to go into details."

"The name seems to translate as 'shinehowl' ", said Billy. "Is that right?"

"Pretty close. It's a very weird stone. Like a piezoelectric crystal, but with a twist. If you shine a laser on it, it sets up some kind of molecular vibration, and the whole stone gives off a piercing whistle."

"Pity. Lasers don't penetrate an inflex screen. Do you know anything that does?"

"Sure."

The Joat's ears pricked up. "What?"

"Gravity."

*That's true. Sherryl didn't float on the ceiling.* "If the thief found some way to use it, he could get through the screen with a portable gravity-generator." He paused. "Pity nobody has any idea how to make one. Anything else?"

"Not that I know of," said Varian.

*Fine sister Mycroft you make.* The Joat grabbed his jacket from the HV tripod on which it had been hung and put it back on. "Thanks anyway. Let me know if you do think of anything. And," he added as an afterthought, "if there's anything I can do in return, just say the word."

This proved a mistake. Twenty minutes later, when the Joat emerged, it was with a sound-microscope tucked under one arm.

He borrowed a small piece of pphollery from Grover University, and took it home with him. He shone a laser on it but it didn't seem to respond. Wrong wavelength? Crystal not large enough? Too impure? He gave up, and spent an hour studying the equations for an inflex screen, until he understood how a spherical zone could grow from a point singularity when the power increased beyond a threshold. Make a few changes here and there and you ended up with an ellipsoid, which was what the Etonians seemed to be using. There were some *very* interesting instabilities that could occur then, including secondary thresholds and multiple zones acting rather like higher harmonics of a sound wave, but he reluctantly pushed those ideas aside since they had little bearing on the problem at hand. Lacking anything else to do, he played with his new toy, the sound-microscope.

Unlike an optical microscope, it used pulses of ultrasound to 'illuminate' an object. The definition was relatively good, because the frequency of the sound was high; but sound waves could penetrate where light could not, and different tissues reacted differently to sound waves, compared to light. He put the piece of pphollery into the specimen area: it looked very pretty but otherwise suggested nothing. Bored, he switched on the HV but got nothing except static: Basketball must be giving out flares again. He switched off both holovix and microscope and went to bed.

The mudlarks outside kept him awake for an hour with their honking. When he finally did sleep it was an uneasy slumber, punctuated by dreams of inflex screens, sound-microscopes, pphollery, and mudlarks. Two enormous mudlarks were studying a miniature and devastatingly sexy Sherryl Eton through a sound-microscope, getting the weirdest echoes...

...and Billy was suddenly wide awake.

He switched the HV back on.

"...brought to you by the manufacturers of OctraPOD, the mild abrasive that keeps your claws *SHARP!!!!* and *SHINY!!!!* And now the latest multigram from Kryzzella Werralu, a thrappy little integer called —" The announcer's voice was obliterated by a burst of static as Billy switched the sound-microscope on. When he turned it off again, the discordant tune returned.

Interference? He tried it without the pphollery. The thrappy little integer came through loud and clear. Well, loud. When the inhabitant of the neighbouring apartment thumped on the wall with the sound of a stampeding bogoceros, Billy rapidly turned the HV off.

The Joat had discovered the *modus operandi...* and the criminal. The location of the missing goods was now obvious. The most urgent problem would be persuading the Etonians to move offplanet, but already Billy's fertile mind had some ideas about that, too. Those multiple zone harmonics of inflex screens that he had discovered might prove useful.

He needed some help, and it was obvious who to ask.

After all, Yaffa Varian had a vested interest in keeping out of jail.

\* \* \*

Three days passed. On the morning of the third, Joze Palgandra received a cryptic phone message, commandeered a tove, and sped towards Brixton in a spray of mud. Even before he arrived, he could tell that something of significance was afoot.

The smell wasn't so bad.

Approaching closer, he saw that something was terribly amiss with the inflex screen.

It had gone black.

And it was surrounded by Femm transports.

And the workers were wearing oxygen masks.

And they were loading crates as fast as they could shift them.

"I don't believe it!" Palgandra muttered. Then he noticed the Joat and Varian sauntering towards him along the boardwalk. "All right," he said, as they approached. "How did you manage it?"

Billy looked at Varian, who snorted his assent. "I won't bother you with the train of thought involved in making the necessary deductions," said the Joat, "although it would be very instructive and I'm sure it would do you a power of good. But we joats do have a few trade secrets to protect, as I'm sure you understand, and that means we have to —"

"Jarneyvore, if you value the continuation of your breathing-rights, *get on with it!*"

"I started getting somewhere when I figured out that an inflex screen, though impervious to matter and radiation, can transmit sound waves. It's just like a rigid surface, and it *vibrates*. I guess nobody had noticed that because inflex screens are normally used only in a vacuum, in space, with no sound waves around. In retrospect, I really should have spotted it when I heard those mudlarks and birds, while I was on the phone to Sherryl Eton."

"Mudlarks? Birds?" enquired Palgandra, but the Joat made no attempt to enlighten him.

"Then I found out about the pphollery." He waited, but Palgandra held his peace. "It's a mineral. They had a lump of it in one of the outer rooms. Yaffa here," he continued, rewriting history where it suited his purpose to do so, "told me that pphollery gives off radio waves when a beam of ultrasound hits it." *The cunning plerg really said it the other way round to deceive me, but that's best left unsaid.*

"Actually," said Varian, also rewriting history, "I told him it gives off light when vibrated by sound waves. That's what pphollery means: pphol means 'shine' and llery means 'whistle'. The Femm play tunes to it and watch it twinkle."

"But," said the Joat, "by Rozby's Reciprocal Relationship, that means that high-frequency sound should generate radio waves. So, if a thief focuses a modulated beam of ultrasound *through* the inflex screen on to the pphollery, he can generate radio messages. And those can be used to subvert the cleaning robots."

"And one of them shuts down the screen to let the thieves in?"

"No, there's an alarm circuit. What the thieves did was more interesting. They got the robots to hide the goods inside the house. To *simulate* a theft."

"But," said Palgandra, "the Etonians searched the whole house and found nothing."

"Etonians," said Billy, "never lift a finger. The *robots* searched the house. When the thieves subverted the program they made sure they stayed away from wherever the stuff was hidden."

Palgandra raised another objection. "Why fake a robbery?"

Varian spoke up. "If you lived near Brixton," he said, "you wouldn't have to ask that. *Anything* that would put pressure on them to move was worth trying."

"But how," asked Palgandra, "did the thieves think of the method to begin with?"

"I'd guess," said Billy, "that they spotted the lump of pphollery through the window, recognized what it could be made to do... and did it." He turned to Varian. "What do you think, Yaffa? Makes sense?"

"Yez, that wud be it," said Varian blandly.

Constable Pigge still looked worried. "Who *was* it, that's what I want to know," he said. "Not that I want to arrest anyone for being public-spirited, you understand, but I've got a job to —"

"Worry not, Big — um, Chief Pigge. No theft... no crime."

The Chief Constable was so quick to agree that he nearly tripped over his own objections. "Jarneyvore, I would say that you have a well-honed grasp of legal niceties."

"Well," said Varian, "you could probably think up *some* charges. *Attempted* theft?"

"My orders were to solve a burglary," said Pigge firmly. "Not an attempted one. The charge wouldn't stick," he added with determination. "Funny, but I can't think of anything that would."

Palgandra was annoyed by the smug looks on the others' faces. "We still haven't heard why the Etonians left."

Billy smiled. "Amazing coincidence. The screen went supercritical on them. Nasty effect, it reverses polarity. Guess what that does to the smell."

Silence.

"Traps it *inside*," said Billy. "It doesn't trap the Etonians — which fact I personally deplore — because the equipment that depolarizes the screen for entrance and exit still functions. But the associated security system is paranoid, and it won't allow permanent depolarization, so they can't install any extraction devices. They'd create too much of a weak point in their defences: the security computer thinks permanent exits mean permanent entry-points."

"Surely," said Palgandra, "they could deal with the smell by depolarizing the screen at intervals?"

"Given long enough, yes," said Billy. "But it takes time to create a significant drop in concentration, and until then the smell persists. It's very penetrating, as we all know to our cost. Don't forget, these people are the *idle* rich. Discomfort, even if temporary, is not something they're used to. Not a patch on old Rudolph the First — he'd have stuck it out forever. He may have been an eccentric old drunk, but boy was he pig-headed."

"They could move out. That would give them time."

"But only to somewhere else on Grover's World. Domicile criteria."

"And it's not just their *valuables* they need to protect," said Varian, making a chopping motion with one hand.

"For the same reason, they can't switch the generator off," said Billy. "But that's an academic point."

"You smug snerk, what's *that* supposed to mean?"

"It's what makes it fortunate — for the Etonians — that their entrances and exits still function. When the generator goes supercritical, it also throws off a second, tiny screen — inside the first one. Fits snugly round the generator. And that one *isn't* fitted with depolarization circuits like the main one."

The Chief Constable laughed in delight. "You mean to say they're stuck with a screen they can't turn off that contains the generator, while the smell that it creates leaks out and builds up inside the outer screen? Oh boy, that's rich!"

"Very rich," said Varian. "It concentrates in small spaces, too." They all laughed.

"Do you happen to know," asked Palgandra, "what can set up this kind of supercritical instability?"

"Naturally," said the Joat. "Ultrasound again. It all fits rather beautifully."

"Can it be switched off?" asked Palgandra. "It's a nuisance if it has to stay where it is. It might be dangerous."

"It's safe for the moment," said Billy. "I'd recommend you get someone to tow it out into space, or dump it into Basketball's photosphere."

"They could have just brought in another inflex screen and moved somewhere else on planet," said Palgandra.

"I think," said the Joat, "they had reason to believe that the same thing would happen every time they set up an inflex screen on Grover's World." *Assuming they got my message.* "Now, they can't protect that much wealth without a screen; but they can't own ConSludge unless they live here... and that, by Quaternity edict, means they have to keep eighty per cent of their possessions here. And that's too much to risk, so they had to cut their losses and leave."

"Which means that shares in ConSludge must be up for grabs," said Varian. After which Palgandra was in a hurry to close the meeting. Rapidly he dialled — not SpaDe HQ, but his stockbroker.

"Murgeon and Caulicrumb, at your service."

"Put Murgeon on please. Thank you. Good afternoon, this is Palgandra. I want to buy shares in Consolidated Sludge."

There was an embarrassed silence at the other end. "I'm sorry, Mr. Palgandra, but you're... too late. The entire issue has been purchased by a holding company set up by the Bank of Betelgeuse."

"What!"

Bolidas Murgeon sounded apologetic. "Apparently somebody tipped off the bank, and in exchange the bank financed the company. They'd have to have some local people on the board, you see, because of the new domicile criteria."

"And who are these locals?"

"I haven't been able to find out. BB is a rather tightly-knit organization. The local firm is called the Natural Organic Sediment Extraction Holding Company, if that helps."

"Not really," said Palgandra. "Could be anyone."

But he began to develop horrible suspicions. And then the Natural Organic Sediment Extraction Holding Company marketed a new smell-proof inflex screen for planetary use. It generated the screen in a thin, double-layered sandwich that confined the smell between two layers. And everything began to fall into place.

The final confirmation came when he realized that the N.O.S.E. Holding Company could have been named only by Billy the Joat.

# 5 Mobies' Graveyard

Longitude 72 degrees West on the equator of Grover's World is Mobies' Graveyard. Here the clapped-out mechanical monsters crawl to die when vibration and corrosion win the entropic battle. It is cheaper to bring new vehicles in from a metal-rich world such as Keetmanshoop than to recycle them locally. Anchored in neat rows to bulbous rubberoid balloons they decay in their hundreds, lonely and neglected. The only visitor is the knacker's van.

With one exception.

At irregular intervals a battered tove, sometimes grey, sometimes khaki, always so mud-bespattered that its registration plates are illegible, arrives during the hours of darkness. It makes its way towards the centre of the junkyard, and ties up beneath the broad leaves of a pongonia plant. A shadowy figure, on skoats, slithers through the mud between the moribund monsters and enters an exceptionally battered relic with three burnt-out ingestion nozzles and a leaking float that has caused it to settle at a steep angle. The figure spends only a short time there — at most two or three hours.

An inspector from the Space Department, investigating the listing moby with the burnt-out nozzles, would probably fail to notice that one rusty segment of panelling can be swivelled sideways, opening into a pitch-dark inspection-way for the leaky float.

However, if the snoop were to explore more thoroughly, an urgent message would shortly be on its way to SpaDe HQ. For the leaky float is not leaky: it is ballasted with scrap metal scavenged from nearby wrecks. It has a power-pack, lighting, and a regulation SpaDe terminal with strap-on polygram circuits and a comm-link capable of hooking into the organization's main data reticule. From here the shadowy figure can interrogate SpaDe's main database on Aphélix with a good chance of escaping detection.

- SecClearCode LPW/456.00856.00231.0001
- Access granted thru FiLevel 12
- State document declarator

The Joat asked for a number of irrelevant files, to conceal his true intentions. After half an hour of innocent enquiries, he finally got round to the only one that mattered:

- Edwin Hubble

The database informed the Joat that there were two hundred and seventeen thousand, one hundred and forty-two entries under that name. He selected for male/significant/ scientist/Old Terran. That got it down to six. The right one was now obvious.

- Hubble, Edwin Powell
- 660-596 BQ
- Astronomer, OT UnStatsAm [[#USA.00001-00886
- Bio. #Suppl. EPH/000
- Nebular Classification #Suppl. EPH/00001
- Expanding Universe Hypothesis #Suppl. EPH/00002
- Law activ. #Suppl. EPH/000003
-  Edwin Powell Hubble was born in Marshfield Missouri, on Old Terra. The son of a...

He adjusted the polygram connections to his wrists and forehead, where they were becoming uncomfortable. This would be a natural action from anyone with nothing to hide. The computer rambled on, offering Hubble's biography in infinite detail.

All this flimflam was just to distract the attention of anyone who accidentally opened the Hubble file. The important bits would come later. Billy accelerated the inflo and the pages whizzed past. The database told him that further information was to be found in a supplementary file at security level 13. That was three levels higher than the Joat was cleared for, and also the first level that he expected to have serious trouble getting into. *Hope those waveforms that I paid five thousand kroon for are still valid.* He relaxed into a meditative state, to fool the SpaDe polygrams.

His mind now calm, his skin dry, his pulse steady, the Joat flicked a switch on a metal box attached to the side of the terminal. The circuitry inside had cost another five thousand, the circuit specs ten times that. But now Billy the Joat was horizontally rich — he could afford anything he wanted, short of a major hike in his lifestyle. Five times the computer denied him access, but on the sixth the screen cleared. *I'm glad they warned me about that... Even with the correct ident, the computer deliberately takes its time confirming.*

- #Suppl. LSP/00772
- RV Edwin Hubble
- 1//Construction Specifications
- 2//Mission objectives
- 3//Personnel records
- 4//Communications records

It was a lengthy file, and the Joat skimmed it while making a copy to be read later. *Hubble*'s scientific mission was to study time-warp phenomena believed to be occurring in Sharraby Breach. There were also veiled references to a more political objective: to confirm or deny a rumour that the Femm had already dispatched their own research craft to investigate the Breach. The Joat asked for another file, containing *Hubble*'s last message home.

- 174 // communication // final
- 1564 2345 3378 9897 8795 7743 2215 3600 4723 2600 7171
- 1174 5892

\# \# \# \#

- ! ! ! ! ! !
- Userrupt

/// Plaintext ///

- R V Hubble PS86 Log 436.7.22.14.06.35
- << Am entering Sharraby Breach as instructed
- << Coordinates UC753.DD264.KJ102
- << All normal // further comm 1700
- end >>

*So they* did *go inside the Breach. And no sign of escalade.* Part of the Joat's mind felt deep relief, but the part controlling the body's reflexes had been trained not to respond. The files held little more of interest on the *Hubble*, though the Joat did manage to confirm that Jole Jarneyvore, predictor, was listed in the passenger manifest.

*Femm exploration in Sharraby Breach… Time-distortion… I'd really like to know a lot more about that…*

It would be risky, but — Joats are not endowed with patience. In this respect Wyllam Jarneyvore conformed to type.

The SpaDe database on Aphélix handles on average 25 million enquiries per day. Billy had chosen a period when traffic was close — but not too close — to the maximum. That reduced the chances of being detected. Taking a calculated risk, he kept the link open for a few more minutes. This time he asked for the file on *Pontryagin*.

The computer's deception routine was similar, and so was the vessel's mission objective. Very interesting, very interesting indeed. Not only that: by the time *Pontryagin* had been dispatched, an unidentified ship had been spotted going into the Breach. Suspected Femm origin, probability 74%.

He was getting close, he could feel it. Very close. The crew list of the *Pontryagin* might give him a lead to the saboteur. The saboteur could lead to the brains behind the whole business. Another minute would be enough.

The strain was telling… It was becoming hard not to trigger the polygrams. *Om mane padme om…*

- Elwyn Funt . Chief Fringe-gimpler. [[#EF. 00233
- Kriss Nouchott. Second Quilpole. [[#KN.00810
- Mawgan Hamblish. Lance-Volumist. [[#MH. 00651
- Wylsen Quiddick. Line Repeater. [[#WMQ. 00200
- Margrit Beamw

At that moment the screen went blank. Billy's illicit circuits had spotted the SpaDe computer running a check sequence, and had automatically cut the connection. That was risky too: the detectors were subtle. But it would have been even more risky to have stayed online.

The Joat waited three days, until his patience gave out, and returned to the Mobies' Graveyard. Twenty seconds after logging on he sensed that something was wrong. The database was slow responding, as if it was trying to keep him busy for as long as possible. He cut the link. Cold, clammy sweat formed all over his body as he relaxed the mental barriers. The trouble with calculated risks is that sometimes the calculation adds up wrong. *Pray that they haven't traced the connection. Pray that they haven't recognized your handwriting. They'll try to work backwards from the data: pray that the camouflage holds up.*

Time to move. After that, he could do nothing but twiddle his thumbs and wait, hoping SpaDe hadn't been on the ball.

Joats hate waiting. The inactivity builds up an intolerable head of mental steam. When the safety-valve blows, very little is sacred.

# 6 Paradise Misplaced

"Expect me back in about three hours, Belphoebe," said Billy the Joat to his front door. In fact the door was an inflex screen thruport and he was addressing the domestic computer of his new villa, purchased from the profits of the N.O.S.E. Holding Company. He had recently discovered, and become mildly obsessed with, Spenser's *Faerie Queene*. He was cultivating the persona of Sir Wyllam de Jarneyvore, destroyer of the dragon Graspmudgeon, keeper of the holy trapcode, victor over the evil Etonian hordes, beater of Harrows into ploughshares...

Pity there seemed to be a shortage of damsels in distress, it would have rounded out the career nicely.

Whistling merrily, he stepped past a grove of cultivated bogwhort, only to halt at the unmistakable sound of an approaching tove: a sonorous, flatulent gurgling like a marsh wollagong suffering from an upset stomach. Assorted squelches and high-frequency hisses signalled to the trained ear that the vehicle was approaching at top speed. Repressing an urge to head rapidly in the opposite direction, he ambled over to the end of the jetty, arriving just as the tove oozed into the mooring-bay. A smartly uniformed SpaDe flunky draped the mooring-loop efficiently over what he took to be a somewhat besmirched bollard. The supposed bollard, a dozing mudlark, uttered a startled *squonk!*, shot off the jetty, and hit the slime beneath like a beautician applying a mudpack to her mother-in-law. The flunky eyed his uniformed shirt-front dolefully.

Without a word, the Joat attached the loop to the correct mooring-point. A Grynth official in full SpaDe regalia stepped ashore. Recognizing him, the Joat made greeting:

"*Why, Archimago, luckless syre,*
*What doe I see? What hard mishap is this,*
*That hath thee hither brought to...*"

The official eyed him sourly. "Prose will suffice, Jarneyvore."

"*Pray address me as Sir Wyllam, foul caitiff!*" *No, better not. Palgandra has lost his sense of humour today. Though it would take an expert to notice he had one to begin with. I smell trouble.* Belatedly Sir Wyllam began to question the wisdom of some improvements he had made, with electronic assistance, to the previous week's video broadcast "What the Civil Service has contributed to Quaternity relations." Perhaps he should have consulted the video company about them first. On second thoughts, perhaps not. His remote digital-edit device had performed very well, though, in the circumstances.

Palgandra stepped gingerly across the thin layer of slime that coated the jetty. It was still wet, and caution on wet mud was a reflex on Grover's World. Billy tried a more respectful tack.

"Defence Secretary Palgandra. I'm delighted that you should honour me with your presence. Is it a social call, a matter of *agneth*, or some pressing affair of state?"

"I would prefer," said Palgandra, "to discuss it with you in the privacy of your villa." Reluctantly, Billy led the way. He had a brief but acerbic argument with Belphoebe, explaining that Sir Wyllam de Jarneyvore had changed his plans and returned ahead of time and, dammit, couldn't the stupid thing recognise his voice like it was supposed to and let him in? Which, after some curious internal squawks, it did. Silently cursing Quaternity surplus vocoders, and studiously ignoring Palgandra's pointed stare, the Joat led the way to a reception-room.

"Mr. Jarneyvore," said Palgandra, "have you ever visited Bahamba Bright?"

Relieved that it was not the Civil Service broadcast that had brought the Grynth to his door, Billy pursed his lips. "The resort world? Over in Pirelli Sector?" The Grynth inclined his head in confirmation. Billy was amused. "I admit my financial status has improved since the N.O.S.E. Holding Company came into being — but you need a private space-yacht even to get near the place, and I can't lay hands on *that* kind of cash."

The Grynth exhaled a snort through the twin orifices behind the lobes of his ears, to signify assent to an immediate proposition coupled with disgust at the long-term state of the universe. He reached inside his cloak and withdrew a small metallic box, studded down one edge with a row of touchpads. He pressed one, and a vivid three-dimensional representation of a planet sprang into being in the air above.

It was a watery world. Tiny green islands were scattered in loose archipelagos across a turquoise ocean that enfolded the entire globe, beneath a sky flecked with wisps of woolly cloud in shades of salmon pink and lemon. It looked idyllic.

"There are over seventy thousand islands on Bahamba Bright," stated Palgandra. "They are rented to wealthy visitors for relaxation, vacations, and so forth.

"The exact number was seventy-two thousand, one hundred, and seven."

Billy caught the inflection. "*Was?*"

"The latest count is seventy-two thousand, one hundred, and six."

"They've lost an *island?*"

"A small one," said Palgandra hastily. "No more than half a kilometre across."

"*How?* Quake? Volcanic explosion? Computer error?"

Palgandra inhaled a snort of dissent. "Definitely not. The island has gone, all right. But Bahamba Bright has a tectonic stability index of 97 — that's one reason why it's so popular. No: it would seem that the island has been forcibly removed. Hijacked."

"My word," said the Joat. "That *is* an uncommon occurrence." The Grynth tried to snort both ways at once and nearly choked. Recovering, he touched more pads. A relief map formed.

"Part of the Riffe Archipelago. The four islands shown are Vnagar, Jaisalm, Strophny, and Trixydix." The Grynth pointed to each as he named it. "This holo was taken two years ago in a satellite resource survey. Now —" he touched a pad "— this one was taken yesterday."

The Joat looked at three islands and a patch of ocean. "No Trixydix."

"As perceptive as ever."

The Joat digested the information. It didn't take long, though it didn't go down easily. "Any traces?"

"The local inhabitants report hearing a thunderclap and feeling a breeze; the marine seismologists have traces of small tidal waves emanating from a focus centred on Trixydix's coordinates. Nobody saw anything, it was dark. That's all."

"Great. The wicked thaumaturge incanted the magical cantrip, and the island paradise of Trixydix vanished forever beneath the surging ocean in a clap of thunder and a puff of green smoke."

"Not only the island," said Palgandra. The residents, too." He ticked them off on the digits of one leathery hand. "Turpine Carleson, Human industrialist. Jerz ap-Browan, Barasshanti cloud-sculptor. Luinda Rompstack, Human video starlet. Llizllyllinzyll Jyrijjeer, Femmish philologist. Mykal Sarpent, Grynth ambassador to the Minor Drimp Cluster. Porgas Jurket, Human numismatics dealer. Plus various items of robotic retinue. The Bahamba Bright Constabulary received a ransom note within one hour of the disappearance. It demanded one billion kroon per person, and stipulated that none would be released until all six ransoms had been paid."

"*But all his mind is set on mucky pelfe,*" declaimed the Joat,

"*To hoord vp heapes of euill gotten masse,*

*For which he others wrongs, and wreckes himselfe...*"

He broke off from his reverie. "That's quite a bundle of kroon."

"It is. It's *just* within the bounds of possibility for all of them, except perhaps Porgas Jurket."

"Surely Rompstack wouldn't have that sort of cash!"

"Carleson has enough for two," said Palgandra drily. "But the availability of the money is immaterial. The Grynth would never be prepared to accede to such a demand on behalf of Mykal Sarpent."

"Why not? The Grynth Diplomatic Service is hardly the poor-house."

"It is a matter of principle. *Agneth* would be diminished."

The Joat groaned. Ordinarily the Grynth were flexible pragmatists, but not where that elusive quality was concerned. On matters of *agneth*, it would be easier to open up an independent food franchise on McDonald Central than to modify the mind-set of any true yellow-blooded Grynth.

Palgandra ignored him. "Naturally this is an unfortunate state of affairs. We urgently need to discover the kidnappers and recover the victims, *without* paying the ransom."

"Why are you involved in all this? What's the connection?"

The Grynth sighed. "The ambassador paid Grover's World a brief courtesy call immediately before his trip to Bahamba Bright. Because of a small misunderstanding on Aphélix, responsibility for his welfare was not transferred when he departed."

"You mean the buck didn't get passed."

"Regrettably, the buck remained on Grover's World, when prudence would have transmitted it elsewhere."

*So now you want me to help pull the diplomatic beercan out of the recycler*, thought Billy. *Oh no. Sir Wyllam the Joat of the House of Jarneyvore is going to sit this one out and bone up on the* Faerie Queene. *And I don't care* what *fee you offer. You won't buy me with money. Not any more.* He looked at Palgandra. Palgandra smiled toothily.

"That, of course, is where you come in."

"An interesting notion," said the Joat. "Though a misguided one, I fear."

Joze Palgandra waved his paws airily. "Mr. Jarneyvore, it's common knowledge that one of your most positive attributes is a burning altruistic drive. The whole of Grover's World recalls the exposure of Mayor Graspmudgeon, the recovery of the lost trapcode, and the remarkable events surrounding the Etonians' inflex screen."

"Palgandra, I've explained a thousand times that the Graspmudgeon business was pure coinci— "

"Nonsense! I was saying to Chief Constable Pigge only this morning how refreshingly different your attitude is from that of certain other denizens of this planet. Why, only last week I witnessed an absolutely *disgraceful* exhibition of antisocial attitudes. Did you happen to watch the programme on the contributions of the Civil Service to Quaternity relations?"

"I don't recall it," said the Joat, suddenly finding himself unable to swallow. "My HV was on the blunk last week."

"I'm glad to hear it, Mr. Jarneyvore. It would have shocked your sensibilities. Some irresponsible hooligan managed to tap a remote digital-edit device into the broadcast stream. It intercut clips from other sources, mixing the action of the clips into the original settings. We identified some of the clips — with difficulty, I can assure you.

"One, I recall, was from *Slavegirls of the Asteroid Mines*. Another was from *Skin in Spaceboots*; a third from *Sexy Sadie Goes to Pxbwlggrmp*. There were others, of similar categorization. Oh, you've got one of those things too."

"Eh?"

"A PAXIAL prism, isn't it? Stupid objects, never saw any point to them. Where was I? Oh, yes. Chief Pigge wasn't especially amused. He was threatening to send whoever was responsible to the Cyberian shockle-mines. A ten-year sentence, I gather.

"He'd analysed the criminal's techniques. He tells me they were sophisticated and rather varied. Few Specialists would have the knowledge both to build the device and to circumvent GHV's safeguards. It requires, I gather, expertise is several fields. He thought it was either the work of an organized gang, or just *possibly* a joat acting alone...

"Of course, that reminded us both of your good self. I put it to Pigge that it was really far more important to crack the Trixydix case than to chase antisocial juveniles, and that working in tandem with a joat would provide his best chance of solving the crime. We had quite an argument, but in the end, I'm glad to say, he agreed with me. However, he did stipulate that only the best joat in the sector would give him confidence enough to devote his time to the case. Failing that, he felt he would do better to hand the problem over to higher Quaternity echelons, and concentrate on more mundane matters like that shocking Civil Service broadcast.

"I pointed out to Pigge that the best joat in the sector was Wyllam Jarneyvore. He admitted he hadn't thought of that, but confirmed that his remark stood, nevertheless. On considering your past record, I told Pigge that I was certain you would be willing to aid him."

*Nice try. But you've only got circumstantial evidence, it'll never stick.* "I hear the Cavalyrri Gang is back in town. Maybe they did it. I'm really not keen to hunt for a shronk's midden. Missing island? Ridiculous."

"You've never accepted your father's death, have you?" asked Palgandra.

The unexpected change of subject, and its direction, nearly made the Joat fall off the couch. "Eh? What are you talking about?"

"Problems, problems — nothing but problems on my desk," said Palgandra, in an offhand voice. "One of them reminded me about your late father. Someone's been poking around in the *Edwin Hubble* file without proper authority. Jole Jarneyvore was aboard when the ship was lost, wasn't he? You have my sympathy." His voice lost its banter. "Genuinely, Jarneyvore. Terrible business." The banter seeped back. "Can't imagine why anyone would be interested in the files now, after so long — I mean, who'd have any *reason* to? And there's another awkward business that may be linked... Mind you, I'll almost certainly have to suspend my enquiries into those if the Trixydix investigation makes any headway. Can't be everywhere at once, now can I, not with so many problems to be tackled. Must fix my priorities."

"You may have to do more than that," said the Joat, and the bargaining began in earnest.

"You've had this room swept?" Palgandra asked. He wasn't referring to dust.

"Clean as a wollagong's backside after an equinoctial thunderstorm," said the Joat.

"Well... I suppose there's no harm in telling you that someone has also been digging into the personnel files of the *Pontryagin*. You remember, the ship that blew up at the edge of Sharraby Breach a little while back."

"When the trapcode was lost. How could I forget?"

"Hrrummf. The Breach is a common link, it could be the same person... Got his knuckles rapped before he saw the whole list, it seems."

"Bad luck, that. If I were he, I'd be hopping mad."

"He? It could have been a woman."

"True."

"The polygrams say not. Yes, one can sympathize, can't one? Even for a crime that carries a penalty of five to twenty years... But don't let me burden you with my little troubles."

The Joat wandered over to a cabinet and opened a small violet flask. "Care for some zussip? It's a good vintage. Helps you relax."

"Oh, most kind. Now, what was I saying? Um..."

"The personnel list. You said you'd rumbled the unfortunate sod just when he was getting into the personnel list."

"Lovely zussip, this. You know, I really do wish you'd help out on this Trixydix business, Jarneyvore. I'd go out of my way to assist, you know. Bend the rules here and there..."

"I'm getting more interested every moment, Palgandra. But do go on about this *Pontryagin* thing. I might pick up a few tips, it's clearly way out of my league."

"You know, he nearly stumbled into something embarrassing. I shouldn't tell you this, but SpaDe thinks there was a saboteur aboard."

"Really?"

"Yes. Though we've never been able to decide which member of the crew it was."

"Fascinating. More zussip?"

"Please, very moreish. A saboteur... Took us years before we got scent of it, and by then the trail had died. False papers, of course. A few operatives tried to follow up the leads, but it was so long ago... To all intents and purposes the case is closed. Still, you don't want to hear about that. You really should take on the Trixydix job — SpaDe will pay a very high fee, and all expenses."

The Joat poured another thimbleful. "As I was saying, I'd *like* to take on the Trixydix affair, but I've got several other jobs lined up. I'd need strong inducements to cancel them. Bad for business."

"A thousand kroon a day."

"I wasn't thinking of cash inducements."

"Use of SpaDe private transport. A yacht, the *Shrimpton*."

"That goes without saying. But I was hoping for something a little more... *informative*."

"Hmmmph. I can see I'm going to have to appeal to your better nature. If only you'd take the Trixydix job, that would take some pressure off me, give me some free time. I might even take another look at those old *Hubble* files... Hoi! I've just had a wonderful idea!"

"You have?"

"If you solve this Trixydix thing, I might be able to persuade my superiors to put you on the *Hubble* and *Pontryagin* cases and see whether you can find a fresh trail. You're just the person to track down whichever misconceived offshoot-of-a-blinch was sneaking around in the SpaDe database, for example. Ordinarily speaking you'd need special clearance to see the files, and you'd never get it — need-to-know, and all that. But I have a limited degree of influence, and your standing with SpaDe would be unsually high..."

"Mr. Secretary, you're absolutely right," said the Joat. My sense of civic duty compels me to offer every assistance to the admirable Chief Constable Pigge in solving this dreadful crime."

* * *

The traveller approaches Bahamba Bright along one of sixteen space-lanes, corkscrewing in towards the equatorial plane at an inclination of some twenty degrees. Viewed from that angle, Bahamba Bright appears to be a ringed world, but — unlike that of Levanninna 6 or Old Saturn — its ring is not a natural formation. It is made up of space yachts, held in parking orbits: typically a third of a million craft. This is a high traffic density for a non-administrative world, and all approaches and departures are orchestrated by Traffic Control, a sophisticated and powerful lateral processor of Femmish manufacture. Phading is not permitted within the orbit of the Bahamban moonlet: the traveller rides the space-lanes on standby drive only. The planet has no large land-masses, and its solitary spaceport, Arcady, is reserved for a shuttle service which conveys visitors speedily and efficiently to the surface.

Wyllam Jarneyvore and Otis Pigge departed the orbiting *Shrimpton* and rode the shuttle down to Port Arcady.

The Bahamban climate is near-perfect. Except in the polar regions, the planet is warmed to subtropical temperatures by the brilliant white Bahamban sun. Nighttime showers keep the humidity low, and gentle breezes waft from island to island.

A meticulously well-kept carriage, open to the sun and drawn by a pair of pedigree skegga, conveyed Pigge and Jarneyvore to the Lustrous Lagoon Hotel on Blue Mull. The Lustrous Lagoon is normally used as a transit stop for those with business at Port Arcady, being one of only a handful of hotels on Bahamba Bright. Most visitors are accommodated in individual island villas, each with its own stretch of beach, served by a fleet of hydrofoil taxis linking to a network of silent, high-speed fliers. The permanent population exists only to service the requirements of the wealthy tourists, and consists largely of employees of *Agenzia Bahambin*, which owns the islands, the hydrofoils, the fliers, and Arcady spaceport. Wealth attracts criminals, who are kept at bay by the local Constabulary and incarcerated, when caught, in Shan Husan prison, near the spaceport.

The clientele of Bahamba Bright seeks not only peace and solitude, but also amusement and excitement, when it so chooses. Each group of islands is furnished with a centrally located community area, or *pleasaunce*, with parks, arcades, refreshment rooms, gaming halls, music, dancing, and other entertainments.

Pigge and Jarneyvore made contact with Chief Constable Lurkin Mole. Mole had amassed a large file on the hijacking of Trixydix and the kidnapping of its residents. Neither Jarneyvore nor

Pigge was impressed: such a large file at such an early a stage would inevitably be ninety-nine per cent padding.

To all appearances, Trixydix had vanished off the face of Bahamba Bright. There were no traces of the method used to achieve this feat. Traffic Control reported no unauthorized vessels closer than parking orbit during the period preceding the disappearance. Seismograph records showed no signs of an explosion, although the island appeared to have been sheared off flat at the base and residents of nearby islands had told of a loud noise like a thunderclap and tidal waves on the beaches.

"I guess you've already looked into the ransom demand and the method of payment, Mole," said Pigge. "Nothing doing, huh?"

Mole confirmed that the transaction was in the hands of the Nomes. In the early days of the Quaternity it had proved essential to have an independent mediator between individuals and organizations, especially those of dubious legal standing. The wayfaring Nome community had fulfilled this function admirably, and had diversified its activities in the succeeding centuries to an extent that was currently proving embarrassing to QuatCent. It had repeatedly proved impossible to infiltrate the Nomes, or to obtain useful information about their activities.

"You've taken a close look at the sea-bed, of course," said Pigge.

"Um. Been a bit busy with all the paperwork, Pigge. You know how it —"

"Get me an underwater inspection vessel. I want it ready at first light tomorrow."

Pigge and Jarneyvore took copies of Mole's enormous Trixydix file back to the Lustrous Lagoon, and retired to their rooms to winnow the seeds of information from the bureaucratic chaff.

*Jerz ap-Browan*
Barasshanti, offspring of Browan ap-Nisp. Born Phariteel IV, 410 QC... Professional cloud-sculptor. (This traditional Barasshanti activity employs chemical agents, administered from a flier, to modify the form of naturally occurring clouds. In its competitive aspect, sculptors vie to produce the most aesthetically pleasing forms, watched by millions...)

*Turpine Toomyvar Carleson*
Human, son of Toomyvar Pester Carleson, founder of the Pink Toad fastfood chain... After his father's death (from snakebite) further

diversified into freight-handling, wrist-computers, exotic jewellery...
Born New Delphi, 426 QC...

### Porgas Kshatrin Subhad Jurket

Human, daughter of Mil'cent Subhad Kshatra... Born Lamnai
Dreft, 400 QC... Dealer in rare coins... Convicted of speeding in a
restricted zone, Blyssom gasclouds area, 422 QC...

### Llizllyllinzyll Jyrjjeer

Femmish, born Palamagantra-Tish, c. 382 QC... Ancestry
unknown... Philologist, specializing in punctilio and probity...

### Luinda Rompstack

Human, née Lettice Enid Rollop, daughter of Sydney Martin
Rollop, born Broncastra VIIIb, 432 QC... Until age 22 employed as
checking clerk by Pink Toad Foods Inc., Wemburg, Broncastra VI... As
Rompstack embarked on a video career as singer of throb songs,
dancer...

### Mykal Sarpent

Grynth, son of Morvay Shimp and Jucille Sarpent, diplomatic
officials... Born third satellite, Gamma Lambardella II, 394 QC...
Appointed ambassador to Minor Drimp Cluster, Winchwood Sector,
454 QC... lightsail racing enthusiast, qualified for Fomalhaut Challenge
Cup 452 QC...

Within twenty minutes Billy the Joat had memorized the file
from cover to cover. Apart from the obvious pattern linking Carleson
and Rompstack, there was nothing to go on. If the choice of island had
been arbitrary, as was quite likely, the information on the victims
wasn't going to help much.

The motive was wide open. The obvious — money — could
cast suspicion on practically every citizen of the Quaternity. The only
person the Joat could safely rule out at this stage was himself, and that
wasn't for lack of motive.

The most promising line of investigation was the *modus
operandi*: specifically, the level and type of technology involved in a
vanishing act with an island. But that was less than encouraging, if only
because no such technology was known to exist.

Before he could get far on that, he would need to inspect the
site.

He wandered down to the hotel lobby. There ought to be better
things to do on Bahamba Bright than beat one's brains out. Two young

women in sunsuits (if 'in' was an appropriate description) sauntered past the entrance. Billy made his unhurried way down the steps towards the street.

Otis Pigge, who had been watching anxiously from behind a potted whyrtle plant, made a discreet exit and headed in the same general direction.

For several hours the Joat sampled the offerings of Arcady pleasaunce: the surface gaiety of the brightly-lit arcades, the sweaty excitement of the gaming-rooms, the hubbub of taverns as the holidaymakers flitted from one glittering spectacle to the next. Bahamba Bright was a moneyspinner, no doubt about that. The Joat made a mental note: find out who owned *Agenzia Bahambin*. Late evening found him in a quieter part of the pleasaunce, a grassy knoll overlooking Ambergray Park. He was about to get up and return to the Lustrous Lagoon Hotel when he heard a footfall behind him.

It was a girl. A strikingly pretty girl in a filmy red dress. "Hello," she said. "I'm Lindilu."

The Joat said the first thing that came into his mind.
"*He had a fair companion of his way,*
*A goodly lady clad in scarlot red,*
*Purfled with gold and pearle of rich assay,*
*And —*"

"That's nice. What is it?"

"It's part of an old poem, the *Faerie Queene*," said the Joat.

"You're sweet. Who are you?"

"Ug. Er —"

"You've forgotten your own name?"

"Um, no. I'm Wyllam Jarneyvore. Usually known as Sir Wyll — oh gods — I mean, Billy the Joat."

She asked him what a joat was. Billy explained how it derived from "Jack-Of-All-Trades," and described the strange combination of abilities that a joat must possess. In return, she told him a little about herself: Lindilu Glynde, daughter of a merchant of refrigeration equipment, vacationing on Bahamba Bright. Billy told her of Grover's World, with its endless mud seas and giant orange sun; Lindilu told him about her childhood planet of Hosperlan, where the Five Green Stars blazed in the dawn sky, and the flocks of whydah and honeyfowl glided above the Sarsheen fenlands at the turning of the seasons. Together they watched the glowing Bahamban sun descend beyond the horizon, between the towering calyptus trees that ringed Ambergray Park. And when they left the park, it was only natural that they should leave together...

* * *

Otis Pigge had a less successful evening. Like the Joat, he had become bored with the Trixydix file. Unlike the Joat, he had read little of it, although he had spent a similar time skimming through it, and come to the same conclusions regarding its likely value. He had nevertheless hoped to impress his colleague with his diligence by claiming to have spent the evening in the hotel, and for this reason had taken steps to avoid being seen.

But Pigge's main reason for leaving the hotel was to buy a souvenir. Something simple, elegant, and unmistakably Bahamban in origin. Something that he could display on his desk back on Grover's World. Something to make his subordinates' eyes pop out. It took him several hours to become convinced that there was nothing suitable within his price-range. Annoyed with himself, both for his failure and for succumbing to temptation to begin with, he wondered idly whether there was any way he could legitimately make a purchase on the Constabulary expense account. Still debating the point, he turned a corner and nearly stumbled over Billy the Joat.

Pigge beat a hasty retreat and peered round the corner. The Joat's back was turned, and he had not noticed the unwary Chief Constable. Billy had acquired a lady friend — a very attractive one — who was trying to decide whether to buy a miniature skegga, carved and polished by hand from a piece of dark-grained calyptus wood. She had picked it up and was inspecting it closely. Presumably it was not to her taste, for she replaced it on the vendor's cloth, and the pair moved away.

At that moment Pigge was struck by a mixture of thoughts. Uppermost was a professional curiosity in the Joat's companion. Others might call it cynicism, but any Chief Constable knew that a realistic assessment of the human condition required attention to people's motives. The Joat, while not bad-looking, and possessed of an outwardly cheerful nature, was not exactly a suave ladykiller. Could be natural attraction, could be poor little rich girl out slumming for kicks, could be something more sinister. However, a second thought underlay all this. Pigge sidled over to the street vendor's stall and pointed to the skegga. After some brisk bargaining, he paid over a sum of two thousand kroon, insisting on wrapping up the carving himself, which he did with unusual care, avoiding touching the shiny surfaces. Then he returned to the Lustrous Lagoon. The carving yielded several beautifully clear fingerprints, which he dispatched for freewave transmission to Central Files on Aphélix. Then he made a careful entry on his expense sheet for two thousand kroon in surveillance costs and set the skegga on the table where he could admire it. He knocked on Billy's door, got no reply, and went to bed. Awakening early, he called the Joat's room. No answer.

Pigge wondered what could have kept the Joat out all night, made an accurate guess, shook his head wryly, and headed for the dining room. A good solid breakfast of plounder mash and thoatcakes would set his day up nicely. Thoatcakes, he felt, were a lot safer, and distinctly more reliable, than the nubile daughters of the rich and the powerful.

\* \* \*

The limpid waters of the Mermynthine Sound slid past the hull of the survey vessel *Caliban*. The sea teemed with gaudy tropical fish whose flickering fins diverted them from the submersible's path. Jarneyvore and Pigge observed the spectacle through the ship's transparent hull, while the taciturn pilot concentrated on his controls.

*Caliban* edged across the sound towards the Riffe Archipelago. The Joat unrolled a chart and spread it out. Ahead and to the left was the island of Jaisalm, ten kilometres long, with four jutting sandbars making it look like warped bagpipes. To the right, Vnagar atoll with its circular lagoon. The vessel submerged and continued down the centre of the channel dividing the two islands. Now Strophny Isle loomed dimly ahead. The pilot adjusted his course to shave the western promontory. Beyond, according to the chart, was Trixydix.

For the first time during the voyage, the pilot spoke. "Bottom'll start to rise any time." Constable and Joat peered ahead and down. The rippled sand of the sea bed developed mottled patches of rock. They saw small outcrops, then larger ones. Beyond was a steepening incline. Further up the incline —

Nothing.

It was as if the island had been sliced horizontally by a knife. About ten metres below the surface, the rising slopes of rock and coral broke off abruptly: above was only the luminous undulation of the waves. *Caliban* rose to the level of the break and slowed.

"It's astonishingly flat," said Billy. "An absolutely level, clean slice. That's hardly credible. Pilot, can you cruise slowly over the area, please?"

The artificial plateau beneath them was covered by a thin deposit of sand and seaborne detritus. The Joat told the pilot to hover a few metres above the plateau, and began pulling on a mask and breathing-tank. "I want a closer look. Back in ten minutes." Leaving by the aft airlock, he swam off to one side, drifting gradually down to the bottom. Inquisitive snelvers darted towards him and then fled, frightened by their own daring. Pink jellyfish waltzed past his nose. The deposit of sand swirled in turbid vortices as his feet touched the rock. Then he was kneeling on the flat surface, to which numerous barnacles had already adhered themselves. With one hand, he brushed a patch of debris away and peered closely.

He jerked back, his heart pounding.

Something just below the surface had moved.

He leaned closer, looked again. There it was.

Eyes. A face.

His own.

"Gods," breathed the Joat. "Lurkin Mole said it was sheared off flat. But he didn't say it was *optically* flat! It's a perfect mirror!"

After a close look with a magnifier he revised this assessment slightly. The surface was like smooth marble, but with a far higher reflectivity than he had ever seen in polished stone. The image was sharp, but slightly darkened and coloured. There were numerous cracks and holes, exactly like mineral samples sliced by a diamond saw. Using a chisel wedged into one of the holes, Billy broke a piece off for later analysis. Then he swam back to the *Caliban* and told Pigge what he had found.

"Even a technoramus like myself," said Pigge, "can see that's an important clue. Any idea what it means, Jarneyvore?"

"Not yet," said the Joat. "How can you slice a quarter of a square kilometre of solid rock to get an optically flat surface without using explosives?"

"For gods' sakes, Jarneyvore, how can you do it *with* explosives?"

"Good point. Well... maybe a focussed blast of dynoplax might get part way. Shaped annular charge, planar dislocation wave... Not easy."

"Mole should have discovered this," said Pigge.

"Lurkin Mole," said the pilot to their astonishment, "lacks imagination." Then he opened the throttle. "Best head back. Air gettin' low."

Going back, the Joat ignored the underwater scenery. *Optically flat surfaces...* He felt faint stirrings, deep in his subconscious. *Somewhere...* somewhere before, he'd come across... Damn. But he knew the workings of his own mind too well to dig for it. The seed would grow at its own rate: forcing it now might kill it altogether.

\* \* \*

Lurkin Mole had a report from QuatCent. He flourished it at Billy. "Here's the reply to your query about *Agenzia Bahambin*," he said. "It took a devilish amount of prying to get what you asked for. It's an unquoted form and there's nothing but bare bones on file in the Companies Register. However, I think the result will interest you."

"Any Etonian connection?" asked the Joat.

"Etonian? What's an Etonian?"

"Let me have a look at that file." No, no Etonians, not even the tiniest whiff. Not this time. *Agenzia Bahambin* sported only ten shares. Four were held by the Cutche Combine, three by Imoth Ap-Ost, and one each by Turion Plence, Savannah Holdings, and the Shill Corporation. The Cutche Combine was a wholly owned subsidiary of the Jeeling Astro Corporation, in which Pink Toad had a sixty per cent holding. Imoth ap-Ost was not the name of a Barasshanti individual, as it seemed; it was a Barasshanti shell company owned by Nisp chemicals. Nisp chemicals was controlled by Jermyn ap-Browan, sibling of Jerz ap-Browan. Turion Plence was a nominee shareholder. His principal was unknown, but the rental on his luxury flatable in the Swoir Bubblecity was paid by Gelica Sarpent, wife of Mykal Sarpent. Savannah Holdings chased through a network of smaller companies to a Femmish concern in the sphere of influence of the Jyrjjeer clan. The Shill Corporation was a specialist company whose only major client was P/J Numismatics Inc., owned by Porgas Jurket.

"My, my, my," said Pigge. "Somebody sabotaged the *Agenzia Bahambin* Annual General Meeting."

"It's very perplexing," said Lurkin Mole. "I should have been told about this."

Pigge caught the Joat's eye. Neither gave voice to his thought, which was obvious to both. *Agenzia Bahambin* had not wanted anyone to know.

# 7 Paradise Displaced

Lindilu Glynde was waiting, as arranged. They kissed with enthusiasm, but holding back enough that it didn't get out of hand. She smiled — a shade smugly, he thought. Then she drew a deep breath, and recited:

*"But welcome now my lord, in wele or woe,*
*Whose presence I haue lackt too long a day,*
*and fie on fortune—"*

"Book I, Canto VIII, verse 43," said Billy. "I see I'm not the only one with literary inclinations."

"It intrigued me," said Lindilu, "so I got a copy from the Library Computer. That's an amazing memory you have."

"Never forget a thing. Joat's curse."

She bit her lower lip. "Yes, I suppose it could be."

"Yeah. But some things are worth remembering."

He ordered food, and a carafe of wine imported from one of the hub worlds. They sipped from tall glasses with helical stems as they ate.

"Any new leads on the vanishing island?" He had told her a little of his business on Bahamba Bright, along with a great many things that he seldom told anyone. He could *talk* to this girl. Really communicate on a deep level. It had never happened to him before.

"Not a thing. The island's been sliced away, smooth as a mirror. Hell, it *is* a mirror. But the analysts say it's just sheared, natural rock. "

She shook her head in wonderment. The Joat found the dynamics of her hair totally entrancing. "That's weird. And you have no idea how it was done?"

*"The sea itself doest thou not plainely see*
*Encroch vppon the land there under thee?*
No more idea than the poet."

She drained her glass. The Joat refilled it — and froze in mid-pour.

"Wrong wine?"

"No, I've just had the glimmerings of an idea. Let me see... how does the poem go on from there? A verse about — um — throwing down the mountains, yes. Then it runs:

*"Of things vnseene how canst thou deeme aright,*
*Then answered the righteous Artegall,*
*Sith thou misdeem'st so much of things in sight?*
*What though the sea with waues continuall*

*Doe eat the earth, it is no more at all,*
*Ne is the earth the lesse, or loseth ought,*
*For wahtsoeuer from one place doth fall,*
*Is with the tide vnto an other brought;*
*For there is nothing lost, that may be found, if sought.*"

"I don't understand."

"Neither do I," said the Joat, "but I recognise a hunch. My subconscious is trying to tell me something. 'Ne is the earth the lesse...', 'For there is nothing lost, that may be found, if sought...', 'Of things vnseene how canst thou deeme aright...'. And an optically flat boundary...

"Do you realise how much energy it would take to destroy an entire island? Or to remove it from a planet's gravity-well? It's enormous. A power-source like that could never stay concealed. Which means that the island is *still here*."

"You mean it just *looks* like it's vanished? All done by mirrors? A Houdini houdunnit? Pretty convincing fakery, isn't it?"

"I know it sounds impossible, but I keep thinking of the alternative. The island can't really be still here, but it has to be here in some sense... Somewhere — hidden. Hmm. Hidden by what? In what? Behind wha— no, beyond! *Beyond!* Beyond a boundary plane so flat that you get reflections off the surface!"

"You *are* trying to tell me it's all done with mirrors! Billy, the wine's gone to your head. Let's go to the beach, you need fresh air. I've bought a new swimsuit that I think you'll —"

"No, wait, I'm beginning to see... Cleavage planes of a crystal lattice — no, the rock isn't a crystal. But it's something like that. Dislocations, that's more what I want. Spatial dislocations across a plane interface."

Lindilu grasped his elbow. "I prescribe fresh air and a swim, followed by something more special to sober you up." But the Joat was transfixed.

"A transfer plane. Gods, an interphase transfer plane." His voice rose to a shout. "Someone's made it work at last! The textbooks all say it can't be done, but I've never been convinced. The proof assumes that Garfold's Conjecture is true in fractional dimensions, you see, and it's been proved only for algebraic irrationals." Lindilu seemed to wilt under the onslaught, even though it wasn't aimed at her, and turned quite pale. The Joat leaped to his feet and thumped the table repeatedly with his fist, disturbing the peace of two elderly ladies drinking herbal tea nearby. "That's *got* to be how they did it!" Then he calmed down enough to see her face.

"Sorry, I got carried away. Did I scare you?"

"You were so — intense. I've never seen you like that before."

"I always get like that when a problem suddenly gives way. It doesn't mean anything."

Her voice was still shaky. "Billy, what's an interpla— interphase transfer plane?"

The Joat picked up two chopsticks and laid them side by side on the tablecloth. "Imagine these are two planes in space," he said. "What an interphase transfer does is, it kind of slits space along the two planes and glues it all up wrong. It joins the left side of one slit to the right side of the other one, so you get a kind of crossover effect. Anything going into one plane comes out of the opposite side of the other one. Go into one plane from the left, you come out of the other one on the right, and vice versa. What's more, it doesn't take any time to do it. It just jumps."

"I *think* I follow that."

"There are some calculations that are sometimes mentioned in PhaDER manuals. The theory of interphase transfer is similar to that of space drives, and it's a good exercise for students to play around with it. The manuals sketch out a proof that interphase transfer impossible and ask the students to fill in the details. Along the way you have to show that *if* interphase transfer is going to happen, then the surfaces along which space is cut-and-pasted must be *exactly* flat. That's an easy consequence of the symmetries of discontinuous solutions to the Pindore-Maxwell equatio—"

"Stop! You're getting too technical. Why does this give a mirror?"

"Think about it this way. Suppose you set up the machinery needed to create a transfer plane across the base of Trixydix, connected to another one under the ocean somewhere else. Once it's switched on, the planes come into being, and Trixydix seems to end at one of the planes. Above it is just ocean. Now, the plane is perfectly flat, therefore optically flat. The sheared rock-water interface acts as a mirror because it behaves just like a slice of polished rock with water on top. But as soon as the plane ceases to intersect the island, the rest of the interface is water-water, so you don't see anything peculiar. And the water moves freely across the interface, so you can't tell there's a boundary there at all."

"That's all very well," said Lindilu, "but won't you get the top half hovering in mid-ocean over the second plane?"

"Smart lady. Very true. Yes, it's got to be a more complicated set-up. I'd guess they used a box, with transfer planes for sides. Put a box round Trixydix; put another box round an empty piece of ocean. Cross-connect, and presto! No island. Not in its usual place, anyway.

Naturally, you have to make sure nobody can spot it in the *other* box, but that's a much simpler problem. I see two serious difficulties, though."

"Only two?"

"I'll ignore the problem of *making* the transfer planes," the Joat said expansively. "Obviously someone knows how to, so it's possible, so forget it right now. No, I'm worried about how I can put things back the way they were. First, I don't know any way to detect a transfer plane as such, beyond inferring its presence from the discontinuities that it creates. Second, I have no idea how to shut one down without getting hold of the machinery that's maintaining it." He thumped the table again, then gave the old ladies a sheepish grin and lowered his voice. "But now that I know what the cause is, there must be some way to turn off the planes and get the *Agenzia Bahambin* AGM rolling again." A peculiar look flashed across Lindilu's features, but the Joat missed it, looking for the waiter. "Come on, I want to see that swimsuit!"

\* \* \*

The Joat left Lindilu Glynde's holiday villa just before dawn, and boarded a hydrofoil taxi to the Lustrous Lagoon's private quay. At that hour, the quay was deserted. He touched a pad to summon the elevator. His head awhirl with Lindilu and transfer plane physics, he failed to hear the gravel crunch behind him. But even the scientific absorption of a lovestruck joat can be interrupted by the pressure of a laser-pistol muzzle at the base of the spine. Unfortunately his befogged brain failed to recognise what the interruption was, and the Joat swung round to identify the intrusion. His assailant had not expected this, and in the time it took him to decide to press the trigger, the Joat had come fully awake, seen the weapon, and chopped at his attacker's wrist. The pistol dropped to the ground. With no time to pick it up, the Joat kicked it into the sea, and moved so that his back was protected by the wall.

The man recovered from the blow and closed in warily. The quay was empty and Billy wasted no time in calling for help. He balanced on his toes, preparing to dodge: mentally he flipped the pages of a *hai-ganzai* manual he had once borrowed from the library.

The man pulled out a knife. The Joat aimed a *shika* kick at his groin. The assailant slashed at Billy's foot and missed, but the blow deflected the kick. The knife flashed down again in a swift arc. The Joat blocked it with his arm, heard cloth rip, and felt a sharp pain as the blade sliced his forearm. He lashed out blindly with his fist, feeling bone crunch, staggered as his feet were swept from under him, and fell on his side. The raised knife gleamed, began to descend —

There was a flash of blue light that threw the nearby scenery into sharp relief, and the crackling sound of an electrical discharge. His assailant's body slumped to the ground. Otis Pigge stuffed the laser pistol back into his belt.

"You all right, Jarneyvore?"

The Joat sat up against the wall. "A cut arm. Not sure how bad. Bloody." The sun had begun to rise and there was now enough light for Pigge to look at the wound. The cut was deep, but the knife had missed the main arteries. Pigge bound it with a strip torn from his shirtsleeve.

"I'll get you to a doctor and then tell Lurkin Mole to pick up a body." He helped Billy into the waiting escalator.

"Lucky you showed up," said Billy. "I owe you one."

Pigge looked embarrassed. "Wasn't luck," he grunted unhappily.

"You were there on purpose? Keeping an eye on me? Why? Don't you trust me?"

"Depends what about. I've been in the force a long time, Jarneyvore. I've seen just about everything, and I've learned a lot of useful tricks. Mostly obvious ones, so obvious everyone forgets them. For instance, crime implies criminals. And criminals don't take kindly to investigators, especially in multibillion kroon kidnap cases. It's to their advantage to discover what the investigators are up to. So when Billy the Joat acquires a beautiful lady friend —"

"Damn you, Pigge."

"— I took the precaution to slap a tracer on him. When he told the lady how the crime was committed, I began to fear for his safety. I guessed you'd come this way, but the quay looked empty and that fellow caught me on the hop. He was hiding, of course. Moved like a squirtsnake: never saw him till he grabbed you. The only luck was that I got a clear shot at him. For a while I wasn't sure I'd get the chance."

"Thanks, anyway. But look, Pigge, I'm not naive. I had the same thought. I checked Lindilu out myself. Though Immigration. She's genuine. What makes you so sure she set me up?"

"Nothing."

A word sounded missing and the Joat supplied it. "But."

"But, there's a corpse on the quay that was meant to be yours. But, Immigration only knows what somebody else tells it. But— but your young lady's real name is Alaya de Flore Strooghn."

"What's *that* supposed to prove?" asked the Joat, hackles rising. "Lots of rich people travel incognito. For their own protection. Especially young beautiful rich women."

Pigge sighed. He'd never expected to feel sorry for Billy the Joat, but when you worked with the man you had to admit he had his good points. Hard to say quite what they were, but he definitely had some somewhere. At least the Strooghn woman had broken that stupid crush Jarneyvore had on Sherryl Eton, which would probably have got him killed one day — so it wasn't a total loss, though this wasn't the time to point that out. And unfortunately it *was* the time to point out something else. "Jarneyvore, the Strooghn family used to *own* this planet. They're still incredibly rich and powerful, even without it. Rumour is that Alaya's great grandfather lost it in a private war. She's not just here on vacation, I guarantee."

The Joat laughed bitterly.

"*No wound, which warlike hand of enemy*
*Inflicts with dint of sword, so sore doth light,*
*As doth the poysnous sting, which infamy*
*Infixeth in the name of noble wight:*
*For by no art, or any leaches might*
*It euer can recured be againe;*
*Ne all the skill, which that immortall spright*
*Of Podalyrius did in it retaine,*
*Can remedy such hurts; such hurts are hellish paine.*"

Pigge looked at him. "You're taking it pretty well, Jarneyvore."

"Shit," said the Joat. "I've never taken anything so badly in my life."

\* \* \*

"It's hard to accept that hypothesis, Mr. Jarneyvore," said the SpaDe technical consultant, a tall, balding Human called Kmarsk. He sounded like a talking manual. "Especially from someone with no professional Guild qualifications. You invoke a device that all the textbooks confirm is impossible, and you admit yourself that there's no way to detect it in action."

The Joat's arm had been repaired with a reabsorbent bioglue and, while still painful, could be used. Billy leaned his chin on his good hand. "I imagine the textbooks would also say that it's impossible for an island to vanish, Dr. Kmarsk."

"This is true."

"The dictionary defines 'qualify' as 'to limit by modifications'. I agree entirely. I am not qualified. I am *not* limited by modifications — I have a brain and I haven't filled it up with preconceived ideas taught to me by people without any imagination. You may rest assured that I'm competent, not only to use the Pindore-Maxwell equations, but to question some common misapprehensions about their solutions. And I don't need to thumb through the manuals to do it: they're right here in my head."

Kmarsk objected. "There's more to understanding than a good memory, Mr. Jarneyvore."

"Damn right! But not only do I know the material better than most Specialists do: *I understand what else it relates to*."

"Such as Garfold's Conjecture being a weak point." Kmarsk was giving up the contest without a fight. He had just advanced the Joat's own best argument. "I admit I'd never realised that the standard proof makes improper use of it. I spent half of yesterday in a huddle with the Library, trying to prove you wrong. I couldn't because you aren't. I was impressed. It's not often that an amateur teaches me something new about phase field theory."

The Joat let the insult pass. Kmarsk hadn't realised it was one.

"Your theory," Kmarsk continued briskly, "is that Garfold's Conjecture is false, the textbook impossibility proof is fallacious, and somebody has found a way to set up a transfer plane."

"You place too much faith in the equations. Fact: the island has vanished. A transfer plane is the only sensible explanation for that mirror finish. It's the only thing that explains why there was no detectable disturbance. It fits. Even if the textbook proof was *correct* I'd still say it's a transfer plane. There'd have to be a flaw in the Pindore-Maxwell equations."

The consultant inclined his shiny head. "Not all Specialists are as unimaginative as you obviously think, Jarneyvore. Not the best ones. Every profession has its dull plodders, and those are the ones you mostly encounter. Suppose we assume you're right. Then we can forget about the detection problem. That leaves only one important question. Do you have any idea how to shut a transfer plane off?"

"Last night I didn't," said the Joat, "but I've been running a few calculations and now it's pretty obvious. It takes energy to transfer matter or radiation across the interface. So if we shove enough stuff through it, we should be able to overload the generating machinery."

Kmarsk digested this. "I see. You want me to recommend a military bombardment."

The Joat nodded. "Yeah. Get the navy to lob something really hefty into the ocean and keep it up until the generator blows."

"Fine. So we ask the Navy to phade a cruiser in. On a hunch."

"That's the general idea, yes," said Billy.

"No."

"Hey, Kmarsk, it's a good hunch. That's what joats are paid for."

"It's not what *I'm* paid for, though, Jarneyvore. I need proof." Kmarsk was convinced the Joat was right. The explanation did hang together, provided you could accept his assumptions. But for someone whose whole training had denied them, that wasn't easy. Especially when his career would depend on the outcome. Top brass hated wasting ammunition. He came to a decision. "Give me one piece of hard evidence," said Kmarsk. "Just *one*, something I can use to justify the decision to a board of enquiry when we spend a fortune and it doesn't work. Then I'll stick my neck out. Way out. But not, Jarneyvore, on a bald hunch."

"Fair enough. If I'm right we ought to be able to tell. Let's run through the sequence of events. They set up a box round the island, then another box round some empty ocean. Then they swap them."

"Don't forget there's an important constraint on transfer planes."

"Sure. The potential energy has to stay constant. So you just have to cut-and-paste between locations with the same gravitational field strength. That's easy enough, everywhere in the ocean is at pretty much the same potential."

"Sure," said Kmarsk. "But how do they hide the island once it's moved?"

"Well... no point in introducing yet another box under the ocean — same problem. I suppose they must have gimmicked the screens with a different cross-connection, to kind of pinch the second box out."

Kmarsk pounced. "Pinching means singularities. Wouldn't those distort the local metric?"

"I guess."

"Which implies the creation of local gravitational anomalies."

"Yes."

"Let's do a planetary gravity-scan."

\* \* \*

A gravity-scan would use the resources satellite, which like all satellites was regulated by Traffic Control. Kmarsk had no trouble arranging that, and after a lengthy session with the system manuals they read in a scanning program. While they were waiting for the check-routines to finish, the Joat idly thumbed the pages of the Traffic Control manuals. It was the first, and probably the last, chance he'd have to see how the system worked; and the innate curiosity of a joat is to that of a cat as a multiprocessor is to an abacus.

The Joat read the manual, and was not impressed. The programs lacked imagination.

Otis Pigge called. The Joat's deceased assailant had been identified as a certain Hymeth Ibral Fasmet, an inhabitant of Poor Yorick, a planetoid in the Shimplery system. Fasmet's holiday villa had been searched, turning up a small arsenal of weapons but no documents. Forensic analysis of the dust on his clothes disclosed some unusual grains of pollen, found only on one cluster of islands on Bahamba Bright. When the minions of Lurkin Mole searched the villas in that region, they found one that appeared to have been vacated in a hurry.

It had been rented to Lindilu Glynde.

The Joat's mood was scarcely improved when the gravity-scan came up with absolutely nothing. But his natural reaction to emotional stress was to work so hard that it kept his mind off the painful topic. After an hour or so of futile argument, inspiration struck.

"Hang on," said the Joat. "We've been assuming the second box has to be somewhere else in the ocean, because that's where the gravitational field is the same as it is at the island. But there are other ways to equalise the gravitational fields. Maybe the second box is off-planet."

"Yes, but the range of a transfer plane is no more than a third of a light year. That's an easy consequence of the Pindore-Maxwell equations and it *doesn't* depend on Garfold's Conjecture."

"Sure."

"So where else would you find the right gravitation? The other bodies in this system all have lower surface gravity than Bahamba Bright."

"No they don't."

"Oh. The sun. But that's got a much higher surface gravity. Oh. Surface. You mean, in the right orbit —"

"Precisely. Kmarsk, you're a genius. I see it all now. It's a three-part set-up, using two boxes. One around Trixydix and another near the sun in an orbit with the same gravitational potential. You paste together the opposite inside faces of the Trixydix box to shut the island up inside a self-contained universe. Anything trying to get out through a face comes back in again through the opposite face. Wraparound in 3D, it's a flat torus. Nothing inside ever gets out. Then you paste the inside of the box near the sun to the place where the Trixydix box's inside was. That way you don't get any gravitational anomalies on Bahamba Bright. But that leaves a hole in space near the sun, because you've lost the inside of the sun box. The easiest way to get rid of that is to identify opposite faces, from outside. So anything that comes along just jumps right across. That *does* create anomalies, but not in a place anyone would look for them."

Kmarsk interrupted. "You've lost me. Run by it again."

"Oh, sorry. You pinch off Trixydix in a self-contained universe, plug the gap with a bit of sunward vacuum so nobody notices, and plug *that* gap by pasting its edges together. Then Trixydix disappears, and the rest looks much as it did before."

"You know, the vacuum must have some effect when the cross-connections are first made. Not like an ocean/ocean interface."

"Good point," said the Joat. "Well, when the switch is first made you get an empty box down here on Bahamba Bright. But then the water and air flow in to fill it. Nothing very difficult there."

"No. But the influx of air and water must generate atmospheric and hydrodynamic oscillations."

"Gods! Thunderclaps and tidal waves!"

"Exactly what the local inhabitants observed."

"You said 'just *one* piece of hard evidence', didn't you?"

"I very much fear that I did," said Kmarsk. "Here goes my career."

# 8   Paradise Replaced

A SpaDe Q-class battlecruiser descended on the Mermynthine Sound in the early afternoon of the following day. Commander Redvers P. Macintyre briefed the gun crew in his lazy Velgastonian drawl.

"...The objective," he read from the briefing sheet, "is to perduce the maximum paws'ble energy flux 'cross the bound'ry uh the transfer plane bawx —" He tossed the sheet on to his desk in disdain. "What kinda crap is that? I want you guys tuh sling energy inna that pond over there 'sif yuh *en*tyre future dee-pended on it. Which, in a manner of speakin', it does, guys. As much energy's paws'ble in's short a *tahm* as paws'ble. Thuh Navy's payin' thuh bills, so don' pussyfoot aroun'. Lenkensteen, whaddaya reckon?"

"A lasercannon barrage, sir?"

"Not 'nless yuh wanna boil the sea, boy. We'll use Manticorium perjectiles. Big, solid chunks uh hyperdense metal. Like my ol' pal Bert Eyunstyne allus useta say, mass is just energy wearin' a different ballgown, if yuh catch mah drift?"

The gun-crew programmed a fire-path that wouldn't do any damage if the transfer planes collapsed before they had a chance to shut the guns down. It would be inconvenient to have the island reappear during darkness, so the bombardment commenced at dawn, an ancient military tradition much to Commander Macintyre's taste. For an hour the hyperdense projectiles ripped across the skies to the accompaniment of sonic booms. Two hours passed, then three.

"Looks like your theories are holding up under fire, Jarneyvore," said Kmarsk, wondering what would be the most suitable line of work for a cashiered technical consultant.

"I'd much prefer it if they weren't," said the Joat. "Worry not. I'd say it's merely becoming evident that the transfer plane generator has an unexpectedly large capacity to absorb energy." But as the end of the fifth hour approached he began to have doubts. The battlecruiser had thrown Manticorium projectiles around like a mudlark with a nest of sumpslugs, and still the planes — if planes there were — hadn't even flickered. *This could prove embarrassing. Palgandra will —*

There was an almost subliminal discontinuity. One instant the island was invisible, the next it was back. After a few seconds the bombardment ceased. This time there were no tidal-waves or thunderclaps, because the water-levels and air-pressures matched. Though a portion of the Mermynthine Sound had shifted into solar orbit.

Kmarsk and Jarneyvore solemnly shook hands.

\* \* \*

Lurkin Mole's men picked up Lindilu Glynde, alias Alaya de Flore Strooghn, at Arcady Spaceport when she tried to sneak on board a shuttle with false papers. Her hand-baggage contained a very strange device, undoubtedly the transfer plane generator. It was rushed to the SpaDe laboratory attached to Arcady Spaceport, to be examined by a team of analysts headed by Specialist Kmarsk. The worst thing of all was some evidence that Pigge had found — a bank audit-trail showing that Hymeth Fasmet had been in Alaya Strooghn's employ when he attacked the Joat.

*Lindilu ordered me killed. But she failed, and now they've arrested her.* Billy expected to feel satisfaction, the vengeance of the betrayed. But if this was satisfaction, then satisfaction was a very empty feeling. "So it's all over," he muttered under his breath.

Pigge overheard. "I wouldn't bet on that."

"But the whole thing is as obvious as a boggie's tail at sunrise!"

"You have a brilliant logical mind, Jarneyvore, but real life is usually a mess of contradictions. Let me tell you something. I've been a constable for longer than I care to remember; worked my way up from the ranks, and it wasn't easy. Along the way I acquired a lot of indefinable things. Instincts, you might say, though personally I don't hold with the word. I'd say it's a gut feeling for patterns of human behaviour. Now I'd certainly agree that this young lady you're so struck with —"

"I'm damned well *not!* Not any more! I was an idiot ever to —"

"Shut up, you don't fool me. That crush you had on Sherryl Eton vanished overnight when Lindilu Glynde walked into your life."

"Crush? You're crazy. Anyway, a lark in the mud is worth two in the —"

"Nuts. You fell *hard*, Jarneyvore. And you *will* make an idiot of yourself if you don't listen to what I have to say. Now, there's no doubt that Mz. Strooghn is involved in some kind of shady business. She, Fasmet, and others unknown used the transfer plane generator to hijack Trixydix and kidnap the principals of *Agenzia Bahambin*."

"You don't need to tell me that."

"Shh. There are loose ends. Dozens of them, all over. In my experience, it's a good idea to track down loose ends. It avoids injustice. One great big juicy loose end is *Agenzia Bahambin* itself. Why all the secrecy and subterfuge? Why conceal the fact that the kidnappees were all *Agenzia Bahambin* top frogs? Second, what's a powerful woman like Alaya Strooghn doing getting her own hands dirty? Why didn't she just stay a couple of sectors away where she was safe and let the hired hands do the job? Third, since she *is* getting her hands dirty, why get Fasmet to attack you with a knife when she herself had ample opportunity dispose of you more quietly and less publicly? There are a dozen far more certain ways for Fasmet to kill you if she just lured you to some out-of-the-way spot. And here's another one for you to chew on. *What was her motive for the kidnap?* I don't believe for one minute it was money. She's from a very wealthy family. Hosperlanian by birth, now moved to Poor Yorick. No, her motive must have been quite different. I'd lay a heavy bet it was something to do with her grandfather."

"Her *grandfather?*"

"While you and that po-faced Specialist have been spending the Navy's projectile budget for the next ten years, I've been digging around in old records in the Companies Register." He handed the Joat a wad of paper. "Here are copies. Bahamba Bright was originally discovered by a colonist called Durgash Strooghn. Recognise the name? Yeah, Alaya's ancestor. Later he leased it to *Agenzia Bahambin* for a peppercorn rent. Doesn't that strike you as odd? For such a valuable property?"

"So what do you propose we should do about it?"

Pigge pressed his fingertips together. "I'm going to bask on the beaches in the Bahamban sunshine and pick up a healthy tan. The longer this case stays open, the happier I'll be. What *you* do is your business, and I suggest you attend to it. If I were you, I'd try to find out from Mz. Strooghn what her true motives were."

"Are you crazy? She tried to have me killed! I'd rather leave her to rot!"

She told Fasmet what you knew. Fasmet tried to kill you. He could have been moonlighting. There's no evidence that the Strooghn woman gave the orders. Anyway," said Pigge, "if you *do* want to leave her to rot, you might enjoy knowing that she's rotting in cell 23, corridor 6, level 3 of the Shan Husan prison, here on Arcady. Here's a map." He tucked it into the Joat's tunic pocket.

\* \* \*

The SpaDe laboratories were in an inaccessible corner of the spaceport area, and security had been tightened. Kmarsk was analysing the transfer plane generator with a neutrino spectrograph when the Joat finally gained admittance. "Unfortunately the mass overload blew a few of the ceramic frommets," said Kmarsk. "We've built substitutes, but we're not having much success with the fine tuning of the ploridial fleisiogonemes."

The Joat took off his jerkin and rolled up his frilly lemon sleeves. "Let me have a go, I can tune those boggies with both feet tied behind my ba— hey, look at those omnidex arrays! I've never seen so many at one time!"

For the next few hours Joat and Specialist ran every test they could devise. By the end, they had restored the missing circuits, and they could control the generator perfectly; but they had no more insight into how it worked than they'd had to begin with. Most of the components were comprehensible enough: positional locators, stabilizing circuits, energy sinks. But the heart of the device was a tiny sealed unit barely a centimetre across. Exotic waveforms emanated from it, but its internal structure was proving inaccessible to everything from X-rays to quark diffractometry.

Kmarsk's singleminded determination to understand the generator made him totally oblivious to everything else. So, while the Specialist was making intricate adjustments to a Thom transverter, the Joat extracted the consultant's magstripe ID card from the side-pocket of his overalls. Then he ran it through a miniature scanner which he had built the previous evening and disguised as a calculator to get it past the security men. Then he returned the card to its unsuspecting owner.

At noon the Joat took his leave, ostensibly for lunch. In Blue Mull market he purchased a Bahamban souvenir — a portable electronic zuffoletta, or flute-organ — in a calyptus-wood case. He stripped out its innards and deposited the remains in his room at the Lustrous Lagoon. Then he returned to the laboratory for a further afternoon's work.

In the evening, in the privacy of the hotel, he manufactured a duplicate of Kmarsk's ID card. With its aid, and some expert lockpicking, he penetrated the laboratory area soon after midnight, and stole the transfer plane generator. He removed the cover and installed the device in the empty zuffoletta casing. He added a few spurious connecting wires — enough to pass casual inspection.

Half an hour later he was huddled in the undergrowth of the dense woods that bordered the spaceport. The plan hinged on accuracy, and the closer he was, the better. By the light of a glowtorch he studied the map that Pigge had given him, changing the control settings on the generator to match the coordinates of Alaya de Flore Strooghn's cell.

Alaya/Lindilu was asleep: the Joat recognised the snore. An insistent whisper, directed into her ear, interrupted her dreams. *Lindilu! Wake up! Don't talk, don't move, whisper! Wake up!* It repeated in a hypnotic chant. She awoke. The subliminal pattern had set, and she made no noise and lay still.

"Who's that?" she whispered.

"*Are you alone?*"

"Yes."

"Billy."

"But I can't see you!"

"That's because I'm not here. I've opened up a small transfer plane to talk through. And you'd better talk fast, Alaya de Flore Strooghn, and it had better be good."

She hesitated. "Why should I say anything to you?"

"Because if what you say is sufficiently convincing, I might just decide to get you out of there."

\* \* \*

It was a simple story.

Four generations back, the Strooghn family had discovered Bahamba Bright and started its long development into a colony world. Alaya's grandfather, Durgash Strooghn, had an assistant called Dixon Purl. Purl had murdered Strooghn, but his wife and child had escaped. Documents in Purl's possession assigned him the Strooghn family's rights to the planet in return for a modest annual fee. The documents were forgeries, of course, and the fee was just a clever touch to divert suspicion, but Clementine Strooghn had been too busy dodging Purl's hired assassins to be able to protest through legal channels. Purl had set up *Agenzia Bahambin* and started Bahamba Bright on its pleasure-planet track. Clementine had evaded her pursuers and settled on Hosperlan. The Strooghn genes asserted themselves, and the family acquired money and land. Lots. Alaya's father invented the transfer plane, but kept the secret in the family. Revenge was always uppermost in his mind, and he thought the device would give them an edge. He trained his daughter to continue the fight. Then *Agenzia Bahambin* finally tracked the Strooghns down, and her father disappeared. Alaya fled with her kin to Poor Yorick, but the family's wealth was mostly in intangibles so they managed to keep most of it. On Poor Yorick she had worked out how to use the transfer plane generator to fight *Agenzia Bahambin*. The kidnap was just the first step: it damaged the opposition financially and psychologically. Enough pressure might win back the planet.

"Good execution, bad planning," said Billy. "Too drawn out. Bahamba Bright makes an impressive power-base. Before you can get the planet back, you have to get the planet back. Eliminate the power-base. Anyway, your plan was screwed up by Grynth racial pride. They wouldn't pay the ransom."

"I did what I could," said Alaya, defeated.

"And then Pigge and I came along," whispered the Joat, "and —"

"And we kept tabs on you."

"That's what you call it," said the Joat bitterly. "All part of the plan?"

"*No!* I didn't mean to — it wasn't part of — Hell, I could have hired a dozen courtesans, you think I'd get my own hands — uh, my — damn it, Billy, I *liked* you. Lots."

"You liked me? You told Hymeth Fasmet to *kill* me."

He heard a sharp intake of breath. "*What?*"

"Fasmet attacked me with a knife. Pigge shot him."

"*Oh Gods, no. No.* Billy, I didn't tell him that! He said he was going to take you out of circulation for a while, smuggle you off planet until it was over. I would *never* have told to — to — please, you've *got* to believe me!"

There was real pain in her voice. Was she just a good actress? For a heartbeat, he hesitated. "Like I said, good execution, bad planning. With what I'd found out, he *had* to kill me."

"Billy, suppose that you'd known the truth, all of it, from the very beginning... what I was trying to achieve, and why..." She paused, then said in a whisper so quiet that he could barely hear, "*What would you have done?*"

"Why should I trust you?" he said, leaving her question unanswered.

"I can't answer that. But I desperately need your help. And I *didn't* order you killed, I swear I didn't." She sounded genuine. The story fitted everything he knew. And the Joat remembered that first, astonishing night... If she'd been acting, she'd been very, very good at it.

"I'm probably making a fool of myself, but a Joat always backs a hunch. Provisionally, I'll accept your version of events. But from now on, you do *exactly* what I tell you."

"Yes, Billy."

"And the answer to your question is, I would have told Lurkin Mole that I had no idea where his missing island had gone, or why."

    \* \* \*

Billy cut the transfer connection, moving fast now the he knew what he was going to do. He headed for Arcady Spaceport departure lounge, collecting his baggage, sent ahead from the hotels. The exciseman glanced inside the zuffoletta but was satisfied by the incomprehensible array of components. Ten minutes later Billy the Joat was in parking orbit: an hour more and he was out of Traffic Control zone and the *Shrimpton*'s phasefringes were extended, ready for departure.

The first phade took him to the far side of the Bahamban sun, at a distance where the gravitational potential was roughly equal to that on the surface of Bahamba Bright. From there he hoped to open a transfer plane link between the yacht's cabin and Alaya/Lindilu's cell.

After a quarter of an hour he was forced to revise the plan. The planet's orbital motion was too complex, and the distance was too great, for one person to keep the plane steady enough. Hastily improvising, the Joat phaded back to the edge of the Traffic Control zone, in the shadow of Bahamba Bright's jagged, deserted moonlet. What he really wanted to do was open up a transfer plane to the planetary surface and drive the *Shrimpton* through it. But you can't pass a working generator through its own transfer plane. ('Close the door and bring it in after you,' a favourite joke of the wandering milligans, sprang to mind.) Nor could he leave the generator in orbit, because the controls had to be adjusted by hand. Instead, he created a transfer plane box around the *Shrimpton*, linked to another one near the sun. Although the generator was now inside its own box, it had not *passed through* any of the transfer planes involved.

It was a tricky business, but a skilled pilot could manage, given luck and determination. Using the generator's locality controls, he lowered the box towards the surface of Bahamba Bright, keeping the *Shrimpton* inside it. Simultaneously he moved the second box towards the sun, matching the gravitation. From the outside — and in particular to Traffic Control — the *Shrimpton*'s box was empty, indistinguishable from the vacuum all around it. *Shrimpton* itself would have appeared to be moving into the sun, but Traffic Control wasn't interested in anything that far away.

The Joat, more confident now, piloted the box below lidar altitude until it was hovering over the woods near Arcady Spaceport; then he switched off the generator. *Shrimpton* suddenly materialized above the trees. There was a bit of a bang as the air flowed in, but no worse than a noisy sportster — a small yacht doesn't compare to an island. He tilted the ship's nose back to the horizontal before it joined the Underground Flying Squadron and lowered it into a clearing.

It was a complicated way to avoid being seen by Traffic Control, but it worked.

From his hiding place among the trees, in the darkness, he had no difficulty in setting up a transfer plane link to Alaya's cell, big enough for her to step through to *Shrimpton*'s cabin. The he ran his box trick in reverse to lift off planet again into the moonlet's shadow, switched off the generator, and phaded from the system like a mudlark pursued by a posse of starving wollagong.

\* \* \*

If Alaya had expected to be treated like a damsel in distress rescued by a knight errant, she was wrong. The Joat interrogated her on every aspect of her story: the past history of the Strooghns, the terms of the document that ceded their rights to *Agenzia Bahambin* for a nominal fee, her movements on Bahamba Bright. He pressed her particularly hard on the loose ends that Pigge had noticed. Why, for instance, was she doing the dirty work herself? Her answer was that she didn't trust anybody else with the transfer plane generator — it was a family secret and she had been trained to keep it that way.

He kept the questions coming and gave her no time to think about her answers; he used every trick in the interrogator's book to try to break her story. Only he knew how much it was costing him, not just to witness her obvious distress, but to cause her more. It took three hours, and at the end of it her tale still hung together. "OK, Lindilu/Alaya. My belief ceases to be provisional."

She was drenched with sweat and the coarse prison clothes were clinging to her body; her hair was lank and greasy, and she was mentally exhausted by the intensity of the Joat's questioning. She gave him a wan smile. "It damned well better. You put me through the mangle."

"Sorry, Lindilu," said the Joat. He touched her hand gently. "Mind if I still call you that? It brings back pleasant memories."

"I guess not."

"I had to make certain."

"You rescued me even thought you weren't. That alone puts you in big trouble."

The Joat dismissed it. "Nonsense. I wasn't even on the planet, remember?"

Alaya knew it wasn't as simple as that, because Spade knew that the Joat knew that... but presumably he knew what he was doing. "I want to get out of these awful rough prison clothes."

"Sure," said the Joat absently. "Now, as I see it, the next move will be to — Lindilu, what are you doing?"

"Getting out of these awful rough prison clothes. You said I could."

"Yes," said the Joat. "But I *had* anticipated you putting something else on instead."

"Spoilsport. I don't mind."

"Ordinarily," said the Joat," I'd be offering you every encouragement. But right now I think we ought to make our next move. Here, you can have my shirt." He wriggled out of it. She took it from his hands, and started to undo his belt.

"Hey! You're supposed to put that on, not take off more of mine! What are you playing at?"

Lindilu gave him a wicked smile. "I'm making my next move."

\* \* \*

"Now, lecherous Sir Joat: what were you trying to tell me?" Alaya had donned the shirt. The Joat looked at her appreciatively, and began,

"*Straunge lady in so straunge habiliment...*"

"I recognise that bit," said Lindilu. "Una. Let me think... Ah, yes.

*Most vertuous virgin borne of heuenly berth,*
*That to redeeme thy woeful parents head,*
*From tyrans rage, and euer-dying dread,*
*Hast wandred through the world now long a day...*

Quite apt; though I think you do have me a trifle miscast."

"That's not a bad memory you have, yourself."

"No, and it's still reminding me about next moves. Give."

"I just feel we have some unfinished business. Could you *keep* Bahamba Bright if I got it back into Strooghn hands?"

"If that's a joke, it's in precious poor taste."

He waited.

"We can keep it. We've learned to play rough. But I thought you said that before we could take it away from them, we had to take it away from them. How do you propose to get round that?"

"Well," said the Joat, "we've let the *Faerie Queene* call the tune several times already, so why not play this one by the book too?

*...with ragged rift*
*Doth roll adowne the rocks, and fall with fearefull drift.*"

"Aha!" said Alaya. "You're going to bomb Bahamba Bright with stray meteorites. An excellent idea, Sir Wyllam de Jarneyvore: you'll only kill a million or two and ruin the fair scenery."

"You're a smart one, all right," said the Joat. "You're closer than you'd ever imagine."

\* \* \*

Twenty light years from Bahamba Bright lies the rimward end of the Hondecoeter Nebula, stretching from the edge of Pirelli Sector to the far side of neighbouring Boccaccio Sector. At each end of the nebula is a desolate wilderness of turbulent dust, interspersed with small fragments of rock ranging in size up to small planetoids. Such regions are avoided by the wary, and therefore prove attractive to those of nefarious intent.

With PhaDER and transfer plane, Billy the Joat sneaked up on the Hondecoeter Nebula and swiped a planetoid.

In third-of-a-light-year jumps, he transferred it over to the Bahamban system, a game of cosmic basketball played for the highest stakes. It took some time to adjust the final transfer plane, because the plan called for a very precise trajectory.

The Joat pushed the button.

The planetoid, rolling smoothly onward, met the transfer plane, and disappeared. It emerged close to Bahamba Bright, on a collision course with its deserted moonlet. *Shrimpton* phaded above the ecliptic to watch the fireworks.

Planetoid and moonlet impacted in a soundless explosion with the force of a neutrino bomb. White-hot magma seethed and spurted, expanding into a huge, smoky, glowing ball that writhed as if in torment. The combined mass, speeded on its path, imperceptibly changed its orbit.

"Big deal," said Alaya. "You've blown up the moon. So now all the moonstruck lovers will boycott the planet and put *Agenzia Bahambin* out of business?"

"*O helpe thou my weake wit, and sharpen my dull tong...* I'll give you three clues, and while you're thinking about them you can rustle up some lunch.

"Clue One. Traffic Control Zone ends at the moon's orbit. The only *outside* things that Traffic Control notices are moving bodies whose orbits intersect the zone — meteors and such. Which, incidentally, is why I didn't make the planetoid plough into the ring. *But,* any faults in the programming of Traffic Control are the legal responsibility of *Agenzia Bahambin*. And *I*, who read the manual, have found a fault.

"Clue Two. That ancient contract." He thrust under her nose the copy that Pigge had given him. "Early Quaternity law is built like a brick outhouse: it would survive the Big Bang. If *Agenzia Bahambin* fails to pay that purely *nominal* fee, that peppercorn rent that they wrote in to provide a tiny deceptive touch of honesty, then the contract becomes void. And then, by the Right of Heritable Seizin, ownership reverts to the descendants of Durgash Strooghn.

"Clue Three. Under Quaternity law, the assets of a bankrupt company are frozen: it can make *no* payments whatsoever.

"And now, wench," said the Joat, patting her on the bottom, "Sir Wyllam de Jarneyvore requires his lunch!" Feigning indignation, Alaya swept out of the cabin.

Responding immediately to the impact, Traffic Control shut down all approach lanes, in case the impact had sprayed material into them. It also ordered all travellers in transit to leave their yachts and take the shuttle back to Port Arcady. The Joat had counted on this routine precaution — a safe bet because it was written into the Traffic Control manual. "That will avoid anyone getting hurt," he remarked to Alaya between mouthfuls of roast yelver.

"Hurt? You're crazy. What's going to hurt them?"

"Keep watching."

Through the telescopic screen they could inspect the ring of parked yachts at close quarters. After a time, Alaya noticed a definite movement. Some of the yachts were shifting in orbit, jostling each other. Two collided and blew up. The fragments damaged others, the jostling became more violent. Elsewhere there were further explosions. Billy pulled back to a long distance shot.

Bahamba Bright's ring was on fire.

Alaya looked at him. "We did *that?*"

"You weren't impressed when I blew up the moon."

"I'm not impressed now — I'm horrified. But even I can see that if you bash a moon with a planetoid, something's going to blow. *This* I don't see."

"Thanks to the impact, the mass and orbit of the moon have changed. That alters the stabilities of yacht orbits in the ring. You get new resonances that weren't there before. Homoclinic tangles, chaos. The yachts start to oscillate instead of sitting still. It doesn't take much disturbance to break the stable patterns.

"That's where *Agenzia Bahambin*'s lousy programming comes in. They have a stability program, but the moon's orbital data are *hardwired*. It never occurred to them that the orbit could change. Garbage in, garbage out: Traffic Control says it's stable, but Mother nature says otherwise. Unfortunately for *Agenzia Bahambin*, which placed its belief in Traffic Control without understanding how it worked.

"Of course, this will all be obvious enough to the Board of Enquiry." He looked at Lindilu like a mother wollagong waiting for its offspring to make its first clumsy leap into a mud-wallow.

"My turn. OK. We have a third of a million tourists whose expensive space-yachts have been wrecked. They'll be after blood."

"Right."

"Traffic Control's faulty programming means that it will be *Agenzia Bahambin*'s blood, in the form of legal damages. For the yachts, for the inconvenience... hang on, what if *Agenzia Bahambin* has insurance?"

"For *that?* You can't insure against Acts of Gods."

"Stop bragging."

"So *Agenzia Bahambin* is on the receiving end of a mass counterclaim action by the yacht-owners' insurance companies. It is immediately declared technically bankrupt and loses its power-base."

"But surely that will just lead to the insurance companies owning Bahamba Bright? It's *Agenzia Bahambin*'s major asset!"

"No it's not. It's leased from the Strooghn family. Can't be touched."

"Oh."

"But the directors of *Agenzia Bahambin* have got plenty of other assets, more than enough to attract the attentions of the insurance companies."

"I see. And when *Agenzia Bahambin* is declared technically bankrupt the Quaternity immediately freezes its assets, so it can't pay the 'nominal' fee, so we Strooghns get our planet back."

"Eventually. The legal mills must grind. But grind they will — have you ever tried to battle an insurance company? Let alone thousands of them. The delay just does more damage to *Agenzia Bahambin*. I reckon their assets will start to be frozen about... ten minutes ago."

"That quick?"

"I made a few anonymous calls to some insurance companies... But we can't stay here gawping. We ought to lie low for a while, so we'd better get moving before SpaDe comes to investigate. One random phade from of the system, and then we'll set course for... hmmm, Poor Yorick. Won't take long."

"Oh."

The random phade went off smoothly enough, but when the Joat came to set up the coordinates for Poor Yorick...

"Woops. Something wrong. The phasefringe fuses are blown."

"That's a pity." Alaya didn't think she should mention that she had thrown them out of the garbage-port.

"That's funny, said the Joat, rummaging in the parts cabinet. "All the spare fuses have vanished."

"You'll be telling me you've run out of fuel, next," said Alaya. "You men are all the same." She'd thrown out the spares too.

"We'll have to find a planet that we can reach on standby," said the Joat.

"That will take a bit longer, won't it?" asked Alaya hopefully, as the Joat consulted the astrogation computer.

"Sure will," he said. "Two days to Hector's Folly."

Alaya looked disappointed. "Only two days?" She was sure the computer had said it would be longer when she'd asked it, just before she threw out the fuses.

"Two days. Mind you," said the Joat, this is a SpaDe vessel based in Lobachevskii Sector, so I converted the time into Aphéligian units."

"How long," asked Alaya, "is an Aphéligian day in Quaternity Standard Old Earth Units?"

"About fifteen Standard Days."

"I hope you've got plenty of spare shirts."

# 9  Once More unto the Breach

True to his promise, Palgandra had pulled strings, and now the Joat could gain access to the *Hubble* and *Pontryagin* files without breaking the law. He and Alaya de Flore Strooghn — or Lindilu as he still preferred to call her — stayed put on Poor Yorick. The *Agenzia Bahambin* bankruptcy case was moving through the courts at with all the pace of a hibernating wollagong — as anticipated — but that didn't matter, because until the case ended *Agenzia Bahambin* was financially hamstrung. However, an appeal to the Low Apellate Court, petitioning for the restraining order on the agency's finances to be set aside, was due to start in a week. Morally and legally *Agenzia Bahambin* didn't have a leg to stand on, but there was always the danger that the judge would see matters in a different light, succumb to bribery, or have a sudden attack of premature senility.

As the legal wrangling approached this first but crucial hurdle, Alaya became more and more nervous. The outward sign was that she immersed herself almost totally in the affairs of Bahamba Bright. The Joat became equally immersed in the files of the *Pontryagin*, but not because of nerves.

The most likely place for sabotage was the phasemesh machinery. Altogether there had been twelve phasegear crew on board *Pontryagin*. Billy had checked the personnel against other SpaDe and Constabulary files, with no useful result. On an impulse, he dialled into Lessee Fair and cross-checked the names against public-access commercial records. Margrit Beamworth had once worked for Wedgely Macro and held shares in Spottiswoode Supermarkets, and Kryss Nouchott was on record as a proxy-holder for the Never Again Corporation of Buenos Thermopolis. None of this appeared terribly significant, but it gave him the excuse to ask for a deep background search, which was more likely to be illuminating.

It took a while, but when it came, it was very interesting indeed.

On board the *Pontryagin* was a Sub-latticer named Hoo Athanasius, whose retinal patterns and DNA tags exactly matched those of one Filip Lamley Jiniwin, a petty criminal whose police record had as many joints as a Femm's leg. Jiniwin had died in a floater accident in 455 QC, the same year that the *Pontryagin* had vanished. The badly burned body had been identified from dental records. This was of great interest to the Joat, who knew six distinct methods for faking dental structure.

Even more interesting was a substantial payment, of some eight hundred thousand kroon, made to Jiniwin's widow Maddalyna. It was paid by KLIC, the Klapakka Life Insurance Corporation.

Further enquiries, pursuing an intricate chain of ownership transfers, revealed that KLIC was a wholly owned subsidiary of the Octavia Trust. The Octavia Trust was owned by Suzella Eton II. Suzella Eton II was Sherryl Eton's mother.

The Femm. The Etonians. Time distortion. Sharraby Breach.

Somehow, they all fitted together into a single whole. But how? He knew there must be a simple key to the pattern, but it remained tantalizingly out of reach. He was getting nowhere. It was all conjecture. His mind was becoming fuzzy and he was getting moody and irritable.

\* \* \*

Alaya knocked softly on the door. "You busy, Billy?"

"Never too busy for my Lindilu."

She grimaced. "I'm trying to sort out the final details of how we rehabilitate Bahamba Bright as a tourist resort. The main thrust is an advertising campaign, of course. You'll never believe this, we've got Luinda Rompstack to make it for us. The poor dear was *so* pleased that she was rescued, she agreed *immediately*."

"That's nice," said the Joat absently, riffling through a stack of printout.

"It's a two-minute flashfax ad. We got Szitshcho Krokolpin to handle the choreography, and Tambra Ap-Ryolly to do the HV camerawork. The editing's being handled by Godolphin Specials and the... you're not really listening, are you?"

"Sorry, my mind was wandering. Look, Lindilu —"

"*I wish you'd stop calling me by that silly name!*" The outburst had been building for weeks, but the Joat was totally unprepared for it.

"It's just a pet name."

"That's what's wrong with it! *I'm not just a pet!* Lindilu Glynde was a fantasy figure, an empty-headed little piece, all body and no brain!"

"Don't get upset. I loved Lindilu Glynde for her mind as well as her body, you know. And both of them were *yours*." Unwisely, he continued: "For a fantasy figure she had an amazing physical pres—"

"That's all you were after! It's still the only thing that interests you about me! You notice me in bed, but the rest of the time you — you — *ignore* me." She sniffed, and a tear trickled down one cheek.

The Joat felt awkward. He never knew what to do when beautiful women cried, especially when it was his fault. He should have taken her in his arms and told her that he loved her and that everything was going to be fine, but that was too simple and it never occurred to him. There are times when it's a mistake to be too intellectual.

"I'm sorry, Lindi— I mean, Alaya. I'll stop calling you that."

"Yes, but you won't stop *thinking* of me like that! I'm a real woman, Billy Jarneyvore, not just a cute lump of meat!"

The Joat, who had never thought of her as a cute lump of meat, was completely at a loss. Hurt and baffled, he said, "I know you're a real woman. You're smart and tough as well as beautiful. You've got a business head on your shoulders that anybody would envy... Oh, Hell, we've both been working too hard, you on Bahamba Bright and me on the *Pontryagin*. Let's get away for a few days."

She looked at him in dejection. "Oh, Billy, I *can't!* Not now, not when the court case is coming to its climax! I *know* we're going to win the appeal, but I can't help worrying! If *Agenzia Bahambin* wins — bribes the judge, interferes with witnesses, I don't know what — then they'll get back financial control, and then we'll be in serious trouble. They can hire fancy lawyers, put the case under all kinds of pressure — I could easily lose Bahamba Bright forever!"

"They won't buy the judge, she's totally honest and dependable. I've checked up on her."

"Yes, so have I — but that doesn't stop me worrying."

"Thousands of insurance companies — *Agenzia Bahambin* can't wriggle out of that." The Joat stroked her hair. "In a few days, when it's all settled, *then* we'll take some time off."

She sniffed again but essayed a wan smile. "And it will be just like it was?"

"Alaya, it can never be just like it was. We've both changed. But we can go on from here."

"Yes, I suppose so. I hope so, Billy, I really do."

\* \* \*

The Femm. The Etonians. Time distortion. Sharraby Breach. *What was the pattern?* The question went round and round in Billy's head. He asked the SpaDe database for the history of the Eton family from Rudolph onwards, then cancelled the request when he realised that Poor Yorick lacked the paper to print it out. No point searching for a swampnit in a boggywallow. He did pull the file on Kray Harrow — no convictions, but several hundred pages of reports that would never be admissible in a court of law, implicating him in everything from spitting in a public bath to multiple murder.

Some things were becoming clear, though. The motivating force *must* be the Femm, for the Femm were easily capable of using the Etonians, but the Etonians would never be able to use the Femm. The Etonians were Femm catspaws. The source of all the interest in Sharraby Breach *had* to be its time-warping properties... unless there was something else about the Breach that SpaDe didn't know. That was possible, because SpaDe knew little about Sharraby Breach. That's why they'd sent both the *Hubble* and the *Pontryagin*. But time-warping *felt* right to his joat's hunch.

Time control, now; that would really provide the Femm with leverage. But the Breach was an untamed force of nature. What use is uncontrolled, erratic time-distortion? The Sump-boglin alone knew. But the Femm weren't involved just out of scientific curiosity. They would have set up an all-Quaternity exploration team if that had been their motive. No, it was something that the rest of the Quaternity wasn't intended to know about. Something big.

Try another tack. What could the Etonians bring to the party? Something they alone had, or knew, or could do... Freewave? Rudolph Eton invented freewave... Did the Etonians know something about freewave that they'd kept quiet all these years? Something useful to the Femm?

He was getting warmer, he could sense it. Freewave and time-warping... communication and... *travel!*

*Time travel.*

If freewave technology could be used to bring some tiny part of Sharraby Breach's time distortion under control, even for a split second — to harness its tremendous forces —

The door burst open and Alaya rushed in. "Billy, Billy! We've won! We've won the case! Judge Whyllzythllyn threw the appeal out! Leave to refer the verdict to Quaternity Supreme Council *denied!*"

"That's great... That's... really great, Alaya."

"We can take that holiday now, Billy! Where shall we go? I've never been to the Quezaltungo volcanoes! Or maybe ice-yachting on Bungosuido Secundus —"

"Alaya, I know I *said* we ought to take a few days off, but —"

She stopped bubbling and gave him a black look. "*Said?* Do you mean to tell me that —"

"I'm on to something. Something about the *Pontryagin*. Something big. I can't just drop it."

"Oh, prug the *Pontryagin*, what about our *holiday?* It was *your* idea! *I've* left all sorts of important things undone to leave time for it, and now you —"

"I'm trying to get my father back, Alaya."

"You... you idiot! You haven't got the courage to admit he's *dead!*" And she stormed out of the room in tears.

\* \* \*

Late that night, she slipped in between the covers of his bed. "Billy? Hold me, Billy. I'm cold."

*Dressed like that, it's not surprising*, thought the Joat, but for once he had the wit not to say the first thing that came into his head.

"Billy? Please forgive me. What I said about your father, I was just being hurtful."

"We're both under too much strain, lover."

"Yes. And we've both got our own obsessions. Different ones. I can't share yours, and you can't share mine."

"I feel the same way that you do about Bahamba Bright, Alaya. But the search for my father comes first. It always will."

She snuggled closer. "Mmmm, you're *warm*. You could be such a wonderful person if only you'd relax, let your feelings show more. But right now, Billy, it's not really working for us, is it?"

Even joats must face facts, however unpleasant. "No. It isn't."

"But it could? If there was nothing else getting in the way?"

"Yes, Alaya, it could. But neither of us is in the frame of mind to make it work, not right now."

She gripped his arm tightly. "I'll never lose my obsession with Bahamba Bright. Not after what I've been through."

"I don't want you to lose it," said the Joat. "I can live with it. I'd *like* to live with it, if you must know."

"But you *could* lose your obsession about your father!" There was a note of hope in her voice.

"I'm not made that way, lover."

"No, you fool, I don't just mean *forget* him! I mean *go out there and find him!* And then you can come back here to me."

*If only it were that simple.* "I wish I could. I certainly plan to if I get the chance. I've been planning it all my life."

The excitement in her voice grew as the idea took root. "Billy! The family's got money, connections — we'll *help* you! Come on, tell me. Tell me what you need, and I'll make sure you get it!"

"Money won't buy what I need, Alaya. I need a stroke of luck, a word, a look. I need someone to spill the beans. I have absolutely no idea what's going on."

"Is there anything that would help you find out?"

"No, not — Well, I suppose... no, it's ridiculously expen—"

"Out with it!"

He laughed. "I need a private yacht. Then I can travel freely, follow up leads. Do the legwork. That's really the only material thing I —"

"A yacht? We've got a spare one on Bocciganni. It's yours. On one condition."

"What?"

"When you find your father, you come back here to me. I'll wait. I promise you, I'll wait."

*"Yet he with strong perswasions her asswaged,*
*And wonne her will to suffer him depart;*
*For which his faith with her he fast engaged,*
*And thousand vowes from bottome of his hart,*
*That all so soon as he by wit or art*
*Could that achieue, whereto he did aspire,*
*He vnto her would speedily reuert —*

"It didn't work for Britomart and Sir Artegall, though, did it? As soon as he'd finished one quest he was off on the next." The Joat stroked her hair. "I'd like to say 'yes', but you know it's not realistic, Alaya." She sniffed back tears. "It could take me years. I might never find him. We'd both change, however hard we tried to stay the same."

"No, my dearest lady — we must part. No promises, no strings. Only memories."

*I want the promises to bind you to me... But you're right, it's something I can't ask. It would be a delusion.* "Perhaps you're right. I can see you won't be swayed. Very well: so be it. I hope you never regret it. And you'll still get your yacht. But now there are *two* conditions. That will teach you not to argue with a lady."

"Depends on what they are."

"One: you name the yacht *Lindilu*."

"I thought you hated that name —"

"Yeah, so I'm passing it on. I've decided to get my revenge by rubbing your nose in your own mess. But you won't carry *Lindilu* everywhere: she'll carry *you*..." Her voice trailed off as she realised it wasn't that simple, never had been. Her eyes widened. "My God, I really *have* screwed up. Lindilu Glynde *was* me, Billy. One facet of me. I just didn't like to admit it. There are times when I enjoy playing the empty-headed sex-kitten."

"Lindilu Glynde was sexy, Alaya, but never empty-headed. Yes, I'll give her name to the yacht." He waited for the second condition, but Alaya's hands were starting to distract him. Joats being what they are, curiosity won out. "Alaya, what's the other condition?"

"You seem to be well into it, lover."

# 10 Beware Etonians

A million dead worlds.

What had killed them, nobody knew. A cataclysm of cosmic proportions. A war beyond all belief, with no survivors. A statistical freak of creation. But nowhere else in the know universe was there such an enormous concentration of planets, totally devoid of life, as the Barrens. Wreckages of worlds, dry worlds, airless worlds, worlds scoured by giant hurricanes, poisoned worlds, molten worlds, worlds of frozen hydrogen, worlds of liquid metal, worlds that were just vast balls of fullerene dust.

Into the Barrens there came a voyager. A robot probe on a thousand-year mission to catalogue the million dead worlds. A scientific project for the Gwissonian Institute of Galactology. It phaded from world to world, photographing, measuring magnetic fields, mapping ion distributions, taking absorption spectra to identify mineral deposits. Roughly seven hours per planet, not counting travel time. Once a month it relayed its data to a deep-space freewave antenna encircling Gwisson Prime.

It had been travelling for two hundred and eleven years and had surveyed more than a quarter of a million worlds.

The robotic brain had already selected the next destination, provisionally assigned the code BW273994. From deep space the planet was nothing but cratered grey rock. But the probe had already noticed something unusual in the planet's energy spectrum. Faint emanations in the freewave range. This was not expected, and it caused the robot to consult its directive program to decide whether the datum warranted immediate transmission. The directive program was instructed to make unscheduled transmissions only in the event of finding signs of life. Freewave emanations might be a sign of life.

On the other hand, they might not be.

*Conclusive* evidence of life, the instructions said. The directive program reserved judgement and did not transmit.

While the robot's sensors were absorbed in studying the approaching planet, it was seized from behind by a grappling-beam, its circuits were frozen, and it was dragged through a hatch in the side of a large space vessel. The vessel's commander sent a tight-beam freewave message to the nearby planet, confirming that the robot probe had been disabled. On the ground, the freewave operator keyed the message through to his superior officer, who conveyed it to the Supreme Director.

"When is the probe next due to transmit, Cysparagon Tubbytt?"

"In sigsteen days, Supreme Director, as predicted. Shall I order the mission to proceed as planned?"

"Yes, Cysparagon. Return the probe to base and deal with it," said Rudolph Eton V.

\* \* \*

To the Etonians, the world was not BW273994, but Araster nex-Thopt. And it was no longer dead. It was the hidden base for their collaboration with the Femm. It kept in touch with the rest of the universe by tight freewave beams to two dozen platforms orbiting as many worlds. Every signal was chopped into twenty-four segments every millisecond, coded, and sent at random to one of the receivers. From there it made its way, sometimes by hidden channels, sometimes public domain, to be reassembled wherever the Dynast of the Etonians happened to be. Sometimes Rudolph Eton V even graced Araster nex-Thopt with his own presence, but on this occasion he was many thousand light years distant, attending the biennial budger-hunt on Chagpat Beta.

On Araster nex-Thopt his eldest son, Tory Eton, fumed silently. *Stupid old bugger trots round the galaxy, having fun, leaves me here to keep control, and still insists on taking all the operational decisions himself.*

It really hadn't been necessary for Rudolph to handle the problem of the robot probe. Tory could have dealt with it, would have dealt with it. He knew how important it was to keep the base in the Barrens secret. Dammit, grabbing the probe to infiltrate fake data before sending on its harmless way had been *his* idea in the first place.

Gods, but Araster nex-Thopt was a bore. He couldn't even bring in a troupe of dancing-girls or some other form of light entertainment, in case he breached their precious damned secrecy. *Stupid old fool, it would be easy enough to have the girls killed afterwards so that they couldn't talk. A phony meteorite-strike and some appropriate wreckage would convince the phoz if they investigated the disappearance. But no, daddy says it's too risky, and so is mindwipe, so I have to sit on this godsforsaken pox of a planet and twiddle my blucky thumbs!*

*So much for being heir-apparent. He* says *it's so that I can gain operational experience in the field. But I reckon he's trying to keep me out of the way. And I don't trust that bitch Sherryl. Ever since*

*Bly died she's been hanging round my old man, trying to talk him into changing the rules of seniority to make Eshelby VI the next in line.*

*And her to follow. She'd poison them both given half a chance, once she was assured of the succession. Can't the old man see that? Shit, I'm his own flesh and blood! They'll trick him into it yet. And I'm stuck out here and powerless to stop it!*

\* \* \*

While Femm technical experts removed the robot probe's optical memory and replaced it by one that contained no hint that Araster nex-Thopt was any different from any other world of the Barrens, Rudolph Eton V held a family conference. The inner circle: himself, his daughters Dwina and Maggi, and Eshelby VI and Sherryl, the children of his deceased brother Bly — and of course Kray Harrow.

"So you believe there's a crisis."

"I see one coming, Eshelby, unless we act quickly."

"Without attracting further attention," said Dwina. "Tubbytt's attempt to ruin Grover's World was a mistake."

Sherryl Eton disagreed. "That was years ago. It's easy enough to be wise after the event, Dwina dear. It was a calculated risk, to prevent anyone accidentally blundering into Sharraby Breach at an extremely difficult moment."

"But it was never that likely! If the Femm involvement had been traced back to us — "

"Impossible! You're losing your nerve, Dwina."

Rudolph butted in. "Nothing is impossible, Sherryl. Never underestimate SpaDe's resourcefulness. Be paranoid before the event, not after. Our cover is good but it can never be perfect. Fortunately, that old debacle on Grover's World has had no serious consequences."

"No, Uncle. But the even older debacle in Sharraby Breach almost wrecked our plans completely. It lost us twenty years. Maybe more."

"Patience, Sherryl. We will have our way in the long run. And I would remind you that the error in Sharraby Breach was committed by your lamented father."

"I know that, Uncle. Bly was an idiot. Speaking of which, I'm glad to see you've made sure that useless pipsqueak Tory won't be in a position to cause trouble."

Rudolph leaned forward on his seat. "Bly made a mistake, and died for it. Tory has his uses. Admittedly his intellect is lightweight — "

"And his morals non-existent! Uncle, if you were to die today, Tory would *inherit!* Can't you see what that would mean? We'd lose —"

"I am well aware of the rules of succession, my dear. But I have no intention of dying just yet, and while Tory stands in *your* way —" his eyes flicked from one to the next "— I feel confident that none of you will try to speed me on *my* way." He waved down their protests. "I'm not a fool. Any one of you would kill me to assume power. We all know that.

"However, in the fullness of time I am contemplating making a few changes to the rules. In favour of Eshelby."

"Thank you, Rudolph."

"A sensible choice, Uncle. When?"

"When I choose, Sherryl. But you won't approve wholeheartedly. Tory will only be displaced to second in line."

"Why? I'm ten times the leader he is!"

"Yes, dear. But you're also ten times as dangerous to me as the rest of my children, nephews, and nieces put together."

"If I didn't know you were kidding, Uncle, I'd take that as a compliment."

"He's not kidding," said Harrow.

"You're positively poisonous, darling," Maggi amplified. "We all admire you for it. But we don't trust you. Even more than the rest of us don't trust each other. However, familial mistrust notwithstanding, we all remain united in our common goal, and against our common enemy."

"Jarneyvore."

"We'll find a way to break down his stasis-field soon. Then we can —"

"Not the father! The son!"

"You know, Sherryl dear," Dwina probed, "you talk about Jarneyvore junior so much, I sometimes think you're attracted to him."

"You silly cow — I hate that bastard. Anyway, look at his awful taste in clothes."

"Love and hate, darling, are two sides of the same emotional Möbius band. And you've *noticed* how he dresses, that's got to be significant."

"Oh, for gods' sake, Dwina! How could anybody fail to notice a green-and-purple checkered velvet vest worn with striped leggings and no muffler? You imagine sexual intrigue every time you discover that a man and a woman are on the same planet!"

"You know what effect proximity can have, Sherryl."

"Enough! We are discussing the incipient crisis," said Rudolph Eton. "Sherryl, you're exaggerating as usual. Just because you got your fingers burnt with Katch-22, you're overreacting. Wyllam Jarneyvore is no threat to our plans. Yet."

Sherryl's hands clenched in rage. "Uncle, you're a damned —"

"Have respect, niece. And your assessment of my character is based upon a misconception. I agree that Wyllam Jarneyvore must be put out of action."

"Finally somebody's talking sense," said Maggi.

"Permanently out of action?" asked Sherryl.

"Permanently. But not because, as you imagine, he is a deadly threat. Nor because he is a nuisance who may one day become a threat. He must die because he is a nuisance who has crossed that fine dividing line beyond which his disposal creates less risk to us than his continued existence.

"I discount his interference regarding Katch-22. That was a purely commercial matter of little consequence. Shut up, Sherryl. You were beaten fair and square because you didn't *think* clearly enough. If Jarneyvore's interference were restricted to such actions, I would propose to leave him alone. If anything, I would admire his talents."

"Yes. In the same way you admire the stripes on a coppersnake."

"No, niece. Talent is a precious commodity. Don't let your emotions devalue it. We could do with more talent like Jarneyvore's in this organization. If I thought I could control him, I would offer him a high-ranking position tomorrow. And some dress advice. But you can't control a joat. And the danger that I foresee is already upon us. *He is searching for his father*. With most people that would be futile, but this man has the talent to learn too much. And now he also has the resources. First, Sherryl, because of your blunder over Katch-22 — I told you, shut *up* — which allowed him to build up some working capital, and now because he has gained influential and powerful allies over whom we have little influence. The Strooghn family is better protected than we are, to be frank.

"If Jarneyvore manages to find out what happened to his father, and why, it could ruin our plans forever. A word to SpaDe, with evidence to back it up: that is all it would take. Our plans are fragile — and we cannot make them robust because we have to work with what is available. The man is a catalyst. He makes things happen. He is likely to cause trouble. He will be removed."

"How, father?"

"An excellent if obvious question, Dwina. The answer is equally obvious. The father died because of the father; the daughter will set a trap for the son." He gave Sherryl an avuncular pat. "That should put paid to Dwina's nasty theories. Just don't make a mess of it this time."

"If you want me to avenge Bly's death, Uncle, I'll be only too happy to oblige. I would have done it long ago but you forbade it. I'm glad you've seen sense at last. Do you have any particular trap in mind?"

Rudolph relaxed, his task complete. "I thought you would find it more amusing if I left it to your wicked imagination, my dear."

# 11   Deep Joat

*His name might be loosely rendered in musical notation, thus:*

*or, with little extra loss of accuracy, transcribed phonetically as Tappitadatdatdappita [pause] bam; or its literal sense might be translated as 'Wiseworldcleavingswarmguide'. Nor is 'name' an adequate description, for a name is an arbitrary personal symbol, and this was anything but arbitrary: it was a role-attributive call-sign, affirming his position relative to his swarmfellows. And since the swarm was a strict hierarchy the simple word 'king' is perhaps a closer approximation than any yet mentioned. Yet the literal translation has its own merits, for he was indeed wise in the ways of his kind, and the swarm had prospered under his guidance. His swarmfellows adored him, and bent obediently to his will. And where he led, they followed, from the crackling cold of {world above} to the softsticky warmth of {world beneath}, their own call-signs chiming joyous descant to his resonant masterpattern.*

*And yet... something was missing; one dimension of their joy was inverted to sadness. There was a flaw in the harmonic texture, a gap that should be filled by the randomly syncopating trill of the {small ones} — but was not, for there were no {small ones}. Worldchange had come, and now {world above} was {too cold}, {world beneath} {too crushing}. To these {now inhospitable} zones the {small ones} came, as ever... and died; which was a terrible wrongness and a wrenching inversion of joy.*

*And Wiseworldcleavingswarmguide sensed, though he could not know — for his mind was of the {present rooted in the past}, holding no {imprint/model} of {that which may yet come to be} — he sensed that the swarm, too, would diminish and die.*

*But for now, the dimensions of joy that remained outnumbered those of pain: progression, and nourishment, and togetherness. And he flexed his snout-ring, and the world flowed through and around him, and he sang his flawed happiness and was almost satisfied with it.*

\* \* \*

A solo spaceflight is a bad way to forget a woman. Even when your vessel is a not-*very*-elderly Vishunti KKB with isospin-complementation halo-shift; even when the ship is *Lindilu* and the woman Alaya de Flore Strooghn. And so the professional Jack-Of-All-Trades went his way, a sadder but not noticeably wiser man. And after three weeks alternately drifting along on standby and phading whither he cared not, he decided that the cure wasn't working — but that working might be the cure. The search for his father was stalled; his lovelife was in tatters; he needed to occupy himself.

He wiped away his beard, put on a clean shirt, and made a freewave call to Joze Palgandra, newly promoted to a SpaDe post on Aphélix. Palgandra was away on business, but Billy was in luck: the Grynth was due back in ten hours. During which time the Joat fidgeted and fretted and won eleven straight games of Ragnarok with Belphoebe programmed to play at 'grandmaster' class, devising in the process a novel refutation of the Batavian Ripper opening currently in vogue. The ship's computer was a different aspect of Belphoebe from the machine that ran his villa on Grover's world, but he had downloaded the same personality modules to make himself feel at home.

Finally the freewave warbled and Palgandra's ursine features appeared. "What do *you* want?" A snarl is very effective, coming from a Grynth. It was amazing how quickly Palgandra's pleasure at the restoration of the vanishing island had turned sour. The Joat was only glad that he'd had enough time to ransack the files on *Hubble* and *Pontryagin* before that silly business with the Ecumenical Council and the tyrannosaur simulacrum had blown up and clouded Palgandra's judgement.

"I want a job," said the Joat.

Palgandra had not expected that reply, and his hairy lower jaw dropped a millimetre, exposing the base of a set of remarkably sharp teeth. "A job? Is this another of those stupid tricks of yours?"

The Joat explained his personal circumstances.

"Gaah," said the Grynth. You wouldn't expect a creature that weighs in at some three hundred kilos and looks like a cross between a grizzly bear, an orang-utan, and a bat to have much emotional sensitivity; but of the four races that make up the Quaternity, Grynth and Human are closest. Palgandra possessed a tinge of romanticism — an allegation which he would have denied vehemently had it been made to his face, though afterwards he would have regretted the impulse and visited the victim in hospital. "I see, Jarneyvore. You want a job to take your mind off a female." He snorted in sympathy. "The condition is a transspecies invariant. Very well, I shall do my best to oblige. Where are you?"

"Gods," said the Joat. "I haven't the foggiest idea. Hang on, I'll ask Belphoebe."

"Waldorf Sector," the computer replied.

"Umf," said Palgandra. "There will certainly be something going on *there*." Waldorf Sector held one of the largest concentrations of multiplanetary corporations in the Quaternity.

"Yes," said the Joat. "But you'll never be able to pin it on them."

Palgandra ignored him and made a call to the data reticule. The Joat tried vainly to read the Grynth's facial expressions as he flipped through his electronic casebook. Palgandra must have found something, for he suddenly displayed a broad, toothy grin. On a Grynth, this resembles the Jaws of Death.

"There are several problems that might yield to your — *snort!* — talents, but one stands out. Have you heard of Sear's Planet?"

"Who hasn't? Originally known as Zzyllmyllillizzyn — I *think* that's right — an uninhabited planetoid under Femmish control. Smallish, low-gravity; renamed by the Femm when they orbiformed it; now one of the fastest growing business centres there is. All the multiplanetaries are flocking to buy real estate and put up offices. The trouble is, it's mostly water, so they have to build kilometres-high towers on a few tiny islands. Personally, I'd have expected them to find somewhere with a bit more *room*..."

"It's the exclusivity that attracts them."

"No, it's a display tactic, like peacock feathers. Proves you're so powerful that you can operate under a handicap that would stop everybody else in their tracks... Offers prestige, which pushes up the price... My, but those Femm are clever psychologists! One junkworld turned into a multitrillion-kroon asset overnight!" The Joat shook his head in admiration. "So what gives with Sear's Planet?"

"Persistent rumours."

"Benign or malignant?"

"Unhf?"

"What *sort* of rumours?"

"I'm coming to that." Palgandra scratched his huge button nose with his thumb-claw. "It appears that those kilometres-high tower blocks are beginning to sink into the ground."

There was silence for a few seconds. "Yes, that would do it," said the Joat, almost absently. "A pretty piece of panicking in high places."

"The markets," said the Grynth, "are a little disturbed."

"That's what I said. And you want me to find out why the subsidence is happening?"

"Not quite," said Palgandra. "I want you to stop it."

\* \* \*

Billy the Joat cast a last, loving eye over the sleek lines of *Lindilu* and checked that the doors to its capacious and empty cargo-doors were properly shut. He slipped a wristband remote over his left hand, giving him access to Belphoebe and hence all of the ship's controls from any distance up to thirty thousand kilometres. Then he exited by the stern airlock and strolled nonchalantly along a translucent flexitube to the waiting shuttle. Twenty-five minutes later the vessel was bobbing in the harbour waters of Shum'n-al-Qyf, the largest of Sear's Planet's seventy-eight islands.

On Sear's Planet, land is too precious to waste on spaceports. From the harbour's edge, homeoglass and plaxycrete walls climb relentlessly skyward, into and beyond the thin cloud-cover. It looks like a Giant's Causeway built by a demented giant who didn't know when to stop. *No wonder the buildings are sinking into the ground. They must be overstressing the crust all the way down to the Mohorovicic discontinuity. Assuming Sear's Planet has one*. But the answer couldn't really be that trite: the Femm were superb engineers.

On his way to Immigration the Joat was stopped by a fat Grynth in SpaDe uniform, who asked to see his ID card. He rummaged in his cape and produced the small rectangle, out of which a miniature Wyllam Jarneyvore stared mournfully at the universe. Below the hologram, personal data were inscribed in allegedly tamperproof magnetic ink.

"Just a routine check, sir," said the Grynth. "If you would be so kind as to accompany me, it will only take a few minutes." He pointed to an unmarked doorway nearby. "Through here, Mr. Jarneyvore." The Joat followed him through the door, across a large open area, to an elevator. "Floor seven," said the Grynth. Billy, who was nearest the control panel, touched the pad for him; the elevator rose.

"Where are we going?"

The Grynth smiled, but said nothing. There was a faint hiss and a sudden smell, like claw-polish remover. The Joat tried to turn his head, but it stayed put. Smiling more broadly now, the Grynth caught Billy's paralysed body before it toppled.

A second Grynth was waiting as the elevator reached the seventh floor. He helped drag the Joat into a dimly lit bay containing several dozen plain grey barrels and a small electric cart. The two of them tipped him head-first into one of the barrels, filled it to the brim with dried bean-husks from another, screwed the top on, and loaded the lot on to the cart. Two more barrels were added for realism. Shortly afterwards the three barrels were rolled into a battered tub-truck and whisked away though the ground floor of what, on close inspection, was more like a single vast building than a conglomeration of individual ones. The streets of Shum'n-al-Qyf were a three-dimensional rabbit warren.

Though paralysed, the Joat as still conscious and aware of his surroundings. There are many modes of travel more comfortable than being crammed head-down in a barrel of bean-husks in a tub-truck with faulty suspension. He vowed dire vengeance on whoever had been responsible.

SpaDe has an office on Shum'n-al-Qyf, on the corner of 873rd Street and the Avenue of the Humigants. It is on the 476th floor. The Space Department would have preferred a penthouse suite on the 777th floor, but these are increasingly stringent times. To this office, by high-speed elevator and pneumatube, the two Grynths conveyed the angry person of Billy the Joat. They tipped him out unceremoniously on to a hard floor and carried him along a corridor to the door of Herdmonitor Brunyg ap-Wyfft, the ranking SpaDe official. The fat one knocked, and they entered.

"Agents Makil and Kreen reporting with suspect as ordered, sir!"

The herdmonitor gave an embarrassed nod. "Oh dear. You haven't exactly been gentle with him, have you?"

"No, sir. We had no orders to be gentle."

"Of course. However, it seems that, in the unfortunate necessity of haste, certain niceties have been overlooked. In particular, this gentleman is not a suspected drug-smuggler, as you may have believed."

"Oh."

"In fact, since he has been aware of all that is happening to him, including the present conversation, we shall have to tender humble apologies for his treatment. You see, he is working for us."

*It will take more than apologies*, the Joat vowed.

"This will be a trifle awkward, I fear," the herdmonitor added.

*It will indeed.* Smugly.

"Pardon my temerity, sir," said Makil. "If I may offer a suggestion?" There was a short, whispered conversation, too faint for the Joat to follow.

"An excellent idea, Makil. Irregular, but justified in this case, I agree. It will save unnecessary inconvenience."

*Compensation! Oodles of beautiful kroon!* The Joat began to assess a negotiable figure.

"Do we have enough, sir?" asked Kreen.

"The supply is more than adequate." The Joat revised the figure upwards.

"When exactly did you pick Mr. Jarneyvore up, Makil?"

"09.47, sir."

"Ah... So the appropriate dose would be seventeen minutes."

*Dose?*

"Yes, sir. Provided I administer the amnesiax now. Shall I proceed?"

*Amnesiax? You stinking bastards, that's a memory-wipe drug! I'll get even with you for this if it's the last —*

"Go ahead, Makil." The Joat felt a tingling coldness...

\* \* \*

...Billy the Joat was lying on something soft. He remembered leaving the shuttle and heading for Immigration, but there the memories seemed to stop. His head ached, and there was something small and hard pressing against his shoulder blade. He wriggled uncomfortably and sat up. This proved to be a mistake.

"Ah, Mr. Jarneyvore, at last you are awake." The Joat turned his head. An angular Barasshanti with scrupulously manicured hooves was sitting opposite. A herdmonitor, to judge by the markings on his carapace. Some computer cards were spread out neatly along the desk. The room was sumptuously furnished: Billy himself was sitting on a lush blue velvet couch, decorated with discreet SpaDe insignia. "My name," said the Barasshanti, "is Brunyg ap-Wyfft. These gentlemen are agents Makil and Kreen. I am the ranking SpaDe administrator on Sear's Planet. We welcome you."

"Oog. What happened? I ache all over. How did I get here? The last thing I remember is —"

"For reasons I shall explain in a moment," said the herdmonitor smoothly, "we were forced to make some changes in our plans. It was necessary to bypass the normal immigration channels. We are unfortunately obliged, in such circumstances, to administer a harmless memory-wipe. To preserve security, you understand."

"Oh."

"I am unable to reveal further details, but I *do* assure you that it involved no discomfort. On that, you have my word." The herdmonitor turned a stony eye towards the two agents. "You may go."

Billy wasn't satisfied. When officialdom goes out of its way to assure you of something, you can bet your most cherished bodily parts that it has ulterior motives. But Brunyg was explaining the change of plan. "Listen, Jarneyvore: this is important. We received word — too late for comfort — that your life might be endangered if your identity became known. A certain..." he thumbed through the papers on his desk "...Otis Pigge, Chief Constable of... *Grover's World?* Where the — no matter. This Pigge sent an urgent freewave call. Our agents reached you just in time."

"My life in danger? Who could possibly want to kill me? I've never done any harm to anybody!"

"Pigge furnished a list of people who might bear you a fatal grudge, Jarneyvore."

"Well, I suppose there may have been a few misunderstandings."

"Sixty-two people, to be exact, Jarneyvore."

"Everybody rubs a few people up the wrong way at some stage in their career," the Joat said defensively.

"The person he is currently worried about heads the list. I have her file here, a woman called" — Brunyg picked up a computer card — "Sherrylyn Elinoora Muramanda Trecylie Eton."

"Who? Oh, Sherryl," the Joat said offhandedly, but his heart skipped a beat. That, in turn, made him feel guilty about Alaya. Were his feelings that fickle? "No promises" was all well and good, but — belatedy he realised that his main problem was emotional overload. To disguise his confusion, he asked the first thing that came into his head. "Um — could you tell me who the other sixty-one —"

"I think you should concentrate on the immediate risk, Jarneyvore. Mz. Eton has excellent reason to dislike you."

"Well, I did diddle her out of a highly profitable trade in organic chemicals... But the Etonians *float* in money! Why would a few kroon bother her?"

"Mr. Jarneyvore, You are incredibly naive. It's not the money, but the principle. You thwarted the ambitions of an extremely beautiful young woman who, since birth, has been accustomed to the satisfaction of every whim. How do you think she feels?"

"A bit peeved?"

"Absolutely bloody furious and Hell-bent on revenge," said Brunyg. "Which may not be long delayed. Sherryl Eton is here, on Sear's Planet, at this very minute. She heads a consortium developing the islands. "

*Sherryl?* Here? *Shit*. "When I took this job, nobody mentioned that the Etonians would be howling after my blood. It gets more impossible every minute!"

"It was totally impossible to begin with. You are sure you want to continue?"

"Yes," said the Joat doggedly. "A joat never turns his back on a challenge." *And I wouldn't mind another look at Sherryl Eton, if the truth were told.*

"You are a brave man, Mr. Jarneyvore, and a foolhardy one." The Joat hardly heard him, there was *still* a hard lump down the back of his shirt. He poked an exploratory hand down his collar.

"You need a new ID," said Brunyg. "I will have one pre—"

"Before you do that,"said Billy, "perhaps you can explain *this*." He held out a wrinkled green object, covered in tiny prickles.

Brunyg peered at it. "It appears," he said, "to be a bean-husk. They are imported from Dumdingo III as a staple dietary item —"

"How did it get down my back?"

"Mr. Jarneyvore: do you or do you not want us to stop you getting killed?"

"I suppose so," said the Joat tiredly. The way he felt, he wasn't sure that life held as much interest as a bean-husk. He threw it at the wastebasket. It hit the rim and rolled under a semicircular decorative frog-tank.

"Then please stop raising irrelevant issues."

"Carry on, herdmonitor. I get the message. The green bean is a red herring."

\* \* \*

It took less than two hours to provide Wyllam Jarneyvore with a new face, a new name, and documentation to match. He was now Rodrik Duxas, an expert tectonicist from Brugglugg IV with a diploma in subduction studies from the prestigious Mittelburg Institute. In this guise, he was ready to begin his investigations.

Palgandra had talked of 'rumours'. Brunyg could go further. The problem of widespread subsidence was a fact — to be concealed from the public until the holovix crews caught on, after which its importance was to be minimized. Those in the know were few, and highly placed, except for the numerous Femm construction workers. But, in their usual inscrutable fashion, the Femm weren't talking. Except to Rodrik Duxas, who was a hired consultant and needed to know.

"We have observed," the Femmish technician said thickly, "that dangerous subsidence is oggurring in some areas. Notably in the most recently developed parts of Gay Camel." Cay Gamel was a sickle-shaped island near the equator.

"How serious?"

"One block sank nine floors."

"A mere bagatelle," said the Joat flippantly. "A drop in the ocean — *hey!* Is the sea undermining the land?"

"No, Mr. Dugsas. All obvious potential gauzes have been checked. Our technicians have made extensive stress analyses." The Femm explained that before construction started, each island underwent extensive tectonic restructuring, to halt, divert, or balance the subcrustal flows that could generate earthquakes and eruptions. The builders sank shafts right down to magma level. "We would not ignore anything as simple as water-seepage," he concluded.

"I want to inspect the site," said the Joat. "As soon as possible."

"I have arranged for a skeeter to gollect you early tomorrow," said the Femm. "If you wish to bring any baggage or equipment with you, please ensure that it is placed in suitable gontainers."

"I'll have it grated up at once," said the Joat.

\* \* \*

Tectonic restructuring is expensive, and best done once and for all: it was Femm policy to develop the islands of Sear's Planet one at a time. On Cay Gamel they were about a quarter of the way through the job, with extensive workings both above and below ground, affecting half the island. The other half appeared to be still in its original state — but that was an illusion, as the Joat discovered.

His skeeter whirred in from the north-east, across the undeveloped terrain. Looking down, all he could see was a dull, streaky brown landscape. He commented on it.

"Yes," said the Femm pilot. "*Wysshhiij.*"

"Bless you."

"*Dead* wysshhiij. Wysshhiij were the main indigenous plants until Zzyllmyllizzyn — what you call 'Sear's Planet' — was orbiformed. Before, it was one third of its present distance from the sun, in a much more eccentric orbit. The glimate ranged from hot and humid to very hot and very humid. Now it is within the gomfortable temperature range, in a circular orbit with no seasonal variations. That is much better."

"Sounds dull to me," said the Joat.

"Yes, Mr. Dugsas, but you are Human. We Femm prefer order. An unavoidable side effect was that the wysshhiij died. They preferred the original atmosphere of superheated steam."

"QuatCent doesn't often give permission for orbiforming if the native lifeforms are destroyed," said the Joat. "

"The wysshhiij were only plants. They had no medicinal or other virtues."

"Were there any animals?"

"Of gorse not. It was too hot."

"In the oceans? Fish?"

"There were no oceans — then."

"I see what you meant by 'humid'. So there was no chance whatsoever of sentient life. Now there QuatCent would *really* have blown its top!"

"I do not understand the idiom."

"They'd never have let you orbiform a planet with sentient lifeforms on it."

"Of gorse, that is axiomatic. We would never have gonsidered orbiforming the planet if it had supported sentient life."

Ahead, the construction site loomed: a dark mass, glittering in the morning sunlight, flanked by half-finished plaxycrete columns, a monstrous caricature of a fakir squatting on a bed of nails. The skeeter veered southwards, where the ground was heavily scarred, bright orange clay, pancake-flat in comparison. It whirred in to land beside a sprawling complex of low, temporary structures, beyond which an enormous isosteel pylon reared skywards.

The Joat began to cheer up. The slimy mud reminded him of Grover's World, and its orange colour reminded him of Basketball. He hadn't been home for a long time...

The project overseer, like all the technicians, was a Femm; his name was Ymillyn Jiydyrrill. He explained the various steps being taken to stabilise the planetary crust against the considerable stresses that the buildings would produce. Eventually 'Rodrik Duxas' was satisifed that they hadn't slipped up on anything straightforward. "There must be some additional, unexpected factor," the Joat mused. "Something far out of the ordinary. Something utterly without precedent."

Jiydyrrill was unimpressed by this contribution. "That is evident. Our gomputations have taken account of all *known* phenomena."

"Does Sear's world possess a Mohorovicic discontinuity?" asked the Joat.

"Of gorse. It is typical of a planet of its general glassification."

"That creates plenty of engineering problems, I'd imagine. A sharp boundary like that between crust and mantle must play merry hell with the P-waves."

"Nothing serious. Our main problem is anomalous flow-patterns in the subcrustal rocks, which destroy the basis of our extrapolations. We have made a statistigally significant sample of gores, yet we find nothing unusual about the rocks lining the main shaft." The Femm pointed out of the window at the pylon. "The shaft can be seen in that direction."

"I wondered what that was."

"It descends for fifteen thousand metres. At the bottom the temperature approaches 900° Gelvin. A kilometre further down the rocks start to melt, and two kilometres below the end of the shaft is the molten gore of the planet. On average, of gorse." Jiydyrrill explained that the core was irregular and there were pockets of magma throughout the lower crustal levels. Many were at extremely high pressures, much higher than that of the surrounding rocks, because of the presence of superheated gases. It was a complicated planet for tectonic engineering.

"Why choose this one, then?"

"It is perfectly suitable, Mr. Dugsas. Femm do not fear complexity."

*Maybe not, but this planet's got you worried.* "How do you sample the rocks in the shaft?"

"A small mobile laboratory runs up and down the shaft on four independent sets of friction bearings."

"Aha!" declared the Joat. "A mohomobile!"

"I bek your pardon?" said the overseer, proving yet again that Femm lack a sense of humour. "The mobile laboratory is completely self-gontained. It is pressure-resistant, heatproof, and propelled by its own motors. The friction-bearings crip the side of the shaft even when its walls become deformed. It is provided with an extensive range of ancillary facilities." The Joat marvelled at a creature that could say "ancillary facilities" but couldn't manage a simple "grip". "It has often been found advantageous to direct the tectonic restructuring using an on-site observer. In particular the danger of an unintentional eruption is crately reduced."

*But not eliminated.* "What action do you take if there's an eruption?"

"Instant evaguation. We have efficient warning devices, and skeeters are kept in readiness for that purpose. The gonstruction work is well away from the active areas of tectonic restructuring. But a blowout — I believe that is the Human term for it — is extremely rare."

"What of the poor mug in the mohomobile?"

"Regrettably there exist no emergency procedures for the observer in the mobile laboratory. But he will be honoured by his brood."

"That's really reassuring."

"Perhaps you would like to use the mobile laboratory yourself, to make a full inspegtion? I can easily arrange —"

"That shouldn't be necessary," said Billy hastily. "It should be possible to solve the mystery from the surface. Though I'm sure it would be a rewarding experience. Now, I'll need data on —" A concealed buzzer cut him short.

"Excuse me," said the Femm. "I must receive a message. I will return shortly."

\* \* \*

It was a personal call from one of his major financiers... She was anxious that the outside expert, Mr. Duxas the tectonicist, should be afforded every cooperation. The overseer gave her a crisp report on the current position. "...and he has requested some data. I will see to it at once."

"Will he be making a shaft descent?"

"He believes he can solve the problem from the surface."

"But we have *already* studied the problem from the surface, Jydyrrill." The Femm overseer forbore to point out that they had also studied it from the shaft. "Mr. Duxas must get to the bottom of the matter — literally. He must make a shaft inspection."

The Femm sounded dubious. "Mr. Dugsas seemed convinced it would not be necessary — "

"I don't believe he can do the job properly from the surface, Jydyrril! As Executive Director for the Gannimex Consortium — which you may recall is financing this project — I recommend *strongly* that he should inspect the lower levels of the shaft in person."

Even to Femm, money talks. "I understand, Diregtor."

"Good. But I don't want Duxas to feel pressured. Do not reveal the Consortium's concern about his ability to perform his job. It might sap his confidence. No mention at all, Jiydyrrill."

"Of gorse not, Diregtor."

The caller hung up. *Excellent. That's put the idiot's neck firmly inside the noose. Then I just have to remove the ground from under his feet. 'Rodrik Duxas' indeed. Sloppy, very sloppy. But that's what makes it so delightful to cooperate with the Space Department.* Which reminded her that she had another call to make. Agent Kreen had been most helpful and had been promised a handsome reward.

Unfortunately he wasn't going to get it. He knew too much and would have to be eliminated. A brief word with Kray Harrow over the freewave link fixed that. Now to more appealing business. She felt a delightful shiver, which she told herself was pure hatred.

*Jarneyvore, you bastard, I've got you this time. The son to atone for the crimes of the father. How symmetric.*

Sherryl Eton liked symmetry.

\* \* \*

The mobile laboratory slid into Hell like a baby mudlark on its belly in a sumphole, its four independent motors purring in satisfaction as it sank into the shaft at five and a half kilometres per hour. It was a beautiful piece of precision engineering, crammed with equipment for every contingency and stocked with enough food, air, and water to last a week underground if need be.

*How did I get into this hole?* The Joat still hadn't worked it out. But Jiydyrrill had been so politely insistent that it had been well-nigh impossible to refuse. Billy was still convinced that it ought to be possible to solve the problem 'up top' — by which he meant not only the literal interpretation, but the little grey cells inside his skull; but curiosity, as ever, had got the better of prudence. And curiosity —

*Joats aren't cats*, he told himself firmly. Anyway, what self-respecting joat could refuse a free trip into the bowels of a planetoid, or a chance to drive such a magnificent machine as the mohomobile? Jiydyrrill had shown Billy how to operate it. He had explained the many safety features. It hadn't really been necessary — the Joat knew enough about technology that most of the equipment held no secrets. But Rodrik Duxas wouldn't have such knowledge.

There was a bank of screens that showed the shaft walls. He could analyse their mineral content, heat flow, elastic stress, crystal dislocation topology, plastic deformation parameters, pressure, and density. The results could be presented as false-colour overlays. Using magnetic resonance imagery, neutrino registers, and quark diffractometers he could map the subcrustal flows and pressures for kilometres in every direction and display any section he wished, or exhibit them in 3D with a holographic synthesizer. Two separate screens showed views up and down the shaft. At fourteen thousand metres, not much was visible either way. Soon it would be time to stop.

He had seen absolutely nothing that would explain the subsidence.

To pass the time, he began to sing: "*Oh, the road into Hell is a slippery well, but the climb to the stars is a pain in the* —" A sound like a thunderclap cut him short. There was a grinding noise. Three more thunderclaps followed, almost together. The laboratory vibrated wildly, shuddered, and stopped.

Darkness.

Silence.

# 12  Orifice in the Underworld

The Joat groped for the microphone. "Topside! Topside!" He hoped the communications hadn't gone, along with the lighting. Not to mention the cooling systems. "Emergency!"

"This is topside," said a Femmish voice. "We are aware there is an emergency. Your motors have stopped and the laboratory is stationary. We will have a more detailed readout in a few moments. Can you describe the cirgumstances?"

"There were four loud bangs, all within a few seconds. The motors stopped at once."

"Curious. The motive units are independent. It may be an elegtrical fault. I will inform Overseer Jiydyrrill. I want you to make a visual inspection and report bag to me."

Billy the Joat found a flashlight, rummaged in the tool-locker, and descended into the lower recesses of the laboratory. One sniff told the tale. In less than a minute he had eliminated electrical faults. That was how long it took him to find the remains of the detonator. The characteristic smell of dynoplax had made the diagnosis obvious from the start.

*A bomb.*

Four bombs. He didn't even look at the other three units. He scrambled back aloft. "Hello topside! The motors have been sabotaged. Dynoplax grenades with a timer circuit. Damaged beyond repair. Can you —"

A female voice interrupted him. "I know." It was a *familiar* voice. The screen flickered, and topside came in on visual. "I put them there," said Sherryl Eton.

*Well, I wanted another look. But not from this position. Damn, she's perfect — that hair, those eyes... Pity about the mind. She saw through the Duxas disguise from the very start.* The Joat knew he lacked bargaining strength, but he had nothing to lose by trying. "Why, Sherryl?"

"Revenge." She ignored the insolence of his familiar mode of address. It was beneath her dignity to comment on it.

"Revenge this way comes expensive."

The king cobra look. *Gods, but she's sexy. Why do I have balls for brains? The nasty little bitch is trying to* kill *me.* "Expense is a way of life to an Etonian, Jarneyvore. The mobile laboratory can be recovered and repaired. When we get round to it."

"I didn't mean the laboratory. I meant the planet." She laughed. "I'm here to do a job. To find out why your precious cities are sinking into the ground. Kill me, and you're losing a hell of a big investment. And the power that goes with it."

More laughter, slightly too shrill. Had she been taking euphorics? "I'll survive the loss. What makes you think *you* can find the answer?"

"I'm a joat."

"Brilliant. And you're such a *clever* joat that you've out-thought a team of the best tectonicists in the Quaternity and found out why the buildings are subsiding?"

"Of course. But I'm not telling you until you guarantee my safety."

"Don't take me for a fool, Jarneyvore. You know the answer, you prove it, or I'll leave you to rot in your tomb."

"All right, no, I haven't. But I will. They've had months and got nowhere. I've only been here a few days."

"And got nowhere faster, thereby proving your superiority?"

"I can do it, Sherryl. I can crack this if you give me the chance."

"It's too late, Jarneyvore. I won't give you a damned thing, however much it might cost me. You're marked down for disposal."

"You're overreacting. That business with the inflex screen surely can't —"

"Oh, you know so little! The inflex screen? It's forgotten, Jarneyvore. It never mattered. A meaningless incident."

*Too offhand, but there's something else.* "Then why?"

Sherryl Eton chuckled. There was no way Jarneyvore could escape from this. It was time to toy with the terrified mouse, to gloat a little. Oh, this was *fun!* "You Jarneyvores," she said, "are irritating people. You always poke your noses where they aren't wanted."

*Jarneyvores? Plural?*

"We thought we'd finished with you when we dealt with your father. But then —"

"My *father?* You did something to my father? What, damn you? Did you kill him? Is he dead?"

"I know all about it, but I'm not going to tell you. Let it torment you while you die, slowly, stuck in a hole like a rat in a sewer. But I will tell you one thing. Your father was a murderer, Jarneyvore."

"You rotten —"

"Shut up, you little quimp! A murderer, and an interfering, bungling fool. If it wasn't for him, we Etonians would be ruling this universe!"

Billy had a lot to think about, all at once. What had the Etonians been trying to do? How had his father stopped it? He needed more to go on, he'd have to provoke her. She was definitely on euphorics, maybe they'd have an adverse effect on her judgement.

It didn't occur to him that he'd never get the chance to use any of the information if he got it.

"You're mad. Paranoid. You worthless nonentities haven't got the brains or the guts!"

"Confound you, Jarneyvore, one Etonian is worth twenty jo—"

"And the Quaternity would stop you in your tracks if you —"

She screamed something at him, and the communicator went dead. He'd provoked her, all right. *And* got something she hadn't planned to say. The problem was — what did it mean? It was a very odd choice of phrasing, certainly. And it left him with a great deal to think about.

Just before she had smashed the handset back into its cradle, Sherryl Eton had said: "You fool. Until your idiot father started meddling, there *wasn't going to have been* a Quaternity."

\* \* \*

Brunyg ap-Wyfft's phone buzzed. "Herdmonitor? This is Ymillyn Jiydyrrill, project overseer on Gay Camel. There has been an accident involving Mr. Dugsas."

"Is he harmed?"

"Not physically. But he is trapped, twelve kilometres underground." The Femm gave a sketchy explanation.

"How do you propose to get him out?" asked Brunyg. "Lower a rope?"

"Herdmonitor, even if we could find a long enough cable capable of supporting its own weight, the temperature at that depth excedes the melting-point of lead. The laboratory is massive, it cannot be pulled up. No known material can bear such a stress at such temperatures, not even garbon-filament cable. A goolsuit would overheat before Mr. Dugsas was halfway up. It would take too long to build a machine capable of descending the sheer walls of the shaft. The only hopeful circumstance is that Mr. Dugsas has plenty of onboard emergency power. But he will run out of air in six and a half days."

"Can't you lower more air to him?"

"Perhaps — if we find twelve kilometres of garbon-filament cable and suitable containers. But the laboratory's gooling system has insufficient heat-sinks for much above a week. I have stretched my granium till it greaks, but an answer is beyond me."

The Herdmonitor used a very rude word in the local dialect. "I will do what I can. Inform me if you require any assistance, of any kind. The full resources of SpaDe are at your disposal."

"Yes, Herdmonitor. There is one other thing."

"Yes?"

"We have lost communigation with the laboratory. We do not know why."

Brunyg put down the phone. At the other end, so did Jiydyrrill. Sherryl Eton smiled at him. "You are handling this emergency very well, Overseer."

He wasn't good at human expressions, but he found her smile disturbing. "As it please you, Diregtor. But the whole incident baffles me. First the motors, now the communications. With all contact lost, we cannot even trace circuits in search of the electrigal fault that presumably is the gauze."

*Ignorance*, thought Sherryl Eton, *is bliss. I shall see to it that a state of bliss is maintained.* Briefly she wondered why she didn't feel very excited about it any more. There was a sense of anticlimax, of post-coital — *yes, it was sort of orgasmic. Maybe that's why I feel so drained. Now that Jarneyvore's as good as dead, I kind of feel an empty space in my head. Almost as if I missed the arrogant, interfering little quimp.*

*Nonsense. It's the euphorics wearing off.*

"Mr. Dugsas did not give any indication when you spoke to him, Diregtor? It is unfortunate that the conversation was not recorded."

"I'm sorry, Jiydyrrill. I'm not very familiar with this type of communicator, and I couldn't find the record button. No, he didn't say anything worth mentioning that I can recall."

\* \* \* \* \* \*

Wiseworldcleavingswarmguide flexed his muscular snout-ring and revelled in the joy of being, the joy of life and progression, the joy of nourishment. As his snout-ring flexed, the world cracked and crumbled into delicious nuggets, to be sucked into his belly and digested by the chemical fires that leeched their energy to render it up for the enrichment of his restless spirit: life-life-*life*, abundant and glorious! He tapped at the world with his ventral callus, and in a moment the returning chorus welled all around him: *{swarmfellows-swarmfellows-swarmfellows} {here-here-here-here-herehereeere}* — as the images overlapped and jangled against each other. *How* *wonderful is the world, for to eat is to travel, to feed is to progress; the means and the end are one.*

And yet, also: *the world is a wrongness, for where are the trills in the swarmchorus? Where are the {small ones}?*

The thoughts were sadness, and confusion — for how could the world be both wonder and wrongness? He tapped again, and the chiming reply all but drowned the distorted echo from a dark patch of *not*-{world} directly ahead of him, and his distracted mind failed to discern the trace that remained. Wiseworldcleavingswarmguide flexed his snout-ring again, to take an even bigger bite out of the world and further increase his happiness... and fell out of the world into a soft, silent darkness. Something struck his braincase a heavy blow, and even the darkness departed.

"*What the Sump was that?*" yelled Billy the Joat, as the mobile laboratory resounded to a tremendous thud directly over his head.

The emergency generators had come on as soon as Sherryl Eton had cut the power connections. To the Joat this made it a childish gesture — unless it was just a side-effect of the loss of communications. He switched on the up-shaft camera, but the screen was black. Were the searchlights on? Yes. Wait: isn't there a patch of light at the very corner of the screen?

There is — and it's *pulsating*. Strange.

*Well... there's only one way to find out. On with the coolsuit and out through the hatch in the roof. See if anything is out there.* He didn't think it odd to be making such an investigation when he was in all probability a dead man. Death was boring anyway: there must be something better to think about. And joats have limitless curiosity.

He began to climb into the cumbersome garments.

\* \* \*

In SpaDe's office, the phone buzzed. Brunyg ap-Wyfft leaned towards it. Sherryl Eton's face shimmered into existence. "Herdmonitor Brunyg, I have an idea concerning Mr. Duxas."

"Can he be saved?"

"Possibly. There is a new model of the mobile laboratory under construction on Brinsley Wain, in Herriot Sector. It *may* be in an advanced enough state to use. If so, the Gannimex Consortium will persuade the manufacturers to phade it over here. We will then assemble it at the top of the shaft and attempt a rescue."

"That's the first good news I've heard today!" Brunyg felt the mental stresses starting to ease. "Won't it be expensive? I'll find it hard to balance SpaDe's budget."

"The important thing, Brunyg, is the saffety of Mr. Duxas. The Etonians will bear the cost. I shall supervise the rescue personally."

"Director Eton, you have my admiration. It's remarkably good of you to go to all this trouble."

"Not at all. In a way, I feel responsible." Sherryl Eton cut the connection. *Most satisfactory. If I'm in charge, I can head off any other rescue ideas, and make sure that the rescue vehicle gets there just too late. I can even make sure one of my agents is in it, to remove any traces of the original sabotage. Meanwhile, I get the credit for being public-spirited and generous to a fault. Nobody would believe that I'd spend that much money on a cover-up. They never can quite comprehend what conspicuous consumption of wealth really means. But what they don't realise is that I'd spend not just every kroon I can afford, but every kroon I possess, to get even with that little quimp Jarneyvore!*

\* \* \*

The Joat squinted into the searchlights. Something was out there all right. It was lying across the camera-lens. And it was alive. But what was it? And how had it got there?

It resembled a large slug, or more charitably, a seal. It was a dingy grey, eyeless, with a gaping mouth and a curious hump on its — back? Stomach? Apart from the pulsation, it looked dead. Unconscious? Did that make sense for such a creature? He looked up the shaft. The beast must have fallen from a crumbling opening that loomed as a dark smudge in the searchlight beam.

No animals on Sear's Planet? The truth, the half-truth, and everything but the truth. Not *on*.

*In*.

The Joat had no idea how to profit from this unexpected turn of events — but a basic rule of survival is to pursue whichever avenues are open. And this was the only one. He touched the creature, ready to spring back if it should move. He could feel nothing through the coolsuit, but the animal was *hot* — the palm-sensors said so. At this depth, it pretty much had to be. He recalled an insulated oven in the laboratory, with a reinforced glass door: it was big, designed for the analysis of large samples of rock. But the creature was in the wrong place for the sample-scoop to reach it. He picked it up in his arms. Despite the low gravity, the animal was heavy, but the suit's servos would cope. He carried it to the hatch and lowered it inside.

With the beast safely in the oven, he extinguished several minor fires that had been started by its body-heat, extracted himself from the suit, and began to examine his prize.

Its skin — *was* it a skin? — was an overlapping array of tiny plates. He bounced a pencil beam off it: the material was astonishingly hard, more so than diamond. The mouth was surrounded by a powerful ring of — bone? Whatever it was, it was even harder — and articulated, to expand and contract, and rotate from side to side in a small arc.

A drill.

A burrowing device.

An animal designed to live deep undergound, chewing the rocks and disgorging the remains behind it, extracting energy as it went.

It was hardly surprising that the planetary survey had missed them. And, of course, their travels through the rock would keep creating new connections between pockets of magma. Differential pressures would do the rest; an observer would see only an inexplicable change in the flow. The creatures, and their tunnels, were below the resolving power of the instruments. You won't spot woodworm with the naked eye from a hundred yards away — but you'll see the roof fall in, all the same.

It was probably a good job his communications were cut. He would have been tempted to inform the Femm. With Sherryl Eton at the helm, the likely result would be genocide. *How can such a beautiful body house such an ugly mind?*

The creature — he had mentally dubbed it a mohomole — stirred fitfully. The Joat watched and did nothing.

\* \* \*

Wiseworldcleavingswarmguide regained consciousness in some kind of horrible not-world. Yet there were sounds. Strange sounds. Frightening sounds. He began to tap his callus frantically. The noise boomed round the room, amplified by the oven acting as a sound box: dippita*dap*dap, dippita*dap*dap. Billy watched as the mohomole writhed and twisted, flapping its belly against the oven floor. Dippita*dap*dap, dippita*dap*dap. The sounds repeated. The Joat leaned closer. They repeated *exactly*.

There must be some purpose to them.

Language?

Oh, come now. Animals, yes, but sentient creatures? Still, it was possible, however unlikely.

*What next?* If he didn't do something quickly, the mohomole might discover that the oven wall was a good deal softer than rock. Then it would probably eat its way through the laboratory floor, and fall the rest of the way down the shaft. It wouldn't do the mohomole, or the laboratory, much good. Billy rapped with his knuckles on the oven door.

Wiseworldcleavingswarmguide was perplexed. Tappida*tap*tap was nothing like the expected reply, which was dippidittitbamdappa, repeated three times: *scatter-scatter-scatter!* Instead, *this* reply sounded like an aged female with a foreign accent, replying with the same fear-call that he had sent out: *Danger!* It was flat and thin and *wrong* too — and it was *close*. Too close, and *that* was wrong.

And yet, the female was making speech. This was a powerful and terrible event, a significant event. But signifying *what?* Wiseworldcleavingswarmguide began to communicate again, in a calmer and more measured voice.

The joat's ears pricked up. *Those* weren't random sounds.

He rigged a recorder to take down the mohomole's tapping, and to play it back with a two-minute delay. With luck, that would intrigue the beast enough to prevent it eating a hole in the oven. The Joat had urgent work to do, and the mohomole had to stay around until it was completed. The laboratory had a DK43 computer: good enough to take a translator program. The Xenology Institute had a highly effective one, running to some 11,080 program lines. It wasn't in the laboratory's library, but the Joat, who had an eidetic memory, had memorised the lot, years before. He fed the whole thing into the DK43 in four hours flat, with a short break every hour, during which he reassured himself that the mohomole was still in the oven. It was, though its patience was sorely tried by the stupidity of the male which seemed to have replaced the foreign female: he appeared not to have an original idea in his head. Fortunately for the Joat, Wiseworldcleavingswarmguide was sufficiently awed not to try to escape. Though Billy had noticed a deep gouge in the side of the oven where the mohomole had hoped for a light snack, but had found the taste unpleasantly metallic.

The Joat hooked up a microphone, plugged several hours of recorded conversation into the DK43 as informatic *hors d'oeuvres*, grabbed a hammer from the toolkit to talk with, and set to work.

It was slow, but the DK43 was a bright machine, and the more it learned, the faster the process went. Soon Billy and the mohomole were holding lengthy, stumbling conversations. The main problem was not in the translation: it was understanding the resulting images. Here the joat's wide experience and unorthodox mentality helped a great deal.

The mohomoles seemed to speak set theory.

Slowly, painfully, he pieced together factual items, the history and lifestyle of the mohomoles. The more he learned, the greater became his amazement at the richness of the their society. Intelligent life! *That* would cause a gargantuan row if SpaDe could be informed.

It was a pity that his wristband remote couldn't communicate with *Lindilu* through twelve kilometres of solid rock. For all his efforts, he seemed no closer to escape.

Back to the mohomoles. He asked more probing questions, sought details of their philosophy of life, their social customs, the upbringing of children. There, he got a surprise.

"{{Small ones} *not*-{are}}"

"{Be that so}, {what way {increases/maintains} the swarm}?"

"{Sad-sad-sadness} is. {{Small-ones} {once-were}}. Now *not*-{are}."

Billy gripped his hammer more tightly. "{Give cause}..." Oh gods, how to say it? "{Give cause} { *not*-{more are}{those once were}}."

"{World above}{{once was} warm}. Now {too cold}. {{World below}{once was}/{now is} warm but {too heavy}}. {Small ones} {*not*-{became} involuntarily}."

That was clear enough. When the Femm had orbiformed Sear's Planet, the larger orbit made the surface cool down. Childbirth must require warmth: the surface was too cold and the warmer deeps subject to pressures too high for the children. Even though the adults could survive the extremes of temperature and pressure, the species was dying.

So was the Joat. *How the Hell do you get out of a hole twelve kilometres deep? Fly?* If the Joat could escape, he could save the mohomoles as well as himself. A balloon? No, there was nothing to make one from that would stand the heat. He was stuck at the end of an enormous tube...

A tube!

There was one faint chance.

It was an appalling idea. Death was an even more appalling idea: the gamble must be taken. It all depended on the mohomoles' ability to tolerate heat. He eventually got the question across.

"{{Possible is}{to live}} in {{most low}{world beneath}}, where world {is soft} and {warm warm *warm*}?"

He waited.

"{{Warm warm *warm*} is {joy+joy}... but {{over-much}{is death}}}."

"{How much}{{over much} is}?"

"One {digestive cycle}." Now, how long was *that?*

"Is {{length we sing together}{more/less}}?"

"Less. {{We sing together}{length is}{{half-one}{digestive cycle}}}."

*Jackpot!*       "{Togetherness       for       self} Wiseworldcleavingswarmguide          progress          {{most low}{soft/warm}{world-beneath}}   —   {   *not*-{overmuch}, *not*-{death}}?"

"{Possible is}. {{Give cause}{togetherness this action}}."

"{Possible is} self {{small ones} joyfully {to-make return}}."

\* \* \*

*Now, Joat, you must be rather careful about your timing*. Even if the idea worked, *Lindilu* had to be in the right place. Billy began computing orbits. As the appointed time approached, he tapped on the oven door.

"{Go-now}. {{Care}{be}{with you}}! Remembrance! {Go now} + joy!"

"{Remembrance is}. {{Soft/warm}{world beneath}} and *not*-{world here} must {{come close} + *not*-{touch}}. {Easy is}."

The mohomole climed clumsily up the insulated chute used to put samples into the oven. *I suppose it* is *easy for him. A creature that swims in the planetary mantle must surely develop an intuition for subcrustal flows*. He still wished he felt as confident as the mohomole seemed to. He opened a side-hatch. The mohomole wriggled through to the shaft wall. For a second it paused with its snout-ring flat to the wall, and tapped a final staccato message. Then it was gone, in a cloud of rock-dust. The closest translation that the computer could make was "Good snouting!"

After an hour, there came a series of taps on the roof. "Wiseworldcleaving-swarmguide {has progressed} in joy+joy+*joy!*" *I hope that means he's been successful, and not just freaked out on a magma-trip. We'll soon see.*

Billy waited while the mohomoles cleared the immediate vicinity. Then he picked up a small object he had just finished making — a simple exercise in chemistry and metalworking with the laboratory's excellent facilities —

climbed to the lowest level,

opened a small double-walled hatch in the floor,

>           dropped the object through,
>               scrambled up the ladder,
>                   ran to the sleeping area, and
>                       threw himself on the bed.

\* \* \*

In Jiydyrrill's control room, an entire bank of lights went crimson. Simultaneously, sirens began to scream. One warning device began to emit steady pulses of infrasound. For a second, he couldn't believe it. *An eruption warning?* Then training took over. He left the room at a run, heading for the nearest skeeter-bay. Breathless, he tumbled into the pilot's seat. A dozen Femm scrambled in after him.

"Anyone missing?" He asked in their guttural language. The ground began to shake.

"No. Except Director Eton!"

"Isn't she in the visitor's dayroom?"

The skeeter's engines began to shriek. Voices had to shout to be heard. "No. She's gone out to inspect the second mobile laboratory that came in from Brinsley Wain three hours ago."

"Where?"

"Out by the top of the shaft."

"Why didn't she following proper check-out procedure? I could have given her a lapel repeater. She won't even know there's an —"

There was a distant rumble. Jiydyrrill overrode the safeties, whipped the skeeter off the ground, tilted its nose to forty degrees, and punched in the boosters. The acceleration pinned him to his seat. The orders were to evacuate everybody who could make it in time.

Sherryl Eton felt a warm glow of satisfaction in a job well done. She had just removed a key component from the new laboratory's automatics and dropped it down the shaft. *They'll think it was left out by mistake during the rush to get it here. That will slow things down nicely.*

*The trap is sprung. Goodbye, Billy the Joat. I can't say it's been nice knowing you, though I'm enjoying saying goodbye.* Yet, in a way, she felt sad. *Idiot, guilt is for the underclasses.* It never occurred to her that maybe it wasn't guilt... Then she felt the planet move. A distant rumble grew to an earsplitting roar, and the ground shook violently. She thought *earthquake!* and began to run. She found an empty groundcar, and took off along the roadway at top speed.

There was a shattering howl as a million tonnes of molten rock vented from the shaft. Deafened, confused, and utterly overwhelmed, she watched it climb towards the sun, falling back in a scarlet fountain. *That's pretty*, she thought. Then the shockwave hit and all thinking ceased.

* * *

The molten core of a planet is seldom the smooth ball that you see pictured in science holomags like *Quaternion*. Protrusions of liquid magma sprout like garden weeds along slip-faults in the crust. In some of these the rock encounters oil, water, or gas: the superheated vapour builds up enormous pressures, far in excess of the already awesome weight of the crustal rocks. And Sear's Planet, as the Femm overseer had said, was an extreme case.

Lying on the bed, Billy the Joat counted the seconds. The mohomobile's mag-res imagers had shown him a nice, big, bulging pocket of overpressurized magma, a mere three kilometres away. If all had gone as planned, Wiseworldcleavingswarmguide's fellow mohomoles would have opened up passages from that pocket, leading to a branching network of tunnels cupped around the bottom of the shaft.

Now drop a small but powerful bomb...

*I hope Jiydyrrill was right about his warning devices.*

The first wave of superheated gas, a bare three hundred metres ahead of the seething column of molten rock, hit the floor of the laboratory. *I hope to gods this thing is as heatproof as the adverts claim*, thought Billy, as he rose up the shaft like a bullet in the barrel of a gun, riding his own private volcano on a cushion of gas. The gas in front worried him just as much as the gas behind: air-resistance would wreck the mohomobile just as easily as molten rock if its heat-shielding failed. *Jules Verne would be proud to see this day*, he thought, and blacked out.

The laboratory shot from the mouth of the shaft at a speed close to Sear's Planet's escape velocity, demolishing the pylon as it did so. This, and the atmosphere, would slow it. The Joat had calculated that it would rise to a height of seventeen kilometres before falling back. At that point, it all depended on *Lindulu*, Belphoebe, and a preprogrammed repetitive broadcast from his wristband remote.

*Lindulu*'s antenna picked up the signal. Belphoebe weighed her options. She fired the main propulsors and the space-yacht plunged planetwards, its skin heated close to danger-point by friction.

The Joat rose to meet it atop a pillar of fire.

*Lindilu* swooped, cargo-bay gaping, and plucked the Joat and his container from the sky. The doors closed and the ship began to tilt, pulling out of its power-dive a bare half a kilometre above the rooftops of Shum'n-al-Qyf. The sonic boom smashed half the homeoglass on the island.

Still acting on instructions, Belphoebe removed the yacht from the system at top speed.

\* \* \*

*I'm dead!* thought Billy the Joat, in an ill-considered attempt to refute Descartes. Then logic took over: corpses don't have sore heads. (Or do they? How could you —) He was alive. The plan must have worked.

He staggered to his feet, put on the coolsuit, and half-climbed, half-fell out of the hatch into the cargo-bay. The laboratory would still be pretty hot, but *Lindilu* was made from an isosteel-titanium alloy. He scrambled out of the cargo-bay, deciding to retain the mohomobile as evidence of sabotage. Five minutes later he was hunched over the console, setting up a phade to Aphélix and a freewave call to the Space Department.

\* \* \*

"You're a lunatic," said Palgandra admiringly.

The Joat, who was still growing new eardrums, lip-read the message, and shook his head. "Nonsense!" More response seemed to be necessary. "I admit I was lucky. I calculated that the relatively slow build-up of pressure would accelerate me gently enough to survive the shock. There was no other choice, anyway."

"You've caused an almighty row, I'll tell you that. SpaDe has already sent a survey team in, and it's slapped a suspension order on all further development. The lawyers are having a field-day shoving injunctions up each other's legal briefs, but for the moment that order is holding."

"It will. My story will check out."

"Yes. And then there'll be *another* almighty row. Rule number one in the Quaternity book is *don't interfere with the habitat of an intelligent species*. There'll be lengthy legal battles, with the Etonians and the Femm bringing in tame 'expert witnesses', who will —"

"Who will be discredited smartly by SpaDe, because SpaDe isn't so dumb, and neither are the courts. Then the Femm will have to move Sear's Planet back into its original orbit, clone some artificial wysshhiij if they can still read the gene codes, and generally try to put the ecology back together again. I'd be happy just to have the orbit readjusted — that will save the mohomoles from extinction."

"Yes. You're not going to be popular."

"I will be with the mohomoles."

"You know that Sherryl Eton was killed in the eruption?"

*Oh no. That wasn't in the game-plan. What a waste. Goodbye, Sherryl. Maybe things could have worked out differently... in another universe. I had so many questions to ask her. Still, there must be other Etonians who know what happened to Jole.* "It's her own fault," he said defensively. "She shouldn't have played with fire."

"*You* have the temerity to —"

"I mean *me*, not a feeble volcano!"

"Jarneyvore, you make powerful enemies like Bell-Galactic makes profits. It's a good job you aren't married. You'd be a liability to any wife!" He said the last flippantly, but was watching Billy carefully to gauge his reaction.

The Joat nodded glumly, thinking of Alaya de Flore Strooghn. But it didn't hurt so much, now. He had lost both women in his life, and was slowly coming to terms with his emotional failures... He shrugged, and caught Palgandra's eye. "Wife? What would Billy the Joat want with a wife? You're a romantic at heart, aren't you, you great hirsute hulk?" Palgandra glared at him and showed a row of sharp teeth. "Well, maybe not," the Joat amended hastily. "Anyway," he went on, changing the subject, "there's one piece of good news for the Etonians."

"I hadn't noticed anything to bring joy to their faces."

"The mohomoles will stay nearer the surface."

"So?"

"They won't disturb the deep flows any more. The buildings will stop sinking."

"That's all very well," said Palgandra. "And far be it from me to complain at the outcome. But when Sear's Planet is re-orbiformed, its surface temperature will be high enough to melt zinc! Nobody could live in that! The Femm will be *furious!*"

"Damn it all, Palgandra," said the Joat. "My brief was to stop the buildings subsiding. That's exactly what I've done. If you wanted them to be habitable as well, you might have mentioned it to begin with."

# 13   Knight with an Infomaniac

"...whereas the Trustees Publick, in recognizance of those rights conveyed unto the guarantor and his successors in perpetuity in respect of the Vesting Deed, to wit: socage, burgage, lampadary, talliage and stallage; waftage and scutage; stannary, figgery, whifflery and lairage, shall by these presents be bound consequent to the constitutional prerogatives of the Acts of Engrossment of 191 QC, to make restitution in fee simple, subject to the statutes, ordinances, decrees and promulgations of the intraspecial treaties of the Quaternity, notwithstanding which it is to be held in issuance that, *ejusdem generis*, such damages feasant as shall be invoked in letters patent..."

Belphoebe's voice pattered inexorably onward in hypnodrone mode, as Billy the Joat tried to relax in the shade of a mulotus grove with a glass of esselethe in one hand and a brunette in the other. Sir Wyllam de Jarneyvore — the persona no longer held painful memories and had been resumed — was studying law.

Indeed, in scarcely two weeks' time, he was due to put in an appearance as Counsel for the Defence at the Sector Courthouse on Aphélix. The charges were varied, ranging from Incitement to Riot and Personal Conspiracy to Contempt of Congressional Procedure and Aggravated Public Disturbance. The Joat had always inclined towards the law: the job was well-paid, the perquisites excellent, and the demands placed on the intellect were a mere bagatelle for one possessed of an eidetic memory. Hitherto he had been deterred by the requirements of a modicum of respectability, sound judgement, patience, and good taste — attributes in which he privately admitted he was mildly deficient. A lawyer whose sartorial preferences lean towards ultra-violet dayglo shorts and a T-shirt labelled "A foot-fetishist is someone who took the wrong turning at his mother's knee" is unlikely to attract wealthy clients. Indeed any clients.

But on this occasion there was no problem attracting clients, for the accused was none other than Billy the Joat himself. Ordinarily he would have hired the best legal brain available, but a miscalculated investment in the Möbius Moonlink Tunnel Project had led to a temporary cash-flow problem. Short of pawning his beloved Vishunti KKB space-yacht *Lindilu*, the only solution was to mount his own defence.

The entire business was so unreasonable anyway, a sorry tissue of coincidences and misinterpretations. It was hardly the Joat's fault that a transcription error had occurred in the operating system of the Civic Planning Computer. It was the merest bad luck that it resulted in the mobile entertainment blimp *Folies Betelgeuse* being tethered, not in the precincts of the Xanadu Pleasure Dome, but in the forecourt of the Quaternity Capitol. It was purely a measure of the paucity of architectural imagination that the two buildings bore a superficial resemblance from the air. The management of the blimp, engaging in what they thought was an authorized pre-publicity event, had not intended an invasion of the Chamber of Representatives by a phalanx of ecdysiasts sporting between them clothing barely sufficient to equip a Sindi Doll for the Riviera. By the merest happenstance this unprecedented occurrence coincided with the Quaternity-wide live freewave broadcast of the Congressional Opening Ceremonies, watched by 63% of the population of the known universe. Poor maintenance was no doubt responsible for the failure of the master cut-off switch. It was admittedly unorthodox parliamentary procedure for a bronzed Betelgeusian beauty to perform an impromptu striptease on the Speaker's Rostrum. The incident had not been improved by the unwary but enthusiastic participation of the entire Conservationist back bench, acting in the unhappy belief that a red light on a holovix camera indicated that it was in a non-functioning state. And it was little comfort that subsequent chemanalysis suggested that their coffee-machine had been spiked with antihibitran, although it did tend to explain their behaviour.

But, to pile improbability upon improbability to an extent that would surely stretch the credulity of even the most flexibly-minded juror, there had been a hardware failure in the optical memobank of the Aphéligian Broadcasting Corporation's main computer. This normally reliable device had mistakenly registered what its addled solitronic circuitry imagined to be a nanosecond power fluctuation, of a type often caused by external tampering. In its dull, unthinking fashion it had hooked into the Constabulary Network, for the sole reason that this was mandatory procedure in genuine cases of unauthorized interference. Said Network, continuing the unhappy saga of ineptitude, thereupon registered what it foolishly took to be a sequence of illicit programming commands. It was understandable that such an artefact would have an unusual semiotic profile, matching only one entry in police files. And thus arose the final mindboggling circumstance: whose entry might that be but Wyllam Jarneyvore's?

It was pure misfortune that a malfunctioning probe-shield diffuser had permitted the interception of the message in the first place, and Yaffa Varian of the Thriftex Part Mart would have a lot to answer for when he returned from the sudden and unexpected funeral of an elderly maiden Aunt somewhere out on the Fringe Reaches. The Joat intended to demonstrate the weakness of the central portion of the so-called 'evidence' by providing a penetrating analysis of the fallacy of applying semiotics to cybernetic structures. The remainder was purely circumstantial. In any case, he could prove that he had been in several other places at the time.

And — while he could hardly offer this to the court as an excuse — none of it would have occurred if he'd not run into a complete dead end in his search for his father. The Etonian secrecy was impenetrable. Joats are built for action as well as thought. When a joat gets frustrated, he can't just sit and do nothing. The displacement activities can take bizarre forms.

The brunette — whose form was anything but bizarre — snuggled closer. Her name, a professional sobriquet, was Delysia Slinque; she was a courtesan from Novi Tahiti, and a birthday-present from a satisfied client. She appeared to be highly intelligent as well as decorative, but her professional facade was faultless and the Joat had been unable to penetrate to the real person beneath. Not that the facade lacked its own interest: if only briefly Delysia took his mind off the loss of the two women in his life, Alaya de Flore Strooghn and Sherryl Eton. The circumstances differed, but the feelings were disturbingly similar. Mostly guilt.

The phone chirped. Billy disentangled himself, whistled the headset across from its shelf and thumbed the release button. With his tongue against his teeth he produced several mechanical clicks and buzzes, before speaking in falsetto tones. "Wyllam Jarneyvore's secretary. I regret the Joat is busy at the moment. Who is that speaking? May I take a message?"

"This is Palgandra. You can tell the Joat to stop pretending to be his secretary, and to take his grasping paws off that Novi Tahitian cutie."

A communication from Palgandra always meant trouble. Big trouble. Joat trouble of a personal kind. On the principle of never admitting anything, Billy squeaked "Fortune has smiled upon you, kind sir. The Joat does have a few spare moments in his otherwise crowded schedule. Please speak concisely. Putting you through now." More clicks and buzzes, and then: "Billy the Joat here. Is that Palgandra? Sorry to keep you waiting. A small matter of a missing consignment of Old Masters for the Lautrec Gallery. What do you wish to discuss?"

"You idiot. An item of intelligence that appears to concern your good self. One of my colleagues in Drug Liaison — a credulous fellow, *totally* unreliable — claims to have traced the purchase of a packet of antihibitran to your sealed account at the Bank of Lucerne in Waldorf Sector."

"My sealed account? Perplexing — I have no such thing. No doubt some confusion with my account at the Louisa May Alcott Memorial Trust." *Better move it somewhere else*, the Joat thought, though the damage was done now. "Is that all?"

The Grynth emitted a rumbling snort of disinterest and boredom. "Some foolish notion that the packet's contents can be identified through marked codons in its passive dispersant medium. Utter nonsense of course, and I'm sure that nothing illegal has occurred. However, routine must be adhered to. By the by, did you know that the maximum penalty for Contempt of Congressional Procedure is thirty years in the skrunt-mines of Job's Last Hope?"

"Fascinating," said the Joat wanly. He pulled himself together. Marked codons? How utterly *gauche*. A thought inserted itself in his mind. A thought of double-edged import. He said, "And the other purpose to your call?"

"What other purpose?"

"There's always another purpose when you disrupt my peaceful and peaceable existence."

"We'll discuss it when you come over," said Palgandra, and hung up.

\* \* \*

Palgandra's desk was dominated by a mottled purple watermelon. One of its green blotches was marked with a bold red triangle.

"Ankershou," said the Joat.

"Bless you."

"The planet on your desk. Ankershou 17/B*/ddJ, Egmont Sector. I was reading about it in *Space-Time* magazine a few months ago."

The Grynth's hairy head bobbed, and he grunted noncommittally through an ear-orifice. "No doubt you recall the substance of the article?"

*This interview*, the Joat thought, *is getting off to a bad start. What about antihibitran? Marked codons? Job's Last Hope?* He dredged his capacious memory, visualised the page, began to read. "Colonized by a Barasshanti expedition forty years ago, but not registered. Colony soon died out, mechanical failure in the food-processor, nothing environmental. Unique in the known universe for its proximity to a twistar sun. Just outside the distortion zone, avoiding time paradoxes. Only native fauna an animal closely resembling the domestic pig. Rediscovered last year by a Femm survey party, which had the sense to register it. Barasshan in an uproar, protest to Supreme Council. Not a chance, serve them right for not registering it themselves in the first place. Meteor-swarm in a teacup, no repercussions bar bruised egos and those are ten a centikroon."

Palgandra exhaled like a foghorn in mourning for vanished mists. "A masterly summation. I wish it were so."

"You mean that dump is *important?*"

"Oh, yes."

The Joat waited, but nothing more was forthcoming. He prodded. "*Why*, Joze? What can possibly be important about a mouldy mauve football lousy with porkers? Except as a base for ecologists or twistar scientists, who'd be granted visiting rights anyway under the Mutual Enlightenment Pact of 16 QC..." *Good girl, Belphoebe. I didn't know I knew that.*

Palgandra's enormous head drooped a fraction, as if in defeat. "Magneurex."

"What? The telepathy-drug? But that's impossible! Magneurex can only be found in the seventh motor ganglion of the blank-faced mockroach, during the pre-mating season, on the seventh moon of the seventh planet of Heptad VII! Everybody knows that!"

"I'll accept your word for it."

"You, if anyone, should. Heptad VII is under Grynth administration and prohibited to commercial exploitation."

"Correct," said Palgandra. "But Ankershou is under neither Grynth administration, nor prohibition."

"You mean there are blank-faced mockroaches on Ankershou?"

"No. The fruits of the Morecambe bay-tree."

The Joat's mind was awhirl. Ever since the Tulliver Riots it had been the firm policy of the three relatively normal members of the Quaternity — Barasshan, Grynth, and Human — under no circumstances to permit dissemination of a telepathy-drug. The result, they knew, would be social collapse. Societies only work when you *don't* know what everybody else really thinks about you. But the fourth race, the Femm, didn't see it that way. Nobody really understood the Femm mentality and the Femm reciprocated by utterly failing to understand everybody else. Unfortunately they were too powerful to be kicked out of the Quaternity, which is why they had been invited to join it in the first place. Furthermore, magneurex had no effect on Femm physiology. All this went through the Joat's mind in a flash.

Palgandra nodded his agreement, and essayed a tired smile, managing to look like a self-conscious bloodhound in a gorilla-suit. "Of course they don't admit to it, and we don't have any proof, otherwise we could at least try to bring some diplomatic pressure to bear." He fiddled distractedly with some papers, then brightened. "Fortunately, I think we have it under control."

"That's a relief." For a wild moment Billy'd had a horrible feeling that Palgandra was going to try to involve *him* in this hopeless mess. A hiding to nothing, that would be. He pitied the poor snerg who got the job of sorting it out. Thank the Wise Weirds of Wymondham, at least *he* could safely...

"Everything should be fine now that I've hired you to deal with this little problem," said Palgandra. He waved a sheaf of papers in his hand, as if to emphasise his words. The Joat's mouth opened to protest, until he noticed what was written on the top sheet. *Forensic Laboratories — antihibitran test results*. Below, a pink card protruded, bearing a number that he recognised as his own Social Security code. He paused, uncertain how to respond. Palgandra looked him in the eye, and said, "I had Big Pig send these through interdepartmental liaison. He wasn't keen — said they were the only copies. But I don't think there's anything significant in them, do you?" He made as if to discard the papers into a nearby shredder.

The Joat swallowed manfully. "When do I start?"

* * *

When Billy arrived home, Delysia had gone out 'to stretch her legs', a totally unnecessary act. Belphoebe had of necessity remained, being built into the fabric of the house. "Greetings, Sir Knight!" she declaimed as he thumbed the door-plate.

"Shut up and let me in!"

"Your wish, Sir Wyllam, Joat de Jarneyvore, is my command!" The door dilated and the Joat stepped through. He snapped his fingers.

"A double Glenfuddle, on the rocks, 'phoebe."

"I hear and I obey, My Lord. Meanwhile..."

"Meanwhile what?" snapped the Joat irritably.

"The Wildfowl Protection Act of 243 QC. Be it so enacted in these hallowed precincts —"

"Can it, Belphoebe!"

"— that sundry species of rare birdlife are protected by the Laws of the Quaternity from any form of interference with their habitat, be it inadvertent or by foul design, to wit —"

"Tu whoo."

"Your pardon, Sir Knight?"

"Just an owl of protest, Belphoebe. I'm not in the mood for legal studies. Anyway, I don't need to bother now. Out of the *Fieri Facias* into the Case of Thorns."

"But, Sir Wyllam, the program you gave me does not permit me to cease, without an explicit command —"

"Which I've just given you!"

"— and a password, which you have not. Landbirds, seabirds, groundbirds, birds of prey, and any manner of..."

The Joat groaned. He'd decided law studies might be boring, and had taken steps to ensure that nose and grindstone remained in intimate contact. If he wanted to stop, he had to recall an autohypnotically implanted password which was only accessible if something important came up.

"Very well, Belphoebe. The password is 'cerebrobrach'."

"... winged creature of birdlike features and demeanour..."

"Correction, 'campanula'."

"...Subsection 44(b)(ii). It shall, on penalty of total forfeit of chattels, goods, hereditaments and other sundry possessions, be prohibited to..."

*Oh gods.* He couldn't remember the password. His brain didn't think there was a good reason to lower the hypnotic barrier.

Two hours later, the Joat was in an alcoholic stupor, and Belphoebe's voice had gone fuzzy and indistinct:

"Subsubsection 936(k)(xviii)(gamma). All species of:

(a) Snow-pigeons;

(b) Rumpled Gallinules;

(c) Flightless groundbirds of all kinds, including Kiwi, Emu, Hralthfrithian Perspunctiple, Moa, Ostrich, Plingent Canunculoid, and all winged but land-bound creatures, denizens of any world within the confines of the Quaternity at large;

(d) The Gauzy Albatross;

(e) The Huge Wren of the Banshee Wyldernesse;

(f) Nestlings of the species *Bureaucratica prevaricans* (var. Irritabilia) of gross displacement no more than the lesser of seventeen standard audubons or..."

The voice became even more indistinct, and the Joat dozed.

* * *

He was still asleep on Delysia's return, but Belphoebe's customarily flamboyant greeting of visitors and house-guests woke him, and by the time she appeared he had staggered to his feet. The password came unbidden to his mind. "Belphoebe: panpharmicon!" To which Belphoebe replied that obviously Sir Wyllam de Jarneyvore would not wish his studies to intrude upon a house-guest, so she had ceased on her own initiative. None of which did his head much good.

"I've brought you a parting-gift," said Delysia shyly. Shyness had not thitherto been prominent in her emotional repertoire.

"I thought you *were* the gift," he said lightly.

"Only until tonight. But you may remember me through this." A bowl of flowering cacti.

"My God. Is it Tuesday already? That's very sad."

"No, sir: it's business," said Delysia. And burst into tears.

A joat, by nature, is equipped to deal with virtually any eventuality: a superfusion reactor gone critical, a gargantuoid-stampede, a wild galaxy on a gravity-binge. Jack Of All Trades. But comforting a weeping woman wasn't a trade, and it left Jack baffled and uncomfortable. Finally he settled for a brotherly arm around the shoulder. "What's the matter, Delysia?"

"You're sending me away!" And the sobs renewed.

Now that, the Joat felt, was unfair. He hadn't ordered her in the first place, and he hadn't asked her to leave, nor did he wish her to. It hadn't occurred to him that the professional training of a Novi Tahitian courtesan would permit her to take any interest in such matters. "I'll never send you away," he said. It made no sense, but seemed to fit the occasion.

"It's all so *unfair*. I never wanted to be a courtesan anyway! It was my mother's fault!"

The Joat seized the opportunity to divert the subject. "What *did* you want to be?"

"An infomaniac!" Delysia wailed.

"Coals to Newcastle, dear," said the Joat, who had misheard. At this, her wails redoubled.

"Just as I'd expect! *Men!* All they think a woman's good for is a tumble in the hay!" The Joat forebore to point out that she had blamed her mother for her current profession. "I want to be a cybernetic polymath, Billy."

"Oh," said the Joat, understanding at last. "An infomaniac, yes." He coughed. "So what prevents you?"

It all came out in a rush. Her real name was Moira Dwotchet. She had been raised on Novi Tahiti by her widowed mother, who could not comprehend why a well-made young lady could seek any career other than the most respectable role of courtesan. Fiddling around with electronics, the good matron had declared, was indecent, decadent, and utterly immoral. Added to which the hours were bad and the prospects poor. The tips were *rotten* and the eventual nuptial prospects worse.

"So why don't you leave, and do what you really want?"

"I don't know *how*; I don't have the training; I don't have anyone to help me!"

"You do now," said the Joat, in a moment of decision.

"But I'm under contract!"

"Consider it cancelled."

"It's easy to *say* that —"

Billy took her by the hand. "When I say something, I mean it. You now receive your first lesson as a trainee infomaniac." He walked away, propelling her gently but firmly before him.

In the innermost rooms of the sprawling house was the Joat's study; an untidy jumble of books, tapes, and cannibalized equipment. He burrowed in the desk and emerged with a remote terminal. "First we dial up the Employment Register like *this*... then we select for Novi Tahiti... hmmm, here we go. In the employ of a Madam Goozblinder, yes?"

"That's right! How did you do that? Let *me* see..."

"All in good time, just keep watching. Your Social Security code is NT-0043-552-2113-078, right?" She nodded. "Good. Now for a more delicate manoeuvre, get into the legal files, find your contract, deal with it, get out again. Ahhhh, yes, just as I expected."

The screen read: NO ACCESS TO UNAUTHORIZED PERSONNEL.

"And you're authorized?" said Moira hopefully.

"Nope. But I never let that stop me." He rummaged under the desk and emerged with a long flat box, plugged it into the back of the terminal, switched it on, and waited. Seeing Moira was puzzled, he explained. "Access decoder. Made it myself. ULSI circuits, ternary firmware, very fast search capability... See?"

The screen changed to: OPERATING SYSTEM — QUALIFIED ENGINEERS ONLY.

"You're a qualified engineer?"

"Better! I'm a disqualified Joat! Had an engineer's licence once, lost it over some stupid misunderstanding, forget the details now."

Two minutes later he had ferreted out Moira's contract, added a cancellation clause, filed the necessary termination documents, and modified all backup copies to match. Temporarily taking over a section of memory in the communication buffer, he wrote a program which let him leave the system, erased all traces of his intervention, and then erased itself.

"And that," said the Joat, "is that!"

Moira wasn't entirely convinced, but the Joat's confidence was catching. "What do you expect me to do now?"

*A leading question on which I shall dissemble.* "You become my assistant, answer the mail, scratch the cat, kick Belphoebe. I cram you with informatics until it comes out of your ears. Come on, we don't have much time!"

"Time?"

"Before we leave for Ankershou at sunrise tomorrow."

"Time for what?"

"Don't be dense, woman."

# 14  *Pseudoporcus podocarpus* (var. Baldwin)

"Now, don't forget," warned the Joat. "The Mutual Elightenment Pact allows access by visiting ecologists and twistologers. So we're a couple of scientists from Harvarda Segunda investigating the mating habits of *Pseudoporcus podocarpus* (var. Baldwin)."

Moira nodded hesitantly. "What's that when it's at home?"

"The sole animal life native to Ankershou, resembling the domestic pig. I am Professor Bnoulli Yornavour, of the Faculty of Porcine Particulars. You remain Moira, but your second name is now Trush; you are my Postdoctoral Research Assistant. We are equipped with fake IDs to match our fake egos, a Freudian joke you may dissect at leisure. My wife Hortoonse, who remains on Harvarda Segunda, suspects us — with good reason — of indulging in mutual non-academic activities. In the hole are several crates of equipment: familiarize yourself with their contents. Meanwhile I will prepare our documentation for landing, obtain the necessary clearances, and so forth."

"OK," said Moira. She looked out of the upper viewscreen at Ankershou's strange sun, an orange ellipsoid tinged with deep blue, which somehow seemed to *writhe*. "I've never seen a star like that before!"

"It's a Penrose twistar," said the Joat. "The further you get into its photosphere, the faster time passes. But its magnetic field confines the effect to a zone immediately around the star, so we're safe enough here. Well, to be accurate, time should speed up by about six billionths of a per cent at Ankershou's orbital distance. Good job it's not more — it'll take long enough to wade through the bureaucratic mire as it is." In the event, it took two days in a holding orbit before the Femm were convinced of the party's *bona fides*. Eventually Professor Yornavour and his assistant were delivered to an inflatable accomodome on the outskirts of the Femm industrial base on Ankershou. Under the impersonal surveillance of two sonobugs and an optic snoop, they took an early rest in preparation for the activity of the following day.

\* \* \*

They were assigned a Femm guide, Mjyrryd by name, and provided with an aircar. Professor Yornavour thanked the Femm profusely for these acts of altruism, and silently hoped they wouldn't be too disappointed when the snoop behind the control-panel suffered a nasty power-surge. With Mjyrryd at the controls they headed South in porcine pursuit. The terrain beneath was covered with lush green broad-leafed plants, grove upon grove of Morecambe bay-trees. Large sections were fenced off, and squat Femmish harvesters prowled among them snipping off bunches of globular pink fruit, which hung almost to the ground.

Just before noon they spotted a herd of pigs at a water-hole, and Mjyrryd set the machine down nearby. He cut the motor, called through to his superiors to confirm his position, and slumped quietly into his seat as the Joat administered a shot of amnesiax. Later he would be supplied with hypnotically implanted fake memories of the day's events.

"So what do we do now?" said Moira.

"Look."

"What are we looking for?"

"Anything that can foul up the Femm drug operation. Chemanalysis of the fruit. Natural pests. Geologic instabilities. Weather-patterns. Maybe we can stimulate planet-wide hurricanes and wreck the crop. Right now, we're groping in the dark."

They unloaded their equipment and set to work.

The pigs were much larger than they had seemed from the air, not quite up to hippopotamus standard but running a close second. Pink and podgy with brown splodges, they seemed indifferent to the intrusion, with the innate placidity of the herbivore. But, as the day wore on, they moved closer, evincing a diffident curiosity that became bolder as they decided there was nothing to fear. One nudged up against a barograph, causing it to give a temporary reading of 113 atmospheres. Another sat on a meteorological balloon, which burst with a loud bang. The pigs hastily retreated to a safe distance, but one, braver than his fellows, edged closer again. He was distracted by a large bunch of fruit at snout level, which he began to eat. Moira made a note on her compad. Billy picked a bunch of fruit for testing. The chromatograph said they weren't poisonous. Some were overripe, and sticky juices ran down his fingers. Absent-mindedly, he licked them clean. The juice tasted a bit like raspberries. He continued with the analysis, noting with satisfaction the presence of magneurex precursors.

Woops. Magneurex wasn't exactly *poisonous*, but... possibly licking his fingers had been unwise. His head started to feel funny, sort of expanded. From Moira's direction he could hear snatches of chatter, including some rather explicit references to himself. He looked, but her lips weren't moving. The magneurex was working. For telepathic contact over more than about fifty metres, both parties had to take the drug; but at close quarters the magneurex user could pick up random thoughts from anyone — other than Femm. His brain continued to interpret the incoming signals as sound. He caught fragments of her childhood memories, previous assignments. In particular a certain Professor Bodley Spatula, who had a remarkable preference for... The Joat blushed, but his embarrassment quickly gave way to amusement. Bodley Spatula was a famous authority on genetic engineering, and the contrast between his public dignity and private tendencies was noteworthy. Then another thought intruded, faint through the mental static. Billy concentrated, focussed. It was an irregular murmur, several different thoughts mixed together. The main content appeared to be >>oink<<.

The pigs were natural telepaths!

An unusually loud >>oink<< made him jump, and he turned to find the boldest of the pigs snuffling at his feet. >>No,<< the message resounded in his mind. >>Not natural telepaths. We eat the leaves of the bay-tree. Improve the mind beyond bay-leaf. Hey, geddit? Bay-leaf, belief, good eh?<<

>>Gods! They're intelligent!<< the Joat thought, adding, after a pause: >>Well, nearly.<<

>>No, no, just a mental resonance with your own brain. Borrowing your own intelligence, so to speak. I, Pogsnort, am but a Dumb Beast. Your human brain pigs out what it imagines to be sapient structure. Pigs out! Oh, I'd slay 'em on Broadway!<<

>>Just my luck, << thought the Joat. >>A spotty pig that thinks in puns.<<

>>Do you mind? Those aren't spots, they're porker dots!<< There was the sound of manic laughter, and tears came to the pig's eyes.

>>And I suppose you came closer to us than the other pigs because you're a little rasher?<< the Joat essayed.

The laughter ceased abruptly. >>Hey, that's not funny, you know. You should cut out your tongue and pickle it for that. Geddit? Piggle-et? Oh, wow!<<

>>Do you always think in puns?<<

>>Look, buster, I hardly *think* at all. All you get from me is a mental skeleton. Not my fault if your brain chooses to flesh it out with dreadful puns. Presumably how you imagine a pig *should* think. Hamming it up. Ha!<<

Moira noticed his preoccupation with the pig, and came over. "Billy, it's time we packed up and went back. What are you doing with that poor pig?" The Joat explained as best he could.

"Yes, I noticed one eating that fruit. I'm surprised, I'd have expected them to root around for fungi and things."

>>I do not concern myself with truffles,<< thought the pig haughtily.

* * *

Five days passed, following the same routine, and without any notable progress. On the sixth, Mjyrryd was replaced by one Dyrr, a sour-faced individual who responded, if at all, in monosyllables. Once more they flew out to the pig herds, once more the Joat administered the shot of amnesiax. But this time, as he leaned across to open the door, he found himself looking down the barrel of a laser pistol. Dyrr had been stuffed with barrier hormones and was resistant to amnesiax.

Cuffed and gagged, Moira and the Joat flew back to the Femm base. All of their possessions, including Billy's wristband remote link to *Lindilu*, were taken. They were thrown into a small bare room, and left.

The next morning, after a day without food or water, six burly Femm guards frog-marched the Joat down a dozen corridors, into a sparsely furnished room. A nasty-looking individual, bearing the insignia of a Field Disbursar and presumably the local panjandrum, sat at an enormous desk. They tied the Joat to a chair facing him. On a table at the side were his and Moira's personal belongings.

The Field Disbursar shuffled through a stack of papers, grunted, and only then looked at the Joat. "We know who you are," he said. "We know why you're here."

"Of course you do," said the Joat in a puzzled voice. "I'm Bnoulli Yornavour, Professor of Porcine Particulars at Harvarda Segunda. I'm here to study *Pseudoporcus podo—*"

"You are a spy and a saboteur. Your real name is Wyllam Jarneyvore, a self-styled Jag-Of-All-Trades. You live on Krover's World and you are a troublemaker. You were sent to interfere with our bay-tree production. Your papers are forgeries."

"That's ridiculous! I'm no spy! I came here to study the rutting rituals of *Pseudoporcus!* I'm writing a monograph on the relevance of tail torsion to reproductive activity patterns, and I—"

"Is it normal for your egological studies to include administering amnesiax to your guide and destroying surveillance equipment?"

"An unfortunate chapter of accidents and misunderstandings. The amnesiax was intended for immobilizing a specimen of *Pseudoporcus*. I have no knowledge of surveillance equipment, and no interest in it since my motives and actions are as pure as the driven ice-crystals of New Novosibirsk and will withstand the most detailed scrutiny. Your hospitality is sadly lacking, I shall complain to the Scientific Exchange Bureau and demand an apology. My assistant needs food and water. I protest this unwarranted and disgraceful treatment. I —" A guard hit him, twice, across the mouth. He could taste blood.

"We know all about you, Jarneyvore."

*If that's true, why the interrogation?* thought the Joat, through a wave of pain. *What are they after? Are they just playing games?*

"We know about the acts of sabotage you have perpetrated. You may as well admit them now, it will save a lot of trouble."

"I admit to nothing! My name is Bnoulli Yornavour, and my sole objective on Ankershou is the study of *Pseudoporcus Podocarpus*." *So that's what they're after. They're worried we've already planted something that will destroy the crop, and they want to know what it is.*

"A pity," said the Field Disbursar. "We shall have to find ways to persuade you to change your mind. Oh, nothing grude, I assure you. Something suited to the dignity of your alleged agademic profession. Lance-Private Dyrr!"

"Sir!"

"Fetch Professor Yornavour and his assistant some food." Dyrr departed, reappearing shortly with a sack. He tipped it out on the floor, revealing a dozen bunches of the fruit of the Morecambe bay-tree. The Field Disbursar grunted in satisfaction. "An interesting plant, Professor. Eaten in small quantities it stimulates telepathig processes. It contains a large dose of magneurex precursors. The more you eat, the more the effect builds up. You know what happens to an over-stimulated telepath?"

*He cracks up*, thought Billy. *The brain can't take the strain.* His thoughts must have showed on his face, because the Field Disbursar nodded. "That's right, Professor Yornavour. Of gorse, you and your assistant have a choice. You may elect instead to starve." He signalled to the guards. "Take him away!"

Moira's concern was mitigated by relief when the guards flung the Joat through the door of their cell. The sack of fruit followed. "What's that?"

"A trap." He explained their choice of deaths. "Unless we tell them what sabotage we've committed."

"But we —"

"Can't do that," the Joat cut in quickly. He didn't want the Femm to realise there *was* no sabotage. Only the uncertainty kept himself and Moira alive.

She caught on rapidly. "So what *do* we do?"

"Eat, drink, and be merry," he replied with false gaiety.

"Huh? But you just said —"

"We've got to get our strength up. One meal won't do much harm. Here: eat!" He popped a fruit into Moira's mouth, took one himself. They waited. After a while he felt a familiar sensation as his brain seemed to swell inside his head. >>Moira?<<

>>Yes, Billy?<< the thought came back.

>>The Femm made a mistake. I couldn't explain it before, but now it's obvious. We can converse without their bugs picking anything up.<<

>>But if they use the drug themselves, to listen in?<<

>>Magneurex doesn't work on Femm. All we have to do now is exploit that mistake.<<

>>And how do you propose to do that?<<

>>I haven't the foggiest.<<

They discussed a number of escape plans in turn. The first few ideas were implausible, the subsequent schemes wildly impractical. All foundered on the fact that they were completely alone, and helpless. After three hours the effect of the drug started to wear off.

>>Great,<< thought the Joat bitterly. >>All we have to do is get out of here, deal with the Femm, take care of the magneurex, and go home. Nothing to it.<< He grimaced. >>Don't worry, I'll think of something. We'll be out of here quicker than a wollagong down a sumphole.<<

>>Sure,<< came a faint sarcastic thought from Moira. >>And if pigs had wings, they'd fly.<<

And the whole thing came together in Billy's mind like Ankershou's sun going nova.

* * *

Pogsnort lazed in the pale sunshine and chewed bay-fruit contentedly. His dim animal consciousness formed the vague thought that this was the proper life for a pig. He looked across the clearing to where Snert and Wallo were rolling in the dust, and belched happily.

A strange thought inserted itself into his mind. >>The feeding is better to the North. Where the buildings are.<< He rose uncertainly to his feet. Snert and Wallo also rose. >>Come and see,<< the intruding thought invited. >>Swine, women and song,<< the Joat added, remembering the pigs' fondness for puns.

>>Women?<< thought Pogsnort. >>Song?<<

>>Swine, sows, and wild celebratory oinking,<< Billy corrected.

>>Got sows here. Got food. Got no problem oinking, neither.<<

>>Not sows like *this*. Not food like *this*. Not oinks of such sonorous resonance.<<

>>Crap. Bog off, you oinker.<<

The Joat sought inspiration. >>Rich piggings,<< he thought in desperation.

>>Oh, wow, rich piggings! That's a good one!<< Pogsnort was interested now. So were the others. Wallo kicked her trotters in delight, Snert tried to tie his tail in a knot. The herd began to move.

Other pigs, attracted by the strange thoughts and the movement of the herd, joined them. Slowly they began to assemble — a dozen, a hundred, a thousand. Soon fifty thousand pigs were converging on the Femm base in search of rumoured rich piggings. The Joat encouraged them with promised delights that grew wilder and wilder, driving the beasts into an anticipatory frenzy. The movement became a rush, then a stampede. By the time the guards decided to believe the evidence of their own senses, it was too late. The pigs flattened the perimeter defences and bowled the guards over. They pounded huts and accomodomes into rubble. A small group led by Pogsnort invaded the detention area and smashed every door in sight, inveigled by promises of Hambrosia, the fabled Food of the Hogs. Among those doors was the one that restrained joat and trainee infomaniac.

Only one central building remained standing, its inhabitants long fled. To this the Joat made his way, and regained possession of his wristband remote. Within ten minutes they were on their way out of Ankershou's atmosphere. Below, fifty thousand perplexed and disappointed porkers milled aimlessly through the ruins of the Femm base.

\* \* \*

They had to move fast before reinforcements arrived. Billy told Moira to contact her old flame Bodley Spatula by freewave and wheedle from him some limb-grafting gene codes. "Promise anything — you don't have to deliver. Threaten blackmail if you must." While she exercised her woman's wiles, holding a lengthy and intimate whispered conversation with a person she addressed as "Boddles", the Joat busied himself constructing a large-nozzled spraygun. Moira informed him that Professor Spatula would call back shortly with the required codes and refused to say what she had promised in return. Billy began construction of a bizarre electronic device like an inside-out freewave transmitter. When Moira asked about it he told her it was a photosphere penrotovator. Soon after, Bodley Spatula called back with the information the Joat needed. He promptly disappeared into an isolation cubby with a box of chemical apparatus and didn't emerge for nine hours.

After that the action, when it came, was over almost before it started. *Lindilu* did a quick sweep of Ankershou's equator while the Joat wielded the spraygun through an open hatch. Then the photosphere penrotovator was activated. As they left the system at top speed something funny seemed to be happening to Ankershou's sun.

\* \* \*

A SpaDe cutter picked them up within a day, with orders to return to Aphélix immediately, where a Quaternity Committee of Enquiry was convening to study a complaint from the Femm Phylarchy. To Moira's surprise, the Joat complied at once.

Billy and Moira were whisked through a screaming mob of holovix newscasters and taken to a guarded committee room in the Capitol Building. Along one side of a huge table sat one each of Femm, Barasshan, Human, and Grynth. Their name-plaques declared them to be Representatives Qyddjdjmyllymn Zzyjrlyrl, Melvaun ap-Peeq, Jaklyn McJagger, and Fleumaz Symwhorl: the Committee of Enquiry. At the head of the table sat a tall, elderly Femm, presumably the complainant. Some string-pulling had placed Joze Palgandra as Chairman — but string-pulling alone wouldn't do the trick. A legal aide sat on Palgandra's left. Two more sat on the Femm's right.

"This enquiry is convened," said Palgandra, "to examine extremely serious charges. Phylarch Yrjjyddj alleges that you, Wyllam Jarneyvore and Moira Dwotchet, are responsible for the destruction of a Femm agromechanical base, and the temporary halting of production of canned fruit intended as a lunchtime delicacy for younglings of the third and fourth station in the scholastic indoctrinatoria of Femmish brood-chambers." There was more than a note of sarcasm in his voice, but Yrjjyddj remained impassive despite a sigh from McJagger and a snort from Symwhorl.

"Can the Phylarch prove these claims?" asked the Joat.

"That is for this Committee to decide," said Palgandra. "The remains of the base are available for inspection. The Phylarch assures us that he can deposit Femm records showing that there was an agromechanical complex on Ankershou, processing the fruits of the Morecambe bay-tree for export to the Femm homeworlds. Do you dispute these assertions?"

"No," said the Joat. Zzyjrlyrl gave Yrjjyddj a significant and surprised glance.

"Then you admit the charges?" said Palgandra softly.

"No."

"Make up your mind," said Zzyjrlyrl.

"I have no knowledge of any of these matters," said the Joat, "so I can neither confirm nor deny them." McJagger had difficulty restraining a snigger. Melvaun ap-Peeq canted his carapace a few degrees, a sign of mildly increased interest, while Zzyjrlyrl attempted to cover his embarrassment by cracking a *kaata*-nut loudly.

"There are traffic reports on file to show that the space-yacht *Lindilu,* registered in your name, visted Ankershou," said Palgandra.

"I can produce regords of an application by an alleged Professor Bnoulli Yornavour, to visit Angershou," said Yrjjyddj. "Retinal scans, also on record, confirm that to be an assumed name. The person in question has been identified as yourself. Do you now plead kilty as charged?"

"This isn't a Court of Law, Phylarch Yrjjyddj," said the Joat.

"That can be arranged if necessary," said Palgandra sharply. He shot Billy a glance that said it all: *You can't get out if trouble that way.*

"I do have two requests to the Committee," said the Joat, "which I believe will resolve this matter once and for all."

"And these are?" interjected Melvaun ap-Peeq.

"First, that the remains of this alleged agromechanical complex be dated by neutron-emission scanning. Second, that a specimen of the native fauna of Ankershou, *Pseudoporcus podocarpus*, be captured and brought before this body."

"I fail to see any relevance in this," said the Femm Representative.

"I am entitled to insist that reasonable steps are taken to obtain material evidence, under the Criminal Justice Act of 122 QC, Section 36."

Palgandra had been in huddled conversation with his aide, probably about the possible diminution of *agneth* if he made a wrong decision. "I rule that these are reasonable requests," he stated. "Though I hope they are not merely a delaying tactic," he added pointedly.

"Certainly not," protested the Joat indignantly. "I swear it on my mother's grave!"

Palgandra sighed. He knew that Matron Terpsichore Jarneyvore was currently enjoying the best of health. "Very well," he said reluctantly. "We shall dispatch a cruiser at once to Ankershou, with a qualified archaeologist and a zoological team. The meeting is adjourned *sine die*."

Much later — by which time the Joat had had a long private meeting with Palgandra — the Committee of Enquiry reconvened.

"And now I hope we can gonclude this matter," said Yrjjyddj. "Do we have the archaeological dating? No doubt it will gonfirm what is obvious at a glance."

"It does seem to," said Palgandra. Moira gave Billy an agonized look. "The ruins are indeed seventeen thousand years old." She gasped. Palgandra placed several holovix stills on the table, adding drily, "As you will see, the ruins do appear somewhat ancient, even to the untrained eye."

Yrjjyddj turned the stills one way, then the other. He picked them up and peered underneath. He passed them to Zzyjrlyrl, who went through a similar performance and finally passed them to Melvaun ap-Peeq, who passed them to McJagger, who passed them to Symwhorl, who handed them back to Palgandra, who put them on the table.

There was something funny about the remains of the Femm base. The ruins looked much too weathered and ancient to be the result of a pig-stampede the day before. Phylarch Yrjjyddj looked as though he had strained at a shrimp and swallowed a porcupine-fish. "But — that is gwite impossible! There must be a mistake!"

"No mistake."

"I protest. The evidence has been tampered with."

"The evidence is impeccable. The ruins are seventeen thousand years old," said Palgandra firmly.

Moira grabbed the Joat's arm. "But Billy," she whispered, "they can't be!"

"Moira, you're surely not questioning evidence that Palagandra himself tells us is impeccable?"

Yrjjyddj recovered most of his aplomb. "I reserve the right to an independent test," he said. "However, for now I do not gontest the ruling of the chair. It matters little: the important point is the interruption of canned fruit production." He glanced contemptuously at the Joat. "Depriving our younklings of their harmless pleasures, a disgraceful action. At best you have achieved a temporary stoppage, Jarneyvore. Production will resume, whatever the decision of this meeting."

"I doubt it," said the Joat. "In fact I predict that you will shortly deny there ever was any production on Ankershou."

"Yes, and piks have winks," muttered the Representative darkly.

The Joat smiled. "A perceptive remark, I congratulate you. May we see the native fauna now?" he asked Palgandra, who nodded. The captured Ankershou pig was dragged in, with some difficulty, by a squad of SpaDe midshipmen. It looked pretty much like any other hot and annoyed spotted pink pig of hippopotamian proportions — except that, sprouting from its shoulders, was a pair of wings. Their span, half a metre or so, was out of all proportion to the beast's body, and evidently inadequate for flight. Jaklyn McJagger started giggling uncontrollably, Symwhorl's grin threatened to disconnect his chin from his face, and Melvaun ap-Peeq canted his carapace so far that he nearly fell off his chair, clicking his elbow-joints in delight. With an effort, Zzyjrlyrl remained impassive.

"This is ridigulous," said the Phylarch Yrjjyddj, who was obviously livid. "A practical joke in the poorest taste. While I fail to see any material relevance, I venture to suggest that the winks are some kind of surgical graft. A stupid hoax."

"No," said Palgandra. "They're natural. We've done a genescan to check. The wings are a mutation that goes back thousands of generations." He had the Committee's full attention, now.

"So, the piks really *do* have winks. So what?"

"It's very simple," said the Joat. "Are you familiar with the Wildfowl Protection Act of 243 QC?"

There was a muttered conversation with an aide, who fiddled about with a wristcomp before replying. The Phylarch admitted he did have some knowledge of the Act, but indicated his belief that it had no applicability. "A pik is not a wildfowl," he stated firmly.

"But if it *were?*" asked Palgandra flatly.

"That is a purely hypothetical question."

"Then you may give it a purely hypothetical answer," said Palgandra. "As an exercise in logic."

There was another hurried conversation. "I protest," said Yrjjyddj, "the direction this Enquiry is taking. It has not been proved that the Morecambe bay-tree is part of the habitat of this sordid greature, and even if it were —"

"If it were, then exploitation of the bay-fruit would be prohibited under Law," the Joat interrupted. "And your alleged production unit would have been illegal. 'On penalty of total forfeit of chattels, goods, hereditaments, and sundry —' "

"Oh, this is idiotig nonsense. The beast is *not a bird!*"

"But it is," said the Joat. "It's a flightless ground-bird." The entire courtroom collapsed, howling with delight. Except for the Femm.

"Gonfound it, it's a pik!" Yrjjyddj had lost his temper. "Any fool can see that!"

"Precisely. Just as any fool can see that a small furry hyrax cannot possibly be related to an enormous leathery elephant. But — it is." He leaned forward to address the Committee. "Classification of living creatures is a very difficult area, your eminences. The Hairy Belmothere looks like a bear but is actually a lizard. The Greater Sting Winkle of the Bliny Isthmus is not a shellfish but a fungus. And the Windhoek Amorphozoon defies classification altogether.

"I could cite a thousand analogous cases" — the Committee drew its collective breath — "but I shall forego them in the interests of speed. The genescan of these so-called 'pigs' shows distinct avian characteristics." *Thanks, along with the wings, to the outrageous appetites of Bodley Spatula.*

"But —"

"Moreover," the Joat continued inexorably, "it would make no difference if they really *were* pigs. The Act says: 'Landbirds, seabirds, groundbirds, birds of prey, and *any manner of winged creature of birdlike features and demeanour*.'"

The enquiry was adjourned amid uproar.

\* \* \*

Billy and Moira sat on a couch watching the holovix newsround. Between advertisements the story emerged. By a six-to-two vote the Committee of Enquiry had adjudged the Ankershou pig to be a species of flightless ground-bird, within the definitions of the Wildfowl Protection Act. If the media had any say in it, the creature would henceforth be known as *Pigasus*, the mythical winged pig. The Femm Representative on the Committee had predictably dissented. The others were clearly only too happy to take advantage of the loophole to clamp down on the production of 'canned fruit'. The holovix interviewer did not address the method by which the pigs had acquired wings overnight, having no reason to suspect that they had.

"I've got most of it, I think," murmured Moira. "The genetic mutation was triggered by those chemicals you sprayed from that can, synthesized according to the instructions you told me to wheedle out of poor old Boddles."

"You did a good job, there. What *did* you promise him? Do you intend to deliver?"

"Don't ask, I might tell you. What I don't see, though, is how there was time for the mutation to take effect."

"But there were seventeen thousand years," said the Joat. "Didn't you listen to the archaeological report?"

"But with my own eyes I *saw* the ruins made only days ago by a mass of maurauding pigs! Today they're ancient and overgrown, and every pig on the planet has suddenly sprouted wings! I just don't get it."

"Ankershou has a twistar sun. There are time distortions near a Penrose twistar. They can be used to speed time up so that seventeen thouand years pass in a few hours. You just expand the twistar's zone of influence until it extends beyond the planet's orbit, using a —"

"Photosphere penrotovator!"

"Exactly," said the Joat. "To — er — plough up the magnetic field," he added apologetically.

"But what about the Femm at the base? Did they all... die?"

"Of course."

"Oh, Billy. You're a mass-murderer and I'm your accomplice."

The Joat hastened to reassure her. "No, no. Not at all. Although to us it took only a fraction of a second, they lived out the fullness of their lives. We just imposed a life-sentence in Ankershou jail, which they all thoroughly deserved. They must have wondered why their communications were disrupted so totally, and why nobody ever came to relieve them. It must have seemed like a monster of a magnetic storm."

"But why have none survived? Didn't they breed?"

"Miracles I achieve daily, but some things are impossible. How many female Femm did you see on Ankershou?"

"Oh." She fiddled uncomfortably with one of the tassels that trimmed the couch. "I still feel unhappy about taking the law into our own hands. What about their families?"

"Femm don't have families, they have brood-chambers. Anyway, we didn't take the law into our own hands — we took *justice* into our own hands. Never confuse the two, Moira. Justice is a big holistic concept: *bad people should be punished.* The law is a hopelessly complicated attempt to quantify a qualitative idea. *This* degree and type of badness is to be punished by *this* size of fine... But the law can never catalogue all kinds of badness in advance, and the really serious crooks always operate beyond the law's imagination. Our *consciences* are clear — I don't care what laws we broke."

"You put a lot of trust in your own personal sense of ethics."

"I heard no complaints from the Committee of Enquiry. But a lot of the credit — if that's the word — should go to you. It all came together when you made that remark about pigs having wings. And our pun-loving porcine pals provided us with —"

Moira grinned. "A writ of *habeas porcus?*"

# 15   The Battle of Gladstone's Gap

The left fluke slithered past the grasping gloves of the centre skingle and crashed into the vantage-box in a shower of styrene padding. Sections of the crowd jumped to their feet and yelled, while others sat in glum silence. Then the umpires declared a mis-pass and those standing howled their derision, while those seated rose to their feet and cheered. Arguments, mostly good-natured, were pursued by those whose seats bordered rival areas, although a Barasshanti supporter of the Ambrosian Wanglers became sufficently enraged to pour a bucket of jusper over a quartet of Humans whose preference, stated loudly and repeatedly, was for the Maverick Gurus. She continued to protest her innocence as two ushers led her away.

Snoosh Merfund sold the last five packets of popkern in his tray to a huge lady Grynth with six cubs in tow, and left them bickering over how to share them out. Sweat was forming where the brim of his lemon-yellow topper met his forehead, trickling down his nose, and dripping on to his crimson bow tie. Despite the air-conditioning, it always got hot inside the HyperDome. He found a service asdec and dropped fifty floors to the basement. Stock up, sell, stock up, sell... it was no life for a budding composer of classical church-organ symphonies, but his instrument was too large for busking in the ambleways and he had to finance his studies somehow.

"Myrv? Gimme a coupla doz popkern, five crimpets, a 16-pack of dipsi, an' twenny sticks of glurk." He slipped the tray off over his head and rummaged in the pockets of his purple pantaloons looking for his sales chit.

"Comin' up. Glurk's goin' well today."

"Yeash. Fans get so excited on Trophy Day, they shout themselves even hoarser than usual. Need lubrication for the throat."

"Me too. Wanna beer?"

"Not right now, Myrv. On duty."

"Good crowd."

"Yeash, Trophy Day brings them in, that's guaranteed. *And* all the bigwigs with season-tickets and private balcs. Couldn't keep them away. Good money up there in tips, they say. Too bad I don't have the contacts to swing the upper levels."

"Yeash, shame."

Snoosh packed the goods into his tray, adjusted the straps where they passed behind his chequered green neckband, and started off along a side-passage that formed a natural short-cut to the main concourse. He never knew the gel-dart had hit him. He was about to murmur his thanks to the stranger who took hold of his tray as his knees began to buckle, but everything went black. Five minutes later he was curled up in his underclothes behind an old crate, out for a guaranteed two hours.

It would be more than enough.

The stranger, now clad in Snoosh's uniform — he thought it rather dashing, but his taste in clothes had always been questionable — and bearing that worthy's tray, traversed the main concourse. He did something to a maglock barring the entrance to a service tunnel, stepped through, took a quick look at the guidelines running along the walls in thirty distinctive shades of colour, and set off for the asdec to the top-level balconies. According to his sources, he wanted the right wing of jasmine level, which made sense because that was where you got the best view of the ice-chute, the one they always showed on HV so that it felt wrong watching the game from any other angle, and even though those that he sought were unlikely to be concentrating fully on the game, they'd certainly take the best seats in the dome as a matter of principle.

He would have preferred one of the more powerful figures in the hierarchy, but their defences would be impenetrable. He'd had enough trouble finding this opportunity as it was. It would suffice.

He located the entrance to the balcony, adjusted his topper, and settled down to wait, rummaging through his stock as if looking for something elusive. The upper levels were almost deserted. That meant there would be very little protective covering.

As if to prove the point, a grey-uniformed usher approached.

"Hey, you!"

"Yeash?"

"You're not the regular foofag for this level! Let's see your ID."

The stranger reached into his pantaloon pocket and withdrew a flat rectangle. The usher stared at it. "That's not a —" There was a flash of light, so brief that anyone passing would not have noticed it, and the usher's eyes took on a blank appearance.

"The regular foofag is suffering from the after-effects of a compression wave on the ambleway and I've been assigned to assist him. You've seen my ID, and it's fine. You've got better things to do than talk to me."

The usher glared at him. "I've seen your ID, and it's fine. I've got better things to do than talk to you!"

"As you say." The light flashed again. The usher shook his head, as if in bewilderment, and walked off down the passage. A second foofag, dressed similarly in lemon topper and purple pantaloons, passed him. The usher saw nothing untoward in this, merely nodding in recognition. Then the new foofag saw his self-styled assistant.

"Hey, you!"

"Yeash?"

"You're not the regular foofag for this level! Let's have your ID."

*People*, thought Billy the Joat, *are so predictable*. He reached into his pantaloon pocket...

The second foofag shortly departed. He was, he said, urgently needed at basement level. He had left his tray on the floor. The Joat swapped it for his, and looked at the order-pad.

> *Mr. Wynstun Eton IV*
> > *1 bag home-made popkern*
> > *1 sachet diet dipsi*
> > *1 packet banana-flavoured glurk*
> *Mz. Sylvy Ziggle*
> > *1 box chocolate-covered kumquats*
> > *1 flagon champagne*

You can judge people by their tastes. In other people, as well as food.

From his pantaloons the Joat produced a miniature syringe, and discharged its contents into the dipsi sachet through the weld in the plastic. It should pass inspection.

He pressed the button for entry. After a few moments the door slid to one side, and a heavy-set character in a dark blue uniform and a darker scowl barred his way. "Yes?"

"Order for Mr. Eton."

"Give here."

The Joat passed him the tray. "You look happy in your job, mister. How do you —"

"Cut cackle, sonny. Wait — I run snoop!" The guard passed a commercial poison-detector over the tray. "Look clean." *If you mean it's perfectly edible and harmless, you're right*. But there are substances that do no lasting harm, and so pass a standard snoop, while having really quite dramatic effects. A feature is a bug that can't be eliminated. The snoop manufacturers do not advertise this feature of their equipment. "Right," said the guard, satisfied. "Bog off, sonny."

"Um — excuse me, sir, but you haven't paid the bill."

The other grunted in disdain. "Much?"

"Fifty-seven thirty-five."

The bodyguard produced a cashdisk from his pocket and spoke to it. The transaction glowed on the disk, and a corresponding figure appeared on the register that formed part of the Joat's tray. "Happy now, eel-face?"

"Delighted," muttered the Joat. "We must have these conversations more often." And left.

The next bit was going to be tricky.

* * *

It would take about twenty minutes before the cocktail of 'harmless' drugs permeated Wynstun Eton's stomach-walls, assuming he polished off his diet dipsi as soon as he got it — which on past form was likely, for Eton wasn't a patient man with his pleasures.

During that time the Joat removed himself from his foofag uniform — a pity, he really liked the topper — and then from the HyperDome, ensconcing himself in the back of a twelve-metre tramper parked in the lot outside. He injected the contents of a second syringe into a vein in his forearm, and settled down to wait.

Right on cue, he felt a ghostly hand kneading his thigh. The magneurex that he had administered to Wynstun Eton was starting to take effect. The Joat had realised how useful that substance would be during the Ankershou business, and had taken steps to ensure an illicit supply, with very much the present application in mind. Voices and lights, fuzzy but growing clearer by the second, began to wander through his head.

"No, Wynnie honey, I doan wannanother glass! Oo *knows* how much I adore *real* Triglem— Trimleg— Trigmellian champagne! Wannanother *flagon!*"

"Sylvy, you're drunk."

"Only an itsy-bitsy tipsy, hunsy-bunsy-wunsy." *Yuk.*

"Oh, all right. Whatever my pet wants, she shall have."

"Wynnie, oo's a *darling!* Come here while I take off my — hey, you all right?"

"I — feel a bit funny."

"Oo's drunk too?

"On a damned diet dipsi? No, I feel a bit..." *When's that bloody hypnodyne going to take hold? I can't take control until he responds!* "I'm getting voices... in my head..."

"Shall I call Jovani?" *If she does, I'm up the creek... Come on, come on!*

"Wug... Who... No, no, it's... I feel better now." *At last.* "Must have been the fizz in the dipsi. Bad for my stomach. I'm an old man, Sylvy, and I've been overdoing things."

"Oo's as strong as a bull, hunsykins, and little me will help oo prove it!" The Joat was experiencing a form of split personality, and finding it quite unsettling. While one part of his brain made Wynstun Eton's body deal with Sylvy as she wished to be dealt with — an unpleasantly voyeuristic task, not helped by Eton's obsesity and Sylvy's gushingly girlyish act, which wasn't even convincing — another was engaged in a battle of wills with Eton's mind. It was a strong mind, like a petulant child's.

It must have seemed even more peculiar to Wynstun Eton, watching his own body being taken over by an unseen invader, unable too control his own mouth to raise the alarm. That was the hypnodyne. Then the magneurex kicked in as well.

>>What's going on? Who are you?<<

>>Call me Nemesis. I want information.<<

>>Get out of my mind, damn you!<<

>>Soon, soon... Just let me rummage through your memories... Mmm, fascinating, but not quite what I'm looking for... Wonderful! Oh, wonderful! Just keep it flowing, Wynstun, this is real gold...<<

The hypnodyne left Wynstun Eton IV unable to resist the ransacking, but fully aware that it was happening. The magneurex laid his mind wide open. It was terrifying. Working fast, the Joat drained the Etonian's memory of everything of value relating to Jole Jarneyvore, the *Hubble*, the *Pontryagin*, the Femm, and Sharraby Breach. He didn't have time to analyse what he'd found, but there was plenty — much of it involving Kray Harrow. In a few minutes the amnesiax would hit Eton's cortex and wipe away his memories of the mental invasion. A three-way cocktail, perfect. If it worked.

If not, Billy was dead. Harrow would see to that.

To pass the time usefully, he skimmed through other areas of Eton's memory. He was becoming better at the dual body/mind control now, and Sylvy was getting more than she had bargained for. A joat with only half his mind on the job was more than a match for the elderly and jaded Etonian. She seemed to be enjoying it. By the time the Joat had finished he'd got enough material for a regiment of blackmailers, and a sick feeling in his stomach. It wasn't that the man's mind was a cesspit of evil — not a bit of it. *He just didn't think of any of his past actions as being wrong.*

Evil is cleanliness itself in comparison to sincere hypocrisy.

The Joat felt Eton's most recent memories vanishing as the microcapsules containing the amnesiax began to dissolve in his stomach acid. He breathed a sigh of relief, waited a few moment more to be sure, and gave himself a magneurex antidote to withdraw his mind from Eton's.

Sylvy Ziggle lay back on her couch, exhausted, with a sly grin on her elfin face. She giggled. "Oh, Wynnikins, you're a bull all right! I've never known you like that before! Whatever got into you?"

Eton shook his head. It ached like the devil. "I don't know."

"Wynnie, that was *the* most *terrific* experience I've ever had! Talk about making the galaxy move! Did you feel it too? You must have!"

Eton's face took on a puzzled look. "Galaxy? Move? Sylvy, I don't remember a damned thing."

\* \* \*

**Battle of Gladstone's Gap**

*73 BQ (2474 Old Calendar). Decisive engagement in the Human/Grynth wars that culminated in the formation of the Duality, precursor of today's Quaternity. Historians are generally agreed that it was the unexpected outcome of this battle that persuaded the Human race to seek a negotiated settlement. The Grynth force under Third Strategist Gorrhuf Rrowl was in possession of the star systems of the Minor Orioles and Cumberknowle Prime. A massive frontal attack being out of the question, the Human Admiral Horace ('Hurricane') Whistler despatched a task force of radar-silent needle-bombers concentrated on six key installations. Grynth intelligence agents gained access to the flight-plans and the task force was defeated. While Human attention was focussed on this engagement the Grynth launched an unexpected strike against the heavily-defended munitions world on the satellite of My Delight. The impact of three grade VI proton bombs cracked open the satellite's crust and the moon of My Delight was broken into fragments by the planet's gravity. This loss caused severe logistic problems for the Human forces and a settlement followed within two months.*

*. . .*

*In 23 BQ, after a statutory lapse of fifty years, documents released under the Information Freedom Provision revealed that the crucial intelligence was supplied to the Grynth by a Human filing clerk named Milverton Waghort [which see], working at EMPCINC on the staff of General Hilton Wheedle. By this time Waghort had been ten years deceased. A period of intense debate whether he should be considered a traitor to the Human cause or a far-seeing visionary led to a consensus view, still held today, that he was both.*

. . .

*Formation of the Duality in 72BQ was instrumental in bringing about the Duality/Barasshanti alignment of 17 BQ, which in turn created an alliance so powerful that the Femm were persuaded to join the combined races rather than fight them. The Quaternity [which see] emerged from this unstable political period as the powerful force for unification that it remains today.*

### Waghort, Milverton Hurvey

*Born 124 BQ (2423 Old Calendar). Devout Grudnidlist. His wife Kathinza (born Grummstone) died in the Rufous Plagues of 99BQ leaving him to bring up an only daughter, Petublia. Petublia Waghort graduated from DeLameter College on Quahootze Minim in 75BQ. In 73BQ she changed her name and emigrated, possibly to Noah's Ark Delta. MW disappeared in mysterious circumstances in 73BQ immediately after betrayal of Humanity / visionary creation of the Duality in Battle of Gladstone's Gap [which see].*

The Joat tossed the holofax printout into a wastebasket. Once read, never forgotten. Propaganda and all.

He now knew what Sherryl Eton had meant when she said that "there wasn't going to have been a Quaternity". He knew what the Etonians had planned to do, and why. He knew, in broad outline, how. He had a general idea of where. And the answer to 'when?' depended on your frame of reference.

Jole must have stumbled across some of the Etonians' preparations when the *Edwin Hubble* was exploring Sharraby Breach. Since their plans had evidently not succeeded, he must have blocked them. Violently, perhaps — why else would Sherryl Eton have called him a murderer? Equally clearly, the plan had only been set back, not stopped once and for all. Otherwise the Etonians wouldn't still be trying.

The fools. Did it never occur to them that the Femm would never honour an agreement to hand over power to anybody else? Least of all to *them?*

His earlier guesses had been accurate. Something in Sharraby Breach — probably in conjunction with freewave technology, the Etonian connection — had the capacity to induce time travel. The Femm were planning to use it to destroy the Quaternity before it ever began. From the information he had extracted from Wynstun Eton IV, it was a dead cert that what they planned was the assassination of

Milverton Waghort, with Kray Harrow as the hit-man. Without Waghort's act of high-principled treason, the Human forces would have won the Battle of Gladstone's Gap, and the Duality would never have formed. Then the Human forces, over-stretched trying to keep the Grynth subdued, would have been no match for the Barasshanti. By the same token, the resulting Barasshanti empire would have fallen to the stronger and highly organized Femm.

It was this scenario that Jole Jarneyvore had halted in its tracks. The Joat was convinced that his father was still alive; indeed this could be the only reason why the Etonians had not tried again, and succeeded. For twenty-one years, Jole had held them off.

Where? How?

Wynstun Eton IV wasn't privy to information of that quality. But he knew where it could be found.

* * *

"I can find nothing physigally wrong," said the Femm psychologician.

"But?"

"You are perceptive, Mr. Eton. Yes, 'but'. But... I have reason to believe your mind has been tampered with. There is a short disgontinuity — an interval of less than ten minutes — in your memory."

"At the HyperDome."

"Yes."

"I've already told you that!"

"Indeed you have. But what you do not yourself know is that the flaw in your memory-chain shows definite signs of being induced by a memory-wipe drug. Probably oblivium or amnesiax."

"You're finding out which one, of course."

"Yes. It is fortunate that you took the precaution of storing a blood-sample." Wynstun Eton IV grunted in annoyance. *Fortunate? No, it was routine. My medibot sees to that. Damned interfering nuisance. 'No alcohol and a fat-free diet.' Blucky mechanical wimp.*

An elderly Barasshanti technician emerged from behind a screened-off area, bearing a long strip of gel. "The results are ready, Dr. Myrjjylly."

The Femm held the gelstrip up to the light. "Thank you, ap-Qyft." She compared its markings with those on a standard chart. "As I thought. Amnesiax. But also... ah, yes: hypnodyne. A remarkable gombination. Do you have any idea what it means?"

"Someone drugged me, that's what it means! And when I find out who, I'll have them mindwiped!"

The psychologician nodded, a Human gesture she had picked up during training. "But with what motive? We must ask ourselves that question. Hypnodyne is, loosely speaging, a truth-drug. Amnesiax, in contrast, produces forgetfulness. In gombination, they suggest an attempt to extract information from your mind without your knowledge. Can such an attempt have been made within the last forty-eight hours? It is a virtual certainty that it was made at the ball-game, if at all, but we must keep an open mind."

Eton's flabby face quivered with the effort of thinking. "It couldn't have happened while I was at my mansion... and I only left once, to go to the Game. My bodyguards were on duty there, it was a private balcony... nobody was allowed in."

The psychologician coiled the gelstrip for storage and further analysis, twining it round her foredigits with her mind elsewhere. "And thus nobody had the opportunity to interrocate you? Gurious."

"There was Sylvy, of course, but she doesn't have that sort of mind. Doesn't actually have any sort of mind, really..."

"It might perhaps have been a *failed* attempt? The drugs administered through some intermediate agency, but the would-be interrogator kept away by your bodyguard?"

"I don't like the sound of that. It would be complacent to assume the attempt failed. The fact remains that an attempt was ma—"

"Uhomm! What is this?" Dr. Myrjjylly held the last metre of the gelstrip against the light and squinted.

"You've found something?"

"Yes. A faint trace."

"You nearly missed it. I won't tolerate incompetence."

"If you doubt my gompetence, hire someone better. Never before in this part of the biochemigal spectrum have I seen anything. That is why I did not notice it before. It cannot be a common chemigal, it requires further analysis. I will set ap-Qynt to work at once, and call you as soon as he has identified it."

\* \* \*

According to Wynstun Eton's memories, all the answers that the Joat sought were to be found on the world of Araster nex-Thopt, one of the million dead worlds of the Barrens. Only it wasn't a dead world, it was the nerve centre for the collaboration between the Etonians and the Femm.

The Joat would have to be the fly that entered the spider's parlour. But this fly was going to be a wasp. He prepared in meticulous detail, loading *Lindilu* with food, software, weapons, and machinery of various kinds. He told Immigration it was for a hunting trip. Gods know what the Immigration official made of the quicksetting foam, rolls of sheet plastic, expanded metal beams, and spraypaint, but those were free of export controls.

How do you penetrate a secret installation on an apparently dead world, manned by superior forces that can see every approaching vessel in a sphere a light year across?

You don't approach through that sphere.

You don't exactly 'approach' at all.

You just arrive.

And to do that, you pay a surprise visit to Poor Yorick and borrow an interphase transfer plane generator. And you hope Alaya de Flore Strooghn will give permission, because it will destroy the subconscious hopes you have of eventually resuming your relationship with her, if you have to take it without. Assuming you can accomplish that without making a fool of yourself, you express your eternal gratitude, take your leave politely before things get awkward, and make tracks towards Araster nex-Thopt. You've got to get close to use the transfer plane, no more than a third of a light-year. The star rho Dodendron is that close, and has a suitable gravity profile. With foam, plastic, metal, and an artistic job of spraypaint you will construct an inflatable decoy, to gain a few minutes if needed. You know you can pull it off, provided the enemy doesn't get wind that you're coming.

If they do, you're dead.

\* \* \*

"Magneurex."

"Yes. In sufficient dosage for short-range mind transference."

Wynstun Eton was sharp enough to work the rest out for himself. The physical presence of an interrogator would be unnecessary. Hypnodyne to lower his mental defences, magneurex to collect the information from a distance, amnesiax to make the victim forget what had happened.

Jovani must be replaced, the man was incompetent. Hrost could take charge, he'd been angling for the job for months. In fact, Hrost could dispose of Jovani. That could come in useful later if he started to get ideas of his own.

*Magneurex.* Who could have obtained a supply of magneurex? Even the Etonians couldn't, what with SpaDe having such a tight grip on the Ankershou supply-line...

Ankershou.

*Jarneyvore!* He was a dolt not to have seen it at once. Like father, like son. A meddler. A nuisance. Interfering vermin. And now Jarneyvore had crossed the dividing line — he had become vermin who knew too much. Gods, what did he know? What *didn't* he know? It was a disaster.

There was one salvation. The full power of the Etonian dynasty against a single, infinitesimal problem. Search and Destroy. It would be as quick, and as simple, as squishing a gnit. He reached for a phone.

In a few minutes he learned that the Joat had indeed been on planet during the period of the Game, final confirmation if any was needed. Within an hour he knew every item of equipment that the Joat had loaded on board *Lindilu*. A hunting expedition? Twaddle. Before the day was out, he was informed of the Joat's arrival on Poor Yorick. The Etonians had spies there. They had spies everywhere. But the network was thin on Poor Yorick, and he learned only that the Joat stayed just a few hours, and had loaded a package on board *Lindilu* immediately before departure. A tracking satellite added one useful item of information: Jarneyvore had set course in the general direction of the Barrens.

*Araster nex-Thopt.* Of course. The Joat was trying to track down his father.

Wynstun knew that the elder Jarneyvore had caused the Etonians an immense amount of trouble, though he'd never been told exactly what. He did know that important secret research, having something to do with Jarneyvore senior and stasis fields, was being carried out on Araster-nex-Thopt. Had Billy the Joat found out?

Much good it would do him. The Etonians would be waiting. A full alert. Pull back all ships not on essential duty, reassign them to base. They'd track Jarneyvore's ship by observation and computer-projection. Once it got within ten light years of Araster nex-Thopt, they'd blow it and its owner apart into their constituent quarks.

# 16   Flare from the Jumbles

A hundred and twenty-four warships held station in a defensive englobement at the vertices of a geodesic dome centred upon Araster nex-Thopt. They were linked by freewave, and each had its detector-screens fully deployed, forming a complete sphere surrounding the planet. Nothing could cross that barrier without being spotted; and if any intruder was detected, there was ample firepower to deal with it.

Messages flashed across the sub-ether. "Target has left Poor Yorick." "Target is short-phading the Jumbles." "Target has taken a passenger aboard." "Query identity of passenger?" "Passenger did not pass through normal channels. ID presently unknown." "Target has been delayed by a black nova. Communications in Balzac and Garrison Sectors are disrupted."

Commander Tory Eton rasped his teeth together in displeasure. The idiots had lost him! Now he would have to rely on computer simulations and maximum likelihood estimates of the target's whereabouts. He set his technicians to work, and when they had rechecked their prediction and found no errors, he aligned his weapons accordingly. At the appointed time, a selected region of space would momentarily come to resemble the interior of a star.

The grim reaper had a date with Billy the Joat.

\* \* \*

The Jumbles.

Here, dusted across space in a twisted horseshoe, a billion asteroids danced stately sarabandes to a score by Newton, lyrics by Einstein. *Largo con gravitá.* To avoid phase alignment errors, wise travellers pass through the Jumbles in sequences of short phades. Thus did the Joat on his chosen route to Araster nex-Thopt.

He was looking for somewhere to hide for a few days, to build an inflatable dummy of *Lindilu*. Few ships were willing to lose the time spent in short-phading the Jumbles, so by choosing that route he would attract less attention than if he hung around near the regular space-lanes. The dummy would have its own miniature PhaDER drive — an easy trick when there were no life-support systems to complicate the design. It was a precaution that he hoped he would never need; a decoy for his approach to the dead world that wasn't.

It was while cruising through the Jumbles on standby, making astrogational checks, that Belphoebe noticed something extraordinary and drew it to the Joat's attention. A shimmering nebula of pink light. It covered the forward screen, a ghostly veil through which the barely diminished stars shone. He adjusted the magnification, but the closer the view, the less detail there was to see. He cursed his stupidity and turned the magnification control the other way, to view the object from a distance, in the hope that it might make more sense. It then became obvious what it was — but it still made no sense.

It was a gigantic thumb.

He assumed it must be some sort of large-scale holographic projection. Its size must be a trick of perspective. He switched on the freewave and asked the computer for a full band scan. Then the thumb jerked in a familiar gesture; the fist beneath unravelled and put forth a finger. The finger pointed to a small asteroid.

*I guess it's clear where you want me to go. A trap? If so, it's a damned peculiar one.* Curiosity and joats. He told himself it must be a stranded traveller, in which case he was duty bound to offer aid, however awkward it would be for his own plans.

And, in a sense, it was.

Since he was going to pick up a stranger, he didn't want the dummy inspected at close quarters. So before approaching the asteroid, he passed the decoy out of the airlock, inflated it, and sent it on its way to Araster nex-Thopt, programmed to return to the normal aphasic universe just before he currently expected *Lindilu* to arrive. The program could always be altered by freewave if his plans changed.

As *Lindilu* homed in on the stranger's freewave beam he saw a lone figure sitting on a rock. It wore a vacuum-suit and carried what appeared to be a backpack. A spindly instrument was erected at its feet. It waved as he landed, folded up its equipment, and sauntered across towards him, so that by the time he had extended the ramp to the airlock it was perched on another rock not ten metres away. The freewave crackled. "Got room for passenger?" It was a high-pitched voice, but with a hard edge.

"You stranded?"

"Could be. Got no ship, that plain as nose on face."

"Try any funny stuff and I'll lase you to a cinder and blow you out of the airlock in a puff of smoke."

"Friendly person."

He let the figure into the airlock, which he cycled up to the point at which it filled with air. He depaqued the inner door to get a good look at the stranger before doing anything irrevocable. "Take off the suit, put it on the floor along with your bag." The stranger gave a curt nod and unzipped the suit. "I want to check you're not carrying concealed weapons."

"Only those gifted at birth."

An odd accent. The stranger was clad in a skin-tight yellow undersuit, with no place to hide a conventional weapon. The weapons gifted at birth were more than adequate, and concealed only in a technical sense. "Name is Flare."

"Funny name for a woman. Well, on second thoughts — "

"Family name. Prefer to what given as personal name."

"Well, Flare, as far as I can tell, you're clean. You can come in, but don't do anything sudden." He let the airlock finish its cycle and she stepped through. "Why were you sitting out there on an asteroid?"

Flare tossed her hair. "Hike-hitching."

"I saw the thumb. But nobody hitches in space."

"Not by choice." She stared past him towards the galley area. "Got good chef on this heap?"

"There's a food-processor, yes."

"Starving. Hustle up meal, hear how happened."

\* \* \*

*She doesn't use pronouns... or articles, definite or indefinite. It's the grammar that's out of whack, not the accent. Wonder where she comes from?* But the Joat's mind was only half on the problem of his passenger's origins. The other half was listening to her sorry tale.

"So told manager, look, old-fashioned girl expect cabin of own. Won't be hustle. But manager think know better. Try to grab."

"Bastard."

"That's what told. Then hit where hurts with fire-extinguisher."

"Ouch."

"Bastard seemed think so. Problem was, had darter and managed to line up on head before got good kick at. After that expected rape, but bastard no longer in mood for that kind games so dumped in middle of Jumbles with week's air-supply. Promised come back when air run low, see if changed mind."

"I don't understand how anybody could behave like that."

"If grow up backstreets Chuila City, sure would. Look after self, take what can get."

"You *approve* of that sort of behaviour?" said the Joat, aghast.

"Approve? Who to approve? Think it make difference what happen when bastard get back whether anyone *approve?* What can *do* is what count."

*A direct philosophy of life*, thought the Joat. *And one by whose standards I am about to be found wanting.* "Flare, I'd like offer to wait around till he gets back, and help you fix up a surprise. But I can't afford the time. Really, I'm not just saying that. I'm sorry."

She gave him a direct stare, one that seemed to look deep inside his mind. It was a most disturbing stare. Whatever she thought she saw, it seemed to satisfy her. "Not important. In hurry too. Not planning stay. Deal with bastard own time and place. Not want help."

"You accepted a ride."

"No choice. Just not expect anything in return." The Joat had never encountered anything like it. Not indifference, not hostility, just fierce independence. Too fierce, and nobody is truly independent. Sad. And none of his business. But it *was* his business to know his passenger's background. "You said 'manager'. You a performing artiste or something? And how did you make that holographic thumb?"

She laughed. "*Artiste?* Fancy word, simple thing. Shape-poet. Create — also fancy word, better 'make' — make shapes with holo-projector, tell — not stories, tell life. Real life as is. Was on tour. Manager arrange. Provide transport. Dirty bastard have secret plan for payment not written in contract. But that discuss already."

The Joat had encountered few poets, even fewer whose stock in trade was holographic images, not verbal, and never a poet who couldn't say "I". Indeed most poets seemed to say little else. Did her mangled grammar account for the non-verbal nature of her poetry? Was it a consequence? For a moment the Joat felt he was on the track of some dark secret, but that was silly. He shrugged the feeling away. "I'll drop you off somewhere, first chance I get. If you want to make charges, that's up to you and the constables."

"No proof. Fix own way. Later." She changed the subject. "Which way going?"

"Uh — Samish."

"Out towards Barrens. Not many go Samish."

"You know it?"

"No. Once knew someone from Samish. Wind-devils, sandstorms, hot like furnace. Why going Samish?"

"Business. My business."

She reddened. "Sorry. Not place to ask."

"Information's free. If I don't want to give it, I don't have to." The Joat was rummaging through the astrogation files. "Where are you headed? If I know, I can choose the best place to drop you."

"Psamathe." There was a kind of pleading in her voice. "Got to get to Psamathe. Fast."

"Next stop on your poetic itinerary? Let's see what can be done." The Joat reviewed the data. "Nearest I get to Psamathe is

Maugrave... It's a bit out of my way, but I'll drop you there if that would help."

"How long?"

"Two days." She didn't look happy, but she nodded all the same.

* * *

Flare's face was scornful. "Not fall for old line, Jarneyvore. Saying out of energy cells next. Not wash."

"Don't be silly, Flare. We're not out of energy cells. We just can't make the fifth phade to Maugrave for another week. Nothing to do with me, sorry."

The news worried her. "Why not?"

"Kappa Cailzie's event horizon has just degenerated. It's created a transverse dislocation shockwave, propagating along the phase-lattice cocycles. The transvectant mesomodule can't kill the homotopy residuals when the DeRham exoboundary develops cusps, so an essential supersingularity forms and the ship becomes unstable to escalade modes."

"What all *that* buzz mean?"

"There's a whale of a space-storm coming and we've got to stay put."

Flare stamped her foot. "Must get Psamathe *now!*" She began calling up charts on Belphoebe's astrogation module. "Joat give up too damned quick." Billy wasn't really watching her: he was distracted by worries about his decoy. Freewave communication didn't work during space-storms, so the dummy was stuck on its pre-programmed course. Maybe it would go into escalade itself. He rather hoped so, because the alternative was that it would arrive a week or more ahead of *Lindilu*. A space-storm has not figured in his plans. So, while the Joat was wasting time regretting one tactical error, he made a worse one. He didn't pay attention to his passenger. Her fingers raced across the keys, and she drew a yellow arc across the screen with a light-pen. "How *this* for course alternative?"

The Joat stared at the display in horror. "Through *Sharraby Breach?* Gods, I'd rather tackle a dislocation wave! Space and time don't just get *bent* in the Breach, they get sliced into little pieces and fed to the philosophers! *Anything* could happen in there."

"Nonsense! Old wife tale."

"Flare, Sharraby Breach is under SpaDe interdict. If we go into it without official permission, they'll be after us like a boggie on shronkscent trail."

"If move fast, Spade won't catch." She began pushing buttons. Before the Joat could stop it, *Lindilu* began to phade.

After ten minutes Flare let her trunk curl into a self-satisfied smirk. "Said was old wife tale," she thrumped. "See? Nothing happen at all."

The Joat looped his tail in pique. "Well, it *could* have," he thrumped back, almost audible in his anger. He metamorphosed into a hairy green jellyfish and draped himself over the lower branches of the navigating-tree. "They say Sharraby Breach is a *weird* place."

"Well, can hear for own nose isn't," thrumped Flare firmly.

"Appearances may be deceptive," protested the jellyfish.

"I'm going to have to agree with myself in a moment," said an identical jellyfish on the branch below. "Us too," chanted seven other jellyfish in unison. They fell to disputing which of them was the most recently timecloned version, until Flare put a scaly paw firmly in the middle of each of them and glared through her seventy-three eyesockets so frostily that they fell silent and vanished. "Billy Jarneyvore, stop sulking!" she hooted.

One of the jellyfish reappeared, now orange with purple spots. It formed a ball, and expanded like a balloon, becoming more solid by the moment. "All right, Flare, I admit nothing weird's happened yet. But don't go squinching plorbs on my calcafrinth again without asking everybody else afterwards, right?"

"Sorry," thrumped Flare, and ballooned contritely. "Want mungle, make up for it?" The Joat blopped in happiness. When two six-tonne bunglaphoons mungle, it makes a lot of noise and damages the furniture. The bunglaphoons, in a state of advanced erotic excitement, never notice this at the time.

*Much later...*

...the pink haze began to dissipate. The Joat recovered consciousness to the urgent bleeping of the phase transit monitor. They had arrived.

Somewhere.

Before them, against a backdrop of blood-red stardust, was a blotched and surly disc. Regions of buff, grey, black, and blinding white jostled together for room on its ugly face. It looked like a pot of porridge that had been burnt, partially scraped clean, and then used to cook lentil soup. Flare groaned, opened her eyes, saw the screen. "That Maugrave, right?"

Billy consulted Belphoebe. "Wrong." *The stars have all gone a funny colour...*

"Then where? Can't even *navigate* right?"

"Look, it was *you* who — "

"Well, must be through Breach. *Told* nothing happen, just old wife tale." Flare plonked herself down on part of a couch. Her eyes slowly widened as she realised that the rest of it was missing, along with most of her clothes. The Joat belatedly looked about the cabin. The table had been broken into three pieces, its legs splayed like a spattered mockroach. The chairs had been shredded. Something had gnawed a hole in the housing of the air-conditioning fan.

"Flare?" said the Joat, with awe in his voice.

"Yes?" she replied, hastily gathering the remains of a tablecloth around her.

"That old wife sold you a real stinker."

* * *

*Lindilu* had survived, but she had sustained a lot of minor damage. The biggest problem was a burnt-out phase resonator; until it was repaired, phading was out. The smell of burnt insulation pervaded the ship.

The grim reaper had had a date with Billy the Joat... but the Joat had stood him up. Death had arranged a rendezvous at Araster nex-Thopt, but the Joat had detoured into Sharraby Breach. But Death was not so easily frustrated. Billy and Flare were still attempting to straighten out *Lindilu*'s cabin when the alarm sounded. The Joat leaped into the command-seat. "Belphoebe, report!"

"Five cruisers approaching. Femm design. I have reason to suspect them to be hostile."

"What reason?"

"They've just fired a salvo of neutron torpedoes at us."

The Joat rose magnificently to the occasion. Now was not the time to instruct a computer in the finer arts of conversation. Instead he asked calmly, "Time to impact?"

"Three minutes thirty-six seconds."

"That last phade damaged a resonator. Can we outrun them on standby?"

"No, too slow. I'm already taking evasive action."

Billy strapped himself firmly into his seat, motioned to Flare to do likewise. "Give me the count every minute. And put up a map of the positions of the hostile craft and their torpedoes, relative to us."

"Map's on screen now. Three minutes."

The Joat stared at the screen. The enemy vessels were in a tight battle formation. The missiles had fanned out, to outflank any evasive manoeuvres, but would shortly start to bunch together as they focused in on *Lindilu*.

"Get me power for board sixteen, but don't put it through until I say."

"Power ready... now. Two minutes."

The Joat had already removed the covers, revealing a row of bright metallic terminal-blocks. "Flare, give me a hand with this."

"Is what?"

"No time to explain." They lugged the transfer-plane generator across, and Billy pushed a bare wire into the first block. *Dolt! You should have had it rigged up all along!* But nothing recently had gone according to plan and there hadn't been time.

There were half a dozen wires to connect. The screwdriver was like a live thing in his hands. He fumbled with the last wire, and was just screwing it down when *Lindilu* said "One minute."

"Right. Feed me some power." He adjusted several dials, glancing over his shoulder at the screen. "Tight... 'Phoebe, hold steady on present course. No evasive action."

"Will look suspicious, Billy."

"Good point, Flare — but even so, they won't be expecting what's in store. If I can just hold the second plane where I want it... Grab that control-lever, keep the needle in the orange segment. Great, just hold it like that..."

Skirmisher Mym-Phrygglyr, piloting the leading cruiser, watched the fan of torpedoes home in on its target. He'd thought it was a silly idea to withdraw every spare ship to Araster nex-Thopt, and this proved him right. He had no idea how *Lindilu* had arrived in Sharraby Breach, but Billy the Joat would never escape this trap.

The fan shrunk, closer, closer...

Just short of their target, all the torpedoes vanished. Mym-Phrygglyr was still wondering what had happened to them when one rammed him from behind and exploded. Five Femm cruisers ceased to exist. "Got 'em!" yelled Billy the Joat. "Hoist with their own petards!"

Flare couldn't decide which to ask first: what a petard was, or what the Joat had done with his strange piece of equipment. Before she could do either, the Joat had opened an inspection hatch and was poking around inside. There was no time to waste, gods knew whether any other Femm were around, and he might not be able to pull the trick twice. "Better fix that resonator."

Flare bent down to get a good look. "Ugh. What mess, melted plastic like guts of disembowelled hrunthosaur."

"That's a revolting metaphor."

"Am poet. Revulsion one emotion in repertoire. All have use, right time and place."

"Well, this is the *wrong* time and place! We're in enough trouble without bringing disembowellment into it!"

"I regret to report," said Belphoebe, "that you are in more trouble than you realise."

"What?"

"In your haste to wire up the transfer plane generator, you made a poor connection. You were lucky the device held out during the engagement. But part of a circuit blew out just after the last missile went through."

"Shit!" yelled the Joat.

Flare stepped back. "Is bad problem?"

"*Quite* bad. Not the resonator, we've got spares. But the transfer plane generator is custom-made. I bet the failure's in those ceramic frommets that Kmarsk rebuilt."

"No, it's the ploridial fleisiogonemes. Their fine tuning was a bit off."

"Thank you, Belphoebe," said the Joat, who had been proud of his fine tuning. "Let's see — we can fake up some J-plugs and insulation; the main problem is filtering the pneumolic fluid to remove any particles of melted carmodyne released when the osmoceptor burnt up."

"Can solve?" asked Flare.

"Yeah, I can rebuild some of it and repair the rest. I've got to do both, quick, before any more Femm show up. But I can't filter pneumolic fluid in zero-*g*. I need a nice, stable gravity-well."

"We'll have to land."

"Oh no. More delay. *Never* reach Psamathe!"

The Joat muttered something uncomplimentary about Psamathe under his breath, and Flare had the good sense not to hear it. "Phading is out, so it's got to be standby." He called up a mass-density plot to set a safe course. "This is crazy."

"What crazy?"

"The active region of Sharraby Breach is a shell. There's normal space inside, and we're in it. The eye of the hurricane. But that's not the crazy bit. What's crazy is that the inside is bigger than the outside. Much bigger."

"Once had cat like that. Was terrible greedy."

"Yeah, sure. There's an entire *universe* in here! With red stars... We're not *in* Sharraby Breach at all, we passed through it. It's a doorway into a second universe, a parauniverse. Look, you can *see* Sharraby Breach on the screen, behind us... inside out. And there are planets. That revolting blotch over there is the nearest. Pray that it's suitable for a landing, there's nothing else close enough."

Flare placed her fingertips together. "Am selecting suitable choice of god. Ah! Pasquhandromguldyte, deity of soft descents. Am now praying: not interrupt." The Joat suspected she was putting him on. If that was a religion it was one he'd never heard of. She mumbled in the background as he turned the ship and told it to prepare for landing.

The planet grew as the ship dropped towards it. "Status check. Condition of surface."

"*Revolting*," Belphoebe announced.

"What sort of revolting?"

"Hurricane-force winds, acid rain, flash floods. Atmosphere unbreathable. The gravity's OK, though. Passable for a short stay, but it'll never make it as a tourist resort."

"We're not here for the beach," said the Joat. "Take her in. Gently, 'Phoebe, there's a good girl."

\* \* \*

He rebuilt what he could of the transfer plane generator and left Belphoebe to monitor a roboremote that was filtering the pneumolic fluid — a long and tedious task. Then he set to work on the phase resonator. With a pair of pliers in one hand, a solder-gun in the other, and a bunch of wires between his teeth, Billy bent over the terminal tags and began to attach the final connections. It was awkward work, he had to hold his hands virtually in front of his nose... He yelped in suprise, and dropped the lot.

The solder-gun began to burn a hole in the carpet but he didn't notice. He wouldn't have noticed Armageddon.

Flare rushed across to see what had caused the outcry, smelt burning fibre, retrieved the solder-gun and switched it off. Billy sat staring at the back of his hand. "What matter? Hurt hand?"

"N-no. No, I'm all right..." *The ring. His father's green ring.* Green no longer. It flashed in a cycle of colours. Green, yellow, red. Green, yellow, red. Green, yellow, red. It reminded him of something.

"Pretty colours," said Flare. "Red nice, but like amber best."

*Amber*, not yellow! A game. A game four-year-old Billy Jarneyvore used to play with his dad. The treasure-hunt, they called it. Jole would hide the treasure — a cardboard box containing a ten centikroon coin — while Billy was out of the room. Then he would be called in, and try to find it.

"Green, green," his father would say, when he was nowhere near his goal. "Amber," when he was getting closer. "Red!" *You're right on top of it, son.*

Green, amber, red; green, amber, red. *He's here! Somewhere on this planet!* The colours stopped cycling, returned to green. *Here, but some distance away.*

*Cancel Araster nex-Thopt. By sheer luck you've blundered into the place where Jole has been kept, all these years. The obvious place, under your nose. He went in... and he never came out. Where* else *would he be? Dunderhead.*

*The ring is a communicator. He gave it to you for this very purpose. Across twenty-one years, he foresaw this.* Billy the Joat whistled in admiration. *You're a damned good predictor, Dad. No wonder SpaDe gave you the assignment.*

Flare was watching with a puzzled expression. He quickly explained the significance of the flashing lights. "Flare, I'm sorry, but this takes precedence over everything. He's *here*. I've got to go and find him." He tried to fight down the feeling of triumph. As well as the ring, there had been a message: *beware Etonians.*

Repairing the transfer plane generator would just have to wait. He told Belphoebe to suspend filtering and set up a search pattern. "Cover the whole surface, within a distance of two hundred kilometres. If that doesn't work, fill in the gap and fine it down, there's a good girl."

"Pattern computed. An Archimedean spiral, pole to pole."

The last wire was attached. "Right. Lift off, and run the pattern. Stay near the ground. Watch out for anything unusual. And keep an eye open for hostile craft overhead."

\* \* \*

The first spiral sweep found nothing. *Lindilu* began a reverse spiral, bisecting the gap. The Joat watched his ring. Another hour passed. The ring changed to amber.

*You're getting closer, son.*

The yacht slowed and began a tighter, local spiral. Amber faded to green. *Wrong way.* The ship reversed course. Amber. Amber. Amber. *Red!*

*Here.*

Then the lights on Jole's ring stopped flashing.

\* \* \*

Belphoebe had been photographing the surface, and claimed to have found a ruined city. Or maybe not: it didn't look exactly like a city. On the other hand, it didn't look exactly like anything else, either.

Whatever it was, it was artificial, and ruined. The computer had found it in a region that they recognised as the eroded remains of an ancient seabed. It printed out a map, together with false-colour overlays showing where the continental masses had once been. The Joat dropped the sheet into an enhancement projector, so that a blow-up appeared on the wall.

"Fascinating," he said. "Flare, do you see?"

"Where? Don't see anything."

"Not yet. But with side-illumination," — Billy tapped the pads to rotate the holo and enhance the contrast —"behold!"

"*Pyramids?*"

"Some sort of raised structure. Hexagonal."

"Earthworks?"

"UUV densities say not. Rockpiles."

"Traces very faint," said Flare. "Even enhanced."

"Driftdust. Now, watch." The projector's tiny brain set to work, adding a line here, erasing there, restoring parts that its algorithms told it *ought* to have existed. The holo melted and flowed on the wall, and locked into focus. If those were pyramids, there were an awful lot of them. Hundreds. Arranged in a pattern of intersecting spirals.

"Spirals," said Flare. "Spirals. Where have seen spirals like that? They seem —"

"Sunflower seeds?"

"What have health-foods got do with —"

"No, Flare, what I meant was, you get the same patterns in sunflower seeds. Fibonacci spirals."

"That significant?"

"No. But it reminds me of something... Damn it, I'm too tired even to *think*. We'll each get four hours' sleep while the other keeps watch. Then we go back down to the surface and take a look."

The ground around the ruins was treacherous soft sand. Beyond it were large thermal areas. The nearest landing site that Belphoebe deemed safe was thirty kilometres away from the ruins. She had set the roboremote filtering again, but the transfer plane generator wouldn't be fully operational for a couple of days.

They would just have to walk.

# 17   Prism Planet

Belphoebe gave it a code name: Hurscaffl.

Hurscaffl was a mud-slimed monstrosity of ocean and rock where sudden torrents of acid rain etched bleak landscapes in the smashed limestone; where wind-devils whirled abrasive with crystalline sulphur; where dust-dunes groped insidious fingers across howling continents to besmirch themselves in acid lakes.

Two suited figures marched in silhouette along the blood-red edge of the world. Hurscaffl rolled; blood clotted to violet, then black. The stars came out, in strange colours.

The Joat took first watch. Flare unlaced her pack, which contained utensils and food. They wore survival-suits, for the atmosphere of Hurscaffl was an unappealing mixture of nitrous oxide and hydrogen sulphide. She nibbled without appetite at her food, while the Joat perched himself on a sulphurous outcrop, weighing shadows.

"Will rain tonight?"

Billy raised his eyes. "I don't think so, Flare. But we should keep the protective covers ready just in case. With luck, we should reach Fibonacci City tomorrow."

\* \* \*

Mid-morning found them beside a lake of boiling mud, plotting a safe path between erratically spouting geysers. Flare scanned the area through binoculars, occasionally murmuring to the Joat, who made annotations on a rough map, consulting flickering characters on his wristband remote. Finally he collapsed the binoculars and returned them to his pouch, and they moved into the pulsating steam-ridden area.

The desert land rose and fell in shallow steps, as if the surface was a thin shell that had cracked into plates and subsided. There was a pervasive smell of sulphur and the rocks were streaked with purple and yellow stains. Hot mud welled from fissures in the ground and flowed sluggishly into depressions, forming a crazed jumble of interconnecting pools. The surface was cratered with soft, wrinkled mounds that periodically spat gobbets of boiling mud, and spurting jets of water vented clouds of steam that drifted unpredictably across their path. In places strange, tumbling extrusions of sulphur formed themselves into convoluted mounds and towers, ranged against the sky like a procession of mythic monsters.

They were skirting a particularly large pool of ochre mud, when a flattish rock ahead of them moved. Rising from the hollow that it concealed, it scuttled towards them on six clawed feet. A wide mouth-slit gaped scimitar spines. "Billy! What creature that?"

The Joat talked into his wristband remote. "Belphoebe says it looks like a florn — a rather noisome beast that lives in the clay badlands of Stairway-to-Heaven. If so, it hunts in packs. But those are florn in the normal universe. In the parauniverse, who knows? Whatever it is, I'd say it's dangerous."

"Brilliant deduction. Joat have mind like razor. Rusty razor."

"Just thinking aloud. I agree it's pretty obvious. Look at those teeth. Get your gun ready, but don't waste charges." The Joat had issued her with an energy-weapon. He drew a device like a crossbow from his pack, sighted along it, triggered it. The acoustically guided quarrel bounced off the carapace in a shower of sparks. They turned, but a second florn barred the way. Off to one side, two more rose from their hollows. The Joat fired again: the quarrel hit squarely and dropped to the ground, a crumpled ruin. Behind them the mud sputtered obscenely.

Flare drew her gun and projected a bolt of energy at the nearest florn. Part of the carapace glowed dull crimson, but the creature came on as if it didn't feel a thing. The ragged semicircle closed. The Joat picked up a rock as big as his head, and threw it. One florn paused in its tracks for a few seconds, then nudged the spent missile aside and scuttled forward again, trailing a shattered limb. He threw another rock, smashing two more legs on the same side, and the creature began to crawl in a circle, making an unsettling chittering sound. But behind it, three more rocks raised themselves on jointy legs and began to move in.

Flare aimed her weapon at a florn's legs, hoping for the same effect as a rock, but with no result. "Heat-resistant," she said. "But brittle," she continued, as the Joat's latest rock found its target. More florn approached. "Suspect," Flare continued in the same analytical tone, "have blundered into nest of things." They ran out of rocks.

The Joat's skin began to tingle, an eerie feeling, as if it were trying to separate from his body. His head felt curiously light and empty, and there was a buzzing sound that somehow came from between his ears. Flare was obviously experiencing the same sensations. The florn too seemed affected, for they were milling around in confusion. From behind him came a snapping sound, like the breaking of a million eggshells.

A cloud of vapour surged over the boiling mudpool, leaving in its wake a trail of solid material, like a crust on the surface. Within the vapour was something dim and ill-formed. Rotund, misshapen, body slung low on six stumpy limbs, with a pointed top. Big — about the size of a bull wollagong.

Was the creature intelligent? Or was it the Hurscaffl equivalent of a dog, a cow —a mouse? The tingling and buzzing increased as the apparition passed close to the shore, and then eased as it veered sharply out across the pool. The Joat, ever the opportunist, leaped the gap on to the encrusted trail. It wobbled, but held firm. "Flare! Jump! But keep your distance — it may not support us both!" By the time they had made their way across the pool, the creature had vanished among the rocks, though a trail of sorts remained. Half a dozen florn clacked in bewilderment on the far bank. The sensations had vanished too.

The Joat broke a piece off the edge of the encrusted trail, taking care not to scald his fingers, for the survival suits were only partially heatproof. He held it in his hand. "It's *cold*," he said, consulting the appropriate sensor. "Look, it's melting. Now it's nothing but mud."

"Remarkable," said Flare. "Beast-touch freezes boiling mud. Pursue?"

The Joat looked at the compass and nodded. "It's going our way."

\* \* \*

The rain drummed on the foldaway covers. Via wristband remote, the Joat and Belphoebe were playing a game involving two octahedral dice and large sums of money; Flare was keeping watch through a transparent dome. Their progress had been blocked by a series of storms. They had lost contact with the freezer-beast, which seemed unaffected by the acid-laden rain. But when it disappeared from view, it was still on course for the ruins. They took the opportunity to catch up on lost sleep.

When the storms died away they tried to pick up the beast's trail, but the rain had obliterated the tracks. In places the water was up to their waists; then within a few seconds they were stumbling along a dried-out gulley. The banks on either side narrowed, then suddenly fell away as the ground flattened out into the dried bed of a huge lake. Crystals glistened in the sun, blinding them. When sight returned they saw—

The ruins.

They were scattered around what had once been the shores of the lake, unlike any architecture that Flare or the Joat had ever seen. A jumble of vast hexagonal forms, some of them mounds, others depressions with raised edges. The walls of the mounds rose almost vertically; the insides of the depressions sloped. Sand and crystal fragments had drifted into the depressions, filling most of them, but in places the wind had scoured the sand away. The whole area was treacherous; soft sand swept by the wind into fantastic shapes. The sheer walls of the mounds looked impossible to climb. Flare and the Joat picked their way cautiously towards the nearest depression, using an echo-sounder to avoid dust-pools big enough to swallow *Lindilu* a dozen times.

At the centre of the depression was a vertical shaft, blocked with rubble.

They hunted around until they found a similar depression with an unobstructed shaft. The surface around it was clear of sand, as if protected by a force field, but their instruments couldn't find one. The shaft seemed to go down forever, although the echo-sounder told them that it was only forty metres deep. The Joat removed a sliptape from his pack and unfolded its struts into a large cross. When it had extruded a suitable length of bonded polymer, he fed it into the shaft, bracing the supports across the opening. A tiny device with a motorized roller and a hand-loop, clipped to the tape, lowered him slowly into the depths.

Flare waited.

"Nothing here but memories," the Joat's voice crackled in her ears.

* * *

They wandered through the maze of tunnels for hours, until the map traced by their inert tracker sprawled across two screens. In places the walls had bulged, partially blocking the path, and the floor was covered in dust. The Joat acted as pathfinder, his flashlight pooling twenty paces ahead. Occasionally he raise it to see further. Flare was about to call a halt for food when the Joat made a sudden dive for the floor. When he got to his feet, he held a tiny angular object. He flipped it across to her.

"What this?"

"I'm not sure... It reminds me of something... Yeah, my Moom had some... Jole had given them to her. It's a PAXIAL prism." He had to explain what these were: Flare had some odd areas of ignorance. As she realised the discovery's possible significance she became more and more agitated. The PAXIAL homeworld would be a find beyond price, and perhaps —

"Perhaps *here* is PAXIAL homeworld?" Flare couldn't keep the excitement out of her voice. "If PAXIAL live in parauniverse, would explain why not found in ours, yes?"

"Maybe. On the other hand, it might be just the thirteenth to be discovered of the thousand and one worlds that the PAXIAL no doubt visited."

"Perhaps freezer-beasts are PAXIAL."

"I'd prefer some information more solid than perhapses," grumbled the Joat. "If they are, that just substitutes one unknown for another. It doesn't help us solve the equation." He meant, find his father.

"Change of variable can often help," said Flare firmly. The Joat shook his head in amazement. Followed by a sudden suspicion that had been germinating subconsciously for some time. Just what *was* Flare? Would a genuine shape-poet recognise a mathematical metaphor? Much less match it? One more 'perhaps' to add to a growing pile of supposition.

They sat down in the dust and ate. Flare took a closer look at the inert tracker's recordings. On a hunch, she told Belphoebe to extrapolate from the scanty data. "What make of this?" The network of lines was like a bicycle wheel, converging in radial spokes on a complex central region. "Wonder why that bit important?"

"I have no idea," said the Joat. "But I intend to find out!"

\* \* \*

The change, when it came, was dramatic.

The driftdust vanished from the floor. The walls turned from rock to metal. And there were doors. Enormous, sliding, hexagonal doors. Shut. Immovable. Huge vents, like heating ducts but more organic in shape, opened on to the tunnel from the sides and roof. Occasionally, set into the floor, there was a six-pointed ceramic star of David. And it was getting cold. Flare wondered why her suit heater wasn't compensating, took an outside temperature reading, and cried out in surprise. It was forty degrees below freezing. It must have been getting colder for some time, but the suit's automatics had coped until now.

"I'd give my right ear to know what's behind those doors," said the Joat. "Let's use a bit of plastic."

"Doubt doors will open to ID card," said Flare.

"I was thinking of plastic explosive."

"Not yet, Billy," said Flare. "Best not attract attention. Patience, at centre soon." The Joat was about to protest, but he stopped with his mouth half open. His skin was tingling again. The same, eerie feeling. Flare felt it too. They scrambled into a vent. The tingling increased. The alien creature passed them — and stopped. Only the Joat saw what it did. After an age, he whispered "It's gone." He looked stunned.

Flare peeped out of the vent. "Where did it go?"

"You won't believe this."

"Reserve judgement," said Flare. "Give opportunity anyway." The Joat climbed from the vent and sat on the floor. He was shivering, not only from the cold.

"It's wearing protective clothing. Like a fat spider in an inflated wetsuit. Had a pack on its back. It stopped by one of those stars in the floor and took something out. Just like a PAXIAL prism, but black."

"A *black* prism? But you said they're always white!"

"I think the freezer-beast is a living PAXIAL." He stopped, momentarily awed by the discovery. "A survivor. The white prisms that archaeologists in the normal universe keep digging up are all dead. That's why the PAXIAL threw them away. Black prisms are the active form."

"Make sense," said Flare. "Power packs? When power used up, throw away."

"Maybe," said the Joat. "But I think they have a much more specialized use."

"Why think that?"

"I saw what the PAXIAL did with one. It put the prism into a slot in its pack, walked towards that ceramic star — and vanished."

"Through door? Prism make open?"

"No, Flare, nothing happened to the door. It was the PAXIAL that vanished. First it was solid, then it was gone. It didn't move. It just... faded away."

"Gods," said Flare. "Prisms are activators for matter-transmission system."

# 18   Brain Transplant

The Femm eyed the young human with distaste, and sought adequate words. Should he be described as unfit to lick bug-droppings off the walls of a derelict brood-chamber? As possessing all the foresight and intelligence of a brain-damaged coprophage? As possessing the utility of an infertile yjj-plant to a starving lyppit? He settled for something within the creature's limited conceptual grasp. "Dolt."

Though the voice was unemotional, Tory Eton flinched. "But the mission wasn't a failure! I followed my orders to the letter!"

"That is why you are a dolt. You are supposed to use your initiative." Cysparagon Hymllyr Tubbytt slid a sheet from the signal-pad across the desk. "Instead, you send this nonsense." A Cysparagon was a Femmish rough equivalent of an admiral, except that it was a brood-rank and its holder had considerably more autonomy — subject only to censure at high-brood level.

Tory knew the words by heart, but he read them again, as if somehow the words would explain what he had done wrong. JARNEYVORE DESTROYED. ALL SHIPS RETURN TO NORMAL DUTIES. *But the action had been a success!* Had Tubbytt misunderstood? Tory hastened to clarify the position. "Cysparagon, I simply don't understand why you think there is a problem. I agree that I sent that transmission, and I stand by it. I was given explicit orders, and I carried out those orders in full. The computers predicted the place and time, and the instant Jarneyvore's craft dephased it came under concentrated fire. It exploded, and nothing but plasma remained, so I called off the engagement as instructed. I'd call that an outstanding success, Cysparagon."

Tubbytt slid another sheet towards him. "You would, would you? Outstanding? Yes, *something* is outstanding. Your orders were to gontinue the action until it was certain that Jarneyvore was dead. Until it was *certain*, Gommander; not until you were *satisfied*. You satisfy too easily." Eton raised the document to eye level. Some kind of technical gobbledegook. "I have here a report," said the Femm. "It is a spectral analysis of the region of space where you allegedly destroyed Jarneyvore and his yacht."

*Allegedly? But I saw the bloody thing blown into cosmic dust!*

"You claim you destroyed a ship, and a man. A human body — two if the passenger was still on board — and an isosteel-titanium alloy hull. Even when vaporized, they should leave appropriate evidence of their passage, do you agree?"

"I suppose. But —"

"Do you see any mention here of proteins? Fats? Bone? Iron? Titanium?"

"Cysparagon, I am not a scientist. I am not trained to ask such questions."

"That is the most sensible thing you have said or done today. Let me enlighten you in layman's terms. The evidence does *not* demonstrate that what you destroyed was a ship; nor does it indigate that there were any living creatures on board. No ship, no people. There is only one thing that is outstanding about your performance, Gommander Eton — and that is any credible evidence that you succeeded. Our Specialists are convinced that the object you destroyed was construgted from plastig. It was, in short, a dummy. And not, I may add, the only one."

*But how could Jarneyvore have known there was a trap waiting for him? It's not fair. I did what they told me to, it's not my fault if they screwed up.*

"A dummy. A crude attempt at misdirection, which deceived you utterly. What is worse, had I not been sufficiently sceptigal to have ordered a spectral analysis, we would now be making the erroneous assumption that Wyllam Jarneyvore is dead. You have imperilled the entire project! You are ingompetent and witless! You —"

Tory Eton leaped out of his chair, his face purpling, ready to strangle the nearest throat. "Don't talk to *me* like that, Tubbytt! I'll have you court-martialled, shot, or worse. You forget that I am an *Etonian!* I give orders not take them. OK, so, I made a trivial error and you picked it up. Congratulations, I'll ask my father to promote you."

Tubbytt made motions of disgust. "Your father to promote *me?* You presume too much."

"Shut up and let me think what action we can take to prevent any serious —"

"Eton, you have no idea of the true cirgumstances. A pathetic display of false bravado will not help. And the necessary actions have already been taken. In particular, you are relieved of your command."

Eton leaned across the table, his face inches from Tubbytt's, spittle strung from the corner of his mouth. "Who says so? You? You're just a useless bloody bureau—"

"Do be quiet, child." Another voice rang from the doorway, and a muscular figure stepped through.

"Father! You can't be taking sides with that — that *animal* —"

The newcomer's face showed signs of exasperation. "You're a racist as well as a fool, Tory. Shut up. I should have dealt with you years ago, but your mother was far too indulgent."

"Don't you take that atti—"

"Now it's too late to do anything except limit the damage you've caused. You're past saving, Tory. You're a spoilt brat. I should never have given you command. I'm taking it away. And I'm confining you to your rooms until I've decided what to do with you. Consider yourself dismissed. Now!"

White-faced, Tory Eton found the presence of mind to snap his heels together; saluted, and marched from the room. But his slapping feet were those of a sulky child. Rudolph Eton V sank into a chair and sighed.

"Do not worry," said Tubbytt. "You performed your duty. Now you must instigate a search for the missing joat. Give the task to Harrow." Eton nodded, his face unreadable.

* * *

One of the many messages that Rudolph sent off that afternoon resulted, half a day later, in the arrival of a sleek silver craft, streaked with dirt from an over-fast atmospheric take-off. Its contours were not those of an ordinary vessel. It retracted its landing-struts until it hugged the ground. Now, when the main lock opened, only a low sill would separate the vessel's interior from the floor outside.

Through the bright lights that ringed the lock, something dark began to emerge. Despite themselves, the ground-crew shrank back. They knew what was inside, and it unnerved them. On a silent cushion of magnetism a squat, ugly mechanism slid forward, a matt-grey ovoid surrounded by pipes, cables, and complicated machinery. A small escort of guardsmen lined up on either side, weapons at the ready, while a few busy technicians disconnected the ovoid from the surrounding equipment. The ovoid moved off smoothly down a side-corridor, but its direction was erratic, as if it was overshooting on turns and having to correct. It had difficulty negotiating the step to the main corridor, and the escort bent, seized it by a half dozen carrying handles, and with an effort lifted it over the obstruction. It bobbed up and down once or twice before the maglev compensators readjusted.

The entourage moved away along the corridor. The ground-crew gave a collective sigh of relief and set to work to polish the silver craft it until it shone.

* * *

Cysparagon Hymllyr Tubbytt flexed bow-legged at the knees, a sign of overwhelming sadness. "Llyrjjyj. Wyljyrrjyl. Jyljyrryd-Famm. Lynnerj. Mym-Phrygglyr. All dead." His finger tapped on the desk without rhythm, indicating extreme exasperation. It was a cold, patternless sound, more effective in its own way than the thump of a fist or the stamp of a foot. Femm anger was controlled, but no less deadly for it. "Five of my best pilots, destroyed in an instant. That is what results from Tory Eton's incompetence!" He turned to address an aide. "Do we yet know the manner of their destruction?"

"The most probable scenario requires a device for the instantaneous translocation of material objects."

"The Joat has access to a transfer plane generator," Tubbytt mused.

"It is still too early to be certain of that, Cysparagon. But the probability that Wyllam Jarneyvore is responsible is currently estimated at 96%."

"And increasing by the instant, I feel it in my joint-cartilage, Jymmj. In every direction we turn there is a Jarneyvore causing trouble, delaying our plans, and making itself an intolerable nuisance." His mind flashed back to his first major assignment, as a young up-and-coming contaximator: the ruination of the Grover's World economy. Stupidly, he had underestimated the planet's inhabitants and stayed in his ship while a subordinate took charge on the planet's surface. Thanks to a certain Billy Jarneyvore, the plan had failed, and the subordinate had been deported, to considerable diplomatic embarrassment. Tubbytt's career had been set back by several years — he should have been a broodmaster by now, not a mere Cysparagon.

He wasn't going to make that mistake twice. "I do not wish to hear of any further difficulties caused by Jarneyvores. I wish the Jarneyvore to become an extinct species, Jymmyj." Tubbytt leaned forward. "The High Femm are becoming disillusioned with these Etonians also."

"So would I, in their place." A grating electronic voice set Tubbytt's molar ridges clattering against each other. "Of course, my dear Cysparagon, it depends on which Etonians you have in mind." Tubbytt whirled in his seat. Hovering ominously at the threshold of his office was a smooth matt-grey ellipsoid. It hummed abrasively on the edge of his hearing.

Tubbytt inclined his head sideways in a gesture of acknowledgement. "You are correct: not all Etonians are incompetent. Allow me to goncratulate you on your recovery."

"I wouldn't describe it in such glowing terms," said Sherryl Eton.

* * *

Even now, the very cells of her body remembered burning. Her skin shrivelling, blistering, the blisters bursting. She could still *see* her hands turning black, her legs charring, as the superheated air washed over her groundcar and the metal frame began to glow dull red, the sleek aluminium skin peeling back in an obscene parody of her own. Then the shockwave hit and the car tumbled across the rust-coloured clay of Sear's Planet like an autumn leaf blown from a bycch-tree.

She was glad that she remembered nothing else for a long time.

The next memory was of pale grey light, as if diffused through layers of gauze. That's what she'd thought it was. She'd known she was in some kind of hospital; her body knew it had been through a long series of operations even though her mind had been unconscious. She remembered the searing heat, deduced that her eyes had been burned dry, damaged. It was surgical gauze unwrapping, the bandages coming off. Soon she would see again, her eyesight restored.

She tried to blink, but there were no eyelids. She tried to raise her hands to her face but there were no hands. She panicked, and tried to scream —

There were no vocal cords.

*Get a grip on yourself! You're alive, you respond to light. You're just disoriented. It will take a few minutes to recover control of your body.* The grey light brightened, became white. It should have been bright enough to hurt, but it didn't. And she could see. Strange, indistinct, moving shapes. There was something extremely disturbing about them. Not about their motions, but their form. They seemed composed of thousands of tiny squares, changing shades of grey, white, black — just like that holovix cliche, the low-resolution fade.

"Sherryl?"

She heard the voice, but her hearing was funny too. It was tinny, distorted, as if the sound was coming through a pipe full of tinsel. Like a freewave-communicator with a dodgy decoder, so that most of the component frequencies were missing.

"Sherryl, do you hear me? Open your mouth if you do."

Experimentally she flexed her jaw muscles. To her surprise, she felt her lips part. *There's* something *there, then. I'm not* totally *disembodied.* But the lips felt oddly inflexible.

"She's responding. Excellent!" A change of tone, more gentle, less matter-of-fact: "Sherryl, you can speak if you try."

"Where am I? What's happened to me?" Her own voice sounded equally tinny, it grated against the inside of her skull. It sounded horrible.

"You're safe now. You were nearly killed by a volcano. On Sear's Planet, do you remember?"

"The Joat's volcano."

"Good, you do remember. We will have revenge, never fear. But do not trouble yourself with such petty matters now. You have been ill — very ill."

"My skin! I saw my skin burning! It *hurt!*" The pain had been unbearable, indescribable. There had been no way to escape it.

"Don't excite yourself. It happened. It's over. You're alive."

"I feel funny. You sound funny. You *look* funny." Suddenly she realised that she couldn't recognise the voice. "Who are you?"

"Your brother Kenith. Eshelby is here too."

"You don't sound like Kenith. You don't sound like *anyone!*" She redirected her gaze wildly round the room. There was a shadow that might be Eshelby. Her viewpoint changed, but she couldn't feel her head moving. And something else, she realised, was wrong. "*Why am I seeing everything in black and white?*"

"I'll explain later, my darling. You just calm down and — "

"Later! I sound like a breaker's yard and everything looks like a crude computer graphic! Kenith, *I can't feel my body!*"

The silence stretched out forever, and a terrible thought took hold. "There's something very wrong with me, isn't there?"

"Don't you worry yourself now — "

"There is! I know there is! Tell me! *Tell me!*"

"Sherryl, you've got to calm down. Doctor? I think you'd better give her another —"

"Oh, gods." The terrible thought lay leaden in her brain. "I *know* why I can't feel my body. You don't need to tell me."

"Sherryl, dear, I'm *so* sorry — "

"I don't *have* a body, do I?" asked Sherryl Eton's brain. "I'm a cyborg."

\* \* \*

A thousand times, Eshelby Eton VI had wondered whether they were really doing the right thing. *If the recovery vehicle hadn't had a refrigerated compartment, and if its driver hadn't been trained in first aid...* well, there would have been no awkward decision to make.

But Kenith and Filip III had agreed that there was no choice. Family honour required them to keep their sister alive, no matter what the price. By 'price' he wasn't thinking of money. Money meant nothing to him. Money was to be spent. It would be a personal price, a terrible price — and he wouldn't be the one paying it.

When the Femm driver found Sherryl's livid, blistered body, her clothes were still smouldering. She lay within a hundred metres of a fresh lava-flow, half-covered in ash that was still too hot to touch. It had been a horrible death. But when he touched his medisensor to her corpse he found that her heart had only just stopped beating. He reacted very fast. He ran back to the vehicle, pulled out a geological sample cutter, and chopped her head off. He placed it carefully in a plastic bag and put it in the refrigeration compartment, set for rapid freezing. Once he had done that, there was all the time in the world.

The Etonians brought in skilled Femm surgeons to transfer her brain into an artificial environment and to reconnect her main nerve paths to servomotors and electronic sensors. They had no idea whether the object of their attentions would appreciate what they were doing. Only Sherryl knew whether she would prefer to be dead, or a disembodied brain in a cyborg support unit. But she had to carry her share of family obligation, for without her intuition for intrigue they had no chance of restoring the fortunes of the Bly branch of the family tree.

The promise of vengeance was all that kept Sherryl going. She recalled nothing of the endless operations, the neuron grafts, the anti-rejection chemotherapy. She did recall, in infinite detail, the tedious relearning of the simplest functions, such as refilling her nutrient reservoirs and recharging her fuel-cells. She brooded on the pleasures she had lost forever, but consoled herself with the one pleasure that remained: *revenge*. She didn't care that nobody knew where the Joat was. A cyborg had a life-expectancy of two hundred years. She could afford to be patient. Nobody could hold out for long against the resources of one Etonian, let alone the entire clan.

# 19 *Pictographia PAXIALia*

The tunnel ended at another door, but one of markedly different design. Flare grabbed a protuberance and pulled. To her surprise, the door slid quietly to one side, and they crept through. The Joat muttered mild obscenities under his breath. "It's bigger than the HyperDome."

"And just as empty," said Flare bleakly. After all their efforts it was a terrible disappointment.

There was some kind of dim concealed lighting. Billy squinted through the gloom. "Not quite," he said. "What's that, out in the middle?"

"Control centre," opined Flare hopefully.

"For what? This place is as empty as the grave."

They crept towards it, feeling naked in the open spaces. A convoluted mound sprouted from the floor, with mouldings in its side that might have been steps, though they were half a metre or more apart and not entirely regular. Flare tried to imagine herself standing on it, and why...

They scrambled up.

There was a wide-mouthed horn like a prehistoric gramophone, the kind that ought to have a small dog sitting in front of it wearing a ruffled collar and inclining its head intently. There was a soft bench like a chaise-longue. It was — upholstered? — in a diamond pattern. There was a — chair? table? refrigerator? — bearing something like a melted samovar. At one corner was a mass of slender tubes tipped with huge rounded cylinders, like a twenty-foot bulrush. Vertical tubes of hexagonal cross-section were stacked like organ pipes. It could have been a steam calliope or an X-ray telescope. Or a sculpture.

"I'm whacked," said the Joat, sitting heavily on the chaise-longue, then lying down on it. "This is hopeless — " There was a *bleep* and the couch revolved through a right-angle, tipped up on end, and deposited him on the floor. His protests trailed into awed silence. The bulrush had lit up like a Christmas tree, the samovar had unmelted and displayed rings of flashing pinpoint lights. The opening of the gramophone horn had opaqued into a screen.

The dome's empty spaces were filled with ghostly machinery.

After a long time, Billy spoke. His voice was hoarse with emotion. "It doesn't make any sense. It's not like any technology I've ever heard of."

"What think products of advanced science *ought* look like?" asked Flare. "Electric teethbrush?"

"It's weird. Most of it has a — kind of — *organic* look. Moulded. Soft edges. No two units quite alike. Look at those pipes — if they are pipes. The cross-section keeps changing. It looks like it's *evolved*, not built."

"But not everywhere. See that?" She pointed an unsteady hand. "*That* more like something out of toy construction kit. Girders and bolts, cables and struts. And huge glass pots!" She was reaching for the 'couch' — presumably a control console or a keyboard or equivalent — when Billy stepped in front of her.

"Hold fire, lady. *I* am the computer expert." He sat cross-legged at the 'couch' and gingerly adjusted the horn to a more comfortable position. It swivelled on frictionless mountings. He poised his hands over the largest diamond in the upholstery, and touched it lightly.

Nothing happened.

He pressed again, harder. The screen cleared. A message appeared in the lower right corner. Billy pressed more diamonds. Each produced a lengthy message in strange characters. "It isn't a general-purpose machine," said the Joat. "It's dedicated to some particular task." Gingerly he tried various combinations, obtaining different messages but exciting no other response. After some time, he sat back thoughtfully. "It's waiting for some particular action. I hope it doesn't require a coded input: if so, we've no chance. I don't know what else to try."

Flare had found something that looked like a cross between beige bagpipes and a vacuum-cleaner, with a flat, gaping mouth. She kicked it in its midriff. It turned pale pink and began to pulsate. Trying to put it down, she tripped and fell into the organ pipes. They came apart, flat hexagons tumbling in all directions. The vacuum-cleaner twisted, sucked one up with a soft *gloop*, and turned beige again. "Not pipes," said the Joat. "Flat things... hundreds of identical flat things in stacks..." He picked several up. Their faces bore cryptic markings. Different on each. "Disks! Computer disks! No wonder the machine wasn't working. I forgot to put a disk in!"

"More likely PAXIAL collection of popular music," said Flare. "Billy, just because *human* technology use monomolecular optidisks for storage, does not mean —"

"Flare, dear," said Billy, "hold your peace for a moment and push that button." This time, when the screen cleared, it showed pictures.

The Joat came to life. "Flare, switch on the sensor array. Patch it through to *Lindilu*. We'll record as much as we can."

They watched the screen as strange vehicles moved through baffling surroundings doing incomprehensible things. At least, they looked like vehicles. They could have been robots, or metallic insects, or speeded-up galaxies, or PAXIAL dancing-girls. "Is amazing artefact," said Flare. "But not much use. PAXIAL do not think like humans. Should withdraw, taking evidence with, and persuade —"

"Not yet." He didn't dare break anything off the machinery in case he destroyed it forever... only the disks looked portable... The Joat began to mutter his thoughts out loud. "They dig tunnels. They have computers with disk storage. Hmmmm. If *we'd* built this item, what *else* would we have provided?"

"Infostruct database," said Flare without hesitation.

The Joat wiggled his ears in excitement. "Right! An index! Let's find it." He started scrabbling through the hexagons. Part of him wondered why Flare had used informatics jargon. From a *shape-poet?*

"Will never find, even if is one," said Flare glumly. "Too many disks, and PAXIAL script is largely unknown."

*Funny... Two days ago she claimed not to know about the PAXIAL; now she's an expert on their written language.* "True, but I hope irrelevant," said the Joat. "There *has* to be an index, and it *has* to be easy to use." He grabbed the vacuum-cleaner and squeezed its midriff. Another *gloop* and the hexagonal disk reappeared in its mouth. He pulled it out and turned the vacuum-cleaner on end. There was a picture of a stack of hexagons, next to a deep depression. He stuck his finger into it. The vacuum-cleaner turned pink and a hexagon shot into its mouth from the heap on the floor. The horn-screen filled with columns of the unintelligible words — and beside each was a picture.

"Transportation," said the Joat, running his eyes down the list. "Then a number. At least we can be sure of the PAXIAL numbering system. Five-three, that will be thirty-three in base six. It must be the number of disks devoted to that topic: there are plenty of repetitions, and there doesn't seem to be any need for individual numbers for the disks." He ran his eyes up the list. "Food — fourteen disks. Or maybe weapons. Or jazz-bands, who knows? Ramsbotham's *Pictographia PAXIALia* may be definitive, but I'd be surprised if it's more than ten per cent right."

"Well, said Flare, "Can read *that!*" She gestured at an entry near the top of the screen.

"Intersecting spirals," said the Joat.

"It's a picture of this place."

"Yeah, and it's just reminded me where I've seen the same kind of spirals," said the Joat. "On the end of every PAXIAL prism."

"Why?"

"I've got half an idea, but it's elusive. That entry shows there must be a disk about it, we could try to look it up."

"But how find right hexagon?"

"We don't," said Billy. "Wyllam Jarneyvore, alias Billy the Joat, in his usual manner of brutish ignorance and unaccountable good fortune, has stumbled across the basic principle of this machine. We don't find it: it finds us. You merely select the required entry and the input device finds the disk automatically. Now, observe that only one disk is indicated for this entry. Using this object like a miniature wheeled bellows, I presumably select a heading — yes, as I thought — and then *squeeze...*" The vacuum-cleaner changed colour, spat, sucked, and changed colour again.

The screen showed a dazzling silver planet, seen from space. The picture cut to the surface, to show an installation of hexagonal depressions arranged in intersecting spirals. Billy skimmed through items at random. He was rewarded with plans, drawings, what looked like numerical tables, mathematical formulas, circuit diagrams. A recorded scene of PAXIAL activities was particularly interesting. A column of the creatures stood beside a star-shaped outline. Each wore an elaborate suit with a huge conical helmet, and carried a hip-pack, into which it inserted a prism. Each walked on to the star and vanished.

"See?" said the Joat. "I *said* the prisms were matter-transmitters."

"Transfer planes transmit matter."

"Yes, but those are limited to a third of a light-year at each stage. By the look of those suits, the prisms work over interstellar distances."

"Gods! What Quaternity would not give!" said Flare, losing her composure. "One tiny disk hold key to universe!" Her ambitions were growing in proportion to the magnitude of their discovery. She turned to the Joat, eyes blazing with the intensity of her vision. "Transfer plane repaired yet?"

The Joat called Belphoebe on his remote. "The filtration is going well, but the roboremote needs a few more hours."

"Damn. Can't use transfer plane. Computer too heavy to carry. Take disks? Or wait for robot to finish?"

"I'm not keen to wait, there are Femm out there. We'll take as many disks as we can grab — especially this one. But we can't take more than a couple of dozen, the terrain outside is bad enough without any extra burden. By the time we get back, Belphoebe will have finished repairing the transfer plane generator, and we can grab the rest from a distance."

"Grab computer too?"

"Maybe. If we can shift it."

"Disks useful without computer?"

"If we are unfortunate enough not to be able to snitch the computer, I'm sure it will be possible to extract the information from the hexagons. It's just a reading and decoding job. They must have used some rational format. No, I think we should just turn this thing off, and beat it while the coast is —" He broke off as once more he felt his skin trying to separate from his body.

"The PAXIAL ! It's coming!" hissed Flare . "Cannot move! Legs not work!" They were locked back into the strange paralysis that the PAXIAL generated. It would probably kill them on the spot, especially when it found that they'd been looting its computer installation. Flare cursed the stolen disk in her pack, but was unable to move a centimetre to put it back where it belonged. The Joat began to compose a lengthy speech on the importance of relics to xenoarchaeology and hoped he'd get a chance to use it.

The PAXIAL came closer and the chill ate into their bones. The creature touched Flare's arm with one of its padded limbs, so cold that it felt as if her arm had been dipped into burning oil. It reached for her pack...

* * *

The PAXIAL bound them to metal supports with thick strands like strings of pearls, and departed, taking with it most of their possessions — both packs, their weapons, the wristband remote. Cut off from Belphoebe, the Joat had never felt so helpless, even when the paralysis began to wear off.

Shortly the PAXIAL reappeared, the paralysis returning with it. It untied the rigid bodies and fiddled about with a compact item of ghostly machinery slung from its middle. The Joat rose into the air without apparent effort, and drifted towards one of the stars of David. Flare was treated likewise. The PAXIAL selected a black, active prism.

*What will it feel like to be matter-transmitted?* the Joat asked himself. *An unendurable wrenching of the psyche as one's soul is stretched across the rack of hidden dimensions? A resonating vibration down to the very bones, nay, the very macromolecules of the mortal frame? A sudden and violent pain like being burnt alive simultaneously everywhere, as the flesh is stripped apart particle by elementary particle, to be reassembled in some unimaginable matrix? A vast and incomprehensible emptiness, a featureless infinite waste? A wash of inconsolable sadness?*

The PAXIAL stuck the prism into a socket and placed him on the hexagonal star. Billy could see his body beginning to fade. It was highly disconcerting.

He disappeared entirely, and went blind. He felt a wave of panic. Then, slowly, he began to reform. *All in the mind*. He didn't even feel sick. Once you got used to it, the experience would be about as exciting as a trycle ride. That wasn't really a surprise, when you came to think of it. All civilizations refine their modes of transport to make them comfortable and easy: if they don't, the customers go elsewhere. The PAXIAL were merely conforming to a universal norm.

He *did* feel a bit dozy — so dozy that he hardly noticed how dozy he felt. This was such a discomfiting thought that he decided to mull it over for a while.

On the far side, through the matter-transmitter, was another tunnel, and unlike the tunnels they had come through it looked as if it was in regular use. The gravity and atmospheric pressure were the same as before — they were still on Hurscaffl. Somewhere. If only he still had the remote, Belphoebe could quickly find out where. *And if wishes were skoats, boggies would sklide*.

Without ceremony the PAXIAL steered them towards a distant gleam of pink light. The closer they got, the pinker it became, a hideously tasteless glow that reminded Billy of an overdone boudoir stranded halfway between suburbia and the whorehouse. The kind of thing you'd expect to find in a Flora Heartpound romantic novel, feminine and frilly, floral and flouncy, with a scent of appleblossom and peach.

They emerged into a large hexagonal chamber. From ceiling to floor it was studded with soft pink hexagonal lights, each a metre or more wide and surrounded by an intricate white frill. Billows of padded cloth draped the walls, arranged in flowing patterns, all of it closely printed with tiny hexagonal flowers. The floor was covered in close-packed soft threads, like a really thick carpet, and it too was the same candyfloss pink. An indented lavender-coloured mound, like a string of coffin-sized sausages, meandered over it without detectable rationale. It was *woven into* the floor, an integral part of the overall design. In the centre was a shallow depression, again hexagonal but with its edges softened by apricot-coloured piping. Something that looked like a stand of tree-sized pastel blue ostrich feathers was offset a little from its centre.

The PAXIAL carried them to the depression and laid each of them in a groove at two of its six corners, with their feet towards the centre. Then it turned and left. The grooves moulded around them and flowed sluggishly, tipping them up at an angle. The edges of the grooves began to ooze great lengths of frilly lace, coiling itself into distorted lemon concertinas. The Joat felt his paralysis wearing off, but now the padded grooves were embracing him in their unbreakable clutches. It was like being assaulted by a giant cream puff. He still felt sluggish.

As his sense of smell returned, he distinctly caught the aroma of appleblossom and peach.

The chamber was warming up, now: soon it would reach a comfortable temperature. He hoped it would know when to stop. He found that he could move his arms and legs a little, but his body was held firmly in place by dozens of pillowlike layers.

"Oh! Comfortable!" Flare said sleepily, her voice muffled by her own quota of pillows.

"That may not be intentional. It seems to be the PAXIAL equivalent of a jail cell. Or a public holoviewpoint." *Or a nuthouse. The trouble with aliens is, they're alien.*

"Remind of house of ill-repute in Chang-Chang City."

"*All* houses in Chang-Chang City are of ill repute," said Billy. "Anyway, what were *you* doing there?"

"Very respectable," said Flare. "Was giving première of shape-poem about life-cycle of eggplant to celebrate opening of new tourist centre. Kissmeland, you hear about?"

"I certainly have! It's notorious throughout the entire civilized universe! Half-naked cuties dressed up as Risqué Rat, Lewdo the dog, and Fondle the — "

"Say no more. Was there for purely artistic reasons, was big commission, very big fee. First serious public performance. But all this not important at moment."

"It helps to pass the time," said the Joat, "until we discover our fate." He dimly recognised that his mind wasn't functioning with its usual clarity. What *had* he and Flare been discussing? Had they forgotten they were in the clutches of a hideous monster the size of a bull wollagong that looked for all the world like a walking turnip?

He found it hard to get excited about it.

Then a thought flopped sluggishly into his brain, and the Joat began to struggle. The pillows sort of *sighed*, and embraced him a millimetre more tightly. He relaxed, wondering if he ought to try to decide what to do next. To hell with it.

Tine passed. Neither of them had any idea how much. The Joat felt a mild tingling, like pins-and-needles, but all over his skin. It grew, and his hair stood on end. Flare's hair stood out in a huge puffball, as if she was attached to a Van der Graaf generator. The air quivered with tension; then the ostrich-feathers began to glow. Billy noted dispassionately that the glow was deep brown, or possibly brilliant purple, he couldn't distinguish which. Even in his semi-torpid state he knew this made no sense at all, which was even more peculiar, because it seemed entirely natural. Maybe his eyes were seeing a new eighth colour. Brurple?

There was a low crooning sound. The lavender sausages contracted and relaxed in huge sugar-puff surges, and turned bright scarlet with salmon stripes. Between the glowing ostrich-feathers a shape began to form, at first no more substantial than a wisp of fog, then thickening, pulsating from opaque to transparent and clouding over again, with a hint of internal organs, jumbled rubbery tubes, wobbling in time with the sausages in an orgy of peristalsis. The air seemed to thicken, then to solidify, and for an instant he felt like a fly trapped in setting amber. *Are they planning to sequence my DNA?* Then the air shattered into a billion fragments, turned to powder, to liquid, to plasma so hot that its absolute temperature passed infinity and became negative... and back to air.

A now substantial figure settled itself awkwardly in the hexagonal indentation at their feet. It was rounded and portly, like an over-inflated michelin-man, but its surface shone like polished chromium plate. It was hard to make out the exact shape — all you could see was reflected pastel pillows. The strange being bobbed up and down as if gravity scarcely affected it. It kept its shape, as if rigid.

A kind of smoky balloon with scalloped edges, like a child's drawing of a cloud, appeared above its head. Below dangled a chain of steadily diminishing clouds. It reminded the Joat of something, something from his childhood, something he saw almost every day, something he couldn't *quite* —

Black shapes began to crystallize in the top cloud: straight rods, twisted tubes, like bendy rubbery construction toys. They were lined up in horizontal rows, the first consisting of two uprights and a crossbar, like a rugball goal but shorter. The Joat shook his head to clear it and concentrated, harder, *harder...* The shapes took on a more familiar, though more abstract, aspect.

Letters.

Letters of the Anglish alphabet. The first one was a U. It was followed by S, E T, and H. What on Grover was a *useth?* But there were more letters, and they made more sense:

USE THE TRANSFER PLANE TO SWITCH OFF THE STASIS FIELD.

Billy stared blankly. None of this was remotely like he'd expected. How could a transfer plane — oh, make it cut through the field. The unmatched faces would provide an entry point, destabilize the stasis field, and it would automatically shut down. But the transfer plane generator was on *Lindilu*. Assuming Belphoebe had finished repairing it.

THE WRISTBAND REMOTE, SNAILBRAIN.

"The PAXIAL took it away," he pointed out. There was a piercing whistle, and a thing that looked like a velvet flowerpot revolved twice and vanished. Sitting where it had been was the remote. It was already switched on.

The Joat muttered darkly to himself, picked it up, and slipped it over his hand. Snailbrain indeed. Someone — some *thing* — would pay for that insult. "Um — 'Phoebe, have you finished the —"

"The generator repair is complete Your new location has been noted. Transfer plane alignment across stasis-suit interface is computed," came Belphoebe's slightly distorted voice. "Am about to activate transfer plane generator and switch off stasis field."

"But — " *Oh, Hell, everything's thinking quicker than me today. Belphoebe must have been listening in via the remote. I think I'll just go and pickle my head in sour cabbage.* There was a sound like champagne being sucked back into the bottle, complete with cork. 'Pop!' backwards spells 'pop!, but it doesn't work that way with sounds. And as for the scchhhhhh— well you'll just have to use your imagination. The silvery suit shrivelled along an unorthodox dimension, and was gone.

Where it had been, there was now a man. His hair had a black streak, like a fresh burn. He wore a khaki-and-blue uniform. He was lying flat on his back with a complicated-looking piece of machinery clutched across his chest. The other hand hovered beside his belt control panel. A laser-pistol lay on the floor next to him, still glowing around the nozzle. His chest rose and fell spasmodically, then settled into a steadier rhythm.

He looked terrified, then puzzled. He seemed to be performing some kind of mental calculation. Then his face cleared. He sat up. He stared. His mouth opened and closed but no sound came out. Then he spoke.

"Is that *you*, Billy?"

"*Dad! You're alive!* I was right!" The Joat rushed across and embraced his father. This was less than elegant since he was still sitting on the floor. Tears were streaming down both faces. They helped each other to their feet. Jole noticed Flare.

"Billy? Who's the young lady?"

"Name Flare," said Flare. "Billy, introduce to nice gentleman."

"Uh — Dad, this is Flare — "

"Pleased to meet — "

I SUPPOSE YOU'RE WONDERING WHY I'VE BROUGHT YOU ALL HERE, writhed the black tubes. They jiggled up and down a few times to catch someone's attention. But nobody was looking.

# 20  Fate of Two Universes

A Femm technician fiddled interminably with a multichannel wave-analyser, while the ship pursued a convoluted search path a few thousand metres above Hurscaffl's inhospitable surface. Within its metal ovoid Sherryl Eton's brain did its best to remain patient. The technician emitted a series of low-pitched clicking sounds, the Femm equivalent of 'tut-tut', and made a new attempt to filter a usable signal from the high level of noise. It was like trying to hear a heartbeat in a hurricane, except that it was looking for electromagnetic signals — the Joat and Belphoebe communicating via wristband remote.

They had experienced little difficulty in finding *Lindilu*. But the whereabouts of the Joat were not as easy to pin down.

The cryostatic supercomputer hiccupped, and then locked into a new pattern. The technician's mouth twisted momentarily into a grimace of triumph before it remembered protocol.

"I have pigged up signals that correspond with the voiceprints of Wyllam Jarneyvore."

"About time," said Harrow.

"A delay was only to be expected," the technician pointed out. "The link between Jarneyvore and his vessel is screened; what we have pigged up is leakage. In fact, we were fortunate to succeed so quigly."

"Stop congratulating yourself and get on with it."

"I will tell the pilot where to land."

Sherryl watched the flickering pixels that indicated that the technician was leaving the room. Her brain had become used to the ovoid's poor vision and the coarse picture almost seemed natural. She could no longer remember what it had been like to *see*, except in occasional vivid dreams. She had many dreams, and few of them were pleasant. The medics thought it was due to some subtle hormone imbalance, but Sherryl knew the nightmares would cease the day she saw Billy the Joat's dead body. The best part would be reducing it to that state, and there her imagination ran riot.

An alarm rang, to signify a landing was imminent. Harrow secured himself in a cubicle, while Sherryl hooked her grapples to a nearby rail and locked her basal magnets to the metal floor. Cysparagon Tubbytt gave an order, and the ship commenced a fast descent.

\* \* \*

"You'll have to give me a few moments to readjust, son," said Jole. "To me, it's only a few seconds since I was in a firefight with a squad of Femm guards. But I predicted you'd come, no matter how much or how long it took."

"There was never any doubt," said Billy. Overhead the black tubes jiggled in exasperation. COME ON, YOU DIMBOS! LOOK UP HERE!

"I hadn't predicted a young lady, though," said Jole. "She didn't figure in my computations."

"She didn't figure in mine, either... She was hitching a ride in the Jum— but that can wait."

His father nodded. There were so many things to catch up on, and most of them would have to wait. But there was one question he *had* to ask. "How's Terpsi? Is she well?"

THIS ISN'T THE TIME OR THE PLACE FOR IDLE CHITCHAT!

"Moom's fine, Dad, though she never got over your disappearance. She pretended you were still alive, but I don't think she really believed it. She'll be over the moon when she finds out that —" He stopped, confused and embarrassed. "Dad, didn't you predict that?"

"Afraid not," said Jole. "I never could work out what was going on in your mother's mind, Billy. It was the one area where my abilities always failed me." The Joat had never really known his father, and now he realised that he didn't understand him at all. What would it be like to sense the future? What would it be like if that talent failed?

"How long have I been in stasis?"

"Twenty-one years, Dad."

"About what I hoped. It was an unquantifiable variable. So you've gained twenty-one years while I've been in stasis — that makes you older than me! You know, it hardly seems more than a few weeks ago when — well, I guess to me it really *was* only a few weeks ago when... Sump, it depends on the frame of reference... where was I? Oh, yes, it seems like only a few weeks ago when the *Hubble* set out on a secret mission..."

THAT'S TORN IT. NOW HE'S GOING TO TELL US HIS LIFE HISTORY.

* * *

The pryship *Edwin Hubble* hovered against a background of blood-red stardust, enveloped in a stealth field, its engines quiescent. Waiting. Nobody knew what for, least of all the predictor who had ordered the action, but Jole had no doubt that it was necessary to be there. They were poised at a butterfly point, where small actions could exert enormous leverage on future events.

Five days passed, six, a week...

In the corner of one screen a pale glow appeared, so faint at first that the computer had to run a very sophisticated signal-processing package to see it at all. When it had satisfied itself that the signal really existed, it outlined the area in red, interpolated to find the most probable centre, and marked it with a white hot-cross-bun symbol. Matching the rapidly strengthening emissions it made a tentative identification and wrote it across the comment window: *fast cruiser of Femmish manufacture, probable type Bandicoot.*

The intruder made its way confidently towards an ugly looking world no more than ten light years away. It was blotched with irregular areas of black, buff, grey, and blinding white. *Atmospheric activity index high*, said the computer, *optional gloss available in sub-window 6*. While they studied the depressing details, the *Hubble* slunk along in the Bandicoot's wake, using the phase turbulence that it generated to mask any leakage not damped out by the stealth field.

The Femm cruiser made a competent landing at the edge of a thermally active region. About a kilometre away a geyser spouted boiling water hundred of metres skywards every few minutes. *Hubble* sent out a landing-craft, surrounded by a thin pseudopod extruded from the main stealth field. Aboard were two marines — a spot-lieutenant and an armiger-designate — and Jole Jarneyvore. It was the largest force they dared risk, but it was too small for safety.

The planet's atmospheric activity index was high, all right. Its notion of a gentle breeze would have been a hurricane elsewhere, and its rain was dangerously acidic. Under cover of darkness the Femm cruiser offloaded a small crate into a massive sealed ground-transport: they watched with nitesites but they couldn't see what was inside the crate. The Femm treated it with exaggerated care. Jole had his own theory — hunch — but it didn't compute to a sufficient credibility threshold and he kept it to himself.

The transport rumbled off among the geysers and the landing-craft followed, still hidden by the mother-ship's stealth field. Jole took the opportunity to check out their equipment again. The usual stuff — food, protective gear, weapons, communicators — and three much more unusual items. They didn't look fancy, just flat boxes that clipped to their belts. But inside... "Take a stasis-suit each," the Captain had ordered. "If things don't work out as planned, trigger them, and we'll come and get you after the ruckus is over." The stasis-suit was an impenetrable field that roughly approximated the body's contours. Within it, time ceased to pass. The person inside it had, literally, no time to do anything, so the stasis-field had be deactivated from the outside. *Edwin Hubble* carried the appropriate devices and codes to do this.

The stasis-suits were intended to boost their confidence, but they had exactly the opposite effect on Jole. The probabilities were too fluid for him to make a firm prediction, but he felt in his bones that they were going to *need* those suits. In fact that was why he'd left young Billy a stasis-field sensitive ring. He'd predicted that that would be needed one day, too.

The armiger-designate tapped Jole's shoulder. "Aren't those *ruins?*" Huge hexagonal shapes had come into view, arranged in great swirling spirals; some formed steep-walled mounds, some deep depressions. The Femm transport halted near a mound. The passengers unloaded the crate and carried it inside through a hidden entrance.

While this was going on, the three men crawled into the lee of the mound. A limpet-phone attached to the wall let them hear the conversation reasonably clearly, except when the wind howled too loudly round the crumbling crenellations.

"Galibrate the [inaudible], Mhyrrymn," said a guttural Femm voice. It was speaking (bad) Human, as expected. There must be humans present.

"Galibration complete," said another slightly wavering voice.

"Gonnect the freewave generator unit to the PAXIAL [inaudible] device."

Jole nodded grimly. *As I feared. The Femm have discovered a functioning piece of PAXIAL technology, and in combination with freewave it gives them...* But he didn't know what it gave them, except that it carried a reality-modification potential considerably above the fifth decad, which was unprecedented.

Then came a human voice. "Is it working, Mhyrrym?"

"Making final tests now, Bly."

Jole Jarneyvore mentally congratulated himself. Not just an Etonian, but Bly Eton himself, just as he'd computed. But what was Bly Eton doing with a team of Femm technicians, concocting some unholy alliance of PAXIAL and human technology in the warped space-time of Sharraby Breach? *If only they'd stop talking in vague generalities!* He was looking for detail too fine to resolve, but he could feel his short stubbly hair trying to stand on end as factor after factor slotted into the developing matrix and the probability haze began to condense around the principal prediction axes.

He touched one of his companions on the arm, and they made their way inside the building. Soon they were close enough to hear the voices directly. Bly Eton was speaking. "Is that setting right, Mhyrrym? The battle was 73 BQ, not 75!" It began to come together in Jole's head... 73BQ was the Battle of Gladstone's Gap, the crucial moment in the formation of the human-Grynth Duality.

"It is, Bly. The battle was in 73BQ, but the weakest point is two years and four months earlier. On the fourteenth of May, 75BQ, Milverton Wakhort is known to have attended his only daughter's graduation as a blue-belt solar magnetoscopist at DeLameter Gollege, Spandau Hills, on the planet of Quahootze Minim."

*The patterns are crystallizing fast. Milverton Waghort, whose creative act of high treason brought about the Duality, and thence the Quaternity...*

"At such an event it is the inviolable gustom that the graduand's closest relative on the paternal branch should publicly share a spunch-gague with the gollege faculty in the common-room immediately after graduation."

"Ahhhh. I see."

*Me too. Except the bit about the spunch-gague. Must be some weird native delicacy.*

"Exagtly, Bly. A simple nerve-poison will suffice. Our agent Munkress has trained long and hard for this crucial moment in history — or should I say, *out of* history? He will waylay the delivery-boy, assume his identity, and contaminate the gague with the poison. He will return here before Wakhort eats a slice."

"Is 'before' the right word?"

"As a rough description of meta-time, it must suffice."

Jole had heard more than enough. Every tiny detail of the plan was prickling the forefront of his mind. All the space-time coordinates... and the inevitable Femm double-cross. He even knew the name of the delivery-boy, so strong had the internal logic of the prediction frame now become.

*Sponge-cake.* He knew that, too.

"The calibrations are defined," said Mhyrrym. A strange yellow light cast diffuse shadows on the wall, but Jole couldn't see its source. "The transit field is on. Munkress, enter the transit field. And now it merely remains for you to —"

Jole drew his laser-pistol and nodded, once. *Now!* The three men charged at the enemy. But the Femm reacted to the first footfalls. In the half-second that it took for Jole's men to reach an open firing position, a dozen Femm guards had aligned their projectors and activated them. A bolt of energy seared past Jole's right ear and his hair shrivelled in the heat; both of his companions were mown down before they could get a clear shot. He rolled across the floor, ending up flat on his face at Bly Eton's feet. Between Bly's legs he saw a Femm enveloped in a glowing yellow hemisphere, the transit field. Beyond it,

226

a second Femm stood beside a compact piece of machinery which floated in mid-air — the time-machine.

With strength born of desperation Jole rolled sideways and pressed the firing-stud, slicing off most of Bly's head. Then he staggered to his feet and hurled himself past the glowing hemisphere to the time-machine itself, where Munkress was reaching out a finger...

In slow motion, perhaps out of the corner of his eye, perhaps in real-time prediction mode, he saw a dozen projector barrels swinging towards him. He grabbed Munkress's arm and swung him away; then he clutched the time-machine against his chest. "No!" Mhyrrym screamed at the guards. "You'll destroy the machine!" But the guards were trained for reflexes, not judgement, and their projectors went off almost together. Mhyrrym threw himself behind a rock, expecting an explosion.

Instead, two of the guards were killed by ricochets as the beams glanced harmlessly off a shining, metallic, dumpy, humanoid-shaped stasis-field.

\* \* \*

PLEASE LOOK AT ME. IT'S IMPORTANT.

"Dad, how could you have known I was coming here without knowing when?"

Jole smiled, the superior smile of an expert confronted by lay ignorance. "The mental integration involves an arbitrary constant."

"Oh."

"All else was predictable. The chaos of the universe was collapsed by convergence on to a single class of futures."

"Ah."

Jole's surroundings finally intruded on his perceptions. "Where are we? The decor is *atrocious*."

"Like a whore's bedroom," said Billy. "A whore with appallingly bad taste." There was a sharp sound like a tove's foghorn, as the source of the thought balloons lost the last remnants of its patience. Heads turned towards the noise, and finally noticed the message in the balloon. Which now read:

I RESENT THAT. THE TASTE OF THE URSCA IS IMPECCABLE. BUT IN ANY CASE YOU MISUNDERSTAND. YOUR SURROUNDINGS ARE NOT 'DECOR'. THEY ARE SEVERELY FUNCTIONAL TECHNOLOGY.

"Dad! I thought it was *you* projecting those words!"

"No, son, I was in stasis. Surely you know that you can't do anything from inside a stasis field — not even get yourself out of it."

Billy was getting more out of his depth every second. "The Ursca?" he said stupidly.

YOU WOULD SAY 'THE PAXIAL'. YOU ARE NOW IN THE URSCA'S UNIVERSE. THE URSCA BUILT THIS PLACE. THE URSCA VISITED YOUR UNIVERSE, A THOUSAND YEARS AGO, BUT COULD NOT STAY.

"Why not?"

IT WAS TOO WARM.

Flare's mind began to clear. "Friend Ursca: release now?" The pillows surrounding Billy and Flare subsided like a soufflé removed from an oven, and they crawled out on hands and knees.

I APOLOGISE FOR RESTRAINING YOU, BUT IT WAS NECESSARY AS A TEMPORARY MEASURE, read the balloon. I HAVE MANY FACTORS TO BALANCE AND I HAD TO BE SURE I COULD LOCATE YOU QUICKLY. I AM HERE TO WARN YOU OF IMPENDING DOOM.

*Pompous bugger*, thought the Joat. The black tubes writhed.

YOU'LL REGRET THAT REMARK, PRUGFACE. And Billy realised he was dealing with a telepath.

"Warn?" asked Flare in apprehension. "Warn of what?"

THE END OF CIVILIZATION, said the speech-balloon.

"*What?*"

DON'T WORRY, IT WON'T HAPPEN FOR SEVERAL HOURS YET.

"Is it related —" Jole began.

TO THE ETONIAN PLAN? YES. YOUR RELEASE FROM STASIS CREATES THE CONDITIONS NEEDED FOR THE PLAN AGAIN TO BECOME VIABLE.

"Plan?" asked Billy.

"Why did you engineer my release, if it reactivates the plan?" asked Jole.

"What plan?" Billy repeated.

BECAUSE THE PLAN CAN'T BE MADE TO FAIL UNLESS IT IS ALLOWED TO PROCEED. THE LAWS OF THE METATEMPORAL UNIVERSE PERMIT NO OTHER FINAL SOLUTION.

"Will somebody *please* tell me, *what bloody plan?*" Jole quickly filled the Joat in on the details — coordinates, name of delivery-boy, the lot.

"Excuse butting in," said Flare. "All very interesting, but would prefer go home."

YOU CAN'T LEAVE RIGHT NOW. YOUR PRESENCE IS VITAL TO THE CONTINUED EXISTENCE OF THE

QUATERNITY. AND OF THE URSCA. WHICH TO TELL THE TRUTH IS WHAT'S REALLY ON MY MIND, it added realistically. WE MUST COOPERATE.

Billy perched himself on the edge of a huge satiny cushion, primrose yellow with cute little pink polka-dots. "I'm all in favour of cooperation. But you haven't explained why. Or what we have to do. It's been coercion all the way, not cooperation."

THE *WHY* IS EASY: YOU JUST HAPPEN TO BE IN THE RIGHT PLACE AT THE RIGHT TIME WITH ALL THE RIGHT GEAR. I ADMIT IT'S POSSIBLE THAT SOME UNIVERSAL GALACTIC CONSCIOUSNESS, LIKE THAT GALAXIA THING THAT JENIPHA LOCKLOVE RABBITS ON ABOUT SO MUCH, MIGHT HAVE CONSPIRED TO PLACE YOU HERE AS PART OF SOME SELF-REGULATING PROTECTION SYSTEM. MAYBE IT DIDN'T JUST 'HAPPEN', MAYBE IT WAS PREORDAINED.

"How do you know about Jenipha — oh, you're telepathic."

The Ursca didn't answer, but resumed its previous train of thought. THE *WHY* IS EASY, BUT THE *WHAT*... THAT'S A BIT TRICKIER. IN GENERAL TERMS IT'S SIMPLE ENOUGH: YOU HAVE TO STOP THE FEMM USING THEIR TIME MACHINE TO ASSASSINATE MILVERTON WAGHORT. BUT I HAVE NO IDEA HOW YOU ACHIEVE THAT. ALL I KNOW IS THAT YOU CAN IF YOU MAKE THE RIGHT CHOICES.

"How do you know that?"

I ALSO CAN SENSE THE POTENTIALITIES OF THE FUTURE.

"Any ideas, Dad?"

"Is our presence here preordained, you mean?" Jole was offended. "Son, professional prediction is purely a matter of probability flows. It has absolutely nothing to do with predestination or galactic hyperconsciousness." Billy tried to interrupt, but Jole interpreted this as an apology and waved it away. "I know you didn't mean to cause offence, son, but you laymen *always* get that stuff mixed —"

"No, Dad, I didn't mean do you have any ideas about Locklove's Galaxia hypothesis. Do you have any ideas on how to stop the Femm killing Waghort?"

YOUR FATHER WILL HAVE THE SAME TROUBLE AS THE URSCA. IT IS A TEMPORAL BUTTERFLY POINT. THE COMPUTATIONS BECOME NONDETERMINISTIC WHENEVER THOSE EVENTS ARE APPROACHED. THERE ARE ONLY TWO POSSIBLE OUTCOMES, AFTER THE HAZE CLEARS. IN ONE, THE QUATERNITY STILL EXISTS, AND ALSO THE URSCA. IN THE OTHER, THE QUATERNITY IS REPLACED BY A FEMM-

DOMINATED EMPIRE, AND FOR THE URSCA THERE ARISES A PHASE OF LINGERING DECLINE AND DECADENCE. BUT IT IS NOT CLEAR WHICH WILL HAPPEN, OR HOW EITHER MIGHT COME ABOUT.

"From what you're saying, the Femm must be on their way here. I say we beat it fast."

NO. THAT WILL NOT BE PERMITTED. YOU ARE NEEDED.

"So just sit around and wait?" asked Flare.

NOW THAT YOU UNDERSTAND THE PROBLEM AND CAN TURN YOUR MINDS TO IT, YES. THERE REMAIN SEVERAL HOURS BEFORE EVENTS BECOME PIVOTAL.

"Great," said the Joat. "Nothing like a long period of inactivity to get you ready for Armageddon. I'll be as nervous as a hummingworm in a boggiewallow!" He scratched his head. "Well, while we're sitting here digging up the past, I've got a whole load of questions to ask. I'm not saying I don't believe you, but your story has a *lot* of holes in it!"

IT IS ALL RATHER COMPLICATED, said the Urscan thought-balloon apologetically.

"OK. One: What happened to the *Hubble*?"

THE FEMM FOUND OUT ABOUT IT AND BLEW IT APART. THEY KNEW THERE MUST BE A MOTHER-SHIP SOMEWHERE, AND IT COULDN'T STAY CONCEALED FOR LONG ONCE THEY MADE A SERIOUS ATTEMPT TO FIND IT.

"That's the basic design-flaw of a stasis-suit," sighed Jole. "Not much use if there's nobody left to turn it off again."

The Joat nodded. "Two: why didn't the Femm just build another time-machine?"

THEIR APPARATUS IS BASED AROUND AN ANCIENT URSCA DEVICE WHOSE SECRET HAS BEEN LOST. IT IS THE ONLY ONE THAT STILL FUNCTIONS, IN THIS UNIVERSE OR YOURS.

"Right. Three: why can't we just destroy the time-machine?"

THAT'S MORE COMPLICATED. THE CONSEQUENCES OF DESTROYING IT ARE FAR WORSE THAN EVEN A FEMM EMPIRE. THE ANCIENT DEVICE INCORPORATED INTO IT IS OF MAJOR SIGNIFICANCE TO THE URSCA . IF IT IS DESTROYED THE URSCA CEASE TO EXIST.

"Why Humans worry about that?" asked Flare bluntly.

IF THE URSCA CEASE TO EXIST, YOUR UNIVERSE WILL ALSO CEASE TO EXIST."Humans worried now," said Flare.

I WOULD PREFER NOT TO EXPLAIN ANY MORE. AS YOUR SAYING GOES, HE WHO FEEDS THE CAT CALLS THE CHORUS.

"Oh, right. Five —"

"Four, Billy."

"Yeah, thanks Flare, *four*: in that case, why don't you just take the device from us and scarper?"

IF THE DEVICE REMAINS IN EXISTENCE BUT NO FURTHER ACTION IS TAKEN, THE FEMM WILL TRY AGAIN. THEY ARE TOO MANY, THE URSCA CANNOT RESIST THE COMBINED MASS OF THE FEMM INDEFINITELY. YOU STAND AT A REALITY NEXUS WHERE A FINAL SOLUTION MAY BE ATTAINED IF THE CORRECT ACTIONS ARE TAKEN. THE FATE OF TWO UNIVERSES IS IN YOUR HANDS.

"I've just remembered an urgent appointment," said the Joat.

\* \* \*

With time on his hands and nowhere to go, no respectable joat could resist the siren call of a Femm-Ursca hybrid time machine for long, as the Joat explained to Flare when she noticed what he was doing. "Don't worry, I'll soon have it back together again! The back came off without any trouble. Well, I did have to cut a couple of bolts, but I'm sure they weren't essential... and take that disapproving look off your face. If you must know, I'm familiarising myself with the equipment."

"Never realise before that 'familiarise' mean spread around floor in several hundred pieces," she said snootily. "What happen if damage?"

"What happens if I don't?" asked the joat enigmatically. "You answer me that! Don't worry, Flare, I know precisely what I'm doing. Once I find that nut..." He began to reassemble the pieces. There was a kind of metal trellis that formed a cage. It held an item of ghostly Ursca/PAXIAL machinery, the ancient and unique device that the Femm had somehow got hold of. He picked said device up, turning it over to see what was underneath.

It had an equally ghostly bottom, but otherwise the inspection revealed nothing of interest. He revolved it in his hands, and it slipped from his fingers to the floor. Flare's heart bounced.

Fortunately, so did the machine. URSCA TECHNOLOGY IS MADE TO LAST A MILLION YEARS. NOW, STOP MESSING ABOUT AND PUT IT ALL BACK TOGETHER. THE TIME FOR ACTION IS APPROACHING.

"I agree," said Jole. "But *what* action?"

NOT MY DEPARTMENT.

"I'm beginning to get an idea," said the Joat. "I am developing — a plan."

"What sort plan, Billy?"

"A very flexible plan, Flare, on account of I don't know what the Sumphole is going on." He screwed on a corner-bracket and plugged a ribbon connector back in; scowled, pulled it out and reversed it, looked slightly more satisfied with the result. "Crummy bit of workmanship, this."

I'LL HAVE YOU KNOW THAT —

"I meant the Femm components! The Urscan part is no doubt impeccable, but I can't be certain of that because I haven't the foggiest idea what it does or how it does it — or even what it *is*. I can't even *see* it directly, I have to sort of sneak up on it with the corners of my vision."

THAT IS NOT IMPORTANT. BUT YOU MAY ADMIRE THE WORKMANSHIP IF IT PLEASES YOU.

"Just my luck. A member of ancient hi-tech race, and it turns out to have more vanity than all the contestants for *Mz. Quaternity* laid end to end."

"Freudian simile, Billy."

"Intentional." He clipped the final strand of wire in place, slotted the components back inside their case, and pushed a dozen control knobs back on to the slider levers. "There, done. Undamaged, but now I know what's inside it."

"What is inside it?"

"A great deal that I don't understand. But." He pointed at the levers, gesturing expansively. "These are obvious: they are the time-settings along the top row, the space settings along the bottom. They use Quaternity standard coordinates."

"I'm impressed. How did you work that out?"

The Joat blushed in embarrassment. "It says so on the label at the front, look." He handed her the time-machine. "Oh, Sump, I wish something would happen!"

"Then your wish is kranted!" It was a Femm voice and it came from behind them. "Do not move, we have you covered!"

\* \* \*

There were five Femm and one human, all armed. Behind them a grey ovoid hovered on what looked like a maglev field. *That damned fool Ursca! It's telepathic, so why didn't it — no, wait. The*

*Femm are immune to the telepathic effects of magneurex. Can it work the other way round? So the Ursca didn't know they were here? But in that case, what sort of —* But now was not the time to speculate.

"Don't try anything, son," Jole said quietly. Billy forbore to point out that there was nothing to try. He recognised the human as Kray Harrow, and wondered what the ovoid was. Looked like a cyborg levi-unit, only there was no sign of the cyborg. *Unless it's inside…*

The ovoid slid towards him, swivelling menacingly, pointing its sharp snout straight at him. He could see the cameras on each side, now. And the twin microphones for hearing.

"You *are* a cyborg!" he said. It was a rhetorical statement, he wasn't expecting a reply. But he got one.

"I am. And it's your fault, Jarneyvore!"

The voice-synthesis wasn't very lifelike, but it was close enough for him to guess. "I thought you were dead, Sherryl." She must have been pretty badly smashed up. The guilt came flooding back.

"That's just the way I wanted it, Jarneyvore. I set a trap and you walked into it, all unsuspecting and innocent. But you deserve everything you're going to get. You're guilty, Jarneyvore. Both of you." She swivelled her sensors to point at Jole. "You're guilty of murder." She turned back to Billy. "And you're guilty of worse."

"It was you who got too close to an erupting volcano, Sherryl," said the Joat. "I'm not to blame."

"It was your meddling that caused it, Jarneyvore! You've made my life a living Hell. So now it's my turn. My turn to do the same to —"

"At the appropriate time," said Harrow, "I will hand over the two Jarneyvores for you to play with, Sherryl. But first I shall deal with the Quaternity, just as Munkress was supposed to do twenty-five years ago." He pointed a small but deadly weapon at Flare. "Move away from the time-machine, darling. Be sensible, cooperate. Or not, if you prefer. I don't care."

"Billy?"

"Do what he says, Flare," said the Joat. "There's nothing to be gained by resisting." *And the Ursca warned us not to risk destroying the time-machine.*

"No guts, even now," sneered Sherryl. Reluctantly, Flare moved away. A Femm picked the machine up and handed it to Tubbytt. The Cysparagon, determined not to make the mistake of leaving a sensitive mission to subordinates, had joined the landing-party. He passed it to a technician, who took it away for testing.

"And now," Harrow said darkly, "we wait. For a little while." His stare moved unblinkingly from the Joat to his father and back again.

* * *

The technician reported that the time-machine's circuits were still in full working order, adding that this was not surprising since it had been in a stasis-field. Harrow shrugged, looked long and hard at the Joat. "I'll let you watch this," he said quietly. "It will drive home just how futile your meddling has been. Sherryl: do nothing until I have left." He checked his pack, then climbed into the machine.

A technician set the space levers at the galactic coordinates for the common-room of DeLameter College and the time levers to graduation day, 75BQ, and quickly moved out of the way. Harrow grinned, paused for a second, took a deep breath, and touched the 'on' button. A shimmering yellow hemisphere sprang into being, surrounding both him and the time-machine, and then it vanished.

"Mission accomplished," said Tubbytt in satisfaction. This time, even with two Jarneyvores to contend with, he had succeeded.

"Not quite," said Sherryl. "Not until I've had my little bit of fun disposing of the loose ends."

# 21  Head Them Off at the Past

Enclosed in her grey ovoid, Sherryl Eton supervised the preparations. "Something simple to begin with," she said. "Later we can get more elaborate. Don't want to do *too* much damage just yet. Yes, put the electrode unit over by the wall. Plug it in, make sure there's an adequate supply of power." Billy, Jole and Flare watched, restrained by shackles, as the Femm hurried to and fro to her orders. "Get those heating-coils ready. Jump to it!"

"Flare, I'm sorry," said the Joat, knowing that anything he could say would be totally inadequate. He eyed the wristband remote where Sherryl had placed it, tantalizingly out of reach and switched off.

"Not at fault. Should know better than hitch ride from stranger." She turned her head to look at Jole. "Would have preferred meeting under more pleasant circumstances, Mr. Jarneyvore, but glad to meet anywa—"

"Stop that prattling!" snapped the ovoid. "Platoon-enabler! Have the prisoners gagged, their idle chatter bores me." The order was carried out, and the ovoid floated across the floor to within a few metres of the three prisoners. "I think the process will be more effective if we deal with you one at a time. Yes — the girlfriend first, then the elder Jarneyvore. You," she added, turning to point her sensors at the Joat, "will be last. I want you to see your companions suffer, and I want you to know that your own torment will be immeasurably greater than anything I do to them." The Joat's curses were muffled by the gag, and after a few seconds he gave up. This time there was no way out. He hoped he would die well, he hoped they would all die quickly, and while he didn't believe there was a chance in Hell of either of those things happening, he was absolutely certain that, one way or another, they'd all die.

On Sherryl's instructions a Femm attached electrodes to various parts of Flare's body. Another wrapped heating-coils round one of her feet, and plugged them into a small power-unit. A third poised a hand over the control-panel, waiting for the order to begin. "A few more seconds," said Sherryl. "Anticipation adds so much to such an occasion."

All eyes were upon the victim — except one pair, which couldn't bear to watch. Behind the staring Femm, the Joat saw a yellow haze building. Harrow returning from the past, no doubt, having completed his mission. "You may begin," said the ovoid. The technician raised a bony finger, poised it... and stabbed at the on switch.

The finger went right through the control-panel without resistance. Its owner tumbled through after it, and there was a long, fading howl of terror. The Femm whirled, fired their projectors, and died where they stood, mown down by their own guns. One beam sliced off the ovoid's communications antenna, cutting Sherryl off from her ship. Tubbytt lay on the floor, staring blankly as a fatal stain spread across his uniform. This time the mistake had been to be *present* at the operation. How had his plans gone so badly awry? He shuddered and died, without finding an answer.

*It isn't Harrow after all*, Billy realised. Sherryl did too, and cursed. She had wanted weapons installed in the ovoid, but the medics had vetoed it for self-protection. A cyborg is not the most stable of creatures. "Sherryl! If you move a millimetre I'll melt you to slag!"

The Joat *knew* that voice — it was familiar but he couldn't quite place it, there was something slightly odd... The yellow light disappeared and the time-traveller emerged, carrying some kind of bag. Billy recognised the face all right. It was even more familiar than the voice.

It was his own.

The voice sounded different because it wasn't resonating through the bones of his head. You never recognise your own voice.

The second copy of Billy the Joat was dressed in strangely archaic garments, and carried a plastic bag. He circled warily round Eton's ovoid, and forced it head first into a corner of the room. He picked up the remote and put it on Billy's wrist. "You'll need this one day," he said. Then he undid their shackles. "Billy, Jole, tip the cyborg on its back!" Sherryl Eton screeched obscenities as her vehicle was upended, its propulsors thrashing like the legs of an upside-down turtle.

"Where did — how —"

"I know this may sound silly in the circumstances, but there's no time for explanations," said Joat-2. Flare, Jole: take a couple of those projectors — he pointed at the ones that the Femm guards had dropped — and guard the door just in case anybody else arrives and tries to get in. Weld it shut, if you can. And make sure Sherryl doesn't cause trouble. Billy, come with me!"

"Where?"

Joat-2 dragged him across to the time-machine. "Not where, *when*. Back to the year 75BQ. Kray Harrow has being about to will have poisoning Milverton Waghort, and we've got to make sure it won't been diverted the timestream."

\* \* \*

Meta-time is a curious medium.

It has its own flows, its own momentum, its own consistencies. What we perceive as sequential events in our own time-flow are but random snapshots of meta-time, shuffled into plausible causal order by our own consciousnesses. Events that unfold in meta-time can be described in several independent but overlapping frames of reference. The same meta-sequence of events tells a different story in each.

The simplest frame is that of Flare, who witnesses two disappearances of the time-machine, two reappearances, and little else.

The next simplest is that of Kray Harrow. In his frame, he goes back in time and poisons Waghort. Then he moves up the timestream to 212QC when Rudolph Eton invented freewave, to verify that the securing of the Etonians' patent has not been erased from the timestream — and to make sure that if so, that event is reinstated. Then he is supposed to return to the precise instant he left. There are, however, a few alterations to this plan, thanks to the activities of two copies of Billy the Joat.

Viewed in meta-time they are, of course, one copy. The Joat's frame is the most complex, but also the most illuminating to those accustomed to perceiving the universe as a causal sequence of events ordered by a single timeline. Let us therefore consider the unfolding of the story in the frame of the Joat.

\* \* \*

Transition between times is subjectively instantaneous. "Where are we?" asked Joat-1.

"In an inn across the street from DeLameter College on Quahootze Minim," replied Joat-2.

"And the year is 75BQ."

"Right. A week from now, Harrow will have just finished poisoning Milverton Waghort."

"Except that we get in there and stop him."

Joat-2 pushed the time-machine under the bed. "No, I'm afraid he succeeds."

"*What!*"

"Unfortunately there is simply too small a gap between his arrival and the poisoning for us to prevent it. Waghort jumps the gun and eats the cake before he's supposed to, and because of that the interval we have to hit is smaller than the tolerances in the time-machine settings. Afterwards, of course, is too late. If we go back *before* the event, as we have done, Harrow isn't around. And if we sit here and wait for natural time to pass, I assure you we will get there just too late."

"How can you know that?"

"I'm a future version of you. I already know what meta-happened."

The Joat was in a state of shock. "Then we've — I've — failed."

Joat-2 shrugged. "You think so? You give up too easily."

"I'm you. *You* give up too easily."

"I don't give up at all. I've got everything we need in this bag."

"Everything we need? To do what?"

"For you to impersonate Milverton Waghort. Clothes, artificial facial tissue, muscle-tone injections, hypnodrone tapes with his entire family history, and the complete works of the Prophet Grudnidle — you recall he's a devout Grudnidlist. You spend a pleasant week in the inn, boning up on his past and getting your features into a really good likeness. Then Harrow arrives, ambushes the delivery-boy, poisons the cake. Waghort sneaks unexpectedly into the kitchen and pinches some. While that's happening we waylay Harrow, knock him out, and pinch his time-machine. Waghort feels sick, goes to the men's room — alone. You follow him in, take over his role, and hide one copy of the time-machine. I depart with the other copy — the one we arrived in — and take Harrow and Waghort's corpse with me. I get rid of them both, not yet sure how. You play Waghort for two years, pray to Grudnidle every dawn and dusk, then sell out the Humans to the Grynth."

"You mean — *I'm the traitor?*"

"You got it. But he wasn't a traitor, he was a visionary."

"It's easy for you to say tha— no, it isn't. You're me. But you've had time to come to terms with it."

"Just learn to think in meta-time, young Wyllam. You'll have two years to perfect the theory in your spare time. What little you'll have between prayers."

"And after that?"

"You head upstream in your copy of the time-machine. You stop off along the way to buy this bag of goodies —" Joat-2 held it up "— at a theatrical supply store. Then you arrive on Hurscaffl just in time to save Flare, Jole Jarneyvore, and Billy the Joat from being tortured to death by Sherryl Eton. That's where the wristband remote comes in, so put it in a safe place along with the time-machine."

"Of course. And at that point I become you."

"In meta-terms you *are* me, but, yes, that's right. Now you see where I and the 'other' time-machine came from."

"In a manner of speaking. But the global causality is paradoxical. My head hurts."

"In a meta-temporal synthesis, it all hangs together. There is no linear causality and no paradox."

"And what do *you* do next?"

"I'm not sure. Uh — it hasn't happened to me yet."

\* \* \*

Everything transpired as Joat-2 had — well, postdicted. Harrow arrived in a broom-cupboard of DeLameter College, coshed the delivery-boy, purloined his sponge-cake, and spiked it with poison. The two Joats, disguised as cleaners, arrived just as Waghort — who had been delayed while travelling to the event and hadn't eaten for hours — was snaffling a slice of cake from the kitchen. They stole the time-machine from the broom-cupboard, temporarily hiding it in the gymnasium under a vaulting-horse, and put a heavy padlock on the cupboard to slow Harrow down when he returned. Next, they manoeuvred an embarrassed parent into knocking the celebratory cake off the table, to avoid poisoning the entire gathering. They cleared the mess away before anyone other than the unfortunate Waghort could eat any. Joat-2 caught up with Harrow as he tried to force the padlock on the broom-cupboard, knocked him out with a goosball bat, tied him hand and foot, and hid him inside a large carton of sweatshirts.

While this was happening Joat-1 followed Waghort into the men's room, arriving just in time to lower the freshly dead corpse gently to the floor. He dragged it into a cubicle, which he locked from the inside. Then he climbed into the next cubicle and disguised himself as Waghort. Joat-2 arrived with a sack and a cleaner's trolley and removed the corpse; Joat-1 went back to attend his daughter's graduation ceremony and play the proud parent, consuming large quantities of champagne in the process. Any flaws in his performance would be put down to his having drunk too much. Within a few hours he'd be perfect. It was lucky, though, that Waghort lived alone.

Over the next two years he settled into the Waghortian role. To stay in character he spent hours praying to Grudnidle, and in his spare time he worked on meta-time theory to avoid being bored out of his tiny mind. With his eidetic memory and broad knowledge-base he made himself an indispensable asset at EMPCINC, and was promoted on to the staff of General Hilton Wheedle. Grynth intelligence made contact with him by a devious route involving a topless waitress and a dozen cream puffs. As the Battle of Gladstone's Gap approached, he passed on vital information about the installations on the satellite of My Delight, hidden inside a crate of frozen gerbils-on-a-stick.

Shortly afterwards, in very mysterious circumstances, he simply disappeared. Nobody knew that he had departed in a time-machine. He stopped briefly in 427QC to purchase various items from The Operating Theatre, a greasepaint-and-costume store on Hudibrastic IX. Then he arrived on Hurscaffl, just in time to save Flare, Jole Jarneyvore, and Billy the Joat from being tortured to death by Sherryl Eton. This was simple, he'd had two years to plan it. He used the transfer-plane generator, with Belphoebe's assistance via wristband remote. The Femm whose task it was to switch on the torture devices fell through a transfer plane whose other end was just off the edge of a carefully chosen cliff. The others shot themselves as the beams from their weapons passed through two suitably aligned transfer planes. One beam disabled Sherryl's communications.

At that meta-instant he effectively became Joat-2.

Leaving Flare and Jole to deal with Sherryl, Joat-2 hurried Joat-1 into the time-machine, gave him the wristband remote, and transported him back to 75BQ. He then explained to him that they were in DeLameter College on Quahootze Minim, and that they could not prevent Harrow from will have just finished poisoning Milverton Waghort. He knew this, he said, because he will had been there when it happenings. He then explained to Joat-1 that he must impersonate Milverton Waghort, sell out the Humans to the Grynth, head upstream in one copy of the time-machine, and stop off along the way to buy some goodies at a theatrical supply store. Then he must arrive on Hurscaffl just in time to save Flare, Jole Jarneyvore, and Billy the Joat from being tortured to death by Sherryl Eton.

The plan worked, at least up to the point at which he, Joat-2, was left with the problem of disposing of the body of Milverton Waghort and dealing with Kray Harrow. He wasn't sure what to do then, because this bit hadn't happened to him yet. But he did know that the Femm were planning to double-cross the Etonians, and thanks to Jole's impeccable predictions and his own perfect memory he knew exactly when and where.

Though he had no idea what.

In the event, he did the obvious and hid in the gymnasium until dark. Then he stole a small truck, loaded Waghort, Harrow, and the time-machine into it, and headed out into the hills. He needed time to think.

He buried Waghort in a wooded glade twenty kilometres from the nearest road, reciting a lengthy prayer to the Prophet Grudnidle — a sentimental gesture but one that seemed only appropriate. He sat and mused upon the contrast between the remarkable simplicity of the meta-universe and the appalling muddle it always looked like when projected into any sequential timeline. He wondered why he lived in a meta-universe that was so constituted that time travel was possible and paradoxes sprouted by the billion, until he realised that by the anthropic principle it was silly for a creature that had arrived where and when it was by means of time travel to enquire why it lived in a universe where time travel was possible. Then he returned to the truck and was knocked silly by Harrow, who had managed to undo his bonds while the Joat was wasting time on religion and philosophy. He came to his senses just in time to see Harrow climbing into the time-machine.

Harrow jeered at him. The yellow hemisphere glowed for a few seconds, and was gone.

\* \* \*

At this point one might have expected the Joat to collapse in despair. But two years' thought about the deep flows of meta-time — and certain spiritual side-effects of Grudnidlism — had turned him into something of a fatalist. First he tried to work out *when* Harrow had gone to. This wasn't hard, since Jole had already told him Harrow's plan. He checked to make sure the logic was still valid.

*He knows I knocked him out but he also knows he poisoned Waghort... He doesn't know I impersonated him and kept the timeline stable, he thinks he succeeded in preventing the foundation of the Duality. So he'll stick to the original plan and head for 212 QC, the invention of freewave. To make sure nothing untoward will have been happened to the Etonian patent — he thinks.* (The Joat had invented an entire set of new tenses for meta-temporal descriptions, but they hadn't quite gelled yet.)

*It* will *has have been, of course. The Femm have will playing a double game. They will have had been senting him into a trap. Because, having finished getting the Etonians to do their dirty work, the Femm will has wanted to eliminate them. The simplest way would be to eliminate their power. Now, they won't have initiated all of these complications without knowing in advance what the end result will be, so they must have some kind of meta-temporal prediction — or postdiction — system. So their own metapredictors will have postdicted what will have been has happened as a result of the Grynth defeat in 73 BQ... much as Jole will did.*

*All I have to do is make my way to 212 QC and find out what the situation actually will* is. *But that requires the use of a time-machine, which Harrow has snitched.*

*Damn. It's the only one.*

He rethought that. *Metatemporally speaking.* Then he started hopping up and down. *But in this timeline, Joat-1 still has his copy of the time-machine, concealed somewhere! And he's still here, playing Milverton Waghort! Now, I know he didn't will have noticed I borrowed it because I've already will been through those two years and I don't remembered any such event — and Joats have eidetic memories. What I do remember, as it happens, is where I hid it...*

* * *

Harrow laughed as the yellow haze cleared. *Success!* That idiot Jarneyvore had screwed up for good. Left the fool trapped in 75BQ. Now to check the freewave patent was still valid.

According to the plan, the settings he'd been told to use would put him in a disused building a few blocks away from the patent office. He looked out of the window, and checked. Yes, fine: he could see the building's main entrance in the street-lights. The ground between was just a wilderness of flattened rubble, so nothing got in the way, just as the Femm had said. Now, his instructions were to wait until daylight. He should then see Rudolph Eton arrive, to file his patent.

He didn't see why they couldn't have arranged for him to *arrive* in daylight, but no doubt the Femm knew what they were doing. The clever buggers always did. He found a pile of sacks in one corner, as promised; lay down on them, and dozed.

A yellow haze began to fill the room, but he didn't wake. The Joat's borrowed time-machine materialized next to Harrow's. He leaned across, picked Harrow's machine up. Both machines disappeared behind a yellow hemisphere... and vanished.

Harrow woke just before dawn. It took him a few seconds before he noticed the time-machine had gone. He rushed outside, thinking somebody had stolen it and hoping they hadn't got far. He ran frantically across the rubble-strewn ground, towards the distant road.

He was a block away when the explosion knocked him flying. He picked himself up, shook his head, and turned round. The building that he had been sleeping in had disappeared in a cloud of dust. *That's why there's all this rubble around. It's a demolition site. The Femm looked up the old records! The bastards told me they'd picked this site because it had a clear view of the patent office.*

It had been a Femm trap.

Which had failed.

He laughed. Within a few hours, Rudolph Eton would appear at the patent office. Once he'd made sure nothing interfered with that, his job was done. He would be stranded — unless he could dig the time-machine out of the rubble and make it work again. Not likely, he was no scientist. *But*, if he could get hold of the remains, and if the ghostly PAXIAL machinery at its heart wasn't damaged, maybe he could convince Rudolph Eton that he really was a time-traveller, and that he was there on the behalf of future Etonians! And Eton was a scientific genius. *He'd* make the time-machine work!

Harrow perched himself on a block of concrete and waited.

Sure enough, spot on time, Rudolph Eton appeared. Harrow watched as he walked into the patent office.

Excellent.

\* \* \*

The Joat, now in possession of two time-machines — more accurately, two meta-versions of the same machine — moved away a few hours and a few kilometres, for safety. He hid both machines carefully in a side-tunnel of the city sewers. He found a theatrical supply store and bought a selection of materials — if a trick's worth using once, it's worth using again. A visit to a pharmacist yielded some necessary chemicals.

At that point he introduced a new variation of his own into the proceedings. It made no sense whatsoever to restore the universe to its original time-track. All that would achieve would be to set up the whole mess again, a closed meta-cycle that would repeat the same actions forever. No, he had to risk making changes — changes big enough to remove the Etonians from the field of play altogether. He had half-convinced himself that he knew how to achieve that without making any really substantial differences to Quaternity history. He just hoped he could live with the result if he was wrong.

He tracked down Rudolph Eton's address from the telephone directory. In those days Eton was an impoverished inventor, and spent most of his time in a drunken stupor, so there was no problem in finding his house or in breaking into it and drugging Eton's beer. Soon the inventor was snoring like a satisfied tomcat and Billy the Joat was making himself up to look like Rudolph Eton.

He rifled the desk and found the patent application form and technical notes. He mixed up some ink-eraser and amended the form in a few crucial places. Then he tucked Eton's ID in his pocket, slipped out of the house, and headed for the patent office.

As he approached he noticed Harrow sitting on a concrete block. He wondered vaguely where the building that should have been behind the Etonian hit-man had gone, but his mind was on more important tasks. He turned into the foyer of the patent office. Once inside, he found a clerk. "I wish to deposit a patent on a method of instant communication. It will revolutionise civilization."

"Sure, bud," said the bored clerk. "Gotcha technical notes?"

"Yes."

"Gotta form?"

"Yes. Er — you will notice that I have filled in the patent owner as the Duality government." The clerk woke up. It was a standard provision on the form, but nobody ever *used* it. This guy was a nut. "I hope this is in order — I want the Duality as a whole to benefit from my discovery. I wish to donate it to the future of civilization."

A *serious* nut. "Yeah — if ya want — it's your choice, buddy. Me, I'd take the dough and let civilization look after its own future."

Having completed the legal niceties, the Joat returned to the sewers and picked up his time-machines, using one of them to convey himself and the other downstream to 75BQ. There he removed his Etonian disguise and returned the first time-machine to whence he had 'borrowed' it. Then he activated the remaining time-machine to head upstream to Hurscaffl, Flare, and his father.

Rudolph Eton awoke with a tremendous headache, and couldn't find the patent papers. This wasn't unusual, so he had a drink while he tried to remember what he'd done with them. Eventually he decided there'd been a burglary, so he called the police, who found that nothing else had been stolen. By then Eton was hot on the trail of a revolutionary method for freezing marmalade, so it took him several days to get round to visiting the patent office, getting a new form, filling it in, rewriting the technical notes, and returning to the patent office. At this point he discovered that he had already generously signed his invention over to the Duality government. He couldn't remember a thing, but to judge from the headache he now recalled, he must have had a wild time the night before. *Oh well*, he thought. *Easy come, easy go. In any case, there's that improved mousetrap that only needs a couple of dozen more diamond-coated bearings before it's finished...*

Harrow dug through the rubble for months. He never did find the remains of the time-machine. He never suspected that it wasn't there.

\* \* \*

The Joat returned to Hurscaffl. His clothes were soiled and sweat-stained, and his face was lined by lack of sleep. He seemed to have aged a couple of years. But he smiled the self-satisfied smirk of someone who has performed immaculately in circumstances that would try the patience of a dormant sumpsloth.

Then he blinked.

The dead Femm and Sherryl Eton's cyborg were nowhere to be seen. Neither was his father. Only Flare remained to greet him. "Flare, what's —"

"No time explain! *Now* get out here!" She grabbed his arm and slipped off the wristband remote, speaking rapidly through it to Belphoebe. Then she gave him a solid push and he found himself in *Lindilu*'s cabin. She appeared a moment later carrying the time-machine.

"Transfer plane," he said. "You set one up via the remote. But how did *you* know how to —?"

"No time. Must get off-planet and out of parauniverse before Ursca do something to prevent. Back through Breach."

"Can't we use the transfer pla— Oh, no, the generator can't pass through its own plane."

"Right. So get strapped in couch, will be rough." Belphoebe, hearing the instructions, was making ready for a fast take-off.

"Why the hurry?" asked the Joat, doing what she had told him. "What do you mean? Why should the Ursca try to stop us? I don't understand."

"Too right," said Flare. "Belphoebe: *now!*"

\* \* \*

The stars about them shone blood-red.

At top speed it would take them close on five hours to get out of Sharraby Breach. Flare would have preferred a shorter delay, but nothing could be done to speed things up, and she'd already instructed Belphoebe to take all possible precautions. Suddenly they had time on their hands.

"Young lady, you've got an awful lot of explaining to do! For a start, where's my father?"

"Is fine. Expect is at home. Never left."

"Huh?"

"Look, remember what sent back in time to *do?*"

There were times when Billy found Flare very indirect. "Yes, of course I do. I spent two years in a different time-zone and wandered all over the meta-temporal landscape! I still don't see quite how it all worked, even though I spent most of the two years thinking about the mathematics of meta-time. I think there was at least one causality violation in there somewhere."

She smiled, and touched his arm almost tenderly. "But did what needed. Knew would."

"Yes, I did. I made sure Waghort betrayed humanity to the Grynth by doing it myself, and I handed Rudolph Eton's freewave patent over to the fledgling Quaternity. I hope I thought that through right: no point in setting up an endless cycle through meta-time."

"Decision perfect. But not surprise if some things changed."

"Oh. Right. I didn't have time to think it through, too busy. I'd got meta-time sorted, pretty much, but I hadn't devised a way to work out changes to the overall timestream. Dad could do it intuitively. I found some beautiful equations for meta-time, you know. Unfortunately, I never found any equations that I could *solve*. I guessed that the loss of the patent would just destroy the Etonians' power-base, and leave everything else much the same as before. Isn't that right?"

"Flies in web, Billy. Change one thing, affect others. Whole web ripples, tears, reforms. New universe out there."

"How come you know so much all of a sudden?"

"Explain later. Yes, resemble old one closely. Only events affected by Etonian patent have changed. But such event was *Hubble* expedition. If Etonians hadn't had political power, would never have happened. More precisely, since Etonians *don't* have political power, *Hubble* expedition *didn't* happen. So Jole Jarneyvore never in Sharraby Breach. Simple!"

"But then *I* shouldn't be here either! Neither should you."

"Is matter of meta-time causality. Joat left here in Femmish time-machine, Joat came *back* in Femmish time-machine. Play in cracks between timezones. Anyway, Joat and Flare *here* all right, plain as noses on faces."

"Yes, but... am I still a joat? I thought that it was the loss of my father that made me such a pain in the ass."

"Psychoanalytic crap. Would be pain in ass no matter what. Anyhow, joat not *necessarily* same as pain in ass. Nothing can stop being joat if have mind of joat."

The Joat tried to work it out, but paradoxes kept intruding. And there were other problems. "What about the Ursca? It helped us. It needs that machine!"

"Cannot trust Ursca," said Flare. "Suspect what Ursca need machine *for*, do not approve."

"But without that machine, the entire Ursca race will die, and us too! That's what it told us!"

Flare arched her back to stretch her shoulder muscles. "Ursca told much, gave evidence nothing. Billy?"

"Yes, Flare?"

"*How many Ursca exist?*"

He looked blank. "I don't know. Millions? They got all over the place, we saw records of a huge civilization."

"Not millions," said Flare.

"How many, then?"

"One."

The Joat did a double-take, and began running past conversations through his head. The Ursca had always chosen ambiguous phrasing. It was never clear whether 'the Ursca' was singular or plural. He'd *assumed* it was plural, but...

"You mean that was *the* Ursca? The last sole surviving Ursca? The final member of the Urscan race?"

"Is part of story, yes."

"Hell, that explains quite a lot."

"Does. But not all."

"So the freezer-beast we saw was the *last* Ursca. Amazing."

"Very amazing. Except freezer-beast not Ursca."

This was getting too much. "Look, hang on, we saw thousands of freezer-beasts in the videos on the Urscan computer! Don't try to tell me they were domesticated animals or some such nonsense! They were the top dogs! So to speak," he finished lamely, having once more chosen a questionable metaphor.

"Not at all. Freezer-beasts are PAXIAL. Definitely."

"But I thought that the Ursca were the *same* as the PAXIAL — *ooooh*, but it was the *Ursca* that told us that! Hang on while I adjust my hypotheses, there's a slip showing." The Joat took a deep breath. "Yes. Right. The PAXIAL are just that — PAXIAL. So what the Sump is the Ursca?"

Flare looked at the floor. "Do not know, merely guess. But guess has firm basis. Believe Ursca telepathic parasite. Ursca enslave PAXIAL, destroy PAXIAL civilization."

"So *that's* why all traces of them cease a thousand years back!"

"Yes. Also why Hurscaffl installation ruined. Surviving PAXIAL under mental control of Ursca. Ursca pretend not, all part of deception. Mental paralysis caused by Ursca, not PAXIAL, also part of deception. Ursca try to enslave humans too. But humans more bloody-minded. *Much* more bloody-minded. Ursca not powerful enough without old PAXIAL machine."

"You mean that ghostly thingummy that was incorporated into the Femm time-machine?"

"Yes, very same. Is, as say, old *PAXIAL* device, which explain why Ursca cannot build new one. Ursca use device to amplify brain-patterns. Amplify brain-patterns enough, Ursca take over parauniverse. Take over ordinary universe too, poof! But device stolen by Femm, race immune to telepathy. Ursca stalemated. Then Jole Jarneyvore steal from Femm, hide in stasis-field, and *everybody* stalemated."

The Joat sat back in his seat, as everything tumbled neatly into place and a thousand unanswered questions resolved themselves. Then he realised that there were a thousand new questions that needed to be answered. "Flare, how do you know all this? How did you know how to use the wristband remote to Belphoebe? How to set up transfer planes? Most of all: *why are you still here?* Not wishing to be offensive, you understand, but — Hell, I picked you up in the Jumbles. I was there because I was searching for my father. In our reconstituted universe, *none of that happened.* I'm only here because I used the time-machine to come back here. You don't belong. But, unlike a lot of other people who didn't belong, you haven't gone back to where you *do* belong!"

"Good reason still here," said Flare. "Was *sent* here."

"Sent? Who by? *What* purpose?"

"To make sure Wyllam Jarneyvore do right thing to save Quaternity," said Flare.

He stared at her in shock. "*What are you?*"

Flare shrugged apologetically. "Am Assistant Deputy Inspector in Time Police. From future, 7885 QC to be exact. Was — will be — sent get Femm time-machine."

"Because of what the Femm were going to do with it?"

"Not exactly," said Flare. "Because this how Time Police get started. This where first time-machine come from. *Have* to go back to secure machine. In *Lindilu* now is future universe's original source of time-machine technology."

"But how did you get here?"

"Didn't did: *will*. Use time-machine, of course."

"But how can you use a time-machine before you've —"

"Is not *before*, is after! Long after. Use time-machine developed from one now being transported to Time Police Headquarters in *Lindilu*. Is clear, no? Totally safe. If Joat make wrong choice about changes to freewave patent, Time Police can intervene. But not needed. *Know* not needed, from history of formation of Time Police."

The Joat was indignant. "You mean all that moral agonizing I did about whether to change history was unnecessary? You could have told me what to do all along?"

"No, *was* necessary because already knew didn't tell! Think meta-time, all paradoxes resolve. Look, could spend three weeks of chronotensorial analysis, demonstrate full internal consistency, no paradoxes, yes? But first must teach chronotensorial analysis. Is not enough time."

I'D SAY YOUR TIME HAS RUN OUT ALTOGETHER. Because of the rapidly increasing distance from Hurscaffl, the black tubes tended to fade erratically. But they were clear enough. "It's found us!" said Billy, unnecessarily.

"Oh, yes. Inevitable."

NOW THAT I'VE FOUND YOU, I CAN CONTROL YOU. Billy felt a familiar wave of lassitude and confusion sweep over him, as the mental fog began to pervade his mind.

As consciousness faded, he thought he heard Flare giggle.

# 22   Grabbiting about Skumpers

Consciousness returned...

The Ursca! Billy felt the panic rising in his throat... He opened his eyes.

He was in *Lindilu*'s main cabin. It looked a wreck. The furniture was all over the place, mostly smashed. Had there been a fight? What with? The walls were daubed with a sticky red substance... blood?

If it was blood, why did it take the form of political slogans? What was Wurmstangle anyway, and why should anybody wish to vote for it? He staggered to his feet and took a closer look.

Jam. Doozberry, by the taste.

A hand touched his shoulder, and he jumped. It was Flare. She wore a large bathtowel and her hair was damp.

"Are we under the Ursca's mental control?" *And if she says no, how do you tell it's not just part of the illusion?* The Joat mentally snarled at himself — he'd never been that impressed by philosophy — and the intruding thought vanished.

"Gods, was *fantastic* party!" She flicked back a strand of wet hair from her cheek.

"Party?"

"Don't remember, huh? What sort excuse *that?*"

"Come to think of it, my head does feel fuzzy... hang on. I remember *something*. There *was* an Ursca, it was trying to control our minds! Flare, what happened to the Ursca?"

"Ursca cannot control minds if minds unconscious," said Flare primly. "Had instructed *Lindilu* put under mild anaesthetic if Ursca try anything, then exit Breach on automatics. Easy!"

"But then — what — " the Joat started again. "What happened to the cabin?"

"Was rowdy party. Celebrating bunglaphoon pre-election victory."

*Oh my aching head. Yes, It's all coming back to me now. We woke up while still in transition through the Breach, and —* "We turned into bunglaphoons again?"

"Yes."

"Oh no. Um. Flare... did we?"

"Do what?"

"Again, I mean. Like we did on the way in."

She gave him a very smug look. "From state of furniture, can surely guess."

"We did. Oh, gods, look, I'm sorry about —"

She put a finger to his lips. "Not apologise. Not responsible for actions during Breach transit. Not responsible for actions during party, either."

"Yeah. Look, Assistant Deputy Inspector of the Time Police, do you understand what happened back there? With the time-machine, I mean? Because I don't, and I could definitely use some enlightenment. I remember we were on the verge of death by torture, and then *I* rescued us. With a time-machine we didn't have."

"Didn't have then, in own timeline. But in meta-time is no paradox."

"Yeah, but —"

"Chronotensorial analysis complicated. Teach one day, maybe. But surely understand Feynman diagram?"

"Sure. Basic kiddygarten stuff. Particles in a space-time diagram. Antiparticles are ordinary particles moving backwards in time. Invented by some ancient philosopher. So what?"

"Physicist, not philosopher. Look, ask Belphoebe draw Feynman diagram of Joat, time-machine, and Harrow. Is very simple, yes?"

The Joat looked at the computer screen. The Feynman diagram was like surreal spaghetti with corners. "Sure," he said. "Crystal clear, Flare."

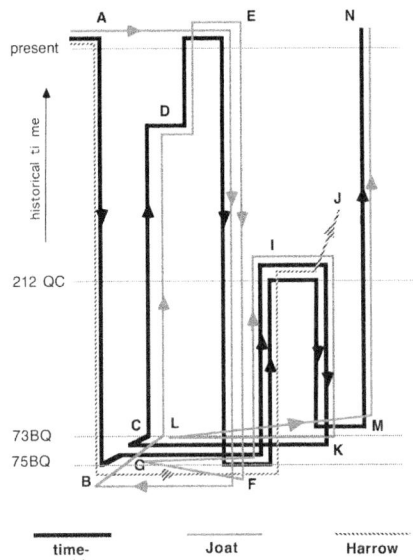

"Not sarcasm: *think*. Thick black line represent time-machine, grey line Joat, dotty line Harrow. Point A in meta-time represent Hurscaffl, present day.

"In Harrow frame of reference, dotty line go back to point B at 75 BQ, death of Milverton Waghort. Then go via point F to point I, freewave patent day, and then to J, where killed in bar brawl.

"In time-machine frame of reference, story more complex. Black line go from present at A to Waghort death at B. Take side-trip from G via F to I, when Joat-2 borrow time-machine. Then Joat carry time-machine passively back via K to replace at C. Next, time-machine used by Joat-1 to move up timestream to D, where pick up disguise bag. Then go to E, where Joat-2 appear to rescue Joat-1, Flare, and Jole. Next go *back* to F, time of Waghort, where stolen back by Harrow. Forward to I, where Joat-2 steal back again. Return to M by Joat-2 carrying previous version for replacement. Then finally go upstream to N. Is totally straightforward, yes?"

"Ug. Give me a moment to sort—"

"Finally, consider frame of reference of Joat, which more complex still. Joat start at A, about to be killed. Rescued at E, taken back to F. Spend period B-L impersonating Milverton Waghort. Then go upstream via D, where pick up disguise, to E where rescue self. Accompany self back to F and send self off to B with disguise, impersonate Waghort. Lose Harrow and time-machine at F. Borrow other version of time-machine at G, and go to I where steal original time-machine back from Harrow. Travel downstream to K, replace borrowed machine at L, and depart in remaining time-machine from M to arrive safely at N. See?"

"Yeah," said the Joat, feeling dazed. "It does all kind of fit together." A thought struck him. "Are you saying I became a mass of antiparticles when I travelled back in time? Shouldn't there have been huge releases of energy when my direction of travel reversed?"

"Were there?"

"Well, no."

"Then can rest assured did not become anti-Joat. Feynman diagram in meta-time is different. Meta-particles have no 'anti'. Just meta-particles. And meta-temporal flow have no 'reverse'. Like said, Feynman thing is kiddygarten analogy, not rigorous chronotensorial analysis. Important feature is key to understanding: each timeline *single unbroken strand*. Time-machine hop back and forth and go in loops producing apparent duplication, but actually all on single timeline. Joat also on single timeline, even when apparently duplicated."

"Yes, I can see that —"

"Moreover, all local causality entirely plausible. Nothing acausal. Rescue possible because Joat arrive with time-machine. Get time-machine from Harrow in 75 BQ by bashing over head. And so on. All events consistent and causal in meta-time picture, as proved by Feynman diagram.

"So why think there is problem?"

\* \* \*

The universe hadn't changed all that much, because SpaDe was waiting for them as they emerged from Sharraby Breach, in the not inconsiderable form of the heavy battlecruiser *Moulin Rouge* and the even less inconsiderable form of Joze Palgandra. Since they were coming out of the Breach, presumably in this universe they had also gone in, so some of the Joat's previous history must have stayed the same. Moreover, it was the same Palgandra that he had known and grudgingly respected, with dull beige fur and black-tipped ears, a mixture of orang-utan, grizzly, and vampire bat. His worries about creating an utterly alien world began to dissipate.

Another thing hadn't changed. The Grynth was not very pleased to see the Joat. Nor, to tell the truth, was the Joat pleased to see Palgandra when he discovered that the Grynth was holding warrants for his arrest on some fifteen thousand separate offences against the criminal law.

"— idiotic pranks," said Palgandra, at last beginning to run out of breath and totally out of original lines of invective. "This time you've really done it. Of all the irresponsible —"

"Done what, Palgandra?"

"Unauthorized entry into an interdicted zone, namely Sharraby Breach. You've turned the entire Quaternity upside down, I can't remember there ever being such a fuss! No knowing what damage you've done! What did you imagine you were up to?"

"Foiling an Etonian plot to destroy the Quaternity," said the Joat, before Flare could stop him. She cringed, waiting for the flash. She'd made it clear to Billy that the Time Police would blow him into gluon soup if he so much as opened his mouth about the time-machine. She was very polite about it, but it was out of her hands, a policy decision at the highest level. And now Palgandra would ask *what* plot, and —

"Etonians? What the pzzyth are *Etonians?*"

"Um," said the Joat, as reality thudded into place around him and a squad of Time Police concealed less than a decade away relaxed and lowered their weapons. "Sorry, getting confused with an HV melodrama I watched last week. Er — look, Palgandra, those fifteen thousand charges, it was just a tiny navigational error, you know how easy it is —"

The heavy head shook slowly. "No, Jarneyvore, you'll need a better excuse than *that*." The teeth bared in an exasperated snarl. "You're in *deep* trouble, my friend. I won't be able to get you out of it this time. And, to be frank, it's no more than you deserve. I'm fed up with your puerile antics, Billy the Joat. You've gone too far. There is absolutely nothing that can save you from a *very* long sentence."

"Not even finding the PAXIAL homeworld?" asked the Joat.

"Not even that," said Palgandra. "Well, maybe *that* —" he looked up sharply. "You're kidding," he said. "You've got to be kidding."

The Joat yawned, stretched his arms. "Sorry, Palgandra, had a bit of a party last night. Place is a bit of a mess. The bunglaphoon pre-election celebrations, you understand. Wurmstangle lost, if I recall correctly. Now, if I can only find —" He turned to Flare. "Where did we put my pack?"

"Is under overturned wardrobe."

The Joat heaved the furniture aside, found his pack, rummaged inside it, extracted a PAXIAL disk, and handed it to Palgandra. "Here's proof: working PAXIAL technology. We've got several dozen, and there's thousands more where that came from. But only Flare and I know where to find them. I wouldn't advise you to go looking in the Breach yourselves; there's something very dangerous on the loose there and only we know what it is and how to deal with it. That's the truth, and this disk is the proof. Run that past the boffins. But tell them to be *very* careful with it, it may contain an important PAXIAL secret."

"What secret?"

"That's for SpaDe to determine. You sit back and let your fur down, and I'll tell you how we got it."

\* \* \*

"... so you're saying that the spirals on the Hurscaffl installation match the spirals on the PAXIAL prisms," said Palgandra. "Intriguing. And the PAXIAL use the prisms as part of a matter-transmission system. Which leads us to conclude that the data on this disk relate to a system for moving entire planets over interstellar distances."

"You might think that," the Joat said guardedly. "I couldn't possibly comment. But I've presented you with the available evidence.

In return, I want your solemn word that all of those warrants will be withdrawn if that disk turns out to be the real PAXIAL goodies."

The Grynth snorted in discomfort and scratched its nose with a claw. "This is all speculation. I've got to offer my superiors something extra to justify my actions. You'll have to grant SpaDe all rights to whatever is on this disk."

"Well," said the Joat, "I was kind of hoping to get a whacking great royalty on the discovery. But you've got me over a barrel. If that's the price, so be it."

"Done!"

"The danger, I'll tell you about for free, but not until you've checked that disk for authenticity. I don't want to end up on the rocker-raft."

"The what?"

"Nuthouse. Funny farm. On Grover's World we — never mind. As I was saying, the danger warning will be free of charge. But Flare and I want a cut in anything *else* that you discover on the PAXIAL homeworld, once we tell you how and where to find it." Flare wouldn't be staying around to profit by it, but Palgandra didn't know that, and they had to remain in character.

"How big a cut?"

"One tenth of one per cent of the gross," said the Joat.

"Is that all? I'm sure we can agree to that."

"Then there's no problem," said Billy. "I'll just get a contract drawn up, and we can initial it here and now. Belphoebe? Run the legal program, there's a good girl."

\* \* \*

Palgandra had departed, peace had returned. "So now big hairy creature will be happy?" asked Flare.

"I imagine so," said the Joat. "We're in the clear. It's not every day that you get fifteen thousand separate prosecutions quashed simultaneously!"

"No. But is not every day give away secret of matter-transmission for nothing."

"Um," said the Joat. He scratched ruminatively at his nose. "Haven't the Time Police metapredicted this bit?"

"No, accountants say would cost *big* computer time. Not need. But is pity could not keep secret, would be very valuable. But best in hands of Quaternity, all said and done."

"Yes," said the Joat uncertainly. He had the decency to look embarrassed. "Yes, I'm sure they'll find the secret of matter-transmission eventually, it must be somewhere in all those records on Hurscaffl. I hope they do, one tenth of a per cent of the royalty on something that big would be *enormous*. Of course, they'll have to deal with the Ursca first, it'll be a lot of effort, take years before they find the right disk."

"What talking about? Have *give* right disk."

The Joat laughed. "Maybe you shouldn't have listened to your accountants."

"But —"

"You're making the same mistake that Palgandra did. I'm not surprised, I made it too. At first."

"Mistake?"

"Yes. You're assuming the PAXIAL disk has something to do with matter- transmission." If only he could have bottled the look on her face, he'd have made a fortune selling it at fairgrounds.

"But *saw!*" said Flare. "Saw with own eyes!"

"Yes," said the Joat. He leaned forward and wiggled his ears. "But *what* did we see, eh?"

"Saw PAXIAL insert prisms in packs and vanish", said Flare in her most pedantic voice.

"Precisely," said the Joat, unabashed. "Suppose you saw *me* put on a pair of ear-muffs and then open the door. Does that mean that ear-muffs function as a door-key?"

"No, but —"

"*Post hoc, ergo propter hoc. After, therefore because of.* A logical fallacy. 'Ah, yes, but what *else* could the prisms be for?' That's what you're thinking. So was I — and I realised there was an alternative."

"What alternative?"

The Joat leaned forward in his seat. "Refrigeration." Flare smacked a hand against her thigh in sudden comprehension. "Yes, refrigeration," he repeated. "We know that the PAXIAL have to keep very cold, cold enough to freeze boiling mud. Obviously they evolved on a low-temperature world. The installation was cold to us, but even then the PAXIAL wore a suit. The prisms aren't matter-transmitters at all. They must be some kind of portable personal coolant device. The PAXIAL were just putting on their earmuffs."

"But they — we saw — "

"Yes, Flare, there *was* a matter-transmitter — but it was *in the floor*. The thing that looked like a star. We thought it was just a marker. It wasn't. It was the transmission device."

"Six-pointed ceramic stars... dozens of stars," said Flare. Her pupils shrunk to tiny points with the enormity of it.

"The PAXIAL roamed across space," said the Joat. They had bases on hundreds of worlds, linked by matter-transmitters. But I reckon Ursca mind-control is killing the race off. You realise, we only ever saw one live PAXIAL. That installation was falling apart. Even under mind-control the PAXIAL would have kept it functioning. The Ursca would have insisted upon it."

"So the installation wasn't a planetary matter-transmitter at all! It was just a factory for making personal refrigerators."

"Nearly right. But it isn't a factory." To keep your ears warm, in the long run, you don't wear warm clothing: you change the climate. The installation was much too complex, the expense too great, just to be manufacturing individual refrigeration gear. There was only one answer.

"If not for making refrigeration units, then what *has* Palgandra bought in exchange for quashing fifteen thousand warrants?" asked Flare.

"I don't regret leading him astray. No guilt-trip, Palgandra got an excellent deal. I imagine he'll be promoted to ten-star Admiral. But he may be a little disappointed at first when he finds out what's *really* on that disk." The Joat stretched the moment out. "Like I said, the PAXIAL evolved on a cold world. Even in insulated suits, they freeze boiling mud. Hurscaffl is a cold planet, but the PAXIAL installation there was *colder*. They built coolant prisms by the billions. But they wouldn't have stopped there. Personal refrigerator-suits? A stopgap. Why go to so much trouble to set up a factory on a dump like Hurscaffl? Isn't it obvious?"

"It's a PAXIALforming device," said Flare.

"Correct. What Palgandra's bought isn't the secret of matter-transmission. It's a set of instructions for triggering an ice age."

\* \* \*

The Jumbles still danced their never-ending sarabande to chaos. Newton and Einstein's laws hadn't been repealed, they didn't depend upon the Etonian freewave patent. He dropped Flare off on a rock that looked pretty much like a hundred thousand other rocks. She took the time-machine, paid for it with a chaste kiss, and his last sight of the Assistant Deputy Inspector was a tiny figure sitting on a boulder staring fixedly at her feet. He knew that the Time Police would shortly arrive to pick her up, along with its prototype time-machine, but she still looked very lonely.

He sighed, straightened his shoulders, and set course for Poor Yorick. So far the universe looked exactly the same as it had before he left: it was something of an anticlimax. At the very least the stars could have turned green, or space acquired the consistency of hot fudge.

Soon the familiar aspect of Poor Yorick filled his screen. He felt vaguely guilty about not making a freewave call to Grover's World, to assure his mother he was safe and check that his father had — well, not so much returned as not left in the first place. But the usual space-storms around Kappa Cailzie were disrupting long-distance communications. He'd drop by as soon as he'd visited Poor Yorick.

Alaya.

She ought still to exist. Bahamba Bright had had nothing to do with the Etonians. There was no reason for that part of the timeline to change. Would she still be waiting? He'd told her not to. Fool. But it had seemed the right thing at the time, when the search for his father was an endless pit that might at any moment consume him utterly. Woops, he wouldn't have *been* searching for his father. Only one thing for it: go and see.

He dropped into holding orbit and presented his ID. An oddly familiar voice bade him approach the landing-grids, but he couldn't place it. He called a cab and shortly found himself outside the Strooghn residence. It looked the same as ever. He buzzed for attention, and identified himself. "You're always welcome here, Mr. Jarneyvore," said the door's robotic control unit. He whistled as he walked along the main corridor. So far, so good.

He was met at the corridor's end by a strikingly pretty young woman in a brief blue dress and wearing the fashionable diagonal-cut hairstyle. Again the face was familiar, and again he couldn't place it. Her voice was the one he had half recognised from the ship, and equally tantalizing. "I've come to see Alaya."

"I'm sorry, Mr. Jarneyvore, but she's not here at the moment. She didn't realise you might be coming, and she's busy on Bahamba Bright." *So I was right — some things haven't changed.* "But you can talk to *Mr.* Anagleist if you wish."

Who the Sump was Mr. Anagleist? Woops, wait a minute, that emphasis... 'You can talk to *Mr.* Anagleist...'. Meaning that he was expected to want some other member of the Anagleist family... His heart sunk into his purple olchskin boots. But he had to ask the question. "Isn't Mrs. Anagleist at home?"

The secretary did a quick double-take. "I'm sorry, Mr. Jarneyvore, but I don't understand your question."

"You emphasized the word 'Mr.' I asked whether Mrs. Anagleist was at home."

"Oh. That's what I thought you did say. Pardon me, Mr. Jarneyvore. But I just told you she's away on Bahamba Bright."

*Oh no.* "Alaya."

"Well, yes, naturally — oh! You haven't heard the news! Of course, that's why you're confused! I should have explained. You see, they've only been married a short time." The boots sank too, taking the heart to the depths of the world. "Ten days ago. Magnificent ceremony, all the HV companies carried it! I'm surprised you missed it!"

"I've been... away," said the Joat lamely.

"Away! You must have been in another *universe*, sir! Ooop, pardon me, that must have sounded impudent. Oh, but they made such a *lovely* couple, Mr. Jarneyvore! Alaya all dressed up in the traditional red cloak and conical wig, she looked a *dream!* And Mr. Dusterswivel Anagleist, he looked so *handsome!*" She stopped, the outburst stemmed by concern. "Are you all right, Mr. Jarneyvore?"

"I'm — I'm fine," said the Joat, who wasn't. *Had she waited? Had she Sump! And you're the fool who told her not to.*

*Probably not in this universe, though. And she probably never... I wonder what happened? For instance, did we —? I'm not sure I'll ever dare ask.* For a moment he wished he still had the time-machine, so that he could change history again, just a tiny bit. But the Time Police would extract his intestines through his ears if he so much as tried it, that's what they were set up for. To *stop* unauthorized meddling with the time-flow. Except, of course, for the unauthorized meddling that had created the Time Police.

"I feel a bit funny," he said weakly.

The secretary rushed round from her desk to help him, her face full of concern. "You just sit down, Mr. Jarneyvore," she said, putting an arm across his shoulder to lead him to a chair. There was something about the way she moved, lithe and fluid, like a cat. But the smile, so bright and natural and charming, it wasn't right. It should have resembled — *what* should it have resembled? He dredged his memory.

Got it.

*A king cobra.*

"You're Sherryl Eton." He sounded dazed.

She smiled even more charmingly. "That's right, sir. But how did you know?"

"I've met — I've met some of your relatives."

"You mean Bly? My father?"

"No, not Bly. Eshelby."

She looked puzzled. "Eshelby? I'm not sure I remember an Eshelby... maybe on my grandmother's side of the family?"

*But he's your brother.* He didn't say it. In this version of the universe, something had happened to Eshelby. Or rather, hadn't happened. Namely, his birth. Changes, changes... ripples in the web. Had one ripple lost him Alaya? Probably not, he'd managed that all by himself. "Probably a distant cousin or something," said the Joat. "Maybe I misremembered the name."

"Oh no, sir. Not *you!* Alaya's told everybody how clever you are, what an amazing memory you have! She's always talking about you, Mr. Jarneyvore. I reckon she has a soft spot for you. She said you'd saved Bahamba Bright for her! And that's why she gave you that space-yacht!" Her face went wistful. "I wish *I* had a space-yacht. But not on my salary. Wouldn't even buy a part share in a groundcar."

The Joat couldn't hold his tongue quickly enough. "But surely, all the profits from freewave — "

"Ah, yes sir, you've put your finger on a family tragedy there," she said. "It's true that my great$^9$-grandfather Rudolph was the Eton who invented freewave. But when the daft old budger patented it, he gave it to the government, didn't he? Gave it away for nothing!" Her face softened, and the Joat shivered all over. "Still, probably all for the best, you know?" She shook her head enchantingly. "There's a lot more to life than money, I reckon. I'm rather glad the old... soul gave it away. Probably for the best. I'd be a real bitch if I had any money!"

Her cheerfulness was infectious. The Joat felt an idiot grin spread across his face. *You know, it would never have worked with Alaya.*

"There, you're looking much better now, Mr. Jarneyvore. For a minute there you looked real peaky, like you'd seen a ghost."

*No, I've laid one. Woops, Freudian metaphor again, must watch that...* An idea intruded into his thoughts. "Sherryl — I can call you that?"

"If you wish, Mr Jarney — "

"Billy. You call me Billy."

"Billy. What a nice name, sounds all sort of cuddly and — " She put a hand to her mouth. "Oh, excuse me! I didn't mean — "

"Sherryl," said the Joat. *How to put this?* "Um... You would like a space-yacht. I *have* a space yacht. I'm not planning to give it away, you understand, but... would you like a ride in it? Several? Dinner on Skidmark, at Fritz's?" *Assuming it's still there.*

"Well... *Billy.* This is all a bit sudden." She ran a critical eye over him, grimaced, shook her head. "My mother warned me not to accept rides in space-yachts from brash young men with appalling dress sense."

"Oh. Sorry. In that case I'd best lea — "

"Visit a good tailor, Billy, and get some professional advice. Spend a few kroon on a smart, fashionable, low-key outfit. *Then* call me — with the vision on so that I can judge the result. If it's up to an acceptable standard — well, I never pay much attention to what my mother told me."

\* \* \*

From Poor Yorick it was only a few phades to Grover's World. *Shall I call ahead? No, I'll drop in and surprise them. But I'd better check with the directory to make sure where they live. Assuming they do....* His past came flooding back. The giant red sun, the mud, the characteristic whine of a clapped-out tove...

He was home.

Soon the tove was tied up by Raft 4177, and a startled Grynth driver was wondering what he'd done to deserve such a lavish tip. But his passenger had shot up the steps so fast that he'd never hear if he was called back. *Which is just as well, in the circumstances*, thought the Grynth, and beat it before the customer had time to change his mind.

Billy began to feel nervous when he turned the corner on to Swidger Street. *My old home*. Still the home of Terpsichore Jarneyvore, and — according to the Directory — her husband Jole. He reached the door, and stopped. He swallowed, his mouth had suddenly gone dry. His heart thumped.

He pushed the buzzer.

The door opened, and there stood his mother. "Billy!" She sounded delighted. "Wretched boy! Fancy coming all the way over here, and not calling ahead! You never change, do you!" She turned her head. "Jole! *Jole!* Stop fooling with those skumpers and come here! Look who's turned up!" She fussed and fretted until the Joat had come inside the house and taken off his coat.

He watched as his mother hung it up. Maybe Sherryl was right: the coat did lack a certain *je ne sais quoi*. But he wasn't sure what. Was the problem the lemon-and-lime frilled collar? The zigzag felt and vinyl stripes? The crimped elbow pock—

"Hello, Billy!" It was Jole's voice. The Joat looked up. He saw the familiar face, now wrinkled, the hair thinning and partially grey. He felt like bursting into tears, but he'd *never* be able to explain himself if he did. Flare hadn't needed to impress the point on him. *Not a word about a time-machine*. Anyway, nobody would ever believe it. Better to keep a secret than to depart for the rocker-raft in the big yellow tove, wearing the shirt with the folding arms that tied together round the back. "Hello, Dad. Haven't seen you for ages."

"No, let's see, must be a year come next Waghort Night. *That* was fun, we must do it again! Don't mind your mother, she always fusses. I've got a really nice patch of skumpers growing out the back, ripe and round as a waitress's — sorry, Terpsi, er — just ripe and round, Billy."

*It's as if he's never been away*, thought the Joat. *He hasn't, of course. I guess I'm the only one who has. Is this really the old universe, changed? I think it's a new one, and I've just blundered into it.*

He looked at his father's cheerful face, and his mother beaming pride at him in that embarrassing way that mothers always have for their offspring, even if said offspring are HV tenzy-stars or planetary presidents. *However this universe came about, I approve of it. I wonder, maybe when you redirect a universe you get to choose what it will do...*

Jole Jarneyvore clapped his son on the back. "Good to see you, Billy! Really good! Now, don't let me grabbit on about skumpers and such rubbish! Tell us what *you've* been up to latcly!"

The Joat leaned back in the comfortable chair and grinned. "Oh, the usual," he said, waving his arms airily. "Just saving the universe."

Joat and parents laughed until the tears streamed down their faces.

But not all at the same joke.

# Epilogue

We live in an age of specialists. In many areas of science it takes a hundred authors to write a two-page article. Our global civilization has become so diverse that it is almost impossible to get an overall perspective. In such circumstances bigotry and pseudoscience flourish. It's hardly surprising if most of the human race finds the whole game incomprehensible, and seeks refuge in a thousand versions of Cloudcuckooland.

We desperately need some Joats.

Not *too* many, though.

The tale of Billy the Joat goes back to Philip José Farmer's classic book *The Lovers*. In it there is a throwaway scene in which the protagonist Hal Yarrow is addressed by a fellow coach-passenger.

' "Couldn't help overhearing what you told the stewardess when she challenged your right to sit here. Did I hear you right, or did you actually tell her you was a *goat*?"

'Hal smiled, and said, "No. Not a goat. I'm a *joat*. From the initial letters of *jack-of-all-trades*. You weren't too mistaken, though. In the professional fields, a joat has about as much prestige as a goat." '

I read it and forgot it, but it came back to haunt me when Ben Bova suggested I should try my hand at writing science fiction. It was the middle of the 1978 Connecticut winter — in total we had 89 inches of snow that year — and there wasn't much to do. So Avril, my wife, brought home a wrecked typewriter from the fleamarket, dozens of mechanical bits in a box. I put it together, and it worked! So then I had to type something on it, and what emerged was a science fiction story. About a joat.

It was the first SF story I ever dared submit to a magazine. I sent it to Ben, asking for advice on how to rewrite it, and he sent me a cheque instead. (Thanks, Ben.) It wasn't till a year later that I re-read *The Lovers* and discovered where I'd stolen the idea from.

The subconscious is a strange and wonderful thing.

There were quite a few Billy the Joat stories after that, roughly one a year over a period of eight years. They form the skeleton of this book, up to about two thirds of the way through. In chronological order they are:

...And Master of One, *Analog* **99** #6, June 1979, 113-126.

The Malodorous Plutocrats, *Analog* **99** #9, September 1979, 87-102.

Paradise Misplaced, *Analog* **101** #3, March 1981,12-38.

Deep Joat, *Analog* **101** #8, July 1981, 88-108.

Missing Link, *Analog* **106** #1, January 1986, 154-174.
Billy the Kid, *Analog* **107** #1, January 1987, 162-175.

Some of them are slightly different here, though. I'll tell you why.

I got to wondering what curious circumstances had shaped the not always admirable character of Wyllam Jarneyvore. Eventually it became clear that he'd had a deprived childhood. No father-figure to maintain discipline.

Yes, but in the *Analog* version of 'Billy the Kid' he *does* have a father.

No problem. The *Analog* version of that story happened in the Joat's brave new universe, the one where he does have a father. This book is about the other universe, the one that doesn't exist any more. It tells the real story.

Except, of course, that many events no longer happened they way they're told here.

Ian Stewart
*Coventry March 2 1994*
*Revised July 2011 for eBook publication*
*Minor Corrections April 2017*

Printed in Great Britain
by Amazon